FAR FROM
THE DREAM

THE GENTLE HILLS / BOOK ONE

LANCE WUBBELS

FAR FROM THE DREAM

BETHANY HOUSE PUBLISHERS
MINNEAPOLIS, MINNESOTA 55438

Published by Bethany House Publishers
A Ministry of Bethany Fellowship, Inc.
11300 Hampshire Avenue South
Minneapolis, Minnesota 55438

Printed in the United States of America

Library of Congress Cataloging-in-Publication Data

Wubbels, Lance, 1952–
    Far from the dream / Lance Wubbels
        p.   cm. — (The gentle hills ; bk. 1)

    I. Title.
II. Series: Wubbels, Lance, 1952–   Gentle hills ; bk. 1.
PS3573.U39F37   1994
813'.54—dc20   94–19920
ISBN 1–55661–418–7   CIP

To Mom and Dad

Thanks for the memories

and love immeasurable

LANCE WUBBELS, the Managing Editor of Bethany House Publishers, taught biblical studies courses at Bethany College of Missions for many years. He is also the compiler and editor of six Charles Spurgeon Christian Living Classic books with Emerald Books. This is his first novel. He and his family make their home in Bloomington, Minnesota.

Special Thanks

to

Carol Johnson

Anne Buchanan

Dan Thornberg

Peter Glöege

Your skills are wonderful.

Your encouragements were invaluable.

Your zeal was contagious.

You made the difference.

CONTENTS

PROLOGUE

Another harsh Depression spring was spreading its misery over the farmlands of southern Minnesota, but the sun in a cloudless sky declined to share in the general gloom, and the exuberant shouts of children in the country schoolyard refused to be silenced.

These were the children whose parents and grandparents had challenged the harshest of winters, homesteaded and tamed the rugged terrain, transforming the landscape into a place of rolling hills and shady valleys and well-tended fields. This land was a part of them, and hard times couldn't dim the optimism that comes with being young and healthy and indisputably at home.

Spirits were especially high on this fine day in late April because there were no classes, only the annual celebration that marked the arrival of spring. This year there would be a spelling bee between pupils of Liberty Bell country school and one of its neighboring schools. But first came the softball game that took on World Series import to some of its participants. Students were spaced strategically around the pasture-turned-ball field, intensely involved in the rhythm of pitch, swing, and throw. Then the loud clang of the school bell brought everything to a momentary standstill.

"We won!" Billy Wilson shouted as the first loud ring echoed through the valley. "We did it again!"

"Three years straight!" Jerry Macmillan returned, clapping his friend on the back. But then his voice was smothered by another peal of the bell, and his face fell slightly at the prospect of the spelling contest to come.

Reluctantly, the two boys joined the clump of players heading toward the white schoolhouse to collect their lunches. Billy and Jerry walked as slowly as they could, busily recounting their glorious exploits. Ruth Buckley, their star pitcher, quickly caught up and fell into step beside them.

"You pitched a whale of a game, Ruthie," Jerry congratulated her. "We nearly shut them out."

"If it wasn't for that one girl with the brown hair," Billy added, pointing ahead to a pretty young teenager who was already halfway up the schoolhouse stairs. "She was killing the ball. And she ran like a deer. Wish we had her on our team."

"Didn't seem very fair to me," Ruth said, shaking her head in disgust. "They never had a chance."

"Why?" Billy retorted. "It was their school against ours. Fair and square."

"But they only had one boy your age, and he acted like he'd never seen a bat before," answered Ruth. "We should have divided you two up so it could have been a real game."

"Forget it!" countered Billy. "We can't help it that their fellas was in the fields already. Two more dry days, and I wouldn't have been here either."

"Who do you think that girl was?" Jerry asked innocently. "You hear her name?"

"Gotta crush on her, huh?" Billy teased. "You been gawking at her the whole game! I think you missed that one ball just for her."

"I did not—"

"Did, too!" Billy whooped and gave Jerry a shove. "And you do got a crush. It's written all over your face."

They were nearly to the schoolhouse doors, and although Jerry wanted to wrestle his best friend into submission, he dared not be late for lunch.

"Stop being so mean, Billy," Ruth ordered. "What's it to you who Jerry likes?"

" 'Cause him and me's never going to get married," Billy muttered. "Gonna work our farms together—got it all planned. So I can't let him get started with some girl we've never met. You keep out of it, Ruthie."

"I'll keep out of what I want," Ruth snapped at Billy, then she turned toward Jerry. "I don't know her name, but I heard she's so poor she brings lettuce sandwiches to school. Nothing in them but lettuce! That's poor."

Going up the steps into the schoolhouse, the threesome was surprised to find the athletic girl waiting for them at the door.

"Hello!" she said, her directness softened by a glint of mischief. "You were talking about me, weren't you?"

The three friends reddened, but Billy recovered quickly. "My friend here, Jerry Macmillan, thinks you're a great ball player. He wants to know your name."

"Is that true?" the girl asked, addressing Jerry.

He nodded, face burning, but the words never escaped his lips.

"My name is Marjie Belle Livingstone," she announced. "I'm happy to meet you. We don't have boys in our school as cute as you. Would you like to share my special sandwiches?"

1

THE OLD FARMHOUSE

A stillness had crept into the old farmhouse dining room and silenced the world of everything except the quiet breathing of mother and daughter. For a time all conversation ceased. Eyes searched eyes—probing and testing, doubting and reassuring—almost a test of wills.

They had long ago learned to read the secrets of each other's hearts by the truth hidden in their eyes. But this was a moment when neither could afford to mistake what was being said.

Sarah Livingstone studied the roughness of her hands. Despite their field-worn wisdom, they were as silent as the depths of her heart. What would Robert say if he were seated next to her now? she wondered. But Robert was gone, and she had never felt more alone than at this moment.

Sarah looked back up into her daughter's confident brown eyes. There was no doubting the sparkle of joy—or the accompanying glint of pain. Only a mother could see and feel both in the twinkle of an eye.

Finally the silence was broken by the mother's whisper, "Marjie, your pa always said who you married was your own decision, and it's plain you've made up your mind. But are you sure it's right to marry him now? Wouldn't it be better to wait till he gets back?"

"You mean *if* he gets back," Marjie said gently, not as a challenge. Her eyes remained fixed on her mother's windburned face as she fumbled for words. Everything had happened so quickly.

"Pa also was fond of saying there's a lot of things in this life we can't plan for—both good and bad things. Something just happens, and you have to make your choices as best you can. Well, no one knew that Pearl Harbor was going to be bombed or that we would be at war today."

"But who says Jerry has to enlist?" Sarah protested. "He's old enough that there's no reason he has to go. And if he loves you as much as you say, then he's crazy to go. Besides, what about his pa? I hear the man's not well. What's gonna happen to their farm? Is Jerry gonna up and leave the old man to take care of that land without any help?"

Sarah Livingstone knew all too well what it meant to be left alone. She and her husband had made it through the worst of the Depression by moving from one rented farm to another with the three children before finally scraping together enough to buy. Somehow they had always managed to feed the hungry young mouths. But when Robert had died of cancer four years previous, she had thought she'd lose the farm for sure. She would have, too, if Marjie's younger brother, Ted, hadn't stayed at home to take over the heavy work. As it was, they barely made payments on the property from crop to crop, and there was never enough money to pay a hired hand. Marjie sent what she could from her waitress job in Rochester, but most months she barely made enough there to support herself.

"Jerry's dad's a lot tougher than they say," Marjie said with as much confidence as she could manage. Her tone changed ever so slightly. "He says he can keep the place going. And if he gets in a pinch, they've got relatives close who'll help."

Sarah raised her hand to chase back some loose strands of gray hair that had fallen across her forehead. She waited, knowing that Marjie was avoiding the harder question.

Marjie glanced around the dimly lit dining room as if searching for a hint of cheer in the dull, gray wallpaper. She picked up her coffee cup and took a long sip of the lukewarm brew. Then, with a deep sigh, she shut her eyes and began to cry—softly at first, then harder. She had no handkerchief and tried wiping the tears away with her hands, but the torrent that fell was more than a match.

Finally Marjie regained composure and dried her eyes and cheeks with a handkerchief her mother had managed to produce. She smiled weakly at Sarah, sniffed, set her chin.

"You're right, Ma. Jerry's old enough to stay home, and his father's health is questionable. And I'm another reason for him to not go. But his brother lives out in Seattle and is so much older that Jerry's the only one from his family who can go defend his country. There's no stopping him, Ma. He's just as determined as Paul was."

Just the thought of her oldest son brought out the tears that Sarah had forced back while Marjie wept. Now it was time for mother and daughter to share the one handkerchief between them.

Paul Livingstone had joined the army six months earlier. "War's coming for sure," he had said. "We're gonna have to defend our families and nation. And I want to be ready to go when it happens."

Through her tears, Sarah found the words she was searching for. "So Jerry's as crazy as Paul. Lord have mercy on both those fools. You know, those two bucks are just like your pa was. Robert was nearly gassed in France during World War I, you know. The man wasn't afraid of anything.

"I understand your kind of man, Marjie," she added with a sniff. "But why can't you wait till he gets back to marry him?"

Marjie laughed a little, wishing she could explain what she felt. Resting her hand on her mother's arm, she said, "Ma, you know what real love is. It's deep and powerful like a river, and it goes pretty much where it wants. I love Jerry like that, and nothing's going to take that away from me. War or no war, he's asked me to marry him, and tomorrow's the day. Even if he never comes back and I only end up living with him for a few days—"

She paused for minute, wide-eyed at the awful thought. "Oh, Ma, I just can't stand the thought of him going away and wondering if I'd wait for him. Whether he lives or dies, I want to be his wife. And besides . . . he's so shy I never thought he'd manage to ask me. This may be my only chance!"

With that, both mother and daughter broke into ripples of laughter that warmed the old farmhouse. Neither had laughed nor cried so hard in a long time, and the shared emotions brought them to a long embrace. Sarah held her daughter as if it were the last chance she'd ever have.

"Well, then, congratulations, my fine lady! You've got your Prince Charming after all. Jerry's a wonderful man. I only wish your pa was here to see the happiness on your face. You were his one and only little darling, you know—always had him wrapped around your little finger. But he'd be worried sick about you, too. You're heading down a road that'll no doubt lead to a pack of worry and fear—maybe grief. And your pa could never stand the thought of you getting hurt."

Silence returned, and all that was heard was the December wind rattling the loose-fitting storm windows. Marjie stayed tucked in her mother's embrace, both of them enjoying a closeness they had not felt in years. But in the silence, even in their closeness, their thoughts began to drift in separate directions.

Marjie's thoughts returned to their vague grasping after what the future would bring. What would it be like to be separated from Jerry for a year . . . three years . . . forever?

Sarah found her thoughts revisiting the pain of her own losses. First Robert. Then Paul. Was there any agony worse than being separated from those you love?

Sarah finally broke through their separate pain with another question that had been bothering her. "So why are you going to the justice of the peace to get married instead of to a minister?"

"We talked about it and decided it'd be a lot simpler," answered Marjie. "I haven't been to church in quite a while, Ma. Jerry's gone more regular, but he says he doesn't believe much of what he hears there. Seems like they specialize in making him feel guilty. We were afraid Jerry's minister might go prying into our views of religion, and I'm afraid we don't have much to say about that. So, we thought the justice of the peace was just a . . . friendlier place to go."

"Seems like going to war ought to scare a feller like Jerry into some serious religion in a hurry," observed her mother. "I'd think he'd be wanting to make sure that everything's squared away with God, so to speak. I remember how stubborn your pa was. I thought sure he'd go to the grave before he let the reverend come see him."

"I don't think Jerry's one to be scared into anything," Marjie reflected. "Besides, he's a good man—just like Pa was. Pa was always there for anybody in the county who needed help. His religion had nothing to do with him not going to church. In fact, I can't say I ever understood why Pa called the reverend during those last weeks before he died. Did he ever tell you what they talked about?"

"Just a window-to-peek-in's worth. Marjie, your pa was the most private man I ever met, especially when it came to religion talk. He hated to listen to people chatter on about religion. He said he figured the Lord would drive most of those folks out of church like He drove the money changers out of the temple in the Bible days. But toward the end Robert kept saying to me that there's more to religion than doing right by your neighbors and providing well for your family. One morning he called me to his bed, and though he was hurting so bad from the cancer, he said, 'Sarah, I know you're gonna think I'm crazy, but I met God in the night. I've been pushing Him away for years. I was reading about how Jacob wrestled with the angel all night. And you know, I think Jacob and I might be a lot alike. I've been so full of pride that I couldn't give in to God. But last night He came to me. He did.'

"Your pa sounded so strange at the time, but I didn't ask any questions on account of he was in such awful pain. Now I wish I'd asked him more. At any rate, it was about then that he told me to call the reverend to bring communion. And Marjie, I gotta say that your pa died the happiest man I've ever seen. He was a changed man—ready to go. Whatever happened to him, I know it was real. Unfortunately, the reverend didn't understand much of what he said . . . and neither did I . . ." Sarah's words trailed off like a wanderer searching for a long-lost treasure.

"You might be right," Marjie deliberated. "But church hasn't really done me any good over the years, and Jerry said it doesn't make any difference to him. Maybe we'll all discover Pa's secret someday, but for now I think I'll take my chances with the justice of the peace. Besides, he's cheaper than the minister, and we're flat broke."

"Well, it's getting late, dear," her mother said with a weary sigh. "You got my blessing, though my heart is already hurting for you. Your pa and I fought our way back through some terrible setbacks, even after the barn burned. But we did it together—and when Jerry leaves, you'll be alone. Honey, I don't think I could survive what you're getting yourself into. But I'm here if you need me."

With that Sarah squeezed her daughter with all the wiry strength that comes from years of milking cows and tending pigs. Their eyes were dry by now, but the tears would return more than once before they finally said good-night.

Am I really ready for this? Marjie sat quietly before the old dresser in the spare bedroom and stared into the age-flecked mirror while she brushed her hair.

This wasn't really what I had in mind for marriage, she admitted to herself, her brush poised for another stroke. Certainly she was old enough; most twenty-two-year-old girls she knew already had a couple of kids. And certainly she loved Jerry.

But this was so different from her fairy-tale fantasies of being swept away by her true love and living together happily ever after. Prince Charming had come, it was true. But in two days he'd be on board a train that would take him to who knew where!

And I'll still be right here. With a sigh she stared past her own reflection—wavy brown hair, long-lashed brown eyes, heart-shaped face—to the tiny country bedroom mirrored behind her. Faded floral wallpaper was pasted layer-upon-layer thick; the woodwork painted a dull gray. The ancient glass globe of the ceiling light allowed only a minimum of light to pass through. The single metal bed was neatly made with musty old blankets, and the shabby wooden table beside it had clearly seen better days.

Having been away from home for the past four years, Marjie found that the dreary atmosphere of the room weighed down her usually buoyant spirit. But it wasn't just the dim light and the dingy walls that dragged her down. This was the room where her father had suffered so much during the last year of his life. This was the room where she and her mother had faithfully nursed him day and night. This was the room where the reality of living and dying had pressed in upon her as an eighteen-year-old and transformed her from a girl into a woman.

Best to shut the light off before it really got to her. She flipped the switch and started over to the bed, then changed her mind and headed for the window.

Peering out through two layers of glass, she could see snow swirling in the moonlight. Beyond the fence line lay the eighty acres of swampy farmland that her father had worked night and day to scratch a living from.

Now her thoughts were drifting like the snow, drifting back to her mother's words. Marjie too remembered the change that had swept over her father in those final days, and brought a brightness to his face that she had never seen before—even when things had gone well on the farm. *Pa said it was worth suffering a lifetime for. But why did he have to go through such hell to experience it?*

Watching her father fade from a strong, robust figure to a pain-wracked shell of a man had left an indelible deadness somewhere deep inside her heart. She remembered the prayers that were said. And she remembered the look of hope and peace on his face, even as the illness progressed. But still he had died. God had not intervened.

"Well," she whispered in the darkness, "I thought I'd put all of this in the past. No such luck, I guess . . . but I've got to get some sleep. Tomorrow I marry the most wonderful man I've ever met. Just in case you're listening in, Pa, I hope you're as happy about this as Ma and I are. I wish you could've gotten to know Jerry better; I know you'd be real pleased. He even loves to fish, and you always said anyone who likes fishing can't be all bad. The two of you had a lot in common."

She turned from the window and crawled into the cold bed. But the anticipation of the day to come held sleep at bay until the early morning hours.

2

FATHER AND SON

The late afternoon dusk had given way to darkness as the two men went about their routine of evening chores. Despite the sudden drop in the outside temperature and occasional gusts of frigid wind, the barn remained relatively warm from the body heat of all the cattle. Between the two poorly lit rows of milking cows, father and son moved with a precision and speed that made their hard work look almost effortless. And they worked in silence. They had done these tasks in the same methodical order for so long that neither required the other to speak a word.

Jerry Macmillan leaned his head into the large black spot on Maribel's side and reflected that he and his father knew the cows about as well as they knew each other—maybe better. Caring for cows seemed so simple: a good supply of feed, a firm word now and then, a tap on the leg to move over, or a soothing scratch on the forehead, and all was well with the herd. But neither man was so simple, neither man was so content, neither man was so very good at getting through to the other. Although they worked together most of the time, the efficient cooperation of their hands bore little relationship to any real sharing of their lives.

It hadn't always been that way. Maybe it had begun the summer that Jerry's mother lost her battle with diabetes. But as the years passed, the father and son had simply stopped expressing their thoughts and feelings to each other.

Jerry was hoping this evening might be different, though. One way or another, he had to make sure that his father meant what he said about working the farm alone. It was true that one man could keep a farm going with an occasional hired hand, but that one man had to be at full strength. And no one doubted that his father could still work most young men into the ground. But the man was fifty-eight. And it was no secret that the doctor had warned him about his high blood pressure—said the condition would kill him if he didn't slow down. That warning, though, might as well have been given to one of the milking cows. Benjamin had no intention of slowing down or letting the pressure in his veins dictate what he did.

"Just about done?" Jerry called over as he dumped his last bucket of milk into the large metal can.

"Yeah, a couple more minutes here," his father answered. "Why don't you head up to the house and fix us some supper. I can finish up here."

Jerry turned to go, then remembered one last thing. "What about that new calf? Did you notice she was coughing when we first started choring?"

"Nope," Benjamin said with a groan as he finished the last cow. "Thought she looked okay. You better take a look."

Jerry walked back to one of several pens that held their calves. Lying in a shadowy corner near its mother was a little Holstein that was mostly white with a few spots of black. A black crescent arched over her left eye like a raised black eyebrow, giving her a quizzical, lopsided expression. Jerry opened the gate, knelt down by the week-old calf, and put his hand on the little animal's chest. There was no mistaking the wheeze and rattle inside.

"Shoot!" Jerry barked in disgust. "Hey, Dad, come on back here."

Benjamin knew what that tone of voice meant. He walked back to the pen. "Let me guess. She's picked up a draft, and it's gotten in her lungs. I better call the vet to come on out tomorrow morning and make sure it don't get worse. Seems like we should rent him a room when the calves are coming in. He's here about every other day."

"Nothing new, I reckon," Jerry added. He stroked the calf's soft coat, and it turned its head to gaze with large, liquid eyes. Jerry wondered if the calf would be here when he returned. *Or will the calf be here and I won't. . . ?*

Jerry figured this was the moment he'd been waiting for. He straightened his six-foot frame and locked determined blue eyes into his father's dark ones. "Dad, I gotta know one thing. Are you sure you can handle all this with me gone?"

"I already gave you my answer. Got some reason to doubt my word?" his father said stiffly.

Jerry was hoping to avoid an argument, but he wasn't backing down. "Well, you missed this calf being sick when you fed her. What if I hadn't caught it? You can lose a herd in a hurry if you're not careful."

"So who taught you that pearl of wisdom? I been tending calves for fifty years, and you think I need you here to tell me what to do?" Benjamin raised his eyebrows and stared back with stoic determination. "I worked this entire farm long before there was a tractor in the country, and I could do it again if you gave me a good team of horses. I can tend the herd, handle the crops, and pay the bills—believe me."

"But, Dad, you're fif—"

"Fifty-eight!" his father cut in. "So what? You gonna tell me I can't hold my own with you?"

"And what did the doc tell you this summer?" Jerry fired back, hoping the doctor might become the target of his father's anger. "Or do I need to give you a reminder?"

Benjamin pushed his cap back, exposing a very red forehead. He shook his head and crinkled his mouth in disgust, then let out a long sigh to blow out some steam. This time his answer was noticeably quieter. "What's that old drunk know? Anybody who hits the bottle as often as he does can't be trusted. He's the one that told your mother if she stuck to her diet she'd have a full life. Lotta good it did her. She'd have been better off eatin' whatever she wanted instead of listening to that old sauce."

"So you're smarter than the doc now. It's a wonder folks don't drive out here to get you to do some examinations," Jerry said through a brief smile. "You know good and well that if you keep pushing your blood pressure up, the rest of you's gonna pay the price."

"Maybe it will . . . maybe it won't," his father responded slowly. "But it don't make no difference either way. I'm not gonna slow down—whether you're here or not. You know that. 'It's appointed once for a man to die, then comes the judgment.' Ain't nothing gonna change that. The Lord said to take 'no thought for the morrow,' and that's just what I'm doing. I'm gonna keep right on working, and if my number comes up, it comes up. I wanta go with my boots on, anyways."

His father had him outmaneuvered now. The day after the doctor had issued Benjamin the warning about his blood pressure, he had gone straight to the hayfields and worked like a whirlwind. And there had been other times when Jerry wondered if his father was pushing beyond the limits in hopes that something inside would break and he could join Jerry's mother in heaven. But this was the first time his father had come right out and said what was driving him so hard.

"You getting cold feet?" Benjamin asked, turning the tables on Jerry.

"You can't mean it," Jerry said with a shake of his head, opening the gate to the pen and moving closer to his father. "I just hate the thought of you suffering because I left."

"There's gonna be a lot of suffering for everybody—already is," Ben mused. "Think of what the Wilsons are going through! And I expect I'll have my share of suffering as well, but that can't stop you from doing what you feel is right." Benjamin turned away and knocked a pile of gunnysacks off a post. "Besides, you're the one who's really going to suffer. And Marjie . . ."

"Marjie's tough, Dad," Jerry intervened reassuringly. "She's been on her own for four years already. She'll do all right without me. And besides, you know I gotta go, especially now. If it's the last thing I do, I've gotta make those Japs pay for what they did to Billy!"

Jerry and Billy Wilson had been best friends almost from babyhood. The Wilsons' farm was just down the hill from the Macmillans', and the two boys had grown up side by side—walking to the country school together, going through catechism, teaming up for softball. When Billy had signed up for the navy, Jerry had driven him to the bus depot. And Jerry was the only person, other than the Wilson family, to get a letter from Billy once he'd gotten underway on a ship called the USS *Arizona*.

And then, just a few days ago, had come the phone call urging Jerry and his dad to turn on the radio and listen to the flash news report. By the time the machine warmed up, the announcer was halfway into the unbelievable story that the U.S. naval base at Pearl Harbor had been the target of a sneak attack by Japanese bombers. That the U.S. fleet had suffered tremendous damage. That the *Arizona* had been hit and sunk . . .

Without saying a word to his father, Jerry had grabbed his coat and dashed out the back door toward the Wilsons' farm. He found Billy's family gathered around the living room radio in ghastly silence. Ella Wilson sat in her rocking chair holding a photo of Billy, oblivious to all but her son's face. Bud Wilson stood like a statue in front of the picture window, his eyes pleading with the brown box for any word to allay his fears. The sight of Jerry broke the spell, and Jerry found himself bobbing in a sea of sobs.

"Billy and I always promised that we'd stand up for each other," Jerry told Benjamin now through gritted teeth. "That if somebody ever murdered one of us, the other'd track down the murderer and pay him back," Jerry said. "That's what I told Ella and Bud. And that's what I plan to do."

"But Billy's alive," protested Benjamin. "They didn't kill him."

Jerry shrugged in disgust. "They say he's burned so bad he wishes he'd been standing closer to where the bombs hit. That's worse than dead, almost. And I've vowed to God I'll make the Japs pay, and I will."

Benjamin straightened to his full height, matching his son's bright gaze with an excited glint of his own. "Son, I swear, if I was a couple years younger, I'd go with you. It's a shame to waste a good man on this rocky old farm!"

At that father and son erupted into laughter, then found themselves locked in a spontaneous bear hug that both shocked and delighted them. Jerry, trying to remember the last time he had felt his father's love so powerfully, found within himself a confusing swell of emotions that simply pushed their way through with another wave of laughter.

The old barn echoed with hilarity, and every cow turned her head to see what the raucous celebration was about. Even the napping dogs roused from their slumber and came running down the aisle to investigate. Tongues lolling and tails wagging, they danced with joy around a father and son who had managed to find each other again before they had to part.

Supper that night was so different from their usual meals together that Jerry half expected his mother to walk through the kitchen door at any time. The food was as dull as ever, but Benjamin's eyes showed a familiar, almost forgotten glow. Jerry last remembered seeing it on long-ago evenings when his father and mother sat talking at the dining room table. But now something that had iced over his soul was broken apart, and Jerry was the amazed beneficiary.

It was late-late before they shut off the lights that night. Son would be leaving in the morning to get married and take his bride on a brief honeymoon before joining the navy. Father had just found his son and suddenly realized how much he had to tell his boy. The conversation was one-sided, but Jerry couldn't have been happier. Both wished they had weeks rather than hours, but both were happy to take advantage of the time they had. Someday, they hoped, there would be time for more talk.

They were deep into the night before the conversation lagged. Then, despite the hour and cold, Jerry bundled on layers of sweaters and his heavy coat and slipped outside. Slowly, he marched down the tree-lined farm lane that led to the silent, snow-covered fields and the hills behind them. He had traveled this lane a thousand times, but no trip had ever been like this one. Every step was an agony of goodbye, spiced with the thrill of anticipation.

"This could be the last time I walk this road," he whispered to himself.

Breaking out of the darkness of the tree lane, Jerry paused to survey his favorite sight—one that never grew old. Even in the moonlight, he could see the entire farm in a long, sweeping survey.

Much of the land was too hilly to farm—steep pasture land rutted with cow paths and darkened with snarly burr-oak trees. Once, skiing down the steepest hill, he had gone airborne and landed face-first in an ice-encrusted snowbank. A little creek running through the valley was where he had once caught a baby fox bare-handed. On the field they named the Seven Corners, Jerry could still see his father and himself diving under the wagon to avoid the golf-ball-sized hailstones from a monster thunderstorm that had caught them unawares.

Every recalling sight tugged at his heartstrings and suggested yet another memory. His mother walking out to the field with a basket filled with the day's lunch. The cow dogs that had, next to Billy, been his best friends. Grandfather under the big willow teaching him how to make a whistle. Nip and Tuck, the workhorses whose gentle strength had kept the farm going before they got the first Ford tractor in the county. His big brother, Jack, who fought him mercilessly and always won, but who defended him against all other comers. Even the darkest years of the Depression, when these fields had been blistered to brown and produced little more than weeds and pain.

Looking out over the familiar landscape, Jerry was suddenly conscious of a love more fierce than anger. It was love for the land, love for its people, love for his family—and it was so strong he was willing to die for it. Nothing could ever pull him away from these gentle hills—nothing except an evil power that had rained down bombs upon unsuspecting people and could bring its bombs here, too. He had to do what he could to stop the Japanese from taking his land, from threatening the people he loved, from doing to others what they'd done to his friend.

Turning back toward the farmyard, Jerry was finally overcome by the wave of building emotions from the crazy day. He let out a yell, but it brought little relief. Then he paused beneath a large old oak where he and his father and mother had shared many noon meals. There he wept, long and deep—wept for the first time since his favorite collie died when he was a boy.

The walk back to the house seemed colder and longer. The only thought that kept his feet moving was the knowledge that Marjie would soon be his bride.

3

WEDDING DAY

Jerry pulled into the driveway of the Livingstone farm just as the winter sun made its late entrance into the new day. The old black Ford's heater could barely keep the windshield defrosted, and despite being in a hurry, he knew he had to go inside and warm up a spell. The car creaked and rattled to a stop, but he wasn't about to turn off the engine while he went in.

He checked the rearview mirror one last time to make sure his lanky yellow hair was still in place. "Should've got a haircut," he groused to himself. "Starting to look like a sheep."

He emerged from the car and hurried toward the house, noting with satisfaction that Marjie's brother's truck was gone already. *This is my lucky day!* he thought. *One less person to say goodbye to.*

The porch door opened before he knocked, and there stood the most enchanting woman he'd ever met. Half-frozen already, he now stopped dead in his tracks to admire her in her tailored suit of woolen tweed and a rayon crepe blouse. In the early morning sun, Marjie almost seemed to shimmer. Every feature that he loved was intensified in measures he hadn't thought possible. But it was the radiant smile that struck him most—or was it the sparkling brown eyes?

"You gonna stand there till you freeze to death?" Marjie laughed. "Come on in and have some coffee."

He stepped into the porch and hardly dared look at her as he pulled off his boots.

"Cat got your tongue, good-looking?" Marjie asked with a loving smirk. "Don't you like my new suit or something?"

"Not so sure I can talk," Jerry stuttered. "You're just so . . . so beautiful . . . can't find the words. 'Course, I've never been too good with words. Guess I feel like a farm hick that's gone and fell in love with a princess. Where'd you come up with the outfit? Makes me look like a bum!"

He wrapped his cold arms around her warm shoulders and kissed her with all the emotions that were locked up in his faltering lips. Both man and woman had waited too long for this day, and it was only the sound of footsteps that brought a halt to their wedding prelude.

"Go on, go on. Don't let an old woman like me stop you," Sarah Livingstone called as she caught them in the embrace. "Been a long time since anybody got kissed like that in this house! Better take every kiss while you can."

Jerry took off his coat and hung it by the oil heater in the living room to warm up, then he followed the women into the dining room. The early morning sunlight streaming in through the windows cheered the drab little room, and the aroma of steaming coffee and fresh-baked cookies tickled his nostrils.

After the first cups of coffee were nearly drained and the cookie plate nearly emptied, Sarah sat back and drew in a deep breath. Jerry took Marjie's hand, and they both looked at her expectantly.

Sarah fiddled with her hands for a bit while she gathered her words. Finally she was ready. "Jerry . . . I wish Marjie's pa was here to give you his blessing. I been thinking about it all night— didn't sleep a wink—and I know that he'd be proud to call you his son. I know he'd only ask one thing from you—that you never stop loving and caring for his little darling. He wouldn't care a straw about whether you were rich or poor, or handsome or ugly, or sophisticated or backward. None of that mattered in his book. But he'd look you in the eye, real serious-like, and he'd ask you if you love Marjie. So do you mind if I ask you?"

Jerry squeezed Marjie's hand and smiled as he looked into her dark eyes, nearly forgetting about Sarah for the moment. "I think I loved you the first time I saw you. You remember when you were twelve—how your school and our school got together to play ball? You could run faster and hit better than any boy in your school. And you were so friendly you nearly scared me to death. I fell in love with you that day, even though it took me near forever to ask you out. Guess I was always scared that you might not be interested in a farm boy that only made it to eighth grade."

"But I fell for you that day, too," Marjie responded, filled with the joy of remembering. "You were so shy and bashful and cute that there wasn't a girl from our school who didn't love you. Do you remember when I introduced myself to you that day? You repeated my name, 'Marjorie Belle Livingstone,' just like you were memorizing it. I'll never forget how you kept standing real close to me and looking at me when you thought I wasn't noticing."

Then she breathed a huge mock sigh, her brown eyes dancing. "But, Jerry, you sure were slow in getting around to showing you were serious. Do you realize I could have married a couple guys while you dragged your feet?"

All three laughed in agreement. Then Jerry fumbled around in his shirt pocket and pulled out something that he covered with both hands. He looked first at Sarah, then at Marjie. "I didn't know what I was gonna do about a wedding ring. We got no money, and it all happened so fast I didn't have time to ask the bank for a loan. But last night my father came out of his bedroom and gave me this—for you."

He opened his callused hands and presented Marjie with a simple gold band studded with a small bright diamond. "It was my ma's."

Marjie was so shocked that she gave no immediate reaction. Tears formed at the corners of her eyes as she reached out to try it on. Slowly she pushed it over her trembling finger, and to her added wonder it was a perfect fit. "I love it, Jerry. But it doesn't seem right to wear anything so . . . so special. How could your father part with it?"

"I don't know," Jerry confessed. "But I do know he loves you. He just said he figured it was meant for you. And once my dad makes up his mind, there's just not much point in arguing with him."

Sarah reached over and studied the ring, tears streaking her cheeks. "Land's sake . . . if that don't beat all. Makes me wonder what I done with Robert's ring. Just a minute."

Jerry and Marjie were looking at each other in silence when Sarah started up the stairs to her bedroom. Then Marjie finally recovered from the surprise and hugged Jerry with sheer delight. When Sarah returned, she embarrassed Jerry again by catching them in another passionate kiss, but this time Sarah was too preoccupied to comment.

Instead of a ring in her hand, Sarah was carrying a large black Bible. She sat down and placed the book on the table ever so gently—like it was a sacred act. Staring at it for the longest time, the bride and bridegroom could only wonder what memories were pouring through her mind. Whatever they were, the secrets would remain with Sarah.

Finally, she took the Bible and opened it about halfway. There—pressed into the center of the page—was a gold wedding band. A few more minutes passed before Sarah spoke. "I knew there was something I was supposed to do last night, and I couldn't figure it out. Guess your father is a step faster than me, Jerry. This was Robert's ring. I put it here the day of the funeral— right with his favorite psalm. I don't have any money to give you as a wedding present, but I'd like you to have Robert's ring, Jerry."

"I couldn't . . . it means too—"

"Please try it on, Jerry," Marjie broke in. "Ma wants you to have it."

Jerry slowly took the ring from the page and placed it on his finger. It was slightly large and easily slipped off again. He looked up, not sure what to say or do next.

"The jeweler can size it for you," Sarah said reassuringly.

"They do it all the time. Looks good on you, *son*."

Jerry reached over and hugged Sarah awkwardly, for the first time ever. But when Marjie joined in the threesome, it made it as natural as if they'd practiced for years.

"One more gift," Sarah whispered in the midst of the hug. "This may be more important than the ring."

With that the embrace ended, and Jerry and Marjie waited in anticipation, wondering what could possibly come next.

Sarah took the opened Bible and pulled it toward her. She read quietly for a few moments, then looked at Jerry again. "Robert was not a religious man. But a couple of months before he died, he started reading this Bible that my mother had given him. He read it day and night—like a man who was starved to death. The only time he wasn't reading it was when the pain was too strong. Jerry, I'd like you to take this Bible with you when you go to war. Robert's favorite psalm—once he started reading the Bible, I mean—was the ninety-first. Look where the indent of the ring was: 'He that dwelleth in the secret place of the most High shall abide under the shadow of the Almighty.' Now, I'm not pretending to understand it all, but I got a feeling that you're gonna need a secret place someday under the Almighty's shadow. War is hell, make no mistake about it. Robert seen things in France during World War I that he wouldn't talk about to anyone—not even me. I hope you never have to face that."

With those words, the three sensed that their special coffee time together was over. Jerry and Marjie moved for their coats. Sarah followed, hoping that the day would come when Robert's ring would walk back into this room, accompanied by hugs and tears—and Jerry.

Mother and daughter embraced and said their goodbyes. Sarah embraced Jerry, too, and the shy young man fell back into a wooden stiffness. Sarah laughed and squeezed him a little harder.

Wishing them the happiness that she and Robert had known in marriage, she waved as the lovers flew out the door and into the waiting car. Then she leaned against the wall and cried a few more tears of joy and trepidation and grief.

4

⸻ ❧ ⸻

FINALLY MINE

As the car crunched off the narrow gravel road and pulled onto the pavement that led to Preston, Marjie was still quietly admiring the surprise wedding ring. Over and over, she'd held it up to the sunlight and watched the little rainbows dance inside the glittering stone.

Jerry was silent as well. So many wonderful, unplanned events had happened in the last twenty-four hours—the change in his father, coffee with Sarah, the rings, the Bible. Still, he couldn't push back his doubts about whether the wedding was the right thing now.

Marjie snuggled up closer to Jerry, who put his arm around her once he got the Ford into the last gear. "A penny for your thoughts," she asked softly. "You look as nervous as a cat. What's troubling you, Jerry?"

"Guess I never been married before . . . never left my father like this . . . never went to war either, come to think of it," Jerry whispered in her ear.

"Isn't it great to be a little crazy!" she exclaimed.

"More like a lot crazy!" Jerry laughed and let go of a chunk of worry.

"Well, if it comes as any comfort, I heard on the radio that hundreds of couples are getting married right before the man heads off for war," Marjie said. "Maybe there'll be a line of folks ahead of us when we get to the courthouse."

Jerry groaned. "Be just my luck. I got plans for you the next couple of days that don't include standing in some cotton-picking line."

"What sort of plans, sweetheart? You are going to clue me in, right?" Marjie pulled back a little and looked Jerry in the face.

He smiled and wrinkled his forehead a couple times, enjoying the few secrets he'd been able to keep from her. "Not just yet."

Marjie punched his arm playfully and mussed his hair. "So when do I get to find out?"

Jerry tried to keep his eye on the road and still hold off her mock attack. It didn't take long for him to give up. "After we're married, okay? Now settle down or we'll end up in the ditch, and the Japs won't need to worry about me."

Marjie snuggled back up to Jerry and turned suddenly serious. "Listen, now. I know this will be tough, but for the next two days I want us to try to not say anything about the war, the navy, the Japs, or the Nazis. For two days I want to forget about everything except you and me. I got some things planned for you, too, and I can't afford to have other concerns getting in the way. I'll give you one warning, though. We're both going to discover just how shy you really are."

"Hmmm, sounds interesting," Jerry said, trying to not blush. "Got a feeling I won't have any problem with the 'no talk about the war' rule."

"You won't—guaranteed," she added. "But before we start the rule, I have one question that you have to answer. What made you decide to report to the navy? If you're scared to death of water, why in blue blazes would you sign up for duty on the water? Doesn't it stand to reason that a man who can't swim a stroke would sign up for the army?"

"Figured you'd already know the answer to that," Jerry answered. "You're right. I'm a rock in the water—never got over falling in the river when I was just a little kid. But Billy went with the navy, and I figure I'll just sorta take his place, in a manner of speaking."

"Reckon you will," Marjie acknowledged, shaking her head

from side to side. "Now I know I'm marrying a man who has all kinds of screws loose in his head. All of this made perfect sense except for the very last piece!"

Then, unexpectedly, she burst out laughing, and he joined her. They laughed with delight, with a happiness that seemed almost enchanted. None of the pieces fit together. So much uncertainty lay ahead. Yet for the moment, everything was perfect.

They crested the last hill into Preston, and the county courthouse loomed into view. "You're sure?" Jerry asked one more time. "There's still time to stop this."

"Not on your life!" Marjie cried. "There's nothing that could stop me now. And don't you say one more word. I love you, Jerry Macmillan, and today you're finally mine."

"That was short and sweet," Marjie said as they walked hand in hand down the dark wooden staircase in the old courthouse.

"Just the way I like it," Jerry replied. "We were lucky we knew that other couple ahead of us. Can't believe I forgot about needing witnesses."

Marjie stopped and tried hard to look upset. "You aren't kidding you're lucky. Makes me wonder if you were trying to sneak out on me. Now give me the wedding kiss you promised. That little peck on the cheek up there was no kiss."

Jerry looked back up the stairs, then down the hallway ahead. "Here?"

"Right here. Right now. Or I'll start screaming," she told him matter-of-factly.

"You gonna drive me nuts like this all our marriage, Mrs. Macmillan?" Jerry worried out loud, taking Marjie into his arms. "Marjorie Belle Macmillan. I love that name, don't you? Marjorie Belle Macmillan, pucker up!"

Whatever had been lacking in front of the justice of the peace was more than made up for in the courthouse hallway. Jerry was so engrossed in his task that he never heard the three secretaries from the county auditor's office who had just returned from break and stopped at the top of the stairs to watch. But when the new husband and wife polished off their wedding kiss, the three onlookers let out a cheer and clapped until Jerry had escaped out the courthouse doors, pulling Marjie by the hand.

"It's true, isn't it? You *are* gonna drive me nuts!" Jerry called back as he ran ahead to the car. "Next time, why don't we post some signs and get the whole town out?"

"If you keep kissing like that, we just might get everybody to come!" Marjie caught him by the arm to slow him down.

Jerry stopped a few feet from the old black Ford and waved his hand toward it with exaggerated formality. "Okay, now it's my turn. And now, madam, behold . . . my first wedding present to you!"

Marjie peeked in the car, squinting through the windows in hopes of a package or something. But it was as empty as when they left it. "Thanks a lot. Try again."

"Behold . . . your wedding present!" Jerry actually raised his voice in a public place.

"What?" Marjie was baffled.

"What do you see?"

"An old black Ford."

"And . . ." Jerry laughed and yelled, ". . . it's yours!"

"Mine? But Jerry, it's your car."

"Exactly! What's mine is yours, don't you get it? We're married!" Jerry could hardly spit the words out fast enough. "The car's the only valuable thing I've got, so it's yours when I leave!"

Marjie blinked, trying to comprehend. Of course, Jerry was right, but this whole situation would take some getting used to. "Jerry, there's just one problem."

"What?"

"I can't drive!" Now it was Marjie's turn to laugh, but to her surprise, Jerry laughed, too.

He pointed once again to the car. "Right and wrong. Right—you never learned to drive. Wrong—you will be driving by the time I leave. Along with the car, I'm tossing in free driving lessons. You can't get a better deal than this!"

"But the whole idea of driving scares me, especially in town," groaned Marjie. "I'm better off taking the bus."

"And water scares me, especially deep salt water," argued Jerry. "But what of it? That's not gonna keep me back. And a little fright's not going to hold you back from using my wedding present, is it? Especially if it will take you to my only other wedding present—right?"

"Jerry, what are you talking about? You know we don't have money for presents. Besides, I don't want presents; I want you— and I won't have you for long. So can't we please stop talking about all this and get started on our honeymoon? Remember, I have a surprise for—"

"You really want to spend our honeymoon in your room?" Jerry asked. "The tiny little privacy palace in your aunt's house where you can hear the person in the next room snoring? Well, that's just not gonna do, I figure."

"It's the best we have, Jerry. In case you've forgotten, we're broke."

Jerry was beaming now. "We were, but we're not. My Aunt Esther found out we were getting married quick and stopped by with some egg money she'd been saving. It's more than enough to put us up at the Kahler Hotel!"

Marjie jumped straight up into Jerry's arms. "Oh, Jerry, it's like a dream! I've always wanted to stay in a hotel. And the Kahler's such a fancy one. Do you suppose we'll look out of place?"

"Probably. Who cares? All they want is our money," Jerry responded, trying to get her back down to earth. "Let's get going. That room's all ours for two days."

"You drive," Marjie pleaded. "This is not the time or the place for me to learn. And I'm really wanting to deliver a few wedding presents of my own."

He blushed at the tone of her voice. "But *this is* the time and place for you to drive, 'cause when I leave, you've got to be able to get your license. C'mon, get behind the wheel. I'll be right beside you."

They crawled in, and he handed her the keys. She looked bewildered, so he launched one more kiss before the driving lesson commenced.

"How did you drive the tractor at home?" Jerry began.

That was easy enough. "I shoved in the clutch, held my other foot on the brake, pulled out the choke, turned the key till the motor started . . ." She threw him a questioning look, as if unsure whether to continue, but he gave her a reassuring nod and she went on with more confidence. "Then I put the shifter into first, let out the clutch real slow while taking my foot off the brake, and away I went."

"Well, that's exactly what I want you to do now," Jerry said. "If you can drive a tractor, why are you so worried about driving a car?"

"I hate to tell."

"We're losing valuable time, lover girl."

"I tried to drive another fellow's car, and I turned too sharp and hit the mailbox," Marjie confessed. "He got so mad, I decided to never try again."

"Shoot! You shouldn't let that slow you down," Jerry said. "There's no worry with this old Ford. If you bash a mailbox or two, it probably won't even show—except maybe on the mailbox! Here now," he added, placing her hand on the gearshift and covering it with his own hand. "Let me show you where the gears are. Shove in the clutch. Okay, now, here's reverse; down for first; up and over for second; straight down for third. See, Marjie, you can do it! Nothing to it!"

Remarkably, Marjie believed him. It took her a while to get the hang of changing gears, and the car jerked and sputtered for several miles, but each shift showed improvement. By the time they reached the next town, she was almost relaxed. Even Jerry was amazed at how quickly she learned.

It took them a little longer to get to Rochester than if Jerry had been driving. But when they pulled up to Marjie's aunt's house so Marjie could pack her overnight bag, Jerry's lessons had given her another gift she hadn't dreamed about the night before—the gift of confidence. And she was looking forward to making the Kahler Hotel worth every precious dollar they were going to spend on it.

5

———— ❧ ————

THE FIGHT

It was just after two in the morning when Marjie lifted her arm to check her watch again. She had discovered there was sufficient light from the street below to let her read the dial as well as to nicely silhouette Jerry's face. For a long while she'd been watching him sleep—studying every line and feature—knowing that this memory would have to last for a long time. Time was Marjie's unmerciful enemy, and her only weapon was to take back every second with undivided attention.

After what had seemed like an unending stream of noisy people and banging doors in the long hallway outside the newlyweds' room, the hotel had finally subsided into silence. Marjie listened intently as Jerry's quiet breathing became the only sound that mattered. His presence was so subtle, yet so full of peace and rest, that Marjie strained to capture the mystery it contained. To a day that had been filled with rare treasures, she added this moment as a gem for saving.

But all the wonders of the day and evening could not stop the dark intruders that had waited patiently for their chance to steal the joys of Marjie's heart. Even now, as she took delight in the lean, brown face, the bright, fine hair, the gently curving lips that had shown her such tenderness and passion . . . unbidden and unwelcome came the sinking awareness that she had only one more day to look at him like this. Only one more day—and there was no way to turn back the clock.

And then came the overwhelming sadness at the prospect of being left alone. The coming lonely weeks seemed to loom before her like a cruel prison.

Finally she felt the creeping paralysis of fear at the thought of her husband at war, in harm's way. She pictured him dodging shrapnel on a shifting deck, fighting fires in a cramped hold, clinging to a flimsy rail over an angry sea. She felt helpless to stop the onslaught of images and thoughts that reeled through her mind like the war clippings she had seen on the movie newsreels. Finally a portent appeared of Jerry as he was now sleeping, but sinking ever so slowly to the bottom of the ocean, where he would rest forever.

With a shudder she reached out to her husband's face with the hope that touching him again would break the spell. It worked. His smooth-shaven skin felt warm and strong, and her panic made its retreat. She lightly stroked his high forehead, his prominent cheekbones. With a whisper that only she could hear, Marjie said, "What will I do when you're not here to chase away the fear?"

Her thoughts drifted back to the wedding vows that they had repeated earlier in the day, *For better, for worse, in sickness and in health, till death us do part*. And she wondered whether, if they hadn't already had so much "better," perhaps the parting wouldn't feel so much worse.

"Would you go away if I told you how much this hurts me?" Marjie whispered ever so quietly. "Oh, Jerry, I don't want you to go. Don't leave me . . ."

But she knew that all the pleading in the world would not change the inevitable. A code of honor was inscribed so deeply inside Jerry Macmillan that to break it would break the man. Like her brother Paul, he would fight for what he believed in, no matter what the cost. *But I'm paying the cost, too*, she told him in her heart.

Sighing, she touched his face again, searching for the strength to face her fear and doubt. But this time not even the feel of his skin could disturb the sadness that had draped itself around her heart. She wondered if this was what her mother had lived with since her father passed away.

Then the rattle of elevator doors broke the silence, and Marjie jumped as a boisterous male voice echoed down the empty corridor. His words were slurred and angry as he poured out a volley of profanity toward an unfortunate female companion. Her high-pitched barrage of protest nearly matched him in decibels but were clearly ineffective in stopping his drunken onslaught.

Jerry snapped out of his deep sleep with a jolt and sat up in bed, looking right and left and then at Marjie. "What's going on?" he mumbled in wild confusion. Then, with another loud threat from the drunken bully that he was going to "knock some sense" into his companion's "dizzy head," Jerry was out of bed and out the hallway door before Marjie could utter a protest.

Without hesitation, Jerry stepped between the shouting man and his victim, looking straight into the man's bloodshot eyes, inflamed with fury. The drunk was a hulk of a man and spoiling for a fight, but obviously out of shape and too inebriated to keep his balance.

"You lift your hand, buster, and I'll drop you so fast you won't know what hit you," Jerry warned with a steely voice. "And if I hear you swearing at the lady one more time, I'll make you sorry your mother never washed your mouth out with soap." He paused and gave the giant his moment to decide.

Bewildered and unsure of his foe, the bully backed up a step and tried to measure Jerry. By now several other hallway doors had opened, and a few brave souls were peeking out. With his pride at stake, the drunk made his biggest mistake of the night: he reached a bulky arm back to take a swing. Jerry met him with a solid punch to the stomach that doubled him over. It was only a warning shot. Jerry could easily have polished him off with more blows. Instead, he stood back and watched the drunk catch his breath, then look up, dazed and shaken.

"You want more?" Jerry barked.

Without a hint of protest came the quick answer, "No."

"Then apologize to the lady," Jerry demanded, pointing to the woman. "Now!"

The red-faced buffoon stood back up and looked over at his disgruntled lady friend. The fire had gone out of his eyes, and a measure of sanity had returned. "Harriet . . . I'm . . . I'm sorry. It'll never happen again."

She looked relieved that the battle was over but did not hint that she believed the promise. She only gave her man a blank stare, then without a word of thanks she stepped around Jerry and steered the vanquished man down the hallway toward their room.

The many doors that had been cracked open to see what was happening began to click shut as Jerry turned back to face a smiling Marjie, who stood in the doorway wearing her long, black robe.

"Guess I didn't notice how skinny your legs were till now," Marjie said with her patented smirk.

Jerry scanned down toward his feet with the dawning realization that he had performed his hallway heroics before dozens of onlookers clad only in boxer shorts! With the agility of a deer, he made a single leap that sailed him into the safety of his own room. The sound of the locking door was music to his ears as he dove into the bed and sought the cover of the sheets.

Marjie was laughing so hard she barely managed to walk back to the bed and flop down beside Jerry, who stared at her in consternation. "You didn't tell me you knew how to fly! The hotel should pay you to come in to do hallway shows!" she said between gasps for air. "Do you do this every time you stay in a hotel, or did you plan this just to impress me?"

She gave him a hug and snuggled up close, then collapsed into another round of giggles.

"Aren't you Mrs. Funny?" Jerry said with the crooked smile of an embarrassed victor. "I could have gotten killed by Frankenstein's brother, and you'd stand there laughing like a monkey. Did you see how big he was?"

"Or how drunk?" Marjie added. "You could've sneezed on him, and he'd have gone down!"

"Wait a minute," Jerry protested mildly, although by now he was laughing, too. "That sucker was mad. You should've seen the weird look in his eyes. We had a bull one time that had the same look . . . weighed about the same, too!"

The newlyweds laughed again, then Marjie took his punching hand and gently stroked it. "What you did made me very proud to be your wife," she spoke softly. "Maybe the jerk will think twice before he hits a woman again. But you scared me half to death, too. How'd you dare do that? You did notice that none of the other men jumped out to help you, didn't you?"

"Maybe all they had on was their underwear," Jerry replied with a snort. "Can you believe I did that? Next thing you know they'll have my picture in the morning papers: 'UNDERWEAR VIGILANTE STRIKES AGAIN!' My mother always warned me that the day was coming when I'd be sorry I didn't wear pajamas."

"So, why'd you do it?" Marjie questioned.

"Didn't have time to think about it," Jerry said with a shrug. "Somebody had to stick up for her. I just happened to get there first."

"Right. Like those other chickens hiding behind their doors were going to step in front of that gorilla. Well, sweetheart, the navy can sure use men like you." Marjie raised up and rewarded Jerry with a kiss that more than made up for not being thanked by the woman in the hallway.

For a long while the lovers held each other. Both were wide awake, and both were deep in thought. Jerry was the first to voice his concerns.

"We were gonna try to not talk about what's ahead, but I've got some things that have been bothering me all day. Do you mind talking about it now?" Jerry asked.

Marjie pulled back, looked into Jerry's eyes, and shook her head no.

"I'm worried about my dad," said Jerry. "Real worried. And it's not just about his blood pressure. Since my mother died, he's never been the same. He's so lonely . . . it's scary at times. I don't know how he'll get along with me gone—not that having me there seemed to make a big difference."

He reached down to pull a long, wavy strand away from her

face. "I don't know how comfortable you feel with my dad, but as soon as you get your car license, would you drive out to the farm and spend some time with him? Maybe help him with some things around the house, but mostly just see how he's doing? Dad hates to talk on the telephone, so you won't get much out of him that way."

Marjie waited until she was sure that Jerry had said all he wanted, then she replied, "You know I think the world of your pa. I'll go out there as often as I can—I promise. I need to thank him for this ring, anyway!" She fingered it lightly and paused with her own thoughts.

"Anything else?" she asked.

"Just one," Jerry said. "Well, two. But both are about you working. I've wondered a long time, but before we were married it just didn't seem like my business."

"You can ask me," she assured him solemnly.

"Well, explain to me one more time why you hafta keep on working at that cafe when you've got a high-school degree? You're smart. You could get an office job, or something better."

"I tried being a secretary, and I hated every minute of it," Marjie replied. "I like being a waitress—I guess because I get to know so many different people. The pay is lousy, but the tips are good. I tried all those other jobs, but nothing seems to fit."

"Okay, but does it have to be the Green Parrot?" Jerry hesitated, then went on. "There's something about your boss that worries me," he deliberated. "Besides being a jerk, I don't like the way he looks at you. He's got more on his mind than just making money."

"He's a married—"

"And I'm a saint," Jerry broke in. "He's a creep, and you know it."

"There's a lot of creeps in this town," she answered. "I've handled worse cases than him before. Besides, the tips are the best I've gotten anywhere."

"Promise me you'll watch his every move," Jerry demanded, "and that you'll quit the moment he crosses the line, even a little."

Marjie nodded in agreement. "That was two questions. My turn?"

"Ah, just one more question—something I've wondered about for a long time. I have to ask it now that we're married," he added. "If the tips are so hot, why are you as broke as me?"

"Well," Marjie responded, "the tips aren't *that* great, and I've got expenses like everyone else. But you're right, I could have been tucking some money away in the bank. I have a secret that explains why I'm broke, but I've never told anyone. Will you promise not to tell another soul? And will you still love me after I say it?"

"I promise," Jerry answered.

She swallowed hard and gazed at him soberly. "I gambled it away," she said. "I can't stop myself."

Jerry swallowed it hook, line, and sinker. Taking in a deep breath, he whispered, "You serious?"

"Of course not! Mr. Gullible." Marjie broke into a renewed gale of laughter, and again it took Jerry several rounds to find the humor. "Seriously, I haven't told this to anyone, especially my mother. When Pa was up here in the Methodist Hospital years ago, he racked up a sizable bill. My folks would've lost the farm if they'd had to pay. So I talked to the hospital administrator and set up a deal where I could pay it off on extended terms. The doctors told my folks that Pa was nearly totally covered because some of the procedures were considered experimental. They never knew a thing, and I've just about got the bill paid."

This secret left Jerry more dazed than her joke. He fumbled around for words. "But . . . but what about *your* life?"

Marjie answered his question with a question: "So why did you stay on the farm? You could've gotten a loan for the Martin farm and gone out on your own, but you knew your pa needed you. Sometimes you just do what needs to be done." Then she flashed him her familiar grin. "Besides, I seem to be doing very well with my own life at the moment."

For a long moment he just looked at her, freshly aware of all the reasons he loved her so much, yet wondering what other secrets she might have. Finally he shook his head as if to clear it.

"All right, Marjie, now it *is* your turn. What was on your mind before I started asking my questions?"

Marjie revisited her thoughts, knowing they would not spill out the way she'd like, but also knowing she had to try. "Before you went parading your body around in the hallway, I was lying here for the longest time, loving everything about you, when I got so scared that I might lose you. I think I'd lose my—"

Her words broke off in a hush. Jerry took her into his arms and held her tightly, stroking her hair. She whispered, "Promise me you'll come home!"

Painfully he fished for the right words. "Marjie, I'm not God. I promise that I will be faithful to you every moment I am gone, and I promise to do everything I can to stay alive, but only God can bring me home."

"Ma was right," Marjie said. "Going to war *has* turned you religious. Are you expecting that sermon to help me?"

"I don't know what else to say," Jerry said. "I don't know what difference it makes, but I believe that much is true."

For the first time, Marjie thought she believed that much as well. "You're right. But promise me anyway."

"I promise," Jerry complied, with a smile and another hug.

"Good boy," she said, then rearranged herself in his arms. "All right, then, enough serious stuff for now. Seeing as we're so wide awake, I was wondering if you were ready for another wedding present?"

6

PARTING

"Now I know why you carry this ugly old blanket in the car," Marjie said as she pulled it closer around Jerry and herself. They'd been sitting cuddled together in the idling car outside the Rochester depot for about five minutes, waiting for the Minneapolis bus. "We didn't have to get here so early, you know. My teeth are even chattering! Are you sure this fine old Ford actually has a heater?"

"Beats sitting outside," Jerry said with a sigh, "but not by much." Then he grinned. "It's a great excuse to sit close, though!"

"You probably unplugged the heater a long time ago so all the girls you took out would have to snuggle," teased Marjie.

"Sounds just like me, don't it," Jerry said. "All the girls—that's a good one. You know you're the only woman I ever took out, and that's only because you gave me so much help. It worked pretty good with you, though."

"I thought so. Ma warned me about men like you," Marjie said. "Too late now, though. So why don't you plug it back in so I don't freeze?"

Jerry laughed. "What you see is what you get, babe. This old buggy is running as well as it has in years, including the heater. But I guess I oughta clue you in on some things. My father wants you to bring the car out to him so he can keep it tuned up. And if you have any problems, call him before you do anything with it. He likes to work on engines, and he's pretty good at it, but mostly it's important that he feels like he can help you."

"You can bet I won't be messing with it!" Marjie replied. "Unless you want to give me real quick lessons. I didn't think I could drive, but your driving lessons worked wonders. Maybe I'm a really good mechanic and I don't even know it. What do you think?"

"I think you're the biggest dreamer in the county," Jerry said, "but you're sure the prettiest. Pretty good driver, too, I gotta admit. Make sure you go to the courthouse to get your license, though. If you get caught without it, you'll have to do a lot of sweet-talking to avoid a ticket."

"I'd rather save my sweet-talking for you," Marjie said, taking Jerry's hands in hers. "Your ring looks good on you. Didn't take the jeweler long to size it. How's it feel?"

Jerry fingered the gold band, trying to pull it over his knuckle. "Tight. What'd you tell that guy, anyway? Least you don't have to worry about me taking it off now."

"You take it off and I'll shoot you," Marjie warned. "I've seen lonely men who didn't think twice about pulling off their ring when they were away from their wives."

"Like your boss?" Jerry asked. "I suppose I'll see plenty of it in the days to come. Makes me sick. But I suppose I'll see a lot worse than that, too."

Marjie shook her head in acknowledgment. "Pa said war does horrible things to men—even good men. Turns some of them into animals."

"Maybe they didn't have someone back home to keep them from doing whatever they did," Jerry wondered out loud. "Well, I don't know what war will be like, but I know I'm not gonna let it turn me into an animal. Besides, I've got your picture safely tucked away. Just looking at it from time to time's all I need to keep me on the straight and narrow. Man'd be a fool to mess around when he's got someone like you waiting at home."

"You better mean that, sailor," Marjie said with a tough-girl accent borrowed from the radio dramas. Then she added solemnly. "I really do trust you, Jerry. But it may be tougher than you think. You're going to see other men—married men—toss away their morals. Some of them will try to take you down with them, tempt you to forget about me."

"It's not gonna happen," Jerry spoke defiantly.

"Well, then, let's do something about it before the bus gets here," Marjie responded.

"What's that supposed to mean?" he asked suspiciously, seeing the familiar spark of mischief return to her eye.

"Let's go in the bus depot and ask the guy at the desk if we can borrow his scissors and buy a couple of envelopes."

"I have a feeling I'm gonna to be sorry I asked, but what do we need the scissors and envelopes for?"

"I want to cut a lock of your hair and save it until you come home," she told him matter-of-factly. "And I want you to have some locks of my hair, too. Then, when we look at each other's pictures, we'll have something extra to make it real. It'll almost be like having you with me!"

Jerry let out a deep groan. "You seriously think I'm going in there and ask that old buzzard at the counter for his scissors? He'll think we're nuts."

"What's new?" Marjie was beaming. "Please . . . for me."

"For crying out loud," Jerry grumped, reaching over to turn the car off and take the keys. "Let's go. But that's it. No more crazy stuff. Okay?"

"Of course."

They jumped out of the car and raced into the depot. Walking up to the counter, Marjie whispered, "You ask him. It'll do you good."

The elderly man looked up from his desk. "Bus ain't here yet. Told you that when you got your ticket. It'll be another ten minutes, if it's on time. Don't set your watch by it."

"It's not about the bus," Jerry responded, lightly scratching the back of his neck. "I was, uh, just wondering if you could . . . sell me a couple envelopes and, uh, let me borrow your scissors for a minute."

"What for?"

Jerry looked at Marjie, already embarrassed. "Well, uh, I'm

leaving for the war . . . and we want to carry a lock of each other's hair with us."

The attendant blinked his eyes and wrinkled his forehead. "You're joking, right? Hmmm . . . guess you're not. That's a new one, mister. But I've heard a lot of new ones in the past days. Yours tops the list, though. Well, here's the scissors, and take these envelopes. No charge. My wife loves these stories, especially the strange ones."

"It was his idea," Marjie told the old man with a shrug.

Jerry took the scissors and looked at Marjie as if he were intending to cut more than her hair. "Let's get this over with fast," he said, handing her the scissors. He scanned the clusters of people waiting for the bus, hoping that no one was watching.

Marjie quickly clipped a section of her hair that was particularly thick and wouldn't show the damage. Then she turned her attention to Jerry. Choosing her favorite lock of hair, which happened to be front and center, Marjie reached out to make her clip.

"Hold it!" Jerry called as he jerked his head back. "You're gonna make me look like I've got a bad case of mange. At least take it from the back."

"Everybody's watching now, Jerry," Marjie said with a delighted smile. "Hold still and let me have the best section. In a few hours you'll belong to the navy, and all this nice hair will be lying in a pile on the floor anyway. You'll never miss it."

Jerry weighed his options and decided that surrender was his only recourse. He bent down, and the scissors did their swift work. Seeing the delight on Marjie's face, he hoped that it was worth the price he had paid.

As Marjie fiddled with the envelopes and precious hair, Jerry turned to hand the scissors back to the clerk. "Thank you very much," he said.

"Don't mention it," the old man replied. "If you ain't a sight! Looks like you got a hole in your head!" With that he burst into laughter, and several close onlookers joined in.

Jerry reached up and felt the gaping chasm, shook his head, and forced a smile for his admirers. "The hole is in the brain," he declared.

Taking Marjie's hand, the newlyweds made their exit as fast as Jerry could negotiate. Hopping back into the safety of the car, Jerry took a peek in the rearview mirror and let out a long groan. "That's the last time you ever cut my hair. I'll scare people on the bus. They'll think I'm from the mental hospital."

"I've seen worse . . . once," Marjie joked. "When I was five, I tried cutting my dog's hair. Believe me, my haircutting has improved."

Jerry laughed at how ridiculous the whole thing was and turned to Marjie. "Was it really worth it?" he asked.

Marjie closed her eyes and whispered something to herself, pausing to find her words. Finally she said, "More than you can ever understand." Her hands came up to her face and massaged her eyes, concealing the first tears of parting. Jerry reached his arm around Marjie and pulled her close to him.

"How am I supposed to live without you?" she said between sobs, burying her face in his coat.

Jerry squeezed Marjie even tighter and choked up himself. He had no answer, though he hoped one might come. His only words were a muffled, "I guess the same way I live without you . . . and I can't."

Marjie felt Jerry's warm tears dropping into her hair, and the two lovers shook together. Silence reigned for the first time in two days. Finally Marjie regained her composure, and she looked up into her husband's tearstained face. She reached out, unbuttoned his coat, then slipped her hand directly over his heart. "We've got to find a way, Jerry. The next time I see your face, I want this heart beating, you understand? Come back or you'll break my heart forever, and I'll . . . I'll never forgive you."

Tears still streaming, she reached up to touch his cheek. "Oh, Jerry, I could never love another man like I love you . . . never. You've got to come back so—so I can hold you again. So I can make a home with you . . . and have your babies . . . and grow old with you."

Jerry cupped his wife's face in his strong hands. It took him some moments to find his voice. "Babe, my heart belongs to you—I'm leaving it here with you. But you've got to be strong, keep on hoping. And we will be together again, just like you said. We will make a home and raise our children on the farm, just like my dad and my granddad and my great-granddad did.

"And, Marjie," he added tenderly as the late bus made its dreaded appearance, "I don't plan on ever getting old."

7

THE FIRST DAY

Marjie sat motionless behind the steering wheel of the idling black Ford. She had completely forgotten both the blanket and the cold. Her puffy eyes had followed the movement of the bus out of the parking lot, down the empty street, until it turned north and vanished behind a line of downtown buildings. All that remained was the ghostly cloud of diesel smoke and a deserted street corner.

For several minutes the only change in Marjie's facial expression was the occasional blinking of her eyes. It was as if she waited long enough, the bus would return around the corner to bring back her man.

But there would be no reappearance, and Marjie knew it. Ever so slowly the truth began to press its crushing weight down upon the center of her heart: *Jerry is gone . . . gone to war . . . for who knows how long . . . perhaps forever. And if he returns, he may not be the same man who left me today.*

Finally Marjie gave up her barren vigil, turning her eyes to the sad reflection in the rearview mirror. Her blank stare struggled to capture any thought that might have hope written on it. *You look a sight* was the only thought she could muster. Marjie watched as the hollowness of her soul seeped up to quench the fire of love in her eyes. "I look like somebody died," she said to herself.

She closed her eyes, scrunched down in the car seat, and pulled the tattered blanket up over her head. Every nerve in her body wanted to scream, but all that escaped was a deep, protracted groan.

She pressed her fingers against her eyelids, trying to hold in the waves of sadness that had surfaced from somewhere deep within her conscious thought. But when she caught the subtle scent of Jerry's aftershave on the blanket, the battle ceased.

All the lofty joys of the past two days and the sudden grief of separation met in an explosion of titanic proportions. How long Marjie wept unabated and unashamedly was lost within the safety of her husband's blanket, but it was more than long enough to drain the well of her tears. And even when the sobs had finally run their course, Marjie did not sit up. Her only wish was that she could stay right where she was until Jerry returned to take her home.

"So what do I do now?" Marjie whispered, trying to piece together her next move. "Stay here and freeze to death?" Her throat hurt, her head throbbed, her eyes burned. Then Marjie remembered that she was scheduled to work the lunch-through-dinner shift at the Green Parrot Cafe. "You are even dumber than you look," she told herself with a sigh. "Two hours from now I'm supposed to be wearing a big smile and—"

A sudden knock on the car window brought Marjie out of her dark reverie. Throwing off the blanket and sitting up, she turned to look into the shivering frown of Harry Backstrom, a city policeman who frequently ate at the cafe. An "Oh no!" burst from Marjie's lips before she could catch it. *Here I sit looking like I'm stone drunk . . . and I don't have a driver's license!* Once again, Harry rapped on the window.

Marjie tried to smooth her hair, then reached over and slowly cranked down the window. She did not have a clue what she was going to say.

"You all right, Miss Livingstone?" he asked. "I got a call from the old guy who runs the depot that this Ford's been sitting here idling for a long time. Said it looked abandoned."

Marjie hoped her voice and brain were still working. "I'm

sorry, Harry," she said, relieved that something came out. "Are you married?"

"Yes, ma'am," the policeman responded. "Twenty-six years. Why'd you ask?"

"Thought it might help explain what I'm doing here," Marjie said with a sigh. She wondered if she could tell the story without any more tears. "Harry, I got married two days ago, and my husband just left on the Minneapolis bus to enlist in—" That was as far as she could go. Surprisingly, another reserve of tears spilled out.

Harry reached out a strong right hand and enveloped Marjie's small hand. The hand was half-frozen, but the words were warm. "You don't have to say another word, Marjie," he said solemnly. "I got a boy who's already left, too."

Marjie dried her eyes and looked into the policeman's fatherly eyes. She was relieved that she did not need to explain the rest of her story. "Thank you, Harry," she said. "Just give me a minute or two, and I'll be on my way."

"Stay here as long as you need," Harry said. Then he added conversationally, "Where'd you get the car? Don't think I ever saw you driving before."

"It's my husband's," Marjie answered, wondering if she should tell him the whole truth. "He said it was my wedding present."

Harry paused, looking intently into her eyes. "You don't have a license, do you?" he asked.

"Well . . . not really . . . not yet. But I was going to get one first thing. How'd you know?" Marjie asked.

"Honest faces don't wear guilt very well," answered Harry with a smile. "I had a daughter who gave me that same look you just did when she was covering up. Are you a decent driver?"

"I'm okay," Marjie said. "I think."

Harry stamped and chafed his arms. "Well, why don't you follow me down to the courthouse, and we'll fix you up with a license in a hurry. I'm gonna turn into an icicle if I stand here any longer. But you've got to promise that you won't tell anyone I let you drive without a license."

"I promise," Marjie said, a slight smile surfacing through the ashen ruins of her grief.

"And congratulations on your marriage," Harry added with a grin from ear to ear. "Who's the lucky man?"

"You wouldn't know him, Harry," Marjie answered with a beam of pride. "He's a country boy. Jerry Macmillan. The finest man in the world."

"I'm sure he is, *Mrs. Macmillan*," Harry said with a chuckle. "I'm sure he is. He's got a fine woman—that I know."

With that, Harry Backstrom nodded his head and walked back to his own car. Marjie was left with the unquestionable impression that Harry had somehow been sent to help her. "Strange," she muttered to her herself as she reached for the gearshift.

Motioning for Marjie to follow, Harry pulled out in front of her and headed for the county courthouse.

Two hours later, Marjie approached the front entrance of the Green Parrot Cafe looking much improved. After getting her driver's license with Harry's assistance, she had gone back to her boarding room and spent some time on her face. A couple of aspirins had taken care of the headache, and a washcloth and hairbrush had helped with her dishevelment, but there was nothing she could do with her bloodshot eyes. She kept wishing she had tried to get the day off, even though she badly needed the money.

The Green Parrot perched on a busy corner a couple of blocks from the Mayo Clinic and served a steady stream of regulars from the hospital staff as well as the families of patients. Mealtimes were always especially hectic, but there was seldom a time when business was slow. All of the booths and most of the stools and tables were filled when Marjie arrived.

Marjie worked behind the counter and took care of twelve stools. Two other waitresses worked the booths and tables. And then there was Gordon Stilwell, "the boss." Stilwell was the owner and manager of the cafe. He ran the cash register, seated diners who wanted a booth or table, and watched over the operation with the eyes of an eagle—or was it a vulture.

Marjie had been told that Stilwell was only forty-two, but she was sure he must be at least fifty. His vain attempts to cover his balding head and hide his expanding waistline, his smooth ten-star smile for the obviously wealthier diners, and the stories of his womanizing exploits turned Marjie's stomach whenever she got too close to him. *Maybe I'll be lucky and he'll be sick today*, Marjie thought.

As she stepped into the cafe, she was startled by a cheer of congratulations from one of the waitresses already on duty. Many of the regulars echoed the congratulations as the woman set down her tray of dirty dishes and rushed over to give Marjie a hug. Priscilla Simmons was none too smart and always too loud, but Marjie loved her warm smiles and her genuine caring.

Wiping her fingers with her apron, Priscilla reached into a deep pocket and pulled out a small envelope, then stuck it into Marjie's coat pocket. "Just a little something from me and Bill," Priscilla said with a laugh. "You shoulda told us sooner! We coulda done something nice, you know."

"It was sort of spur of the moment," Marjie answered. "If I'd have known sooner, you and Bill would have been the first to know."

Priscilla took Marjie's hand and lifted it up to the light. "Let me see your ring," she said. "Lovely . . . lovely. It's a dandy, Marjie."

"Thanks," Marjie responded. "It belonged to Jerry's mother."

"You don't say! God rest her soul," Priscilla said as she paused to push her glasses back up on her nose. "That ring's more than lovely, dear. It's blessed."

Marjie wasn't sure what Priscilla meant or if Priscilla even knew what she meant, but Marjie appreciated the sentiment. Unconsciously she reached to caress the shiny stone.

"You guard that with your life," Priscilla said, glancing around quickly and grabbing her tray back up. "Look out for Stilwell," she added under her breath. "He's acting real strange—like he's got something nasty on his mind. You know what I mean." Without further explanation, Priscilla dashed off to the kitchen with her tray.

Marjie took off her coat and headed for her usual position behind the counter. She was hoping for a normal, uneventful shift, but Priscilla did not dish out warnings without a reason. Just then, Stilwell marched out from the kitchen and came straight for her. Marjie bristled inside and prepared to man her mental battle stations.

"Congratulations ... congratulations ... congratulations!" the manager called out, but his words sounded as wooden as the oak floor. "How could you go and get married without telling us? Let me give you a big hug!"

Marjie had never allowed Gordon Stilwell to put a hand on her, but she could not think of any way to escape. It was obvious that he had been planning this ambush from the moment he arrived that morning and heard her news. Stilwell's arms wrapped around her like an anaconda and pulled her body tightly against his. She suppressed a shudder, wanting to pull away, but was keenly aware of what had happened to the other waitresses who offended him in public. His hug was too long and far too affectionate, and Marjie determined she'd be ready the next time he attempted this trick.

Finally pulling away, Stilwell reached into his pocket and with a greasy smile pulled out an envelope. "Marjie, a little wedding present ... with love," he oozed as he handed it over.

"Thank you, Mr. Stilwell," Marjie said, forcing a smile and wondering what favors he would demand in return.

"Come on now, when are you going to drop the 'Mister' and just call me Gordon?" he teased, pulling his sagging dress pants back up into position.

"I really prefer to keep it *Mr.* Stilwell," Marjie said evenly, stretching out a thin line of defense. "And I really need to get to work now."

But instead of letting her move around the counter, Stilwell stepped in front of Marjie and took her hand. "Let me see your ring," he demanded. He made no comment about the diamond, but seemed to draw satisfaction from holding her hand as long as he could. Then he leaned in toward her face and whispered in her ear, "You look just wonderful this morning. Must have been quite a wedding night?"

Marjie pulled her hand away. It was all she could do to keep from slapping him. She had put up with his "accidentally" bumping into her as she worked behind the counter, but until now he had never made any overt advance toward her. That he would do so now, on the very day Jerry left, pushed her over the edge.

With a murderous glare and a quiet, measured tone, she warned, "Don't you ever speak to me like that again—unless you want me to give your wife a call. Try me if you think I'm bluffing." Then she stepped forward and drove all of her weight down on his right foot. "Get the point?" she asked.

Marjie stepped back and moved around Stilwell, who stood frozen in position. She had successfully backed him off, and no one in the cafe had noticed a thing. But Gordon Stilwell's pride had been damaged far deeper than his foot. Marjie knew he would find a way to make her pay—sooner or later. She only hoped it was later.

Nothing more occurred between Marjie and Stilwell the rest of the day, which turned out to be very busy. Marjie was delighted to share her wedding story with her regular customers as well as to gather in a pile of extraordinary tips. Still, she could not help noticing Stilwell's eyes occasionally following her as she moved back and forth behind the counter, and she was immensely relieved when quitting time finally arrived.

Marjie drove the black Ford to her aunt's house and slipped quietly into her boarding room, where she flipped off her shoes, tossed her purse and her body on the bed, and stretched out. She was sure this was the longest day she had ever lived through, and parts of it easily ranked as one of the worst.

Inside Marjie's purse was the envelope from "the boss." Her curious side was dying to open it and see if it was truly a gift. Her suspicious side warned her to keep it sealed and give it back in the morning. As usual, her curious side won the argument.

Pulling the envelope out of her purse, Marjie held it under the light, then slowly tore it open. Inside was a wedding card and a ten-dollar bill. "Wow! The old cheapskate really coughed it up this time," she said quietly. "Wonder what he has in mind?" She knew the card would tell the rest of the story.

Flipping open the card, Marjie's attention went to his scrawled message: "There's more where this came from. If you're interested, meet me at the Blue Inn at 9:00 P.M."

Marjie uttered a little cry of disgust and flung the note and the money to the floor, shaking her fingers as if she had touched something slimy. "You filthy dog," Marjie spat out the words as though he could hear her. "Jerry would kill you if I showed him this note."

She jumped off the bed and began to pace the little room to work off her rage. Stilwell had crossed the line, just as Jerry had warned, and her first inclination was to quit—or go straight to the man's wife. But she still needed the good tips she could get at the Green Parrot.

"Someday, though . . ." she muttered. As soon as she had that hospital bill paid off, she would find a way to take "the boss" down to his knees.

She paced for another ten minutes while her fury drained into a weary nausea. She could feel Stilwell's eyes following her, his flabby body pressing against hers, and she felt dirty from the man's intrusion. And her resolve still held; she would get the man. It would take time to plot the perfect revenge. But she had plenty of time.

In the meantime, though, she felt wearier than she could ever remember feeling. Maybe that was a mercy, she thought as she sank back on the bed and drifted off to a heavy sleep, longing for Jerry and beginning her count of the nights she must endure alone.

8

THE BUDDY PLAN

The thud of the bus door slamming shut and the sight of Marjie's last wave replayed in Jerry's mind a thousand times as the bus rolled its way north on Highway 52 to Minneapolis. The snow-blanketed fields and woods held little interest to Jerry's blank stare through the frosty window. His expressionless face refused to betray the waves of conflicting thoughts and emotions that pulled his mind and heart in whatever direction they desired.

One wave of thoughts questioned what Marjie might go through without him, whether his father's health would hold up, how long he might be gone, and what would happen to them if he came home maimed or, worse yet, if he never came home again.

Then he thought of the Japanese bombers scorching Pearl Harbor, of Billy Wilson struggling to stay alive in a naval hospital, of the promise he'd made, of his duty to defend his nation and his home. Wave after wave crashed in upon him, battering him around like a chunk of driftwood in a crosscurrent.

Jerry was glad the seat next to him was empty. He was in no mood to talk to anyone about anything. If only he could go home and take a long walk out in the fields to clear his head. It seemed impossible to think at all with the vision of Marjie standing before him and the ringing sound of the door closing still echoing in his ears.

How could he leave behind the one whose love meant more to him than life itself? And would his going really make any difference? Maybe he could serve the war effort better by helping his dad keep the farm going. Maybe he was just being selfish, leaving his dad in the lurch. Jerry knew that no one would fault him for changing his mind, especially given Benjamin's age and physical problems. But could he forgive himself if he didn't go?

Now the waves of thought were a spinning whirlpool that threatened to suck him under. Part of him wanted to yell and pound the window, but instead he sat immobilized by the overwhelming current of his thoughts. He dropped his head into his hands and closed his eyes, but the whirling continued.

Maybe we should have waited to get married until—

Just then Jerry felt someone tap him on the shoulder. Silencing a deep groan, he looked up into the wide-open smile of a man a few years younger than he was. Jerry had briefly noticed him in the seat across the aisle; for some reason he looked familiar.

"Mind if I join you?" the young man asked, then plopped down in the seat before Jerry could respond. "I hate sitting alone."

Jerry relaxed the deep frown on his forehead and tried to find an answer that would not be rude. "Be my guest. But I'm afraid I won't be much company. Got a lot on mind right now."

"I noticed the pretty girl you kissed goodbye back there," the stranger said. "She your girlfriend?"

"She was," Jerry said as his eyes drifted back out to the frosty rural landscape. "We got married two days ago."

"Wow! You got yourself a beaut. Congratulations," the friendly observer added. "And now you're heading off for war, right?"

Jerry swung his attention back to his inquisitive neighbor. He wasn't sure how far he wanted this conversation to go. "How'd you know that?"

"I guess you didn't see me in the bus depot," he said with a grin. "I overheard you trying to explain why you needed the scissors. You should have heard that old geezer at the desk carrying on after you walked out the door. Got right on the phone and called his wife. That lady of yours sure did some damage to your hair!"

Both men broke out in laughs, and Jerry reached up to feel the empty space he'd already forgotten about. He was surprised that the newcomer's comment did not embarrass him.

Reaching out his hand, Jerry said, "My name's Jerry Macmillan. Pleased to meet you."

"I'm Chester Stanfeld," the other man replied as he gave Jerry's hand a firm squeeze. "Pleased to meet you, too."

"You from around here?" Jerry asked. "You look sorta familiar."

"Yep, sure am," Chester replied. "I live south of Chatfield on a farm with my folks. How 'bout yourself?"

"You know where Greenleafton is? Little burg of about eighty people twelve miles southwest of Preston," Jerry answered. "I farm with my dad."

Chester smiled knowingly. "Now I know where I've seen you before. I've been out to the ballpark there a couple of times. You may not remember this, but I played against you in fast-pitch softball. You covered third base like a pro."

Jerry laughed, self-conscious but pleased by the compliment. "You got a better memory than me. I love to play the game, but I got a feeling my ball playing days are over."

"Mine, too. Where you heading?" Chester asked.

"Well, I thought I was on my way to Minneapolis to enlist in the navy, but I guess you'd say I'm going just a little crazy right now," Jerry replied. "I didn't know how hard it was gonna be to leave Marjie at the depot. Plus I left my father to run the farm alone, and he's not in such good health. When you poked my shoulder, that's what I was churning over in my head. Not quite sure what to think about it all."

"Yeah, I noticed you were chewing on something mighty tough," Chester said sympathetically. "That's why I jumped over here. Thought maybe I could help some, but it sounds like I'm butting in where I don't belong. It's a bad habit I inherited from my mother."

Jerry laughed again. He didn't quite know how to take Chester's friendly forthrightness, but he liked it. "To tell the truth," Jerry said, "I already feel better just by saying it out loud to you. Believe me, it couldn't get any worse'n it was. I felt like my head was gonna blow off my shoulders."

Both men shared a hearty chuckle. Then Chester leaned his head back in the seat, stretched his long legs into the aisle, and closed his eyes comfortably. "Well . . . I'm on my way to join the navy, too, but my decision was a lot simpler than yours. I've got brothers still at home to help my dad, and I don't even have a girlfriend—just my nation to defend."

The words were simple, matter-of-fact, but somehow they cut through Jerry's confusion like a knife through butter. Once more he could see things clearly, see where his heart was. No matter what the cost, he had to do his best to defend his homeland and the freedom of democracy. Had to do it for Billy, too, and for all the people he loved. He would be a coward if he didn't go, and he couldn't be a coward and still live with himself. He couldn't let the hurt of leaving and all the "what ifs" surrounding his decision hold him back from taking his stand.

Now it was Jerry's turn to put his head back in the seat. He felt a surge of inner resolve return as the deepest convictions of his heart moved to reclaim their rightful place. Yes, he would fight. And then, no matter how long it took, he would make it home again—alive. Home to Marjie, and his dad, and the farm. And someday their children would be running and playing on those hills that he knew so well and loved so much.

Jerry let the thoughts sink in before he said anything more. Finally he glanced over at Chester, who still sat with his eyes closed, thinking his own thoughts.

Who is this guy? Jerry wondered, looking more closely at his new friend. The strong physique, neat brown hair, and square-jawed face reminded Jerry of a college football player he'd seen once. *Anyway, I'm glad he sat down when he did.*

"I wanna thank you for helping me sort this thing out," Jerry offered.

"What's that?" Chester opened his eyes and turned his head.

"When you talked about defending the nation, well, that sorta put things back into perspective for me," Jerry answered. "I know that's what I need to do, regardless of how I feel. But I gotta tell you, I'm not feeling very good about it!"

Chester's green eyes widened in surprise at Jerry's statement, but now he grinned again. "Glad to be of service," he said. "I'll send you my bill."

"You know," Jerry added, "I think I do recall playing ball with you. Do you remember sliding into third and tearing my ankle up a year ago?"

"Oops! I hoped you *wouldn't* remember that one!" Chester exclaimed. "But the ump called me safe!"

"We lost the game because of that lousy call," Jerry groused good-naturedly. "And I could barely walk the next day."

Chester was smiling from ear to ear. "Well, guess I owe you an apology. But listen, maybe I can make it up to you. Are you enlisting alone?"

"What's it look like?" Jerry asked. "Are you suggesting I can take my wife with me?"

"Don't you wish!" Chester answered, rolling his eyes. "But listen, you've heard about the buddy plan, haven't you?"

Jerry shook his head no.

"Well, what it means is that friends can enlist together," Chester explained, "and the navy'll try to send them to the same assignment. Anyway, that's the way I heard it."

"No kidding?" Jerry said. "Sounds like a great idea. So, what about the buddy plan?"

Chester looked at Jerry as if hoping his new friend could muster the smarts to add one and one together. "Well, I know this is sort of impulsive, but I'm wondering if you'd like to join up with me?"

Jerry shook his head and held up a flat palm. "Whoa—wait a minute. I need some time to think on that one!"

Now Jerry's thoughts were whirling again. Ten minutes ago he'd been having second thoughts about joining in the first place, now he was thinking of enlisting with a "buddy" he hardly knew. He didn't normally make friends that fast. But this wasn't normal times, and he had to admit he liked the idea of serving along with someone from near his home.

He looked at Chester, who had discreetly directed his gaze across the aisle and out the opposite windows. Something inside told him that this man would make a good friend—and he could certainly use a friend.

It really didn't seem like such a tough decision. "I guess I'd like that a lot," he told Chester. "That is, if you're sure you want an old married man like me hanging around. Might cramp your style, you know."

Chester looked dumbfounded. "Are you kidding? I was praying that one of my friends would come with me. But none of them wanted to go into the navy, and I really didn't want to go in alone. Fact is, I really wanted to leave a couple days ago, but I couldn't get up the nerve."

For a brief moment it occurred to Jerry to wonder what Chester meant about praying, but then he dismissed the thought. It wasn't really any of his business if the man prayed or not. And Chester seemed normal enough—at any rate, normal enough to join the navy with.

"I think I know what you mean," Jerry confessed. "I'm kinda scared, too. I don't have any idea what I'm getting myself in to. I just know it's what I have to do. But say," he added, "I sure hope you know how to swim. If we go down together, do you reckon you can stay afloat while holding up a hundred-fifty-pound rock?"

Chester put on a mock-sober face. "Buddy plan or not, if we go down, you better make tracks for the nearest lifeboat." Then he flashed a grin and offered Jerry his hand a second time. "Friends?"

Jerry pumped Chester's hand with all his strength and replied, "You bet."

"Say, your wife doesn't have a good-looking sister who's available, does she?" Chester asked. "I figure this buddy plan might be real helpful to me!"

"No such luck," Jerry answered with a smile. "But she's got a cousin. Not so much to look at, but she's hunting for a good man like yourself. I'll get Marjie to send you a picture of sweet Bertha."

"Swell," Chester said. "Sounds just like my kinda lady."

9

DOC MACMILLAN

Another wintry morning arrived cold and bright in Minnesota, and Marjie took advantage of her Sunday off by sleeping in. A week and a half had dragged by with no word from Jerry. Each day, Marjie had gone through the motions of her life with the vague conviction that nothing really worthwhile could happen until Jerry was back home with her.

At least there had been no problems at work. Gordon Stilwell had said nothing about the note and had made no attempt to retaliate for the foot warming. But Marjie knew "the boss" didn't give up easily. She had watched him make moves on other women at the Green Parrot, and he seemed to enjoy the game even more when it turned to cat and mouse. *But I have the advantage,* she had told herself one afternoon. *It would never occur to him that a woman might strike back.*

Marjie's aunt and uncle had already left for church before she got up. They rarely took interest in what she did, and Marjie was well aware that if it wasn't for the rent money she paid, Aunt Margaret wouldn't give her the time of day. Her aunt had never had any children, and she made no attempt to disguise her dislike for her brother's brood—especially the ones who didn't go to church. Marjie put up with her aunt's attitude only because she couldn't find a cheaper room anywhere in town. As soon as the hospital bill was paid, and as soon as she made Stilwell pay for his sins, Marjie planned to look for another place to live.

She took her time getting ready and sat down to enjoy a leisurely breakfast before going out to warm up the Ford. All week long she had looked forward to driving out to see Jerry's dad. But she figured there was no reason to rush—Benjamin was probably in church.

Just to make sure, Marjie picked up the telephone and asked the operator to put her call through. She was surprised when Benjamin answered after only three rings.

"Benjamin, this is Marjie. I was hoping I could drive out today and celebrate Christmas early with you, but I didn't expect you to be home right now. Is everything all right?"

"No, everything's not all right," he said in a tired voice. "I'm having problems with my baby pigs, and the vet can't get here. I'm afraid I'm gonna lose a bunch of them. You don't know any vets, do you?"

"What's the matter with the pigs?" Marjie asked.

"All six sows had big litters," Benjamin explained. "But the little ones look like they're starving. For sure they've got a bad dose of diarrhea. I can't figure out if the sows' milk is bad or if there's not enough milk to feed them all or what. Never seen anything like it."

"I'll be right out," Marjie said. "Maybe I can help."

And then she hung up and grabbed her coat before Benjamin had a chance to protest.

Marjie rolled into the farm driveway about forty-five minutes later and pulled to a stop by the garage. The rattly old car seemed to settle into the familiar ruts with a contented sigh.

Benjamin stepped out of the farmhouse, pulled on his boots, and waved at Marjie with a smile that managed to be both welcoming and worried. "Merry Christmas!" he called.

"Merry Christmas to you, too," Marjie said, hustling to his side. "How are you . . . *Dad*?" She gave him a hug and surprised him with a kiss to the cheek. "Look at the ring. Isn't it beautiful. How can I ever thank you?"

"My goodness," he said. "I'm so wrapped up with my sick pigs that I even forgot to congratulate you when you called. Guess I'm off to a bad start as a father-in-law. Let me try again."

Benjamin took Marjie's hands, studied the sparkling stone, then looked into her deep brown eyes. "Marjie, I count it a privilege to have you for my daughter-in-law. As beautiful as you are, I can't figure why Jerry waited so long to propose. But I am delighted he finally did, and I'm mighty proud to welcome you into the Macmillan family. And I can't think of a more wonderful place for Martha's ring than on your finger. Wear it proudly, Marjie."

Now it was Benjamin's turn to give Marjie a hug, and he even returned her kiss to the cheek. Both of them paused for a second, stiff and a little embarrassed. Then both broke into laughter.

"Now," Marjie declared with a confident smile, "let's go take care of those sick pigs."

"Right over there," Benjamin pointed to the hog shed. "Like I said, the vet's tied up with sick cows and said he don't know when he's gonna get here. Looks to me like it'll be too late. But you really shouldn't go in—"

"Nonsense," Marjie interrupted, taking a quick step toward the shed. "Let's do what we can."

Marjie followed the deep path in the snow to a long, white building that was surrounded by its own wooden fence. Opening the door, Marjie stepped in, squinted her eyes to adjust to the hazy darkness, and wrinkled her nose; she'd forgotten how much pigs could stink up a place. Looking down, she found herself wishing she had brought her old shoes, but she said nothing as Benjamin closed the door and stepped over into one of the pigpens.

A mountainous sow lay on her side against one edge of the pigpen while a dozen or so baby pigs mobbed around her belly trying to get a meal. At the sight of Benjamin, several of the little pigs broke away. They came on a run for him and immediately began nipping at his boots like playful puppies.

"Did you ever see the beat of this?" Benjamin called out. "Crazy pigs!"

Marjie laughed at the sight. Wherever her father-in-law moved, the baby pigs dove for his boots. "Looks like they think you're their dad or something," she joked.

"Well, I'm not their dad. And as funny as this looks, these runts are gonna die if something don't happen soon," Benjamin said mournfully as he stepped back over the wooden fence. Immediately the baby pigs returned to the mob scene around their mother. "Okay, Doc Macmillan," he asked Marjie, "what do you think?"

Marjie walked down the little corridor past the other pens. What Benjamin had said was true. Each sow had large litters and seemed overwhelmed by the appetites of the little ones. Suddenly Marjie got an idea.

"Give me your boot," she said.

"Why?" Benjamin asked, obviously in no mood for games.

"Just let me have it, please."

Benjamin gave a sigh, then pulled one of his boots off. "Be careful. There's a fair amount of you-know-what on it from the barn."

"Exactly," Marjie said with the satisfaction of a master detective hot on the trail of something big. She broke off a dry piece of manure from the boot and reached down into the pen. One of the little sharp-eyed beggars came dashing up to see what was being offered and snapped it out of her hand without hesitation. "That's it," she said quietly.

"What's it?" Benjamin grumped.

"Don't you see?" Marjie teased.

"See what?"

"Isn't it obvious?" Marjie paused, enjoying the moment. "It might be the milk or the diarrhea or just too many pigs—but those babies are *hungry*, and they were nipping at your boots because they tasted something they need. See, there's more than manure stuck to your boots—there's grain for the cows there, too. Why not try mixing some of the cow feed with some warm water and make a mush for the pigs? Maybe they can eat it as a supplement for whatever they're not getting from the milk."

"I've never fed—"

"Do you want to go get the feed, or should I?" Marjie broke in.

"Well, I guess it's worth a try," Benjamin said doubtfully. "But I've never—"

"I'm the doctor. Right?"

"Tarnation . . ." Benjamin muttered as he headed for the barn. "You wait here. I'll be right back."

When he returned with a large pail of steaming brew, Benjamin still wore a suspicious frown. But he poured some of the feed mixed with warm water into a bowl, set the bowl into one of the pens, and waited.

The results were nearly instantaneous. First one, then another, and finally all of the baby pigs in the pen came running up to the bowl and plunged their noses into the mixture. Grunting and snorting, they lapped up the bowl's contents as fast as their tongues could move. Then more than a dozen happy pig faces looked up to see if the benevolent giver of good things would stoop to satisfy them again.

Marjie was beaming from ear to ear. "Not a bad Christmas present, eh? Wonder what the vet would charge for this advice?"

Benjamin was smiling, too. "Well, Marjie, I believe you've saved the day. But maybe we can split the profits later instead of you taking all my hard-earned cash now. These pigs will fetch a pretty penny when they get some meat on those bones. But how'd you know what to do?"

"You're not forgetting that I spent eighteen years on a farm, are you?" Marjie teased. "Actually, it was just a good guess. Besides, I prefer slopping pigs to working with my boss *any* day."

Benjamin may have not figured out the cure for the baby pigs, but he easily picked up on his daughter-in-law's displeasure with her boss. "Well, why don't you go in and put some coffee on while I finish up here. If you feel like starting lunch, just hunt around for some food. Let me feed the rest of these little beggars, and I'll be right in. Sounds like we've got a lot to talk over."

Benjamin opened the farmhouse door to the smell of frying

ham and potatoes and brewing coffee. In the kitchen, Marjie was singing quietly to herself as she pulled plates down from the cupboard. For a moment Benjamin paused inside the door and longed for the days when it was normal to come home to good smells and good company. Benjamin had begun to hate stepping into a house filled only with ghostly memories.

Pulling off his coat and boots, he washed his hands in the entryway sink and walked into the kitchen. "Smells great," he said. "I'm almost as hungry as one of those runts!"

"Reckon we both are," Marjie answered, turning around from the stove with a spatula in her hand. "Do you have an apron around here? I looked everywhere."

"I'm sorry . . . no, there aren't any aprons," said Benjamin with a hint of sadness. "When Jerry's mother died, we gave all the womanly stuff away. That was a long time ago now."

"Looks like it," Marjie replied as she filled a serving bowl with the ham and potatoes. "When's the last time you and Jerry cleaned cupboards? Getting kinda crusty around the edges—you boys figuring on growing another crop of something up there?"

Benjamin laughed, glad that she wasn't afraid to tease him.

"Sit down and let's eat," Marjie ordered, carrying the bowl into the dining room. "Hope this tastes better than the stuff you were feeding those little pigs off your boots!"

Father-in-law and daughter-in-law sat down at the dining room table for their first meal together. Both were struck with all the empty chairs around the large table, but neither one commented.

Benjamin pushed aside a few strands of straggly hair that had fallen across his forehead, then bowed his head to say grace. Marjie closed her eyes politely. "Our Father, we thank you for these gifts of your care. I thank you for bringing Marjie out here today to save the baby pigs . . . and for her laughter and joy. We pray that you will be with Jerry today, especially as he faces Christmas alone. And we pray that you will protect him and bring him home safely. Amen."

Marjie found herself whispering, "Amen," as well. It was an

easy prayer to agree with. She looked over at Benjamin and said, "You pray like you mean it."

Benjamin was startled by her directness and fumbled for a reply. "I . . . do mean it," he said, dumping some potatoes onto his plate.

"Do you always pray so simply?" Marjie asked. "No thees and thous? No flowery words?"

"Like preachers, you mean?" he replied.

"Exactly."

Benjamin laughed with Marjie. "I'm no silver-tongued preacher, that's for certain. But I do believe God hears prayer— even when we think He don't."

The silence lay gently between them for a long moment. "I wish I could say the same," she finally said. "Tell me why you believe."

It was late in the afternoon before Benjamin and Marjie closed their conversation. If it hadn't been that the cows needed milking, Benjamin would have gone right on into the evening. If it hadn't been that she was afraid of night driving, Marjie would have gladly stayed to listen. But both reasons were compelling.

"What was that about your boss?" he asked at one point in the afternoon. When she told him the story, Benjamin's face turned red; he threatened to come up the next day and have it out with Stilwell. Marjie had all she could do to calm him down, but she did accept his offer to come to the cafe if she ever needed his help (and if it was between choring hours). She also got him to promise to not write Jerry about it.

As Marjie guided the black Ford back down the farm drive-way to the country gravel road, she wished with all her heart that she could stay. For the first time in years, Marjie felt like she was home. For the first time ever, something of a simple farmer's faith almost made sense to her. Whatever it was, it contained an ingredient that drew her toward it rather than made her want to run away. And she was weary of running away. She truly wanted to believe.

But most of all, this place made her feel close to Jerry. He was just as much a part of it as Benjamin and the pigs. And with every mile down the road, she felt farther and farther from her husband's love.

10

THE WASP

For two young men who'd just met on their way to enlisting in the navy, Jerry Macmillan and Chester Stanfeld had grown very close. It didn't take them long to realize that it can be nice to have a partner when venturing into the unknown.

Finding their way around was not the problem they expected at first. Every young man they saw seemed to be heading for Fort Snelling; all they had to do was follow the person in front of them and do what he did. But neither of these country boys was prepared for their immersion into the smothering masses of young men who were pouring into the navy. Wherever they went and whatever they did, they found themselves in a rushing whirlpool of human beings. And once they reported to the Naval Training Center in Great Lakes, Illinois, their world sped up to nearly breakneck speed. At one point Chester wondered if being a new recruit was something like living in an ant farm, and Jerry thought it had to be close.

With the declaration of war, the methodical pattern of training in boot camp at Great Lakes had been transformed into a furious race to get men out to assignments as fast as possible. With the Pacific fleet severely crippled and the threat of attack on both shores, *time* had become another menacing enemy to the nation. Every effort was being employed to speed up the country's defense.

Like every other recruit, Jerry and Chester were issued the standard navy field jacket, which happened to be a size forty-eight, the day they arrived. Some of the men complained that their coats were far too big and were promptly given the only other size in stock—size thirty-six. They were sorry they'd asked, but didn't dare ask again. They were also issued blue shirts, a pair of brogans, a pair of low-quarters, denim trousers, dress whites, shorts, T-shirts, buckles, socks, and a green seabag to carry everything in.

Jerry and Chester met with the typical degrading treatment from the boot-camp petty officers. Neither man had been called a "girlie" for many years, but they quickly learned to keep their mouths shut and just do what they were told. The first guy they saw who dared to talk back got a prompt order to "Hit the deck" and do push-ups while the other men stood around and counted. Jerry took a good round of abuse from an especially nasty petty officer who found Marjie's haircut amusing and seemed annoyed that he couldn't goad Jerry into fighting. Jerry would have never thought that having his head shaved by one of the boot-camp barbers could feel so good.

The few days they had to spend at Great Lakes were filled from morning to night with regimented drills, liberal doses of "double time," and shouted instructions on how to do military tucks on their bunks, spit-shine their shoes, and keep their lockers in perfect order. Sandwiched in between were instruction sessions that supposedly would provide the basic information they needed to survive the war. The only moments they were not on the run were mealtimes and when they were finally allowed to hit the sack in the late evenings. There was certainly no time for writing letters home. The two long rows of bunk beds that ran the length of the open bay of the barracks became the only safe haven of rest for them.

All too quickly, Jerry and Chester found themselves dragging their seabags aboard a military train bound for the Norfolk Naval Base in Virginia. Their orders both read the same: They were to report for duty on an aircraft carrier, the USS *Wasp*, which was undergoing an overhaul. Along with greenhorn sailors from all over the Midwest, they stumbled onto the crowded Pullman coach and quietly took their seats.

All the new recruits seemed drained of the initial adrenaline that had spurred them to enlist in their nation's defense. As the train rolled east across the countryside, most showed interest only in sleeping and lighting an occasional smoke. Despite their fatigue, however, both Chester and Jerry kept their eyes glued out the window, watching some of America's finest farmland pass before them. Every acre of harvest land and every solitary woods, every town and every farm beckoned to be explored and enjoyed. The farthest Chester had ever been from home was Chicago, and Jerry had once made it as far as Nebraska for a family reunion. Both of them hated the idea that if they shut their eyes for a nap, they might miss something they'd never seen before and might never have a chance to see again.

Chester was the first to start a conversation. Gazing out the window at passing landscape, he said, "Guess this is what we're going to war for."

"Just what I've been thinking," Jerry agreed. "Look at what's out there. I never realized just how big this country is. Miles and miles of good farmland. Hundreds and hundreds of families— just like yours and mine. Grandpas and grandmas, and young families with kids, and rich folks and poor folks, and city people and country people, all minding their own business, trying to make a living, and suddenly their lives and their homes and their freedom's all in danger. Hard to believe, huh? But look at that dairy herd," he said, pointing to placid animals in a snowy pasture. "Guess they haven't listened to the radio for the past month or so."

"Must not have," Chester said with a chuckle. "They don't look any too nervous, that's for sure. I'll bet the old man that runs the place has been listening, though. Probably has a son that's packed into this train with the rest of us sardines. I don't know about you, but there's been times these past couple weeks when I wished we hadn't listened to the radio back home."

Jerry laughed and nodded. "Like when the nurse said, 'Drop your drawers, bend over, and keep moving through the line'?

How many shots you think those old battle-axes fired into our backsides?"

"I lost count," Chester replied. "But I'm sure I'll be good'n healthy for the rest of my life. They must have given us something for every disease there is. Maybe my sinus problems'll finally clear up."

"I suspect it's gonna take more than those shots to keep us alive," Jerry suggested. "Did you know that two thousand Americans were killed at Pearl? The Japs sunk the *Oklahoma* and the *Arizona* and crippled six battleships; we were lucky that part of the fleet was out on maneuvers. My best friend's lucky to be alive—least he was alive last I heard. Now it's payback time."

"No doubt," Chester agreed. "At any rate, there's no way we're not gonna see action on an aircraft carrier. You can bet we're gonna do the enemy damage, and we'll be a big-time target as well. What do you think we'll be doing? Suppose they'll be wanting us as pilots?"

"I'm sure," Jerry laughed. "I'll bet I can fly a plane as well as I can swim. But your guess is as good as mine. Don't really matter to me, and I doubt we'll have a lot of choice in what we get. Just as long as they keep me busy—that's all I care about. Whenever I have a free minute, I start thinking about Marjie, and I get so lonely it's like I'm going nuts."

"Well, I thought you'd been looking odd, especially since we got our heads shaved. At first I thought it was just your pointy ears," Chester joked. "You seemed to especially enjoy Christmas in the barracks with the men!"

"Right," Jerry said with a grunt. "I was away from Marjie on our first Christmas and I didn't even have time to send her a present. I haven't even written her a letter! Just look at the letters she's already sent." Jerry pulled three plump envelopes from his pocket. "Can you believe this lady?"

Chester flashed a big smile. "My mother used to burrow her forefinger into my chest and say, 'There's no time like the present.' I hated it when she said that, especially the sharp finger drilling my ribs, but she was usually right. Why don't you try writing a letter now. Who knows what's gonna happen when we get to

Norfolk? You may never get a chance to catch up to the letters she's been sending."

"Shoot—I'll never catch her," Jerry protested. "When it comes to writing, I'm slow as molasses in January."

"So's this train," Chester countered. "And besides, it just happens to be January. Knowing how things go, tomorrow we might wake up and find out it's the middle of July."

"I wish it *was* the middle of July," Jerry said. "Do you know how cold it's gonna be if our ship stays in the North Atlantic?"

"I'd rather not think about it," Chester answered. "But you're avoiding the point. I suspect your wife is not gonna be happy with you if you never write her."

"That's true," Jerry conceded. "She can take a lot, but you don't want to push her too far. Marjie can make you pay if you get her worked up. I've seen her in action."

"Okay, here's the plan," Chester said. "I'll get my notebook out and write my folks. Then you can use it to write Marjie."

"Mighta known you'd bring a notebook," Jerry said with a sigh. "Suppose you brought envelopes and stamps, too."

"You guessed it," Chester declared triumphantly. "And pencils. You got no excuse, buddy!"

When the train pulled into Norfolk, Virginia, both men had finished their letters and caught up on some of their sleep. The smell of salt water hit their noses as they stepped from the train, and the adrenaline began surging through their veins again. Tiredness and loneliness were set aside as Jerry and Chester gathered their seabags and headed for the harbor. Once again they found so many men headed for their destination that all they needed to do was tag along.

Arriving at the navy yard, they stood gaping at the size of the ships and the bustling activity of the docks. Everyone but their group of bewildered sailors seemed to know where he was going and what he was doing. No matter where they stood, they always seemed to be in the way.

Jerry looked over at Chester. "Better push your jaw back up before a fly gets in your mouth."

"This is unbelievable!" Chester exclaimed, managing to finally close his mouth. "Sorta like a monster mechanical beehive."

"You got that right," Jerry agreed, then grinned. "Wonder how much farther till we find the *Wasp*?"

Before Chester could answer, the front of their group rounded a corner, and they all came to an astonished halt as the USS *Wasp* loomed into view. Not a man among them was prepared for the sight of the great ship. Commissioned two years earlier from the Boston Navy Yard as a CV–7 class carrier, she stretched 741 feet from bow to stern and rose 80 feet high from the water line to the flight deck. The hangar deck was long enough to hold two regulation-size football fields.

"Wow!" was the most articulate observation that escaped from the lips of the rookie sailors.

"My dad should have come along just to see this!" Jerry whispered to Chester. "He thought we had a pretty big barn!"

Chester just stood there, unable to comprehend what his eyes were reporting. Finally he gasped, "And I thought the barges on the Mississippi were big!"

"Me, too," Jerry said. "I think I'd prefer trying my luck on that tugboat over there first."

"Looks like you'll get your chance," Chester replied. "I think that's our ride out to the *Wasp*."

Just about every type of warship and naval auxiliary was within their view, but the *Wasp* definitely dominated the harbor. She looked invincible, and the more the men stared at her, the more their confidence grew. This was their ship, and she was clearly a great one.

Finally one of the men at the front of the group yelled, "Let's give'm hell, boys!"

A loud cheer went up from the pack, and one by one the "civilians" stepped forward to be transformed into sailors. Whatever these young men lacked in training would be made up for in heart.

Chester looked over at Jerry. "You ready?"

"Are you kidding?" Jerry said with a shout. "We got ourselves a war to win!"

With a slap to each other's back, the two Minnesota farm boys shouldered their seabags and proudly stepped forward to serve their country.

11

A LIGHT IN THE WORLD

Nearly a month of silence passed before Marjie finally got her first letter from Jerry.

On their last morning together, he had warned her that writing was a painfully slow exercise for him. He had carefully pointed out that it had been more than ten years since he'd seen the inside of the country schoolhouse. So she hadn't expected him to write often—but that hadn't stopped her from dashing home every day to check the mailbox.

Day after day her hopes had been met with stark emptiness. And she had found no consolation in Aunt Margaret's daily reminders that Uncle William had never written her once during World War I. Marjie figured her uncle was probably so relieved to be away from the old crab that he never even thought about writing.

Now the long-awaited sight of Jerry's letter in the box was so overwhelming that Marjie's hand trembled as she slowly pulled it out. One glance at the deeply dented letters on the envelope told her how much effort the letter had cost Jerry. Each penciled letter was carefully shaped and so deeply etched that she was amazed the lead hadn't punched through the paper.

Clutching her envelope, Marjie fled to her room and locked the door behind her. This was a moment she would not allow Aunt Margaret to spoil. Dropping her coat to the floor, she sat down on the edge of her bed and stared at the postmark. *Norfolk, Virginia. That's where the naval base is. Must mean he's already been assigned to a ship.*

Taking a deep breath, Marjie carefully slit the letter open and withdrew the treasured contents. Two neatly folded pages, carefully inscribed on both sides, were more than she had hoped for. Ever so slowly her eyes traced the opening words, *My Dearest Love,* and she imagined Jerry seated next to her on the bed, whispering the words in her ears. *Words cannot express how much I have missed you. I had no idea that my loneliness could be so deep or hurt so much. What would I give to be with you again?*

Mixed tears of joy and sadness dampened the homemade quilt as Marjie pored over the skimpy details of what Jerry had been through and where he was headed. She was not surprised that he had not had time to write. Everything seemed to be happening so fast. In less than a month's time he had left his father's farm, survived boot camp, and reported to a ship that would head for its first war assignment January 14. Marjie ached to be with him, wished she could be there to help him get his bearings. She was relieved to discover that he had made a friend who was headed to sea with him.

She felt pride, too, in his obvious determination to do his job and fight with everything he had. And Marjie could read between the lines that he was thrilled to be assigned to such an important ship as the *Wasp.* If anyone would serve his country well, she knew it was Jerry.

Loneliness seemed to be the greatest problem Jerry was facing, and this worried her. If his loneliness was anything like her own, it could be a bigger enemy than the Germans or the Japanese. But there was nothing she could do about his loneliness or hers except continue to write him letters.

Every evening since Jerry left, she had sat down to write him something from her day. She'd save up two or three nights' worth and then send them off, hoping that the mail was reaching him. Clearly, those earlier letters had gotten through. Jerry's letter reassured her of that; he said he had read them over and over again. But now that he was heading to sea, Marjie was concerned that they might lose communication altogether. Now, sitting on the bed in her tiny boarding room, she vowed to continue writing, whether she heard from Jerry or not. He desperately needed to hear from her—and the act of writing was the only way she knew of feeling closer to him.

Marjie read and reread Jerry's letter until she finally realized she had memorized every word. Placing the letter on her night-stand, she stretched out on the bed and ran through the words again, whispering them to herself. If she never got another letter, Marjie determined to squeeze everything there was out of this one.

Yet the very comfort she gained from reading Jerry's words somehow seemed to sharpen Marjie's own loneliness and fear. Now she had a clearer picture of the man she loved as a solitary figure perched on the flight deck of a gigantic gray aircraft car-rier—a sitting duck for an enemy plane's bombs or a submarine's deadly torpedoes. The mental image of his sinking into the depths of the ocean returned to haunt the deep places of her memory.

Marjie was so lost in her darkness that she nearly jumped off the bed when a knock sounded at her door. Despite the fright, she was grateful for the interruption.

"Marjie, time for supper," Uncle William called. "It's roast beef and gravy over bread. Margaret's in a bad mood, so you better hurry."

"Thanks, but no thanks, Uncle Will," Marjie replied. "Tell her I'm not feeling well. Maybe I'll get something later."

"Suit yourself, Marjie," he said. "But take care of yourself, all right?"

"Yes, sir," Marjie affirmed with a smile as his heavy footsteps trudged down the hallway. Despite his wife's sour attitude, Mar-jie liked her uncle. She had always felt he would have been a great father if he had gotten the chance.

But she hadn't been fibbing about not feeling well. In fact, she had begun to wonder if she were coming down with something. Several times over the past few days she had felt sick to her stom-ach. But she didn't feel that way now; she just felt exhausted. So the queasiness was probably just a consequence of worrying about how Jerry was doing. Now that she'd heard from him, she'd probably feel better in the morning.

Marjie intended to get up and write Jerry a long love letter, but a sudden wave of tiredness stole over her. Within minutes she drifted into a deep sleep. But what she meant for a short nap ended up lasting the entire night. She awoke to discover the morning sun already burning a hole through the frost on her window.

"For crying out loud! What time is it?" Marjie exclaimed as she bolted up from the bed, still in her work clothes, and tried to focus on the alarm clock she had failed to set. To her disgust, she realized she'd also failed to wind the clock; its motionless hands signaled 2:15.

Then, to her relief, Marjie remembered she had the day off. She had planned to drive down to see her mother, but there was no particular hurry. She flopped back onto the bed and wondered how it was possible that she could sleep so long and hard—in her clothes, and without even turning out the light. *This is very odd*, Marjie thought as she tried to fall back to sleep.

She couldn't do it. Her slept-in clothes were rumpled and uncomfortable, and the scent they carried of stale grease from the restaurant curdled her stomach. Marjie was certain she'd be sick if she didn't do something about that smell.

Might as well change my clothes and get moving, she told herself. *No matter how early I get there, Ma'll be up anyway.* Marjie had only made it home once since the wedding, and she was looking forward to sitting at the kitchen table with her mother again.

But the queasiness refused to go away with a fresh white blouse and black slacks. And no amount of breakfast coaxing could overcome her stomach's reluctance to accept the egg she fried in bacon fat; it ended up being buried in the garbage so Aunt Margaret would not go into her usual tirade over wasted food. The most that Marjie could swallow was an unbuttered slice of toast and a cup of black coffee.

I'm coming down with something for sure, she thought, and wondered for a minute whether she should postpone her trip. But the need to see her mother quickly outweighed the voice of caution, and within an hour she was on the road.

There were several times on the road to her mother's that Marjie thought she would have to pull off into a farmer's driveway and be sick. Every mile felt like an endurance test. Marjie couldn't remember being more relieved than when she pulled the Ford to a stop on the snow-packed driveway in front of the silent old farmhouse.

Without knocking, she slipped quietly through the front door and stepped into the entryway. What a welcoming abode this drab, shabby house felt like, especially when contrasted to her aunt's cold, though lovely, dwelling. *Love makes a home*, Marjie thought, and gave a big sigh of unexpected contentment. It felt so good to be home. Especially when you were sick.

She heard someone rustling around in the kitchen and called, "Ma. Is that you?"

"Land's sake, you here already?" Sarah Livingstone replied and stepped out into the dining room. "Didn't know you city slickers got up with the chickens."

"Most of them don't," Marjie said as she hung up her coat. "But don't mistake me for a city slicker. I'll never be anything but a country girl—regardless of where I live."

"I reckon that's true," said her mother as she greeted Marjie with a hug. "Good to have you home. It's just too quiet around this old house these days."

"Where's Ted?" asked Marjie, breathing deeply to ride over another wave of nausea. She had hoped she'd catch her younger brother at home on this visit.

"He picked up some carpenter work at the old Manford place and won't be home till choring time."

Marjie shook her head and said, "Too bad. I haven't pulled anybody's hair out for a long time."

Sarah laughed and added, "That boy's lucky not to be bald after all the roots you plucked out. He said to give you his love, but he didn't hint that he's forgiven you yet."

"As mean as I was to him, I can't say I blame him," Marjie admitted. "Is that *hot* coffee I smell? I'm freezing. I swear that car's heater doesn't give a drop of heat."

"Just be thankful you have a car," Sarah answered as they went into the kitchen and poured their cups of steaming brew. Sarah paused as she took a long look at her daughter. Finally she said, "Marjie, you feeling okay? You're white as a sheet."

Marjie looked down at her arms. She didn't notice anything unusual, but she wasn't about to argue over skin color. "To tell the truth," she said, "I haven't been well at all. I nearly threw up on the way down here this morning."

"If you've got the flu, why didn't you lay low?" Sarah questioned.

"I don't think it's the flu. No fever, anyway. Just an upset stomach, and I've been very tired at night. Maybe it's a case of the nerves or something, from Jerry being gone. Last night I fell asleep with my clothes on!" Marjie laughed with a bit of embarrassment. "Can you believe that?"

Sarah wasn't laughing. She just stared as if she were analyzing secret data invisibly etched on Marjie's face. "I can believe it," she declared with several thoughtful nods. "You been to the doc yet?"

"For a queasy stomach? Come on!" Marjie was incredulous. "You think money grows on trees?"

"I sure wish it did," Sarah said with a reassuring smile. "I got a feeling you could use a couple branches' worth before too long. Marjie, what you've said sounds like how I felt when I was pregnant . . ."

The smile vanished immediately from Marjie's face, and she crumpled into a kitchen chair in disbelief. Sarah locked her gaze onto her daughter's dark brown eyes as she continued, ". . . with all three of you."

"You can't be serious!" exclaimed Marjie, pausing between words. "I can't be pregnant. That can't be!"

"Did you and Jerry sleep in separate beds?" her mother asked.

"Of course we didn't," Marjie answered with a touch of irritation. "But we only had two days together."

"And you can't make a baby in two days?" Sarah pressed.

"Of course you can, but it can't be . . ."

Sarah let the silence do its work. "I started my morning sickness between the third and fourth week like clockwork. Count the weeks, Marjie. But even more important, have you missed that time of month?"

Marjie couldn't believe she hadn't even thought about it. But yes, she was over a week late—and she was never late. She felt so stupid.

Now time seemed to stand still as Marjie squeezed her eyes shut and tried to comprehend the dawning reality of motherhood. She realized she did not need a doctor to second her mother's diagnosis. Her own intuition confirmed that she was indeed pregnant—pregnant with a child whose father was preparing to launch into the stormy and dangerous North Atlantic.

"It just can't be," Marjie whispered. "Not this soon. Not without Jerry here . . ."

Sarah pulled up a chair alongside Marjie and put a strong arm of care around her daughter. Neither one said a word for a long while. Finally Sarah spoke quietly, "No sense getting too stirred up until you see a doctor, sweetheart. Don't go listening to an old woman like me. Did I ever tell you about how I convinced your pa that Teddy was gonna be a girl when he was born? I was so sure that we didn't even bother to pick a boy's name until the minute the doc told me, 'It's a boy, Sarah.' Teddy almost got called *Emily*!"

Mother and daughter laughed quietly together, and Marjie opened her eyes to face the real world again. She picked up the badly chipped coffee cup, studied it for a moment, and then took a long sip. Having found a smile, she looked at Sarah and said, "When's the last time you perked a pot of coffee with all new grounds?"

"Waste not, want not," Sarah replied in a parrot's voice. "Bet you can still hear your granny saying that."

"She didn't drink coffee, though," Marjie argued. "That disqualifies anything she said about it. Didn't she also make you eat moldy milk toast?"

Sarah raised her hands in mock surrender. "You win this one," she said. "Next time you come, bring me a can of coffee and I'll toss out my reused grounds!"

Marjie laughed again, then sighed deeply and went back to studying the chips on the cup. Sarah sipped her coffee quietly, waiting for Marjie to collect her thoughts. Finally Marjie said, "I know you're right about the baby, Ma. I'm sure of it. What am I going to do?"

Sarah's eyes dropped from her daughter's face to study her hands. She rubbed a sore spot on her index finger, but her mind was far away, searching for words that might help her daughter. "Well," Sarah reasoned, "if you're really pregnant, seems like one option is to feel sorry for yourself, worry about it for eight months, and then have the child. Another option would be to be delighted you're carrying Jerry's baby, trust that somehow everything's gonna work out during the next eight months, and then have the baby."

Marjie picked up her cup and just held it in both hands while she mulled over Sarah's practical wisdom. "Got any other options?" she asked with a crooked smile. She paused and took a sip. "Well I think I've done my share of feeling sorry for myself these past weeks. I can't keep crying all the time. How'd you ever make it when Pa was gone?"

"How'd I make it, Marjie?" Sarah repeated. "Not very good, darling. Not very good. Got so bad that I spent a good part of one day sitting right under this table crying my eyes out. Didn't care if I ever came out again. But I know that crying's good for the soul, so I guess my soul got in pretty good shape. And the day finally came when I could laugh again, although I've got to say I never stopped missing Robert. I found it was much easier to cope when I determined to live one day at a time and not worry too much about the next one. Many's the time when I thought we'd lose the farm, but somehow it's always worked out—always. 'Amazing grace,' your pa would say, and I guess he'd probably be right. Fact is, I sometimes wonder if Robert is peeking over the rim of glory and putting in a good word for us down here. So now I try to stop worrying about all the things I can't control and just do the best I can."

Marjie lifted her hand to her mother's face and gently touched her cheek. "Pa'd be proud of you, Ma. Real proud. And I want to make Jerry proud of me, too. I've got to be strong for him . . . and the baby. But, Ma, I'm scared."

Once again Sarah reached an arm around Marjie and gave her a long hug. " 'Course you're scared. Who wouldn't be? But you'll make it, Marjie. You're stronger than you think. I've seen it . . ." Tenderly she reached over and pulled a stray lock of curly hair out of her daughter's face. "Instead of panicking, what if you chose to believe that the child inside you is a gift from God— another light to shine in a dark world."

"A light from God?" Marjie pondered aloud. Something inside her wanted to say yes, but it was drowned by a cacophony of doubt. "You know I'm not much on faith."

"I never said you had to be, Marjie," Sarah said. "I've never been all that much of a churchgoer myself—you know that. But what if the life inside you is God's gift to you and Jerry? Do you see the power and courage that comes from believing that every child is precious? Then no matter how bad life gets, the way we love and cherish that life becomes everything."

Marjie did feel the power that her mother spoke about. She nodded her head and acknowledged its truth. "Well, I'm not sure what I believe about God," Marjie whispered. "But I do believe this little baby inside me is precious. And, yes, I will cherish this baby just as much as I love Jerry."

She turned to face her mother with a look of stubborn, determined joy. "This child *is* our gift, Ma. And we're gonna make it— somehow . . . some way. We've gotta make it! But you'll still promise to help me, won't you?"

The look in her mother's eyes answered any of Marjie's doubts.

12

MR. NO-NECK

With the *Wasp* in dry dock for repairs, Jerry and Chester spent their first week on board ship helping to change the ammunition and taking on provisions for the next duty. The week in dry dock gave them time to find their way around the massive ship. There were eight decks on the *Wasp*—four main decks and four dedicated to storage. The top was the flight deck where planes took off and landed. Below that was the hangar deck, where seventy to eighty aircraft were housed and repaired. The seamen slept on the deck below and descended even one deck lower to eat. The huge ship was an easy place to get lost until one learned all the stairways and halls.

The two new recruits quickly learned it was not unusual to work a twenty-hour day when the ship was in dock, and the rumors they heard about newcomers getting the worst jobs proved true—usually they were buried deep within the holds stacking whatever needed to be stored. They were fortunate to be in good physical condition. More than one of their mates dropped from exhaustion in those first days on the ship.

They were thoroughly sick of stacking sacks of flour and boxes of bolts by the time they received their permanent job assignments. By then, the ship was nearly ready to get underway.

"You have all the luck," Chester groused when he found his name on the list. "Catwalk antiaircraft gunner on the deck force.

I get stuck in the machine shop fixing broken equipment."

"If you recall," Jerry reminded him, "you were bragging about being able to fix just about anything that broke down on the farm. If you hadn't told them you loved to weld, maybe they wouldn't have put you down as a machinist."

"You got me there," agreed Chester. "So when do you think you'll get to fire one of them twenty-millimeter cannons?"

"Who knows?" Jerry answered. "The gunnery division's supposed to learn to fire all of the ship's guns as well as keep them clean and stand watch over them. Maybe it's not as great a job as it sounds."

Chester nodded. "We'll find out soon enough. I have one advantage, though. It's gonna be warmer where I work. Maybe I'll have to come up every once in a while and thaw you out."

"Probably," said Jerry. "Either way, we don't have any choice in the assignment. Guess we'll just have to make the best of things."

It was a thrilling and ominous moment, on January 14, when the tugs finally went to work pulling the *Wasp* away from the docks. Even the sailors who had been on board for nearly two years and had been through countless training runs stood quietly and watched as the great vessel slowly glided out to sea. They had been frightfully close to real combat on patrols before that fateful morning of December 7, 1941, but this voyage marked the beginning of the real war for them. They could only hope now that all the practice and hard work would pay off. The familiar fear of what could happen and the wondering of where they were going gripped the heart of every man aboard.

Jerry gave an involuntary shudder as he felt the ship's engines rumble beneath him, and he pulled his field jacket as tightly around his neck as he could. Although the Virginia sky was fair and the sun was bright, he suddenly felt a chill deeper than he had ever felt on a Minnesota midnight. His teeth began to chatter. Probably his nerves playing tricks on him, but he couldn't stop shaking, and he hoped desperately that no one was watching. Then he noticed he wasn't the only one trying to button his jacket tighter, and his embarrassment was overshadowed by the stark realization of what was happening. He and his crew mates were deserting the warmth and safety of their home port and venturing where death lurked at any moment. And as large and as unsinkable as the aircraft carrier felt, Jerry knew there was nowhere to run and escape if the enemy approached. Every sailor's destiny was tied to the ship's destiny.

It was a solemn group of men who went about their duties that first day at sea. Everyone seemed too preoccupied with their own thoughts to strike up conversations with their fellow workers. Jerry had hoped that he'd get a chance to try out one of the twenty-millimeter guns. Instead, the daily routine of a catwalk antiaircraft gunner on the deck force seemed disconcertingly similar to that of a maintenance man. He and his work crew were assigned to sweep down an area of the deck, mop it clean, scrub off the loose paint, then paint it again. It was an unendingly boring job, and the more experienced hands told him it was an almost daily routine.

Boredom quickly gave way, however, to another experience. They hadn't been long out of harbor before the seas began to swirl. The *Wasp* tilted from side to side, up and down, and back and forth as the waves rose and then fell into swelling troughs. Jerry had heard horror stories about seasickness, and now, with every pitch of the ship he felt himself turning progressively green. Several times a day he found himself dashing for the ship's railing, comforted only by the crowd of fellow greenhorns that joined him there.

Jerry was afraid the day's work would never come to an end, but he was determined not to give in to the relentless nausea. The men who tried to get permission to go to the sick bay were met with a raucous chorus of laughter and labeled as sissies. Jerry knew he would rather fall overboard than have half the deck crew call him a sissy the first day. So he hung in there—and hang was about all that he could do.

Finally, to Jerry's immense relief, the chief petty officer announced his group had done enough scrubbing and painting for the day and could head for the evening chow line. His stomach recoiled at the greasy food smells wafting up from the mess hall, but he knew he had to try to find something that might stay down and give him strength. *A couple more days like this one*, he groaned to himself, *and they might have to bury me at sea.*

Just as Jerry reached the top of the metal stairway leading down to the mess hall, he spotted a weary-looking Chester waiting for him at the bottom of the steps. Chester gave him a nod and a tired smile, and Jerry felt a little better.

"Let me guess why you're as white as a sheet," Chester told him at the landing. "You either had your first encounter with a German dive bomber, or else you've been hanging over the ship's rail all day. From the indentation marks on your coat, I think I can guess which one it was. You sure you want to eat?"

"No," Jerry mumbled in response. "I just hope I find my sea legs before my stomach has to be shoved back down my throat. I have to try and eat or you'll be looking for someone else to do the buddy plan with."

Chester and Jerry managed a laugh and headed toward the chow line. Both men were too tired to be in any hurry and had already gotten sick of the ship's food.

"Rough day, eh?" Chester asked.

Jerry shook his head in agreement. "I've had rougher, I guess; I just can't remember when. I hit the rail five times before the dry heaves set in. Not pretty, believe me. I'm surprised to hear you say I'm white. Most of my buddies at the rail were seaweed green. I think I would have surrendered to the Nazis today if they promised to get me back to solid ground."

Chester's sagging eyes were brightening with every word from Jerry, and he couldn't stop chuckling. "You've gotta forgive me," Chester said. "It's just so horrible that it's funny. One of the guys I work with let 'er fly all over his welder. I just about lost it myself, but I guess I'm lucky. Mom always said she'd never seen a kid with a tougher stomach than mine."

"Count your blessings," Jerry said as they got to the beginning of the food line. The sight of a huge container swimming with beans and bacon nearly sent him scrambling for the stairway, but somehow he managed to force down the wave of nausea and move on through the line. All that he took was a couple slices of bread and some milk. He was fairly sure the bread had a good chance of staying where he wanted it, but he wasn't so sure about the milk.

"You're gonna insult the chef," Chester teased, beaming over a very full plate of everything that was offered.

"I don't think it's possible to insult that guy," replied Jerry weakly. "Did you call him a *chef*? I'm a bad cook, believe me, but you'd have to *try* to make stuff this terrible."

Chester headed for several empty chairs near the end of a long table. "Let me clue you in on a secret I picked up today. The longer we're out from port, the worse the food gets. If you want to survive, you need to eat heavy during the first weeks and then hope you can live on body fat the rest of the trip!"

"Great," Jerry groaned in disgust. "Sounds like a slow, agonizing death for me. I just hope this bread stays put. So how was your day, now that I've spilled my sad tales?"

"Not so great." Chester's cheery voice took on a troubled tone. "I didn't feel so well myself when the ship started pitching around, but that turned out to be the least of my problems. I got into some trouble at the shop." Chester cut it off there and offered no explanation.

Jerry didn't know how to respond. Already he considered Chester a good friend, but didn't know how far he should stick his nose into his friend's business. Both men stared at their food for a minute, then Jerry finally asked, "Do you want to talk about it?"

"Not here," Chester said under his breath. Then he whispered, "Uh-oh, hang on!"

Jerry looked up to see a huge sailor bearing down on them, a smaller crew mate in tow. Red-faced and bull-necked, the big man pulled up beside Chester and leaned over him, staring right into his eyes. Jerry tightened up, figuring they were in for a fight, but then he realized that the other sailor was riding shotgun and watching in case Jerry made a move.

"You're gonna pay for what you done down there today, farm boy," the sailor whispered in menacing tones. "You better watch your backside, 'cause me and the boys, we have ways of dealing with you altar-boy types. You understand?" Jerry could see the sailor's huge knuckles whiten as he squeezed Chester's arm.

Surprisingly, Chester said nothing. Whatever was going on, Jerry figured Chester was playing it cool to avoid getting into trouble. If they were going to fight, the mess hall was not the place to do it.

Chester's lack of response only made the big sailor madder. He glared up at Jerry and said, "I suggest you stay clear of this farm boy for a while. When we mess him up, we're gonna take down anyone who stands up for him. Understand?"

Jerry understood, but was too surprised by the sudden turn of events to say so. Instead he looked around the mess hall to see if there were any officers nearby, and that look was enough to send the red-faced sailor and his mascot toward the doors.

They had been seated far enough away from the crowd in the mess hall that only a few sailors noticed something was brewing. Those who did quickly looked down and applied themselves to their greasy meals with renewed energy.

Chester picked up his spoon and dug into his pile of beans. Jerry just sat blinking his eyes in bewilderment. He took another bite of the dry bread and sipped on his milk, waiting for Chester to explain what the scene was all about.

"It looks like this buddy-plan stuff is a little more complicated than I figured at first," Jerry finally said. "Do you always make such good friends everywhere you go? Like with Mr. No-Neck there?"

Chester looked up with a rueful grin. "I was hoping to tell you about it later, but I didn't think I'd be facing him again so soon. It's a pretty simple story, really. I wasn't sure how you'd respond to it, though. You'll probably think I'm crazy when you hear."

"Why?"

"Because I could have avoided the trouble . . . but I couldn't," Chester explained and raised his eyebrows. "Make sense?"

Jerry shook his head no. "Just tell me the story and don't give it to me in riddles. If I'm gonna be threatened by some slimy goon I've never seen before, I'd like to know why."

"Okay, here goes," Chester said. "Mr. No-Neck, as you call him, is actually Fred Woodward, and he's been working down in the shop for almost a year. So, he's got seniority, right? Anyway, it's my first day down there, and they've got me doing some welding projects on some broken parts from the boiler room. I'm minding my own business when Fred comes over and pulls out some pictures of what I thought at first was his girlfriend or wife. I thought he was just being friendly. Turns out those were the most filthy, disgusting pictures I've ever seen—I mean, really bad. I shoved them back into his hands, told him I didn't want to look at them and I'd appreciate it if he never showed me stuff like that again.

"Well, that made him mad, and he asked me if I was queer or something. I told him no; I just believe that kind of stuff's immoral. Well, then he cussed me . . . cussed me out, and I made the mistake of telling him I would pray for him. Then he blew the roof, and all I could do was turn around and go back to my work."

Jerry stared at his buddy with a quizzical expression. He had to admire Chester for standing up to the guy. But would it have been so bad just to humor Mr. No-Neck along, even if the photos were as bad as Chester said they were?

Chester was continuing his story. "A little later, I heard this loud cracking noise from over at Woodward's turning lathe—like metal breaking. But when I looked up, he was already picking up something from the floor and coming over to where I was. Woodward handed me what was left of the chuck from the lathe and asked me to cover for him. Apparently he'd been doing such bad work that he was afraid he'd get transferred to a rotten job. So he wanted me to say I had used his lathe and broken the chuck. He said I'd be excused because I'm a greenhorn."

"And from Woodward's warm reception here in the mess hall, I'd guess you refused to cover his tracks," Jerry broke in. "And I suppose you brought God into it again?"

"You're very discerning," Chester said with a nervous laugh. "Like I said, this story isn't any too complicated. I told him that even if I didn't get in trouble with the petty officer for lying, I would be violating my conscience. And I just can't do that, Jerry—for any reason!"

Jerry let out a long sigh as he comprehended what was coming next.

"Well, the officer came by to check on what the noise had been, and Woodward jumped right in and started blaming me. He said it was my first day on the job and I had mistakenly jumped in on his machine and forgotten to lock the chuck and broke it." Chester added as he brought the story to its conclusion, "I told the officer that I hadn't touched the turning lathe and that my welding project was all the proof I could offer. He came over and seemed pleased with my work, then he turned on Woodward. Apparently Woodward's got a list of infractions as long as his arm. So Mr. No-Neck's new assignment is sweeping up all the metal filings that are left around the shop. He was none too happy with me, but what could I do?"

Jerry held back from saying that Chester could've gone ahead and covered for Woodward. It didn't seem like that big a deal—surely one little lie wouldn't have hurt. But he just shook his head and shrugged his shoulders.

"I guess I don't know what I would have done. But that guy is bad news, that's for sure. You don't need him for an enemy, and I don't either—and that's what he is now. Maybe you would've been smarter not to bring up the religion part. Sounds like it just made it worse."

"A lot worse. But I had to be true to the truth, didn't I?" Chester asked.

To that, Jerry didn't even attempt a response.

13

THE CONFRONTATION

Marjie received only one more letter from Jerry before the ship left Norfolk, and she carefully tucked it away with her other treasure. This letter was much shorter than the other—he was obviously exhausted from the long days and short nights—but just the reassurance that he was safe gave her a much-needed boost of strength.

A couple of weeks had passed since her visit with her mother, and the daily bouts of morning sickness seemed to be diminishing. The end of every workday, however, found her totally drained. Many evenings she went directly to bed after supper.

A visit to a doctor she knew from the Mayo Clinic confirmed her mother's diagnosis, but as Marjie paid the bill she wondered why she had bothered. She knew full well that she was pregnant, and she didn't need a physician to give a due date. Somehow, though, hearing it from a doctor made it more official.

Marjie agonized over how or when to tell Jerry about the baby. She longed to share the joy of the news, but she also hated to make him worry more than he already was, especially when there was nothing he could do. She was a little embarrassed that they hadn't even considered the possibility of her getting pregnant over their short honeymoon, and she knew that Jerry would feel he'd left her holding the bag. He was already sending home most of the money he got from the navy, but the amount was not nearly enough to cover her needs, and he would know that. She decided she'd wait to make sure the pregnancy was going well before she wrote to him or told anyone besides her mother.

The last person she wanted to find out about the pregnancy was Gordon Stilwell; she knew he'd fire her in a minute if he so much as suspected. He'd done that to a previous waitress, and Priscilla had overheard him telling one of his friends that he "couldn't stand looking at that cow." Marjie figured she could fool him for another month and a half. By then, if the tips kept running as well as they had been, she would finally have her father's medical bill paid off. Then she would have the luxury of quitting the Green Parrot—after giving Gordon Stilwell a dose of his own medicine.

A specific plan for getting back at Stilwell was already taking place in Marjie's mind. She had first gotten the idea one busy noon hour when she was racing behind the counter, trying to keep up with the orders of all twelve diners seated on the stools. She seldom had a problem with any of her customers, but an older man she had never seen in the cafe before had been complaining from the moment he sat down. First, he hadn't gotten his water quickly enough, then the prices were too high, and there weren't enough entrees, and on and on. Marjie occasionally had diners come in distraught after a bad prognosis at the Mayo Clinic, so she always tried to be understanding of people who were truly under stress. When she found out the complainer was a traveling shoe salesman, her small reserve of patience quickly wore through.

While she was taking another man's order a couple stools down, Marjie heard the whiny voice getting louder and louder. "Excuse me, ma'am . . . excuse me . . . ma'am, do you have a hearing problem?"

Marjie had all she could do to keep the lid on the boiling pot inside her head. As calmly as she could, she glanced at him and said, "I'll be right with you, sir. You may have noticed that I was already taking this gentleman's order."

That shut him up for a minute, and he gave her the defiant look of a little boy who'd been made to sit in the corner of the schoolroom. *I wish I had a dunce cap to put on him*, Marjie thought. But she dreaded having to go back to deal with whatever his latest problem was.

When she returned to the salesman, his face had soured considerably, and his eyes were bugging out behind his reading glasses. "I'm sorry that took so long," she said. "What can I help you with? Dessert?"

The little man ran his fingers back through his thinning hair, and his voice crackled this time when he spoke. "You're not the least bit sorry, but I can make you sorry. The bread that was used in my sandwich was stale, and you said your bread was fresh from the bakery this morning. I demand that I get another sandwich."

Marjie stared into his owl eyes in disbelief; she pitied the poor soul who had to live in the same house with this crank. But she hadn't given up trying to reason with him. "Let me assure you that we only use fresh bread, sir. I was here this morning when today's bread was delivered. And it must not have been too bad—you did eat it, I see," she said, pointing to the crumbless plate.

"I ate it because you are the slowest waitress I have ever seen," he barked back. By now everyone at the counter was staring at the disgruntled soul. "Please get me another sandwich and use fresh bread this time!"

Marjie noticed Stilwell moving out from behind the cash register. The look on his face suggested he was more unhappy with her than he was with the salesman.

She looked back at the man and said, "I'm sorry, sir, but that sandwich was as fresh as this morning's bread, and I will not replace it. If you raise your voice again, I will ask the manager to see you to the door."

Pushing his wire-rimmed glasses back on his nose, the salesman again raised his voice as he turned around on his stool. "And where *is* the manager of the Green Parrot Cafe? I'd like to speak with him."

Stilwell had closed in quickly, but not before even the customers in the back booths were straining to see what would happen next. Unfortunately for Marjie, "the boss" performed in true Gordon Stilwell character.

"Yes, sir," Stilwell said quietly as he reached out to shake the angry man's hand. "I am the owner and manager here. May I help you?"

"You can start by getting rid of this insolent waitress who is lying through her teeth," the salesman growled. "I ask whether your cafe uses only morning-fresh bread, and she says yes, but the bread is stale. Then she refuses to replace the sandwich with something fresh. I have never seen such lousy service, and I travel from coast to coast."

Stilwell looked up at Marjie with a scowl. "Get the man whatever he wants," he commanded sharply.

"But Mr. Stilwell, the bread was fresh. You signed for it this morning. And besides, he ate the—"

"I won't say it again!" Stilwell barked, turning the heads of the diners again. "Get the man whatever he wants or *you're fired*. Our policy is that if anyone complains about the quality of our food, we replace it without asking questions."

Marjie was momentarily staggered that Stilwell would publicly shame her and tell such an outlandish lie. There was no policy of automatically replacing food in the cafe. She reached back to untie her apron and walk out of the joint. But then a light went on inside her head—the man had just handed her the ammunition she could use to shoot Stilwell down. If she could just grit her teeth and endure this incident, it was only a matter of time before the score would be settled.

Every eye in the cafe was fixed on Marjie. Giving a loud sigh, she shocked everyone by giving a big grin, then she broke into a hearty, genuine laugh that left the salesman and "the boss" dumbfounded. Returning her attention to the little man who had won his battle, Marjie said, "Thank you, sir. You don't know how much you've helped me today. I had never heard of this policy before, but now that I am aware of it, the cafe will never be the same again. Please . . . here's the menu again. Order whatever you like. Your wish is my pleasure."

Stilwell turned in shock and partial relief. Then he headed

back to his post at the register, smugly aware that his authority had been upheld. And the little man at the counter did his best to select the most expensive entree on the menu while he pondered the strange waitress who had played a card he had never seen before, although he had played this game countless times in cafes all over the Midwest.

A few days later, Marjie cranked up the old black Ford and set in on the road to her father-in-law's farm. She knew the winter days on the farm were long and dull once the chores were done, so she had decided to spend her day off with Benjamin. When she had called the day before to tell him her plans, Marjie had been surprised at Benjamin's delight. Now she was mildly surprised to realize how much she looked forward to tidying up around the farmhouse and doing some cooking for him. One day in the country and away from the cafe, she decided, was just what the doctor ordered.

When she had parked the car in its familiar spot by the barn, she did what Jerry had asked her, and suggested to Benjamin that he might want to look the car over for any problems. His face lit up like a kerosene lamp, and he quickly set to work. Marjie headed for the house and before long had a chocolate cake in the oven. By the time she heard Benjamin rattling the back door open, she had a good jump on washing down the counters and the faces of the kitchen cupboards.

"Smells mighty good," Benjamin called out from the mudroom as he pulled off his boots and coat. "Been a long time since we had a cake baked in this old house. Tell me it's ready to eat."

"It'll be a couple minutes, yet," Marjie said as he came around the corner into the kitchen. "Coffee's hot, though," she added with a wry expression. His face looked like it was nearly frozen in one position, and he headed straight for the stove, numb fingers seeking a source of warmth.

"Boy, this heat does feel good!" Benjamin exclaimed. "Five more minutes out there and I'da been a snowman. Good thing you had me check the car, though. She was low on oil. Gotta watch that, you know."

Benjamin poured himself a cup of coffee and stepped around the counter to the dining room. Stopping at the large picture window, he stood quietly sipping the liquid and letting it warm his insides.

Marjie finished washing the last of the shelves, then checked on the cake with a toothpick. Surprised that it was done so quickly, she pulled it from the oven and cut generous slices for them to enjoy warm.

"Sit down," Marjie said as she set the two plates on the table. "Nothing beats chocolate cake right out of the oven."

Benjamin sat, still cradling his coffee cup for warmth. He quickly picked up his fork and took a large bite, shutting his eyes and letting the warm cake melt in his mouth. Marjie had to laugh at his charm.

"Mmmmm . . . mmm!" Benjamin murmured appreciatively. "This is the best! Thank you for fixing it. Chocolate's my favorite, did you know?"

"Matter of fact, Jerry told me it's the golden key to your heart."

"Should've known it was a set-up," Benjamin spoke with a laugh. "But he was right. You've found my only weak spot."

Marjie jumped up to get the pot of coffee and refilled their cups. Benjamin's attention had wandered out the picture window again, and Marjie wondered what was on his mind. Taking her seat again, she asked, "So, how've you been? You're looking good."

Running his fingers along his cold-flushed cheeks, Benjamin continued gazing out the window and said, "Must be the clean, cold air, I guess. The color in my face always is better in the winter. Yeah, I've been feeling good enough for an old man, but . . ."

His voice trailed off, and the light in his eyes seemed to dim. Marjie wondered if she could get Benjamin to tell her what was bothering him. She felt she had to at least try.

"But what?" Marjie asked.

Benjamin folded his hands very deliberately, like he'd been thinking of doing it for a long time. Then he got up and walked over to the window again. Finally he turned around and looked at Marjie. "You know, when I was younger, I never told anyone about what I was feeling inside. But Martha could read me like a book and pulled it out of me real gentle-like, thread by thread. When she died, I kept it all inside and tried to tough it out, but I suffered because of it and so did Jerry. That last day before he left was the first time in years that I've really talked."

He paused to survey the farmyard, then collected more thoughts and continued. "I regret that I wasted so many years, and now that I've returned to the land of the living, the past couple weeks have been very hard. Seems like it should be just the opposite, don't it? I . . ."

Benjamin thrust his lower lip up over his upper lip and then gave his face a good rubbing before he continued. "This goes against my grain to say, Marjie, but the past couple weeks I've been so lonely here I could hardly stand to be in the house. I don't think I can take it, though I know that sounds stupid. I had no idea what Jerry meant to me."

Whether because Benjamin had choked up or simply run out of words, silence took over. The old man seemed content to stare at the farthest point he could see from his position at the window.

It was Marjie who finally broke the silence, although she had to wait for a wave of emotions to subside and her thoughts to clear again. Her throat was raspy as she said, "I think I know what you mean, Benjamin, and it doesn't sound the least bit stupid. I have never felt so alone in all my life." She shut her eyes and wondered what was next. Benjamin surprised her by sitting back down and taking one of her hands into his cold, chapped hands.

He looked at her and smiled. Then he said, "Why should we both be miserable?"

"What do you mean?" she asked in bewilderment.

"Well," Benjamin went on, the twinkle returning to his eyes, "I've been chewing this over in my head for some weeks now. Didn't you say you'd be quitting your job at the cafe soon?"

Marjie nodded in agreement, not knowing where Benjamin might be headed.

He picked up his coffee cup and swallowed the remaining drops. "Well, maybe this is a little bit crazy, so be gentle with your response, now. But, I'm wondering if, instead of looking for another job and another place to live . . . if you'd consider moving out here to help me with the farm. I'm afraid I just can't go it alone like I promised Jerry. And, well . . . after all, you *are* good with pigs!"

Marjie couldn't have been more shocked if Benjamin had dropped a bomb on the table. When the initial whirl of her thoughts settled down, however, she began to warm to the idea. It was clear that Benjamin really did need someone to help him, but it was even clearer to Marjie that in the very near future she was going to need help, too. She would never have asked Benjamin to take her in, but now her mother's words rang in her ears, "Somehow it always worked out."

Marjie's blank stare troubled Benjamin, and he finally shook his head. "Marjie, I'm sorry to have made you so uncomfortable. Just forget I mentioned it, please. It was just a crazy thought from somebody that's got too much time on his hands."

"No, no, no," Marjie pleaded. "Just give me some time to think it through. It's a wonderful idea, but it's more complicated than you know. Will you listen to my story first?"

"Of course," Benjamin said attentively.

Marjie paused, but her thoughts came together quickly. "You know that I love your son, and I love this house, and there's nothing I'd like better than to stay here and never go back to the cafe. I've come to love you as well. I think we could make a good team here while Jerry is gone. But there's something that you need to know, and it may influence whether you still think your offer is a good one."

Benjamin sat silently waiting for Marjie, nodding his head to go on.

Taking a deep breath of air, Marjie looked deep into Benjamin's eyes as she calmly told her news. "I'm pregnant with Jerry's baby."

It took several moments for the reality of what she had said to reach Benjamin's understanding, but it was obvious when it hit home. It was as if someone pulled a shower cord and down poured the tears. Benjamin tried crying and laughing at the same time, and the result was a mess. He found himself blubbering like a baby.

Marjie caught the joy in his eyes and joined the shower of fresh tears as bewilderment wrestled with elation and concern in her mind. She had never dreamed that someone so staid and quiet as Benjamin could be so overwhelmed by sheer happiness. Still, she did not want him to make his decision based on his emotions.

"I may be more of a burden to you than a help," Marjie whispered. "The baby's going to be here about the time you should be in the fields picking corn."

Benjamin was still having a hard time putting two words together, so he jumped up and started pacing around the table, shaking his head and laughing. "Wonderful!" he called out as if he hadn't heard her warning. "Really wonderful! Congratulations! Congratulations! I couldn't be happier! This is wonderful!"

"Wonderful, yes," Marjie said calmly. "But it's going to be very, very hard without Jerry. Do you understand that?"

"Understand?" asked Benjamin, stopping his pace around the table. "Of course I understand. I did raise two boys in this house, didn't I? All through the Depression—those were hard times, believe me. Of course I understand. But I also understand that if Jerry has to fight for our nation, then there's no one better suited to help you bring this child into the world than me. Don't you see, Marjie, this is your home now. I couldn't be happier."

"Are you sure?" Marjie asked. "Maybe you should give it some thought."

"I've given it too much thought already," Benjamin declared. Then he stopped pacing and bent to take her hand in his.

"Please do me the honor of letting me help in this way. I suspicion my days here on the earth are getting pretty slim, and this is my chance to make them count. Please say yes."

Marjie jumped up and threw happy arms around her father-in-law. "Then we really are a family!" she whispered.

And Benjamin whispered, "Family," in return.

14

ON STANDBY

The *Wasp* had initially set out to Ireland to deposit a group of American troops. For reasons Jerry never understood, however, the ship changed course about two hundred fifty miles from the Irish coast and headed across the wintry Atlantic toward Argentia, Newfoundland.

As the days wore on, and as everyone settled in to their duties, the initial tension on board gave way to a calmer, business-as-usual atmosphere. The weather was calm, and Jerry found to his vast relief that his seasickness lasted only another day. Because their work schedules were so different, Jerry and Chester saw less of each other, although they still managed to talk every day. And beyond an occasional taunt, Chester's friend Mr. No-Neck seemed uninterested in making trouble.

Jerry found his schedule both complicated and tiring. A usual day meant an early manning of the guns, a morning inspection for clean clothes and a good shoeshine, and then a full day of either working with the guns or scrubbing, mopping, and painting. Then there was watch duty, and the watch schedule varied with the guns. The watch on the five-inch guns lasted from eight in the morning until noon, then from eight at night till six the next morning—and that was followed by another stint from noon till four and then all night. The watch on the other guns was equally difficult. Little time was left for anything besides sleeping and an occasional movie.

Jerry quickly grew to hate the night watches. The daylight duties were not so bad. But those hours of "absolute silence" on the pitch-black deck in the wintry sea air were full of a raw torment for Jerry, for it was during those times that he wrestled with his fear and worry.

Sound travels surprisingly far over water. It seemed that no matter which gun Jerry had to man at night, he could hear the steady drone and ping of the ASDIC antisubmarine detector. In the eerie silence of the night, Jerry would stare up at the pitch-black bridge to see the skipper cast into spooky silhouette by the thin green beam that circled the ASDIC's big, clocklike face. The thought of lurking U-boats and the ear-scratching electronic monotony of the sonar combined to keep Jerry's stomach in a knot.

Sometimes, to break the nervous monotony of the dark, Jerry would sing to himself, making no sound but mouthing the words of popular songs by Fred Waring or Bing Crosby or Ukulele Ike. But more often, thoughts of home would dominate his mind. Worries about his father and the farm buzzed constantly through his head, and he imagined dire scenarios—a letter from his father saying he had to sell the farm, or a somber officer approaching with the telegram announcing his father's death.

His only star of hope on those long, cold nights was Marjie. Many nights, it was often the hope of seeing her again that kept him at his post; he kept telling himself that if he could just make it through to another morning, he'd be one day closer to her. His mental picture of her mischievous eyes and her forthright smile had a power over the dark fears that pressed in so closely. But worry colored his thoughts of her as well. He knew his Marjie was tough, but she was also human. He worried about what Stilwell might be up to, whether she was even safe with him around, whether she could handle the car.

Argentia, Newfoundland was a colorful Canadian seaport town. Jerry watched with fascination as an array of routine flag and light signals guided them into the dock. The harbor bristled with U.S., British, Canadian, and Free French warships, either riding at anchor or tied up alongside one of the docks. But no shore leaves were issued, and the *Wasp* was soon back out doing patrol duty.

Nearly a week outside of Argentia, just before an evening movie, word spread among the men that the order had been given to intercept a German raider five hundred miles away. Heads came up and eyes brightened as the news passed from man to man; the movie was forgotten. Then, suddenly, bells began to clang, and over the ship's loudspeakers came the sound of the "bosun's pipe"—a sort of two-note whistle—followed at split seconds with *"Now hear this! All hands! Stand by to man your guns! All hands stand by to man your guns!"*

Jerry felt the ship come about sharply and accelerate toward the south. Even at thirty knots, the ship would take some time to get where they were going, and for now it was only a standby, but nevertheless there was a bedlam of shouts, noises, and rushing feet. Crew members hurried to grab their old World War I tin helmets, get their life belts ready, and collect their valuables. Then they waited, adrenaline pumping, for a possible engagement.

Most of the men, Jerry included, slept with their clothes on that night. Jerry was glad he had not drawn watch duty; he wanted to be ready to man his gun the next day. He tried to get some rest, but sleep was a lost cause.

Lying in his bunk, Jerry wondered if Chester was awake, whether he wanted to talk. A couple of nights earlier, while standing watch, Jerry had suddenly realized that most of their conversations had revolved around Jerry and his family. In all these weeks, he still had not learned much about Chester's life. It struck Jerry that this might be a good time to remedy the situation.

"Chester, you awake?" Jerry whispered after he had sat up and peeked up into Chester's top bunk.

"Are you kidding?" Chester answered. He leaned his head down over the bunk and saw Jerry's dim shadow. "I'm wound up like a top."

"Me too," Jerry said.

"Yeah, so am I," called out a voice from a few bunks over. "But I might have a chance of getting some sleep if you guys'd keep yer voices down!"

Jerry leaned up again and murmured to his friend in a quieter tone. "You scared, Chester?"

"Of dying?"

"What else?"

Chester was silent a long minute. "I guess I'm most afraid that I'm not trained well enough yet to do my part in defending this ship and the lives of all these men," he answered quietly. "But, no, I am not afraid to die. That don't mean I want to, though."

Like so many other responses that Chester had given, this was not at all what Jerry expected to hear. He was so taken aback he didn't know what to ask next. But Chester didn't give him a chance.

"Are you afraid to die, Jerry?"

Jerry squirmed to feel the conversation directed back toward him once more—and on a distinctly uncomfortable subject. But he had come to trust that Chester cared what he felt, so he decided not to cover over his answer. "Yeah, I'd have to say I'm pretty scared. Mind telling me why in the world you're not?"

Chester leaned way over the bunk and positioned his square-jawed face as close to Jerry's as he could. "Just one simple reason, Jerry. It's because I believe that Jesus Christ is the Son of God . . . and that through His death my sins are forgiven."

"Come on! That's it?" Jerry's voice rose again. "I was being serious with you when I said I was scared to die; now I'm asking you to be serious with me. Look, I've gone to church all my life, and that sure hasn't made me ready to die!"

"Shut up!" came the voice again from across the room.

"Oh, all right," Jerry retorted. "Just take it easy."

"I didn't say anything about going to church," Chester continued in a whisper. "To tell you the truth, Jerry, right up until leaving home, I haven't gone to church at all—except for a few times."

"You've got to be kidding!" Jerry blurted. "So how'd you get so religious? You're always talking about God and prayer and stuff. I thought it was because of your parents—thought you were raised that way."

Chester shook his head in the dark. "I don't really consider myself religious, although God has become a very important part of my life. But my folks—they don't believe in God *or* religion. Fact, my dad's the main reason I haven't gone to church. He said that any of his children that stepped foot in a church was no longer welcome to live under his roof. My mom told me that she and Dad used to belong to a church, but they got kicked out when they couldn't afford to pay what the church said was their tithe. So my dad's about as bitter against God and the church as anybody I've ever met. I figured that as soon as I left home, I'd find a church I like, but in the meantime there didn't seem to be any reason to let a church get us in a fight."

Jerry was amazed; the scattered pieces Chester had showed him of his life didn't seem to add up. "All right, just give it to me straight. I don't have a clue as to how you got so religious, or whatever you want to call it. I've always figured that to get to heaven meant you did a lot of good things that had to add up to a big enough sum—faithfully going to church, not swearing, not drinking, giving a certain amount of money. And I know I'm not even close to being good enough. Tell me how you know that what you said is true. Dying is different than talking about theories."

"If I tell you my story and I convince you that there is an easy way to find out if what I'm saying is true, would you be willing to explore it?" Chester asked.

"You're baiting me," Jerry said. "Just tell your story."

"All right," Chester gave in. "Well, back a few years ago, my friends and I were looking to have some fun one night, so we picked up the local town drunk, Donny. None of us were old enough to buy booze, but he'd go in for us and buy us whiskey if we gave him money for a jug of cheap white wine. We'd always haul him down to Lanesboro because the police in our town knew our car. Know what I mean?"

"Yeah," said Jerry.

"Anyway, the whole way down, that guy told one dirty story after another. None of us were all that clean-cut, mind you, but this guy was really disgusting. Anyway, after he'd bought the wine and we were headed down the road, ol' Donny opened his jug of wine and chugged it down like it was water. I was in the backseat watching. And you know, the thought that got to me was this: I could be just like Donny when I got to be fifty if I kept living the way I was headed. I saw myself driving with kids to another town to buy them booze, telling my filthy stories, and slurping down wine like I was dying of thirst. Let me tell you, that thought scared me to death!

"I kept on thinking about that night, and it got so I could hardly sleep. Even though I was afraid of what I might become, see, I didn't have any idea how to change it. But I had this one friend from school who was fun to be with but who stayed clear of the bad things we were doing. Name was Dave Dirkson. Anyway, I knew Dave was different, but I didn't know why. So one night I went over to his house and asked him . . ."

Silence fell then from the top bunk, and Jerry prompted, "And. . . ?"

"And," Chester echoed, "that guy said that Jesus Christ had changed his life and that He could change my life as well. He showed me in the Bible that God loved me so much and wanted me to be His child so much that He gave up His only Son to die for me. Die in agony—and just so I could be forgiven for all the stuff I'd done and so He could find a way to come into my life and help me. But Dave also showed me I needed to make some changes. I had to ask God to forgive me for all the bad things I'd done and help me stop doing them. I had to put all my faith in Jesus as my Savior. But if I did that, Dave said, then Jesus would come and live in my life forever.

"It sounded too good to be true, but I guess at that point I was so desperate I was willing to try anything. So I bowed my head and told God about Donny and the drinking and all the other stuff I was doing. I asked Him to forgive me for Jesus' sake, and then I asked Jesus to come into my life. And He did. I swear to you He did it. 'Cause ever since that night, my life's been different."

Jerry silently took it all in. He wondered how he could go to church for so many years and not get a similar story.

"Well, I guess that's pretty much it," Chester added. "What do you think?"

"I guess I'm not sure what to think. I never heard anyone in church say what you said—never once. What's this easy way you said would confirm whether what you're saying is true?"

"It's right in your footlocker," Chester whispered. "You've got a Bible in there, don't you?"

"Been snooping around my stuff, huh? Yes, I've got a Bible, but I've never read it," Jerry answered. "It's overwhelming big, and I'm as slow a reader as I am a writer."

"Not a problem," Chester said. "I'll show you where to start, if you want, and I guarantee that it won't be long before you can know what is true for yourself."

"I don't know," said Jerry, leery of obligating himself. "I'll think about it, though."

"You do that," said an exasperated voice from a few bunks away. "Think real hard—just stop talking so I can get some sleep."

In the early morning hours, Jerry awoke to the realization that the seas were getting rougher. By daylight he was beginning to understand the power of a great North Atlantic storm. The ship had to slow down in order to cope with the gigantic waves and the gusting, fifty-mile-an-hour winds. And the storm only seemed to increase as the hours went by.

There was little for the men to do but stay low and play cards. Fortunately the ship was well heated, because the outside decks were unlivable.

Soon ice began to form over the ship; even the planes on the flight deck glazed with a four-inch covering. Word spread that the waves were so high that officers inside the covered bridge had completely lost visual contact with the destroyers that flanked the carrier. When it finally seemed to the officers that they would be overwhelmed by the ruthlessness of the ocean's bitter cold and merciless waves, the captain sent a message to the admiral that it was impossible to operate and that they were turning back.

A week later the *Wasp* anchored in Casco Bay just off Portland, Maine, but the storm had followed them the whole way in. By the time calm was restored, water had sloshed through innumerable cracks in the hull and flooded several large sections. Huge pieces of iron were twisted like twine, equipment had been broken off or smashed, and only the toughest of stomachs had withstood a second outbreak of seasickness.

During those stormy days at sea, Jerry pulled out the Bible that Sarah Livingstone had given him as a wedding present. Slowly, as Chester had suggested, he began to read away at the Book of John. He wasn't sure what to think of his friend's story, but after all those years in church he felt he was meeting the man Jesus for the first time.

He knew it was going to take some time before he felt he understood what those pages were saying, and he struggled with the antiquated language. But something in the pages felt strong and real. Something inside urged him to read on.

15

SPRINGING THE TRAP

March 7 arrived like a long-awaited friend, and Marjie greeted the day with delight. More than a month and a half had passed since Benjamin invited her to come live at the Macmillan farm, and now the day had arrived. Today's paycheck would give her enough to polish off her father's hospital debt. Today's scheme, carefully crafted by her and Benjamin over the long winter hours, would take care of Gordon Stilwell. And then the old black Ford, already loaded up with her belongings, would take her away from the Green Parrot and her aunt's house for good.

And none too soon, she observed wryly as she turned sideways to check the mirror. *It's a miracle nobody at work's noticed how much weight I've put on.*

Marjie arrived at the cafe when it opened that morning; she was only scheduled to work through the lunch hour. Stilwell had an odd policy of paying his workers early in the day, and Marjie pocketed her check with a smile. When Stilwell handed her the check, Marjie surprised him by smiling and putting her hand on his arm, telling him that she had never worked with anyone else like him. Stilwell lit up like a Christmas tree and then took every opportunity throughout the morning to get close to her behind the counter. He reminded Marjie of an overstuffed turkey, preening and puffing out his feathers. *Too bad you're just about to get plucked,* she told him in her mind.

As Marjie had hoped, business was slow most of the morning. About eleven o'clock, Marjie asked Priscilla to cover for her while she made a quick phone call. She walked to the telephone in the back and dialed Benjamin's number.

"Are you all set?" she asked when her father-in-law picked up.

"All set," he answered. "Your mother and brother just pulled in. We'll be leaving in a few minutes."

"Good," said Marjie, glancing down the long hallway to see if the coast was still clear. "Remember, come in one at a time and try to spread out at the counter."

"We'll do our best," replied Benjamin. "See you soon."

"Don't be late."

Now all that remained was for Benjamin and Sarah and Ted to make their appearance. They were driving up together, and each had separate roles to play. Stilwell had never been introduced to any of them before, so there was no way that he would be suspicious that Marjie was up to something. As long as there were three empty stools at the counter, the stage would be set. And if they all came in shortly before noon, there should be room.

About five minutes before noon, Ted Livingstone stepped through the cafe doors dressed in the fine new suit he'd borrowed from a friend, his good shoes polished, and his hair slicked back neatly. He pulled off his outer coat, hung it up on the hangers by the cash register like some of the businessmen did, then nodded to Stilwell and took the far corner stool at the counter. Marjie and Ted had loved to play tricks together when they were children, and now Ted pinched his lips together to keep from laughing when he looked at Marjie.

Marjie had just gotten Ted a menu and a glass of water when her mother entered. Leaving her coat on and deliberately avoiding a look in Stilwell's direction, Sarah made a beeline for an empty stool in the center of the counter. She looked over at Marjie with the most innocent of smiles. Sarah had not wanted to get involved in the scheme at first . . . until Marjie told her the details of what Stilwell had done. Now she seemed to be enjoying herself immensely.

A minute later, in walked Benjamin, looking like he'd come straight from the barn. Marjie wasn't quite sure how he had done it, but Benjamin's boots sported large clumps of manure that seemed to be hanging on by a thread. Before Stilwell could stop him, Benjamin was pounding his boots down in the entry and the clusters were flying off in all directions.

Shaking his head in disgust and muttering to himself, Benjamin looked up into Stilwell's unhappy face. "Cotton picker! If that don't beat all. My apologies for the mess. I thought I'd changed boots." Slipping past Stilwell, who was reaching for the broom and pan, Benjamin caught the last stool on the opposite end from Ted.

By the time Benjamin had his water and was ready to order, Ted was just beginning to cut up his meatloaf and potatoes and Sarah's sandwich was on the way. Benjamin scanned the menu and decided to try the fresh fish special. He looked up at Marjie and said under his breath, "You sure you want to go through with this? We can still pull out."

Marjie shot him a look of disbelief. "I've been cooking this bacon for three months, and you think I'm giving up now? Let's get the show on the road!"

Benjamin leaned forward and nodded down at Ted. "Ma'am . . . excuse me, ma'am . . ." Ted called out to Marjie.

Marjie walked down to his end of the counter and asked, "May I help you?"

Ted picked up the tempo by raising his voice to where he hoped Stilwell might hear. "This meatloaf tastes like a rusty tin pan. I can't eat it, though you'll notice I tried drowning it in catsup. I wouldn't give this to my dog."

Marjie shook her head sympathetically, noticing that "the boss" had his antenna up and was watching. "I am so sorry, sir. I'll speak with the cook immediately. Is there anything on the menu we could replace this with? We have a wonderful steak platter you might like."

Stilwell looked pleased and nodded to her. Obviously, he did not want another incident.

Ted smiled as well. "That sounds great! Make it a big one, okay?"

"Coming right up," she said and disappeared into the kitchen.

Stepping back out, Marjie was quickly hailed by Sarah, who had been complaining to the diners next to her that her tuna sandwich was dry as a board. Stilwell was already shaking his head unhappily by the time Marjie got to Sarah's place. Marjie again apologized profusely and offered her anything on the menu. Sarah said she'd like to try that same steak platter that the good-looking gentleman on the corner had ordered.

Marjie headed for the kitchen again and was met by one bewildered-looking cook. Marjie had forgotten how he played into the sting. Hoping that their friendship was enough, she whispered, "Bill, I can't explain, but please play along with this and start frying steaks as fast as you can. I can burn Stilwell if you do."

Bill had endured Stilwell's tirades so many times that he just smiled and winked. "Give him one for me," he said.

Delivering a glass of milk to one of the other diners, Marjie heard Benjamin coughing up a storm at the end of the counter. Thinking there really was something wrong with him, Marjie dashed to attend him, but one look told her he was acting. He finally stopped coughing and shaking his head. "This fish has bones in it! Why in the world didn't you tell me? I just about choked to death!"

"The fish should not have bones in it, sir," Marjie pleaded sincerely. "Let me take the plate back to the kitchen and get you something else. Did you see anything else on the menu that sounded good?"

"By golly, that's real sweet of you to offer," Benjamin said through one last muffled cough. "Matter of fact, I thought the steak sounded good, but it looked a bit rich for my blood. I'll take that now, if it's not too much trouble."

"After all the pain we've put you through, sir, it's no trouble at all," Marjie said. "We'll get it right out."

Marjie winked at Sarah as she headed back to the kitchen again, while Stilwell stood quietly at his post with a stricken look on his face. He didn't know exactly what was happening, but it was pretty clear that he was giving out a lot more than would come back into his precious cash register.

When Marjie emerged from the kitchen again, she already had Ted's steak platter ready to go. Putting it before him, Ted said, "Ma'am, the gentleman sitting next to me here said he thought his roast beef was a bit tough. Isn't that right, sir?"

The man looked a bit surprised, but had obviously noted the results of the others' complaints. "Well, it's tough, all right, but I guess I can finish it off," he said.

Marjie leaned forward and said, "Sir, our policy at the Green Parrot Cafe is that if anyone has any complaint whatsoever about the food, it will be replaced immediately with anything on our menu." Grabbing his plate before he could get the last bite of roast beef, she asked, "What would you like? Steak sound good?"

"Sounds very good," the confused diner agreed with a pleased grin.

Looking at the man seated next to him, who had also observed the strange happenings, Marjie asked, "What about you, sir. Someone said the ham was not the best. Would you care for steak as well?"

He was a bit taken aback but didn't want to miss his chance, so he said, "Sure, I guess. The ham was a bit cold—"

Marjie was gone with his plate before he could say another word. The plan was working better than she had dreamed. By the time she got back out from the kitchen, Sarah and Benjamin had convinced the diners next to them that all they had to do was ask for steak and they could have it. Marjie brought out one platter after another to some very happy customers.

Stilwell stepped away from the counter and hurried into the kitchen to chew out the chef, but the chef argued that he was not doing anything different, and that the food was fine. Stilwell frantically grabbed Marjie by the arm on her next trip in, but she said she didn't know what else to do. "Remember, you told me what your policy was, and these people are all complaining. I'm not supposed to argue with them, am I?"

Before long all twelve stools had steak platters, and Ted was complaining about the apple pie he'd ordered, and wanting it replaced with cherry pie and ice cream. Sarah and Benjamin were calling for service as well, and finally Marjie threw up her hands and asked for Stilwell to please come and help.

Stilwell had worked himself into a fury as he marched around Benjamin's corner of the counter. "What's wrong, now?" the owner grumped.

Benjamin returned Stilwell's scowl with one of his own. "I almost choked to death on a bone from your fish, mister, and now these potatoes are cold. Taste'm yourself. Whatcha gonna do about that now?"

Stilwell just grabbed Benjamin's plate and headed for the kitchen, but he was intercepted en route by Sarah. "Sir!" she called. "These peas must have come from a can. They are not fresh!"

"No one said they were fresh, you picky old—"

"He'd love to get you some fresh ones!" Marjie broke in.

Stilwell raced by her with both plates, then it dawned on him that they didn't have any fresh peas. He turned and yelled for Marjie to come to the kitchen, but she took no notice. And at that moment his wife walked through the front door and stood in bewilderment by the cash register. Elizabeth Stilwell had never seen such chaos at the cafe.

Ted reached over, tapped Stilwell on the shoulder, and said, "If you *ever* yell at her again, I'll be stuffing those big fat peas down your slimy throat one by one. This is all your fault, you know." Then he flashed a big, ferocious-looking smile.

Stilwell looked at him, trying to figure out what Ted's problem was, and then he caught the family resemblance. "What in the—"

But it was too late, and Stilwell knew that he'd been had. He looked over and saw Marjie saying something to his wife. He was so panic-stricken that he froze in place until he heard Ted's voice break through the alarm bells going off in his head, "Hey, Gordy, seen any ghosts lately?"

Stilwell dropped the plates and dashed around the counter with the hope of somehow salvaging this mess, but Benjamin had already gotten up and pretended to trip into him before he could get to his wife. Stilwell went flying into Priscilla, who was bussing a cart of dirty dishes back to the kitchen; the cart toppled with a huge crash and a loud scream from Priscilla.

Every eye in the Green Parrot Cafe was frozen on the raging Gordon Stilwell as he turned to face his wife. Even Bill, the cook, had stepped from the kitchen when he saw Stilwell make his dash around the counter. His greasy hair still sticking up all over from his collision with Benjamin, Stilwell opened his mouth to explain to Elizabeth, but he was so dazed that he could think of no lie big enough. All that came out was "Elizabeth . . ."

"Have you lost your mind, Gordon?" she asked. "Marjie said you were acting strangely today. Maybe you should come home and rest for a while."

Marjie looked over at the disheveled Stilwell and said, "I think that would be a good idea, *Gordon*."

That pushed Stilwell over the edge, and he lunged at Marjie with his fist raised to strike her. But Benjamin stepped between them and grabbed Stilwell by the neck, shoving him up hard against the wall. The hard-working farmer was much more than a match for the pudgy restaurant owner, and Stilwell made no attempt to protest.

"Mighta figured a no-good calf like you could stoop so low as to raise his fist to a lady. If you ever touch my daughter-in-law, if you ever even *think* about coming after her, let me warn you now that I can get real nasty. And I *will* hurt you, hurt you bad—understand!" With that he jammed Stilwell up a little higher on the wall.

Benjamin told Marjie to get her coat, and Sarah and Ted went to the door to make their exit together. Marjie calmly walked behind the counter and picked up some very generous tips, then headed back toward the cash register and opened it up.

"If you rob the till, I'll call the cops," Stilwell squeaked, still pinned tightly to the wall.

Marjie laughed and said, "I don't want your stinking money, Gordon, but I thought maybe I'd fill up the register for you." Grabbing the wastebasket that contained the manure from Benjamin's boots, she dumped the contents into the till and then jammed it shut.

A spontaneous cheer went up from the diners, and a couple of regulars who were fans of Marjie stood up and applauded. Marjie waved and called out "goodbye" as she and Sarah and Ted stepped proudly through the cafe doors into the wintry air.

Benjamin relaxed his hold, and Stilwell slumped down against the wall, rubbing his neck. Before Stilwell's wife could come to his side, Benjamin gave him one last warning: "Don't ever give me the chance to do to you what I'd really like to do."

Turning to exit, Benjamin stopped at the counter, nodded to the diners on the stools, and said, "Been real nice eating with you folks. This has been a meal I won't forget for a long time, and I'm so glad we could share it together. Enjoy the steak. Enjoy anything you like. It's on the house."

When the door closed behind Benjamin, one by one the patrons of the Green Parrot Cafe quickly finished their meals and exited for the last time.

16

FIRST LEAVE

Having weathered their first major storm of the North Atlantic, the *Wasp* spent the next six weeks doing patrol duty around Portland. Jerry spent most of his time painting and scrubbing the storm-damaged decks. That lull allowed him to write a couple of letters and, more important, to allow half a dozen of Marjie's letters to catch up with him.

Marjie's letters usually contained a delightful mix of the everyday things that she was experiencing along with expressions from her heart that left Jerry feeling both beloved and blue. She would write about what it was like to get some of the items being rationed—gas, sugar, coffee, canned goods. Jerry especially loved her story of what it had been like to stand in line for nylon stockings. Then she would write out some of the verses to a song like Jimmy Dorsey's "I'll Never Smile Again," and Jerry would spend the next night's watch humming out the tune and thinking of being alone with Marjie again.

Jerry read the letters in the order of their dating and was doing fine until he read the one dated March 9. Then he found himself caught somewhere between murderous rage and uncontrolled hilarity. When Jerry read about how his father and Marjie's mother and brother had helped take Gordon Stilwell down, he laughed so hard that the tears poured down and his sides hurt. But when she told him about Stilwell's proposition, he was almost glad that he was so far away. Much as he hated not being there to protect his wife from such a vulgar creep, he also knew how explosive his temper could be; it wouldn't take much for him to grab a shotgun and put the dog out of his misery for good. He also sensed that Marjie's scheme had more justice in it and would be a greater punishment than anything he could have dished out, but that did nothing to alleviate his frustration. No matter what happened to Marjie, he was powerless to make a difference.

The good news was that Marjie was going to live with his father. Jerry was relieved that the two people he loved most would be there to look out for each other. But it bothered him late into the night that both Marjie and his dad had held back from telling him certain things. She had not told him what Stilwell had pulled on her months before. And his father had not written a word about being so lonely on the farm. Jerry could understand their desire to not add to his worries, but he couldn't stand the thought of perhaps the most important things being covered up.

Jerry started a letter to Marjie pleading with her to keep giving him all the facts, but it was a letter he never finished. Halfway through he got the feeling that it was unreasonable to demand to know everything. Maybe there were things he was better off not knowing. *Perhaps*, he thought, pulling out paper for a different letter, *I just need to trust Marjie to tell me what she thinks best.*

A whirlwind of depressing emotions wrapped themselves around Jerry and followed him like a bad dog into the long night of March 16. He had drawn duty to stand watch on one of the guns as the *Wasp* left Casco Bay and headed for Norfolk, traveling as a part of Task Group 22.6. During the late evening hours the convoy of ships ran into a dense bank of fog that only added to Jerry's sense of woe. Visibility fell to nearly zero, and the blanket of cold, damp air seemed to penetrate his soul and multiply his loneliness. The hours dragged by with agonizing slowness as he stood by his gun.

Having checked his wristwatch over and over again, Jerry was anxiously awaiting his replacement just minutes before his shift was to end at six in the morning. To get out of the "pea-souper," as one of the men called it, would be a huge relief. Although it was nearly impossible to tell in the dark, Jerry thought the fog was worsening. He could not even see the front of the ship from the gun where he was standing.

Without warning a tremendous crash sent Jerry tumbling into the metal railings that surrounded his gun. Shaken but unhurt, and with adrenaline surging, he picked himself up off the deck and scrambled to stand at his gun, ready to pick off the unseen enemy. Alarms and whistles went off all over the ship but were hardly necessary. Every man on the ship had been tossed around by the impact and jumped into immediate action.

But no gun would be required to cope with that particular alarm. Instead, the sailors on the *Wasp* were rudely awakened to discover that they had collided with one of the destroyers traveling in the convoy. The *Wasp*'s bow had plunged into the *Stack*'s starboard flank, punching a hole and completely flooding the destroyer's number one fireroom. But in the murky gloom it was impossible to tell how badly either ship was damaged, and they could not make contact with each other. It was late afternoon before the *Wasp* crew found out that seven men on the *Stack* had been killed and that the ship was so badly damaged that she had to be towed by another destroyer to the Philadelphia Navy Yard.

The *Wasp* was not seriously damaged, but it was a somber group of sailors who limped into dry dock at Norfolk four days later. The fact that seven Americans had lost their lives not in combat, but in a collision between two friendly ships, seemed senseless and discouraging. Every man on the ship, it seemed, longed for shore leave and the chance to get away from the scene of sadness.

Chester and Jerry wanted off the ship as much as any other man, but as soon as the ship docked they were put to work changing ammunition and provisioning the ship. Repairs went faster than expected, and word went around that the ship would be sent back out as soon as she was seaworthy again. The two men felt extremely fortunate, therefore, to finally get their passes.

Despite a bone-deep weariness, the two friends quickened

their pace in the early evening shadows as they headed away from the *Wasp* for the first time in three months. Jerry was glad to have Chester with him, but he wasn't sure what Chester had planned. And he hadn't told his friend that what he really wanted to do was head for the closest tavern. He knew Chester had given up booze, but Jerry hadn't. And he determined that Chester's convictions were not going to spoil his one chance to have some fun.

At this point, though, they both wanted to just walk freely through the streets and see the city. Chester told Jerry he'd like to head for one end of town and keep right on walking until he found some good fields and woods and streams. After three months' confinement on the ship, to be able to go wherever they wanted and do what they wanted was exhilarating.

It was also shocking. The two young men who'd barely been off their farms in Minnesota were poorly prepared for what they encountered on the city streets. It was one thing to hear the stories of what went on during shore leaves, but it was another thing to actually see it. Jerry heard Chester whisper something under his breath about Sodom and Gomorrah, and what he saw seemed to fit what he could remember of the biblical story. He was reminded of what Marjie had said about men becoming animals, and he wondered if her warning had come for this very moment.

Chester told Jerry that it felt like they were in the middle of one big party that actually didn't look like very much fun. Sailors pulling young women out of the bars and behaving in the lewdest fashion right on the streets. No one seemed to care that what they were doing was in full view of countless passersby. Jerry and Chester saw guys stumbling along the streets in drunken stupors looking for their ships; others were brawling over who knows what; still others were getting hauled away by the shore police. Chester looked over at Jerry, shook his head, and kept on walking.

They thought if they went a little farther they could escape the rowdy revelry, but that was not what happened. Spotting a group of men whom they knew from the ship, Jerry and Chester decided to follow them and see where they were headed. They overheard one of their drunken mates holler about the "red light" district, and the two country boys continued to tag along just to see if it was for real. They had heard stories about the place, but they had a hard time believing it really existed.

Sure enough, red lights began to appear in the windows ahead, and Jerry wondered out loud to Chester why these people still had their Christmas lights on in March. Chester told Jerry that he didn't think the lights had anything at all to do with Christmas. After a few more minutes, Jerry had to agree; he was acutely embarrassed to have been so naive.

Outside the apartment doors of several of the red-lighted windows stood women of various ages, appearances, and races. Some were more beautiful than others, but the one common factor was that they all looked used. Groups of sailors would wander past them, griping about the selection, throwing out rude comments, which the women returned. Then, one by one, the sailors would pick out a "lady" for the moment.

Chester and Jerry stood silently mesmerized as they watched the transactions take place. Occasionally one of them would say something like "I can't believe this," but that was as far as the conversation went. The sailor would make his approach, haggle briefly about a price, hand the woman a sum of money, and then disappear into the dark apartment. In a matter of minutes, perhaps ten to fifteen, he would reappear and head down the street, looking guilty, and often unhappy. A couple of minutes later, the woman would be back on the street too, hailing another wide-eyed sailor who was looking for a good time.

Finally Jerry tapped Chester on the shoulder and said, "Let's get out of here. I think I'm going to be sick."

Chester stood for a few more moments, lost in his thoughts. Then, giving a shudder, he seemed at last to shake off the spell and turned to walk away. Under his breath Chester was whispering to himself. All that Jerry caught was ". . . forgive them . . ."

"You talking to me?" Jerry asked.

"Sorry," Chester said, shaking his head no and stopping to lean against a streetlight. "I suppose it sounds stupid, but I was praying. I know what it is to sin, and I think I know what it's like to be driven by sin, but I never imagined anything like this. Do you remember the story of Noah?"

"Sure," Jerry said reluctantly, not really wanting to go far with this conversation.

Chester took a deep draft of cool air and sighed deeply. "This reminds me of it. It says that God looked on the great wickedness of mankind and was sorry He had made man on the earth. It says that 'it grieved Him at His heart.' Grieved Him. Up to now, what that means has been a complete mystery to me. It didn't seem possible that God could feel grief or sorrow. But I think I understand a little bit of the pain God must feel when He sees what sin can do to the people that He loves."

"You really think that God is like that?" Jerry wondered aloud. "I can't imagine Him feeling pain. Getting mad, maybe, but not hurting. I always got the impression from church that God's all stern and righteous and sorta angry—all the time."

"Oh, I'm sure He's angry—sure has a right to be—but I think He grieves as well," Chester responded. "The best gauge of what God is like is the life of Jesus. He knew what it was to be angry when He saw sin, but look at the continual stream of love that overflowed from His heart! Jerry, lives are being destroyed in that hellhole over there. Women are selling their bodies and their souls, and men are committing immoral acts that will stain them forever. Don't you think that hurts God, who loves them?"

Jerry had recently read the story in the Gospel of John about the woman caught in adultery, but he didn't want to let Chester know he understood some of what he was talking about. "Well, it don't look like they're very interested in God right at the moment," Jerry said, nodding to another group of men heading down the opposite street. "Let's go. I'm getting the creeps in this part of town."

"Maybe they really don't know any better," Chester mused, studying the scene again.

"What's that supposed to mean?" Jerry asked.

"Well, it looks to me like no one is trying to stop any of this," Chester said, still thinking it through. "Looks to me like sheep heading to the slaughter, and there's no shepherd to protect them."

"Did sorta remind me of the stock barn," Jerry agreed. "Hauling in batches of animals, auctioning them off, then hauling them to the meat-packers. You know a lot of those men are married. Seems hard to swallow. But I don't get the drift of where you're heading."

Chester began nodding his head like he'd got the answer, and Jerry didn't like the determined look on his face. Chester said, "What if you and I were to go back up there and try to talk these guys out of what they're doing? Maybe talk with the women, too?"

"Oh no!" exclaimed Jerry. "You've been stuck on the ship too long. We got off the ship to have some fun—not to become some kind of moral police. What business is it of mine if those people want to do whatever they are doing in there? I'm keeping my nose where it belongs."

"I'm sorry," Chester said. "It wasn't fair of me to ask you to come along. But I've got to try. You go on. I'll see you back at the ship later tonight. I can find my way."

Jerry gaped at Chester. "You're kidding, right? What will you say? And why should they listen to you? You going to tell them you're a preacher or what? Somebody'll probably knock your head in or call the shore police. This is very strange, you know."

"I suppose it is, and I don't want to get in trouble," Chester answered. "But I'm telling you, I've got to try. Go on, now. I'll be fine."

Jerry hated to leave Chester, but there was no way he was going to stay, either. He hoped Chester would be okay, but he was determined to find some good entertainment before heading back to the ship. Jerry felt a wave of guilt wash over him as he walked away from his friend, but he reasoned that a few beers would help with that problem.

Heading back down to the area of the taverns, Jerry picked out a decent-looking place with a Pabst Blue Ribbon sign in the window. Inside, tobacco smoke hung heavy from the ceiling, and the place was packed with loud, thirsty sailors and young women who seemed to be traded from man to man. The jukebox was roaring, and the dance floor was a crowded mass of swirling bodies. Jerry found an empty stool at the bar and asked for a beer, then sat looking around for a friendly face. He didn't know a soul, and the noise and smells only seemed to intensify his own aloneness.

Paying for the beer, Jerry tipped up his glass and took a long, deep drink, savoring the rich taste. Quickly pouring down the rest of its contents, he had swiveled around to asked for another when someone tapped his shoulder. He turned and looked into the face of one of the tavern's prettiest brunettes.

"Got a smoke, sailor boy?" she asked, flashing him a radiant smile.

Caught off guard, Jerry wasn't sure how to respond. "Sorry . . ." he sputtered, "I don't smoke."

"One of those, eh?" she said, taking his arm and leaning tightly against him. "I like guys who don't smoke, but you're a rare breed. You're very good-looking, sailor. How'd you like to dance with me?"

Jerry reached back to pay for his second beer, then he took a long drink. The first thought that crossed his mind was *it can't hurt anything*, but then he remembered seeing married men pulling out their wallets to pay the women in the red-light area. He looked down at his wedding ring, and it didn't take long to make up his mind. "Sorry, again," Jerry said, turning his attention back to her and gently pulling his arm from the warmth of her grip. "I'm a married man. I'm only here to have a few drinks."

She gave him a scowl, then glossed it over with a smile. "She'll never know, handsome boy. C'mon, have some fun for one night. She'd understand what you need."

Picking up the beer and draining it dry, he turned and gave a big laugh. "Thanks for the fun, but I've gotta be on my way," he said. "She might never know, but I'd never forget. And what I want is something that nobody but her is meant to give."

With that he went straight for the door and didn't turn around to glimpse the angry young woman shaking her head in disbelief. The fresh air felt good on his face, but the feeling of doing the right thing and escaping a trap felt even better. He wandered aimlessly back down the streets and thought of hitting another tavern, but the possibility of being approached by another woman kept him out.

He realized he was heading back toward the red-light district, and the guilty thought of what might be happening to Chester loomed before him. With nothing else to do, he decided to see how his friend had fared.

When he arrived at the spot where they had first stood and watched, Chester was nowhere to be seen. Jerry walked on past the doors with the reddish glow and disregarded the world-weary voices calling to him, "Hey, sailor, looking for a good time?" He quickened his pace and worried that something bad might have happened to Chester. But he had no idea where to look.

Jerry's choices quickly narrowed down to one—asking around. He stopped to talk with the next woman he saw. Her heavy makeup and perfume repulsed him, but he stepped over to her anyway.

Her voice was a smoky rasp as she fed him the standard line, "What can I do for you, sailor?"

"Nothing!" Jerry blurted back. "I mean . . . I'm looking for another sailor that came up here and said he was going to try to talk with some of you about—"

"That basket case that's been walking around here spouting off about God?" she groused.

"That's him!" Jerry declared. "Where'd he go?"

"What's it worth to you?" she spat at Jerry. "He cost me some customers."

"Five bucks?" Jerry begged and jammed a bill in her hand.

"He's back in that alley, and I s'pect them last two sailors that shoved 'im back there are shutting his big trap," she rasped again, pointing down the street. "They was mean lookers."

Racing down the street, Jerry heard noises and scuffling coming from the alley. Peering into the dim shadows, he could make out two large men beating on another guy, who was lying on the ground. Hearing a shout from the larger of the two, Jerry instantly recognized the voice of Fred Woodward. He figured that Chester must have tried to talk with Woodward, but now No-Neck and his sidekick had finally decided to settle the score with his friend.

Jerry raced down the alley toward the thugs, screaming like a madman, and barreled into Woodward with all his strength, knocking him into the wall. Then he turned on the shorter man and drove his fist into the meaty jaw. The man dropped like a rock, and Jerry turned to square off with No-Neck. He knew that Woodward would not surrender so easily.

Woodward charged like a crazed bull and swung wildly at Jerry, who stepped aside as the wayward blow missed its target. Before Woodward could regain his balance, Jerry brought an overhand right crashing into the other man's left cheek and forced Woodward to his knees. But one blow was not nearly enough for such a thick skull. Woodward returned with an upper cut that caught Jerry in the ribs and sent him sprawling backward. Then he lumbered to his feet, clearly unaccustomed to being challenged further.

But Woodward underestimated the power of Jerry's temper. He didn't even feel the pain as he jumped up, anger propelling him toward his opponent. He felt his hands coming to life like the cannons on the ship in target practice. Every muscle flexed as he delivered one punishing blow after another to Woodward's face and body. It took eight successive blows to send the big man crumbling to his knees again, but this time he would not rise. Jerry gave him a kick, and No-Neck tumbled over onto his back. Pouncing on his chest, Jerry pushed his fist into Woodward's bloody face one last time, and warned him never to touch Chester again unless he wanted another beating. Woodward could only shake his head in dazed defeat.

In the meantime, Chester had picked himself up off the ground but stood slumped over, holding his ribs. He winced and gasped as Jerry helped him stand up all the way, then he whispered, "Man, am I glad to see you. I'm all right; you got here before they could do too much damage. Now let's get out of here before the police come."

The two friends took their time and walked the quieter streets back to the ship, but they made no stops. For the first time, the ship looked like a safe haven rather than a floating prison.

17

RUTHIE

Marjie gazed out the kitchen window while her busy hands made quick work of the morning breakfast dishes. It had taken only a couple of days for her to settle into the quiet routine of life on the farm, and the next few weeks had quickly faded Gordon Stilwell, the Green Parrot Cafe, and her tiny boarding room into memory. She felt as natural and free in this house with Benjamin as she did in her mother's house.

Outside, the first winds of spring were warming the farmyard with the promise of winter's end. She saw Benjamin crossing from the barn to the hog shed with a bucket in hand. Although she had pressed him to change his mind, he had forbidden her to help with the barn work. He said that if she could keep the house clean and do the cooking, she could stay forever. He probably didn't expect, though, that only after a couple weeks she would have scrubbed and cleaned and rearranged most of the farmhouse. She had even thought about asking him if he'd go to town for some paint so they could spruce the place up a bit.

Marjie reached up to swipe at a cobweb she'd spotted at the upper corner of the window and bumped her stomach against the sink. "Oops," she said out loud. "Forgot about you again." Reaching her dishwater-damp hand down and lightly patting her stomach, she studied for the thousandth time the softly swelling mound that signaled the growing child. *I just wish Jerry was here to see this wonder!* she thought, then laughed. *'Course, then he'd have to look at me! If I get to looking anything like some of the women I've seen, he might not think he got himself such a princess after all.*

Having taken care of the cobweb with a wooden yardstick, Marjie headed for her room to change clothes. It had been several years since she had gone to church, and if the truth was told, she had no interest in going this Sunday. But Benjamin had asked her a couple of times, and she had said that she would try once and see.

Benjamin had given her his bedroom by the living room and taken one of the three smaller bedrooms upstairs. He had told Marjie that it was best that she have the first-floor bedroom. She shouldn't be climbing stairs, he had reasoned, and when the baby came she'd be close by all the time. She hated to see him give up his own bedroom for her, but she didn't want to be climbing the steep stairs, either, not if it wasn't good for the baby.

While Marjie pulled from the closet her only nice dress that still fit—barely—she heard Benjamin enter the house and go into the bathroom. The sound of running water started as she pulled on her dress and buttoned it, then she picked up a hairbrush and crossed over to the leaded glass mirror that hung on the wall. Instead of brushing, however, she stood still, staring in the mirror.

What if I don't like his church? she asked her reflection, and the doubtful face in the mirror returned her questions. *What if I don't want to go back anymore—will he mind? Everything's working out so good with Benjamin—I sure don't want to spoil it.*

And then she wondered what was going on with Benjamin lately. Even in the short time she had been there, she'd noticed the change—a kind of mellowing and sweetening. She had told herself it was just from having a woman around the house again, but she knew that it was more than that. Even the prayers he said before their meals had a different sound to them. But Benjamin said nothing to hint at what had changed and why.

Any rate, as good as he's been to me, guess it won't kill me to go to church with him. Even if I don't like it.

With a bit of a smile and a determined flick of the wrist, she set to work with the hairbrush.

The church was quite large by country standards—a lovely wooden building with huge stained-glass windows. Marjie and Benjamin entered together, and Benjamin had to introduce Marjie to several clusters of neighbors and a few relatives before they could find a seat. The news had traveled quickly that Jerry's wife had come to live out at the Macmillan farm, but only a few neighbors had come over to meet her as of yet. Marjie tried to fix a name to each face but quickly lost track of who was who.

There was nothing about the church service that appealed to Marjie, but she found there was little that offended her either. The pastor was a white-haired man who seemed sincere, although his congregational prayer was infinitely longer than any prayer she'd ever heard anyone pray, almost like a second sermon to her. And she appreciated that the organist appeared to be doing her best, although she kept missing notes and losing her timing. Marjie didn't know the hymns anyway, so she didn't mind that much.

Benjamin had told Marjie that as soon as the service was over, they'd go home rather than stay for the Sunday school hour. But before they could make their exit, the kindly old pastor caught them at the door and greeted Marjie warmly, promising to come over soon so they could get to know each other better. Then he asked Benjamin if he could stay for a special meeting of the deacons and elders to talk about some repairs that were needed for the church's exterior. Marjie tried to be gracious and told him to go ahead, so he directed her toward the basement, where the adult Sunday school was meeting.

Marjie headed down the stairs with a sense of mild dread, not looking forward to another hour of empty chatter. The class was already underway, so she was able to grab a chair in the back without too many people noticing. An older man whom she did not recognize began the hour with another long prayer. Then he turned the class over to a woman whom Marjie recognized instantly, even though they had never met. She appeared to be in her mid-fifties, with jet-black hair swept back from severe features and a sour frown pulling down the corners of her mouth. *You have to be the most unhappy looking soul I've ever seen,* she thought. *Just like Aunt Margaret. Why is it that the more religion you swallow, the grouchier you look?*

Marjie gathered that the teacher's name was Edna something-or-other, and just as Marjie thought, she'd been a country school-teacher in the area for twenty some years. At some point in her long career she had developed a deadly monotone that could have droned a teething baby to sleep, and it did not take long for Marjie to drift from the lesson. The woman seemed to be lecturing to herself about the value of faithful church attendance.

Hearing but not caring what Edna was saying, Marjie let her eyes roam over the rest of the class, who sat listlessly in rows of rickety chairs while the teacher droned on. Marjie was most interested in a woman about her own age who sat a couple rows ahead. At first glance she seemed to be just another plain-looking farm woman. But then she turned around and looked back momentarily, and Marjie noticed a pair of the darkest eyes she had ever seen. Even without makeup, she was a striking woman, if not beautiful, and she looked very familiar.

Something else about the woman caught Marjie's attention. While most of the heads were noticeably nodding, this woman seemed to be growing more agitated by the moment.

It finally struck Marjie that although the dark-eyed woman had not spoken yet, she obviously did not like what Edna was saying. Marjie perked up a bit and tried to listen more closely to the lesson.

"Scripture says that we are to do no work on the Sabbath," Edna was saying. "I take that to mean no cooking, no cleaning, or any of the work we do during the regular—"

"Excuse me," the woman with the lively dark eyes broke in. "I wasn't sure if you were going to let us ask questions, but I have to ask you how you do that?"

"Such as?" Edna questioned back, obviously not pleased to be challenged.

"Like not cooking on Sunday."

Edna drew herself up a bit taller and said, "I cook all the food on Saturday, and all I have to do is warm it up and serve it on Sunday. I've done this for years."

"You aren't serious, are you?" asked the woman. "What if there's work that *must* be done, for some reason. Can you do that in good conscience?"

"That's an appropriate question," Edna answered smugly. "Let me give you a real-life example that happened to me a while ago, and it's a confession as well. One Sunday morning just before we were going to leave the house for church, I noticed that the hem on my dress was down. My confession is that, rather than making us late for church by changing my dress, I quickly tacked the hem up. But then on Monday morning, I let the hem out and sewed it back up again. That, it seemed to me, offset whatever wrong I had done by breaking the Sabbath."

The dark-eyed woman nearly stood to her feet in shock. "So, God is counting the slightest violation of what you believe about the Sabbath rest," she stated. "Wasn't that just what the Pharisees thought about tithing?"

By now there were no more nodding heads. A nervous tension gripped the room as the rest of the class waited to hear who would fire the next shot. Whoever Edna's adversary was, she was certainly making a hit with Marjie.

"We are not discussing tithing, Ruth," Edna countered. "But you might guess that I believe the Bible has a great deal to say about that, too."

"I'm sure you do," Ruth agreed. "But can we get back to your view of the Sabbath?"

"Surely," Edna said. "I have nothing to hide."

Ruth's stare intensified and bore down on Edna as she asked, "So, your husband did not milk his cattle this morning?"

"Of course he did," Edna returned, shaking her head. "This is silly."

"Silly? You said we were to discontinue all work that we did during our normal week, didn't you?" Ruth asked.

"I said that, but you've got to—"

"Not so fast," Ruth broke Edna's escape. "Milking is not only work that is done every day; it's done *twice* a day. I agree it must be done or the cows will suffer, so let's chalk it up as a necessary evil, Edna. But, seeing as it's done on the Sabbath, do you then set aside all the money that you earn from the sale of the milk to the creamery and give that to the church?"

"No . . . but . . . well . . . we could never afford that," Edna groped for words.

But Ruth was not finished making her point. "Sounds like 'filthy lucre' to me. I'm not talking about what can be afforded, but I am asking you to be consistent with what you so clearly defined as a hard and fast rule of God. I am not saying I agree with how you have interpreted this scripture, but having interpreted it this way, I fail to see how you can live consistently with it."

Ruth paused and let the force of her words sink in. From her seat in the back Marjie could see other class members shift uncomfortably, and she could practically hear Edna's teeth grind.

"Where and how do you draw the lines practically, Edna?" Ruth continued. "You cook on Saturday, but do you wait to do Sunday's dishes until Monday? Or do you do the dishes on Sunday, then dirty them Monday morning and do them again? Who defines what 'work' means? You, or me—or should we all bring our lists and try to work through all the possibilities?"

Edna stood speechless and defenseless.

Ruth spent the next ten minutes challenging the idea that it was more important to be in church on Sunday than to help a neighbor in true need. Edna contended that Sunday worship was their only priority, and that other needs must wait until God had been properly worshiped. Ruth countered that worship was something that Jesus said was done "in spirit and in truth" and had nothing to do with a place, but very few members seemed to catch on to what she was saying.

The Sunday school hour ended with the sparks still flying, but then the men and women filed away with little more discussion. As Marjie stood up to go find Benjamin, she was surprised when the woman named Ruth ducked out of her row and caught Margie by the arm.

"You're Marjie Macmillan, is that right?" Ruth asked.

"I sure am," Marjie said pleasantly. "And you're Ruth?"

"Buckley. Ruth Buckley," she said, and her dark eyes flashed a lovely smile. "Jerry and I were in country school together. He's a great guy, just a little shy!"

"That's Jerry," Marjie said as they shared a laugh.

"Actually, we met before," said Ruth. "A long time ago. Do you remember the spring ball game . . . the first time you met Jerry. The—"

"Lettuce sandwiches!" Marjie burst out. "I knew I'd met you before."

"I was so rude . . . and embarrassed," apologized Ruth. "I've never forgotten it."

"Time to forget it," Marjie said. "After all, it gave me my chance to meet Jerry!"

Ruth lowered her voice. "And am I right that you're expecting a baby?" When Marjie blushed and nodded, she added with enthusiasm, "Congratulations! That's so exciting."

"Thank you," Marjie said, pleased to feel close to someone from the church who really cared about Jerry. "Exciting . . . and scary!"

Ruth laid a comforting hand on Marjie's arm. "It must be hard with Jerry being away. But, tell you what, I only live a couple miles away. I'm the old maid who teaches the local children in the country school, so I've got time to help you through it. Is that a deal?"

"It's a deal," Marjie said. "But I don't want to inconvenience you. You must be awfully busy, with your work and all."

Ruth laughed and said, "Don't you worry about a thing. I can handle it."

"Oh, I'm sure you can," Marjie agreed. Then she whispered, "You handled Edna whatever-her-name-is pretty good. Do you always start a bonfire in Sunday school?"

"No, no, no," Ruth claimed. "I usually skip out, but every once in a while I come back to see if anything's changed. And of course it hasn't, but then again, neither have I. You'll notice I have a hard time keeping my mouth shut. Edna and I have never gotten along too well."

Marjie nodded her head. "I noticed the heat. But I'm glad you said what you did. You made a lot of sense, although I don't know enough about it to say you are right. Maybe we can talk about it again some time . . . over coffee and cake? Maybe we can work on your old-maid problem as well!"

"I'd love it," Ruth's dark eyes were dancing. "Maybe you've got some prospects for me, eh? Slim pickings around here, especially since Pearl. I'll give you a call. I'm sorry to excuse myself, but I need to run before Edna corrals me and we tangle again."

"Thanks for welcoming me," Marjie whispered, but Ruth was already around the corner and heading up the stairs.

"So, what did you think of church?" Benjamin asked after Marjie had served their lunch meal. "I'm sorry I had to leave you. They could have easily gotten along without me in that meeting."

"Well," Marjie delayed her answer, "it was not as bad as I thought it might be. Which surprises me. But I have a confession to make. I made the lunch after we got home, and I have sinned."

Benjamin looked at her a little cross-eyed. "You sinned? Oh . . . I get it. Edna did her holier-than-thou routine, did she? I suppose she threw in the Sabbath hemline story for good measure?"

Marjie burst out laughing, with Benjamin echoing her sentiments. "How could you know that? Did Ruth tell you?"

"No one told me a peep," Benjamin declared, rubbing his hands together. "No one needs to tell me anything about what goes on in the church. I've been going there since day one, Marjie. I've heard the hemline story so many times I can recite it word for word."

"So you don't agree with Edna?" Marjie asked.

"I don't know that I agree with Edna on much of anything, let alone that," Benjamin replied.

"I'm glad," Marjie said. "If that's what religion does, I don't want it."

"That's exactly what religion does, Marjie," Benjamin stated. "And that's all I've had for most of my life. It's no surprise my boys don't care much for church, even though I took 'em regular when they was little. A person could choke on it, it's so dry. But that's *not* what real faith does, Marjie. I know that for certain now."

"I've been wondering what was different about you the past weeks," Marjie probed. "Does this have anything to do with whatever you're talking about?"

Benjamin laughed and rolled his eyes back. "I'm not sure what you mean by being different. I'm just as ornery an old cuss as I've ever been."

"Wrong!" Marjie exclaimed. "Something's going on with you, and I demand a full explanation!"

"I wish I could explain it," Benjamin told her, suddenly serious. "If I could put words to it, I'd gladly tell you right now. But it's getting clearer for me every day, and as soon as I understand, I'll tell you, all right?"

"You don't give me much choice," Marjie answered. "Just as long as you don't get all strange on me. Remember when those holy rollers went through this part of the country years back? You're not going to be one of those, are you?"

Hesitating with his answer, Benjamin said, "I hope not—no, I'm not no holy roller. Not sure yet what I'm getting to be. Anyway, I'm glad you met Ruthie."

"Yeah," Marjie agreed. "I think she and I have a lot in common."

"You're right, there," Benjamin said. "You can't go wrong with Ruth as your friend. She's got what I'm looking for these days, Marjie—real faith. If you listen to anyone, listen to Ruth."

"I will," Marjie said with conviction. "But I think the first thing I need to do is write Jerry and tell him I'm pregnant before he hears it from someone who saw me in church today. If Ruthie could tell, other people could, too!"

18

SCOTLAND

"Well, here we go again," Jerry remarked to one of his gunnery mates as the newly repaired *Wasp* pulled out of Norfolk.

"Yeah, seems like we was just doing this," the other man commented as he wielded his scrub brush. "Where you s'pose we's heading this time?"

Jerry shrugged. Speculation was always buzzing around the ship about where they might be heading, but only a select few men ever knew for certain. Jerry had pretty well come to terms with the fact that he wasn't one of those men. But like most of the crew, he wasn't immune to the anxious wondering.

The next harbor was a familiar one, though. The ship docked once more in Portland, where it anchored overnight. Then, early in the morning of March 26, they left the sheltered waters of Casco Bay and emerged once more into the choppy North Atlantic. This time they were traveling in the company of nine destroyers, the beautiful new battleship USS *Washington*, and two heavy cruisers. Word gradually filtered down through the crew that they were part of Task Force 39, bound for the British Isles to reinforce the home fleet of the Royal Navy and help cover convoys routed to northern Russia.

They battled high seas all the way, and their voyage across the Atlantic was soon marred by tragedy. Word spread one afternoon that Rear Admiral Wilcox, the commander of the entire task force, had been swept overboard from the *Washington*. Jerry watched from his station on the flight deck as *Wasp* planes took off over the churning water to join the search. Although two pilots spotted Wilcox floating face down in the trough of a wave, his body was never recovered.

On April 3, the American ships were met by an Allied force based around the light cruiser HMS *Edinburgh*, and escorted to Scapa Flow in the rocky Orkney Islands on the northern tip of Scotland. Here the *Wasp* parted company with the other ships and all but twenty-one of her fighter planes and headed south toward Glasgow.

As the carrier glided up the broad estuary at the mouth of the River Clyde, Chester joined Jerry and a crowd of other sailors on the flight deck to get a look at the John Brown Clydebank ship-building facilities, the largest shipyard in the world. It was a breathtaking sight in the misty morning. Every type of warship and naval auxiliary, barges, gigs, whaleboats, and other small craft came to life with the carrier's passing as their crews emerged to give her a tumultuous cheer. Shipyard workers paused long enough from their labors to add to the overwhelming welcome for the American boys.

From the first sighting, something about Scotland brought a feeling of home to the men on the ship. Jerry thought that he'd never seen anything as pretty as the trip down the River Clyde to Glasgow. The green highland hills and the old stone houses with their multicolored roofs blending in with the trees made for a picture he felt no artist could ever paint. The whole landscape had a friendly look, constantly hugged by great clusters of clouds.

Chester and Jerry were both delighted and nervous to be among the first men to get liberty from the ship in Scotland. They had no idea what there was to see, and they wondered how they would get along with people from a different country. It did not take long, however, before their fears were laid to rest.

Wherever they went, the Americans found warm hands reaching out to shake their hands, and friendly voices with un-familiar accents thanking them for coming to their aid. Thin faces and shabby clothing gave a human face to the heavy rationing and acute deprivation Jerry and Chester had heard about. But here, in contrast to the American seaports, everyone seemed happy and contented. The townspeople showed respect and honor to the visiting sailors. Perhaps most startling was the almost total lack of foul language. Having grown so used to the constant barrage of swearing on the ship, Jerry and Chester were relieved to get away from it for a while.

Walking down an old picturesque street, Chester and Jerry met a man clutching a sheaf of small papers. "Could I interest you gentlemen in some dinner?" he asked in a hearty brogue. "Might be hard to find a place to eat, it being Sunday an' all. But our church group's opened a hospitality room fer you lads. Just 'round the corner and down the street a piece. Be worth yer while; those women can cook."

Jerry and Chester eagerly took the tickets and followed the man's directions, expecting the usual crowds of their fellow sailors. To their surprise, they were the first servicemen to enter the room. Feeling a bit awkward, the two men returned a generous round of handshakes from the men and women who had organized the meal. Then they were approached by a diminutive elderly woman who took their hands in hers. They were surprised at the strength of her tiny hands, the tenderness in her smile, and the laughter in her eyes. She seemed to be the group's designated greeter. "Well, an' God bless ye, boys," she declared. "It's so good you Yanks have come. We do need yer help."

Jerry blinked, relishing the homey comfort she exuded. For a moment he almost thought that he was home again, and the war faded from his thoughts. Jerry couldn't describe the pleasure he was feeling inside, but he realized that he was smiling from ear to ear. Looking over at Chester, he was not surprised to see tears forming in his friend's eyes. Jerry figured you'd have to have a heart of stone not to feel like crying.

"Thank you, so much," Jerry said, almost choking up.

"Yes, thank you," Chester blubbered out.

Then they both gave the old woman big hugs.

She directed them to the serving line, then turned to greet

other servicemen who were straggling in. A couple of women had just entered the hall from the kitchen, bearing steaming bowls. At nearly the same instant, both men were stopped in their tracks at the sight of the young woman who was organizing the serving table.

"Wow!" was all that Jerry could whisper over Chester's shoulder.

The petite Scottish lass glanced up and caught their starry-eyed stares. She quickly looked back down, clearly as embarrassed as they were. But they couldn't help themselves. Even without makeup, she could have held her own next to any Hollywood actress with her round blue eyes, shimmering dark hair, and narrow, curving lips.

Jerry recovered quickly, but Chester's feet were nailed to the floor. Jerry moved alongside his friend and gently nudged him on. That seemed to revive Chester's flow of blood, and his face went beet red.

Seeing Chester reeling, Jerry thought it would be fun to see how far this comedy could be extended. As he took his plate, the young woman looked up again and spoke with a lilting burr, "Good evening, sailors. Take as much as you'd like. We're pleased to see you Yanks."

"Thank you," Jerry returned, conscious that at home he would hardly have dared speak to her. *Guess this war's doing something for my confidence,* he mused, *or maybe a little of Marjie's rubbed off.*

"We appreciate your hospitality," he went on. "My name's Jerry Macmillan, and this is my friend, the fine sailor and part-time preacher, Chester Stanfeld."

Chester's mouth was not working yet, but he tried to shake his head that he was not a preacher while the young woman offered a hand. "Margaret Harris," she said, inclining her head like the grandest lady. "I'm pleased to make your acquaintance. So you're in the ministry, then?" she asked Chester, obviously interested. "My father is the pastor of this church."

"No . . . no," sputtered a distraught, visibly shaken Chester. "I'm not a preacher . . . just a farmer from Minnesota . . . but I am a believer. Excuse my imaginative friend; he's been calling me a preacher since our last shore leave."

Chester gave Jerry a "keep your mouth shut" look, but Jerry was not ready to be muzzled. "Miss Harris, my friend here would like to talk with you after the meal, if that's possible."

Chester nearly dropped his plate, but there was little he could do but attempt to repair the damage. "I am truly sorry," he said to Margaret, who had not looked away this time. "I hope this rudeness does not offend you . . . and I *would* like to talk with you later. But so would every other man that comes in here. Please forgive us, if you can."

Jerry had meant it only as a joke, and he'd forgotten they were not in Norfolk anymore. But he noticed that Margaret Harris had fixed her elegant gaze on Chester, who seemed to have lapsed into speechlessness again. "No forgiveness is needed," she assured him. "And we could speak later, if you'd like. But after the meal, we will be having a short service. I do hope you're not in a hurry."

The only response from Chester was a silly smile and the solitary motion of his eyelids blinking. Jumping to the rescue, Jerry assured her, "He'd love to. We have all evening."

Once again Jerry had to nudge his frozen friend on, and they seated themselves at one of the many tables that was set up for the meal. Chester seemed to be in shock.

"The fork and knife are instruments to help you eat," Jerry chided. "Here, watch while I show you how to use 'em. It's really simple . . . see. Now, you try."

"She's the most beautiful girl I've ever seen," murmured Chester. "What am I going to do?"

"You're going to stay later and talk with her, stupid," Jerry stated, taking a bite of bread. "I think she likes you."

"Shoot!" Chester gasped. "You're dreaming about Marjie again. She could never go for a chump like me."

"You're no chump," objected Jerry. "I thought she was going to melt when you looked at her with those big green eyes."

Chester finally laughed. "Cut the jokes," he pleaded. "This is serious stuff. I may never get another chance to see that girl again. What am I going to say to her?"

"Say whatever she wants to hear," Jerry counseled. "Maybe she wants to talk about religion. You're good at that."

"But I'm afraid I won't be able to say anything," Chester worried. "I've already made a fool of myself."

"That's for sure," Jerry agreed with a chuckle. "I know the feeling, though. I always felt like a rusty lock trying to talk to girls—good thing Marjie kept trying. But give it another shot, Chester. Maybe she's not looking for a Casanova."

"I hope not," Chester whispered again as some other servicemen walked past. Then he turned to sneak a peek at Margaret Harris and realized she was looking straight at him. He continued to stare long after she had turned away, and Jerry had to shake his arm again.

"Enough!" warned Jerry. "Don't blow it, Dopey. You've got a lot of competition, you know. Every guy in here is falling over."

Chester turned around and picked at his potatoes with his fork. "Why'd you get me into this, anyway? I'm just wasting my time."

"For crying out loud, what else have you got better to do?" Jerry asked, finally getting serious. "The loveliest girl I've seen since I kissed Marjie goodbye wants to talk with you tonight. So why don't you just relax and try to have some fun for once. You're always talking about praying. Maybe you should try that."

Jerry was joking again, but Chester was not. "You know, that's a good idea!" He bowed his head, shut his eyes, and began praying out loud.

"Try silently," Jerry mumbled. "I'm not interested."

While they were eating, a wiry, balding man sat down at the piano that was close to their table and began to play. Jerry recognized some of the tunes as hymns, but could remember only snatches of the words. The piano music continued while the servicemen finished their meals. Quietly the women cleared the plates away and brought them cups of coffee. With the smell of the coffee and the echo of the music, feelings and sights of home rushed in and surrounded Jerry's every thought. He imagined sitting at the farm table with Marjie, talking late into the night and—

His revelry was cut short as he noticed that the piano had gone silent, and someone was stepping to the small podium at the front. Apparently the church program was beginning. To both men's surprise, Margaret Harris stood there, holding a hymnal with her eyes shut as the pianist began to play again.

All the shuffling and whispering in the room stopped abruptly as she began to sing "When I Survey the Wondrous Cross." Her voice was as clear and as warm as the sun at full strength; the words came with a haunting power—they felt almost as if they were encountering an angel wrapped in humanity. Jerry felt the profound wonder of every word, and like a knife they stabbed into his consciousness: "Did e'er such love and sorrow meet, or thorns compose so rich a crown?" Yet it all seemed beyond his reach, beyond his understanding, beyond his believing.

Men around the room were surreptitiously wiping tears as she ended with "Love so amazing, so divine, demands my soul, my life, my all." Here was pure beauty and goodness standing in contrast to the tragic insanity that raged in the world outside. Here was the eternal, glorified above the howling darkness that was threatening the world. To see such a light, if only for a moment, was almost overwhelming.

Jerry forgot all about his joking with Chester, forgot that Chester was even there. He desperately wanted to clutch the fleeting feelings of the moment before the wonder evaporated. *If only it was true!* he wished.

The man who had played the piano stepped to the podium as Margaret took a seat. He identified himself as her father, the Reverend Thomas Harris, and he asked the servicemen to kindly give him their attention for a brief talk. Jerry tried to regather his focus, but the spell of the hymn was still so strong that the preacher's words were muted and indistinct.

The sermon was only about twenty minutes in length, and as it neared its conclusion, Jerry regained his faculties and caught the ending. Thomas Harris was as skilled a preacher as his daughter was a singer, and Jerry regretted later that he failed to hear most of the message.

"Grace is enthroned this day because Christ has finished His work and gone into the heavens," Harris was proclaiming in strong, rolling accents. "Grace is enthroned *in power*. When we speak of its throne, we mean that it has unlimited might. Grace neither sits on the footstool of God nor stands in the courts of God, but it sits on the throne as the king. This is the dispensation of grace, the year of grace. We live in the era of reigning grace: 'Wherefore he is able also to save them to the uttermost that come unto God by him, seeing he ever liveth to make intercession for them.'

"If you should meet grace as a merchant with treasure in his hand," Reverend Harris continued, "I would bid you court its friendship—it will enrich you in the hour of poverty. If you should see grace as one of the peers of heaven, highly exalted, I would bid you seek to get its ear. But when grace sits on the throne, I beseech you close in with it at once. It can be no higher, it can be no greater, for it is written 'God is love,' which is an *alias* for grace.

"Come and bow before it," he invited, his voice now quiet but clear. "Come and adore the infinite mercy and grace of God. Doubt not, halt not, hesitate not. Grace is reigning; grace is God; God is love. Oh, that you, seeing grace as thus enthroned, would come and receive it."

With that, Harris stopped, and silence reigned. Then he gently asked if any of the men might want to come forward to pray. A couple of rugged-looking British boys stepped out of their chairs and quickly made their way to his side. One of them began shaking and cried out loudly that he was too evil to be forgiven.

At that point, Chester jumped up out of his chair and went to the distraught sailor, putting his arm around him and holding him tight. Other men from the church also stepped out of their chairs and made their way to help. And all of the women began to pray softly, except for the saintly grandmother who stood and began to thank God out loud for His mercies.

All this was too much for Jerry. He was both charmed and

frightened by such a sudden confrontation with overwhelming feelings, and what seemed to be the truth also seemed so foreign and unreal as well. He hated to leave Chester behind, but he could take no more. Slipping quietly out of his chair, Jerry headed for the door. He figured Chester could find his way back to the ship as well as he could.

Stepping into the cold, misty dark was like stepping back into another world. Every emotion fled with a passing cloud of fog, and Jerry stopped to wonder at what had really gone on inside the church hall. *Was that for real?* he asked himself. "Strange . . . very strange," Jerry said out loud. He started down the street toward the ship and added, "Crazy, I guess. Maybe they're all nuts."

Whatever he had experienced, Jerry knew it was different than anything he'd ever heard or felt in his home church. He'd never heard of grown men rushing up and raising a ruckus in church. "Too strange . . . nice people, though," he mused to himself as he slowly trudged down the narrow cobblestone street. "Glad I didn't go making a donkey of myself," he muttered. Then, a few steps later, he decided, "I won't let that happen again."

But although Jerry felt lucky to have escaped the church, he did not like the way the preacher's words, "hour of poverty," stuck in his mind. He could chuck off most of it, but there was too much of truth in these words to dismiss.

19

SPRINGTIME

Easter had come and gone somewhat uneventfully on the Macmillan farm. Marjie had invited her mother and brother for Sunday lunch. Seeing Ruthie at church, she had asked her over, too. They spent a fun afternoon getting to know each other and even managed to play a couple of hands of cards before choring time brought the party to a close.

Benjamin had been working long, hard days, trying to get everything ready for the spring planting. He forgot that over the past few years Jerry had taken nearly all the responsibility for the early field work. The corn planter was in need of repair. The seed corn needed to be purchased, as well as the oats. And then, on top of all the daily chores, there was the mountainous pile of winter manure that had to be loaded and spread on the now-dry fields.

Marjie worried about how exhausted Benjamin was looking, but she could not persuade him to hire some help. She thought his coloring was bad, even though he was spending a lot of time in the warming sunshine.

"I feel better than I have in years," Benjamin told her confidently. "Maybe it's just the long winter. The cold's still in my bones."

Marjorie didn't buy his story. "That's baloney, and you know better," she said. "Something's not right. Why don't you go see the doc?"

"I been to see him," he answered, fiddling with the zipper on the coat he wore to the barn.

"That was almost a year ago, you stubborn old bull," she cried. "You're worse than my father, and worse than what Jerry told me."

Benjamin tipped his cap and smiled. "You shoulda listened to that boy. He knew what he was talking about. You may as well give it up. Besides, the doc's a drunk. I don't like the man."

"So why do you think I should go to him when the baby comes?" she asked craftily.

"Because he's good at delivering babies," Benjamin responded, dancing away from the trap. "And it's too far to any other hospital. As far as we are out here, I'm just praying you make it there in time as it is. There's no way I'm delivering that baby, and you can't have it here. I forbid it. Understand?"

"How about in your car on the way?" teased Marjie. "My mother barely made it to the hospital when Teddy came, in case you're interested in a little history."

"Like I said," Benjamin grumped, "you're on your own, lady. That would be the end of me."

"What a way to go, though!" Marjie exclaimed. "You'd make the local headlines."

"I'd rather not," Benjamin said shortly and headed back to his work. "There's gotta be a better way than that."

Marjie was left with the feeling that she'd pushed the teasing just a little too far. There was nothing funny about Benjamin's mortality, and she regretted even mentioning it. She had come to love the man, and she treasured the days they had spent together. She hoped her children could enjoy him as much as she did.

"Say!" Marjie called to his receding back. "Are you going to dig my garden up today? The ground's warming. Time to get those spuds in."

"I was just getting the tractor now," he called back. "Couple of hours, and it'll be ready for you. Why don't you get back inside and rest awhile? Talk about somebody who overdoes it. You've been going like a house afire."

That was true, she knew. All traces of morning sickness had

vanished, and Marjie felt a gigantic surge of energy. Despite Benjamin's warnings to take it easy, she had taken long walks around the farm and gotten to know the layout of the land. Now, having conquered most of the household tasks and having been forbidden to go to the fields to help with the planting, she had shifted her focus to restoring what appeared to have once been a sizable garden. All that remained now was a batch of tangled, overgrown raspberry bushes that Benjamin had agreed to plow under. Marjie had already transplanted some of the younger raspberry shoots into some wooden boxes and hoped to have enough plants for at least one new row of raspberries that would bear fruit the following year.

It was such a lovely day that she hated to go in and rest. Instead she headed down to take a look at the pigs. She recalled the freezing winds of January when she had first marched down this path. Now that the weather was decent, most of the pigs were slopping around in the pen outside the shed. Surprisingly, nearly all the young pigs that had come so close to dying had ended up surviving the winter. Benjamin had intended to have most of the young ones sold by now, but he had been too busy to take care of it.

"I saved your life, fatty," she said to one of the larger pigs who stood at attention with its curled tail poised and a hopeful gaze fixed upon her. "No more food until tonight. Go on!" She waved her arms, and the pigs jumped and snorted away.

Marjie laughed at the sight, then started back to the house, passing Benjamin on the small gray Ford tractor with the plow behind it. She was almost up the steps when she heard the phone ring. Going inside, she picked up the receiver.

"Marjie, hello, this is Ruth," said the voice in answer to her greeting. "Any chance I can stop by for a cup of coffee after school today?"

"Sure. I'll put on a fresh pot."

"Good. I should be there a little after three. See you then."

Marjie hung up and decided to take Benjamin's advice. They'd already had their lunch, and there wasn't much she could do until he had the garden worked up.

Lying down on her bed, Marjie wondered how Jerry had responded to her letter about the baby, or whether her very special letter had even gotten to him. It had been a couple of weeks since she'd sent the letter, and she tried to meet the mailman every day out at the roadside mailbox to see if Jerry's response had come. She knew it was early, but every day that passed made her worry about his response.

Marjie dozed off and on for about an hour, then she got up to put on the pot of coffee. That done, she headed out to the garden to see how Benjamin was doing. She knew he really needed to be out in the fields and that this garden work was a gracious interlude done on her behalf.

He had apparently gone at the task with a burst of gusto, and she was surprised at how much he'd gotten done already. The plot had been plowed, disked, and dragged until it was as smooth as a baseball field. Benjamin was just tossing out the last big clusters of weeds.

"How's it look?" Benjamin called out, obviously happy with his accomplishment.

"Beautiful!" Marjie marveled. "I can't believe you did this so fast!"

"I gotta get back out in the field," Benjamin said. "But she's ready to go. I'd stay and help you if I had time, but the ground out there's just right for working. I'll spread some fertilizer on this plot a little later."

"Oh, can't you stay till three and have some coffee?" Marjie asked. "Ruth is stopping by."

Benjamin shook his head no as he climbed back on the tractor. "Sorry, Marjie. It'll have to wait for another day. Give Ruthie my love." He popped the tractor into gear and with a wave goodbye he zipped out of the farmyard and down the lane to the fields.

Marjie stood admiring her garden plot. The ground had worked up so nicely that there were hardly any clumps left to break up. It was rich soil—dark and moist—and Marjie could imagine what it would look like in the middle of summer. She could hardly wait to get started, but she guessed she'd have to wait till Benjamin could help with the rows.

Then it struck her that she did not need Benjamin to help do her row of raspberries, and the sooner she got them back into the ground, the better chance they would have of surviving the transplant. She went to the shed and grabbed the spade, pulled the boxes of plants out to the edge of the garden, and set to the task.

Marjie knew it would be best if the row was marked with twine stretched between sticks, but she figured she could eyeball this row in well enough. Guessing about nine inches between plants, she went down her row with the spade and notched out enough soil to drop one plant in each. Then she took one of the wooden boxes and started down the row. Tucking the roots deeply into the hole, Marjie carefully packed the soil around a tender plant. The soil felt good in her hands, especially after having been away from it for so many years.

Standing back up and taking a deep breath, Marjie felt herself relax. She knew there was no reason to rush, so she decided to slow down. Pulling her box along, she placed one plant after another, soiling her hands and knees and legs as she went. Wiping a stray lock of hair away from her face, she left dirt tracks across her cheek without noticing. She wouldn't have cared if she had noticed. What difference did it make, after all?

She was nearly three quarters down the row when she heard a car pull into the driveway and the dogs set to barking at the visitor. Marjie looked up to see Ruthie waving as she pulled up near the house. It was too late to try to clean up, but Marjie was relieved to remember she had already brewed the coffee.

Ruth jumped out of the car, stopped to give some attention to one of the dogs, and headed for the garden site. Marjie had stood up and was walking to meet her.

"Coffee's on!" Marjie hailed her. "I'm sorry that I got so caught up in my garden. I guess I look a sight! It just felt so good to dig in the dirt that the time got away from me. Come on in the house."

"No rush," Ruth said. "You look pretty good to me. I love getting my hands in the dirt as well. My mother used to say that she felt closer to God when she was digging in her garden."

"I think I know what she means," Marjie responded. "I don't

recall you talking about your mother before, Ruthie. Where does she live?"

A trace of pain and sadness darted across Ruth's face. "She's gone, Marjie. Tuberculosis took her two years ago this spring."

"I'm sorry to hear that," Marjie said, taking Ruth's hand in hers. "My father died over four years ago, and there's not a day goes by but I miss him. Your mother must have been a fine woman."

Ruth's dark eyes flashed back to life, and she smiled. "She was the kindest woman on earth. Of course, I'm just slightly biased. But I miss her badly, too. Say, looks like you're almost done with your planting. Let's finish it before coffee. What do you say?"

"Are you serious?" Marjie asked. "You've got your good clothes on."

"Nothing here that some good soapy water won't wash out," Ruth declared. "You go ahead and keep planting. I'll get some pails and carry water out to the plants. They have to have water to get a good start."

Marjie tried to protest that it was too much work, but Ruth was determined. Before long the two gardeners had the row complete and a good dousing of water on every plant.

"Let's get that coffee and cake I promised," Marjie said, having finished her task.

Ruth stopped and took one last look at the row. "You didn't mark it, did you?"

Marjie studied the row and smiled, "Guess I should have. She zigs and zags all right. But it's good enough."

"You wait until Benjamin sees it." Ruth laughed. "It'll drive him nuts. You've obviously not seen his corn rows. Straight as an arrow."

"Then he must deserve one crooked row," Marjie said. "Straight lines get boring!"

The two new friends drank their coffee and chatted on. There was so much to learn about each other and about what was going on in the neighborhood. Marjie found that Ruth could answer just about every question she had regarding the local people she was slowly getting to know.

Finally the conversation switched to how things were going on the farm, and Marjie said, "I love it here, Ruthie. Truthfully, I hope I never have to leave this place. But I'm worried about Benjamin. He's not looking good, and he's been working around the clock since the fields dried up. And that man's as stubborn as a goat. He won't let me help, and he won't hire anyone either."

"Sounds just like my dad," Ruth said. "He doesn't have heart problems or anything like that. But I'm afraid that one of these days he'll just drop in his tracks and that will be the end of it."

"That's Benjamin," Marjie declared. "But what can I do, Ruthie? He won't listen to anyone. What if he has a heart attack? I can't stand to even think of it."

Ruth's dark eyes locked on to Marjie's sad brown ones. "I know what you mean, Marjie. There's only one thing that I know that helps. But not everyone agrees with me."

"Please, tell me," Marjie asked.

"I pray."

That was not the answer Marjie had hoped for, but then she didn't know what else to expect from Ruth. Marjie looked away, then got up and walked to the picture window. She said nothing as she stared into the distance, and Ruth was silent as well.

"I want you to know that I respect you a great deal, Ruthie," Marjie finally began carefully, turning back to the table and sitting next to Ruth again. Fingering the last crumbs of cake on her plate, she said, "But when my father was sick with cancer, we prayed and prayed that God would spare him. Many times I prayed all night beside his bed as he moaned and cried with pain. It was terrible. I begged and I bargained. But it made no difference, and my pa's lying in the ground. I don't mean to offend you, but the way I see it, either God is not there, or He doesn't care, or He's cruel beyond belief.

"Maybe I've said too much," Marjie ended lamely. "Perhaps we should talk about something else."

Ruth took Marjie's hand and closed her eyes. "No . . . please, let's talk. Why should your honesty offend me? I watched my mother cough herself to death, Marjie. I have walked through the same valley."

"And you prayed for your mother?" Marjie asked.

"Of course," Ruth responded, opening her eyes. "And, yes, she died. Our prayers did not stop the disease from taking her."

"And you were never angry at God?" pressed Marjie. "Please be honest with me, Ruthie. I've got to know. I've never dared ask anyone before."

"I was very angry with God," Ruth conceded, gently nodding her head.

"Are you angry today?"

"No."

"But God failed!" Marjie exclaimed. "He failed you, Ruthie. How can you not be mad about that?"

Ruth was not quick with her answer. She shut her eyes again, and Marjie saw the pain etch its way across her lovely features. "It's nearly impossible to describe why, Marjie. If I try, I don't ask you to agree with me, although I hope you will weigh its truth. But if I tell you and you don't agree, please tell me we can still be friends."

"Nothing you say will stop our friendship," Marjie whispered.

"Marjie, whether God answered my prayer is an important question, but not the most important question—at least, not to me." Ruth went on. "For me, the deeper question was God's love. And I nearly gave up believing in His love when He took my mother from us."

"So what changed?"

"I guess I did," Ruth whispered. "But it was painful."

Marjie shook her head. "I don't understand."

"Sorry," Ruth added. "Let me start over." She sat silent for a long minute, thinking hard. Then she reached over and laid her hand over Marjie's. "It's sort of like your crooked row of raspberries. I found that life didn't fit my straight line of how I wanted things to be, and God didn't either. I wanted my mother alive, but that didn't mean it was the best thing for her, or for my dad, or for me. By drawing the straight line of how it had to be, I had set myself up as God. I had to let that go—and it was hard."

"But why believe in God's love? I believe He's cruel."

"And so did I," Ruth said. "I must have thought it a thousand times. But another question came in that challenged me and would not let me keep running away. If God was cruel, or if He did not care, how could I explain Jesus dying on the cross in agony and pain? If Jesus Christ was God, why would He give himself for my sins unless He loved me. A dying Christ on Calvary defied my arguments. How could I see God as cruel again? Does that make sense?"

"I'm not sure," Marjie responded, shaking her head. "I'll have to think it over."

"Please do," Ruth asked. "Oh, Marjie, there are a thousand things that I don't understand about what happens around me, and most of the time I still find I want only straight lines. But they come out crooked anyway. The only thing that I know and believe for sure is that God is love, and that in Christ Jesus God has loved me. Beyond that . . . well, sometimes I can't make sense of anything else."

Marjie had heard enough and asked no more questions that day. But she had promised to weigh Ruth's words with care, and she tucked them away in her mind for further consideration. The icy castle of doubt had felt the warmth of Ruth's belief but not melted. Yet its truth had wedged itself in the foundation, and time would prove its worth.

20

GIBRALTAR

During the few days that the *Wasp* was wharfed alongside the giant King George V dock in Glasgow, there was a constant hum of activity. The longer they were there, the busier the ship got. Communications officers worked over reports and decoded messages from Washington. Instructions were fired off to each division of the ship. Sailors dashed on the double from place to place, preparing to get underway.

Neither Jerry nor Chester had any idea of what was going to happen, but they had realized something big was up when they landed their torpedo planes and dive bombers at Scapa Flow. The picture got clearer and the buzz on the ship increased on the morning of April 13, with the arrival and the loading of forty-seven Supermarine "Spitfire" Mark V fighter planes. Those Spitfires were in no way designed for aircraft-carrier flight, so the sailors knew they must be preparing some sort of ferry mission. Where the delivery was to be made, however, was a complete mystery.

Soon after the first Spitfires were loaded, a contingent of Royal Air Force pilots came aboard. Jerry was amazed at how young the RAF pilots were, ranging from eighteen to twenty-two. For young men who faced death every time they got in their planes, they seemed incredibly easygoing. It was obvious by the way they were looking around that they were not used to life on the aircraft carrier, and at first they didn't know where to go or what to do.

The business of inspecting the loaded Spitfires began, then one by one the planes were lowered by elevators to be stored on the hangar deck. Before the end of the day, it was nearly impossible to get around the hangar deck, which was crammed bow to stern with the Spitfires and *Wasp*'s own Grumman fighters. Finally every available space on the huge ship was taken up, and it appeared the mission was ready to commence.

With the arrival of the harbor pilot on the morning of April 14, everything was squared away and the *Wasp* shoved off. Her protective screen consisted of Force W of the Home Fleet—a group that included the battle cruiser HMS *Renown*, the antiaircraft cruisers HMS *Cairo* and HMS *Charbydis*, eight British destroyers, and the American destroyers *Madison* and *Lang*.

Once again the Scottish landscape beckoned to the sailors as they passed. Jerry stood by his gun, mesmerized by the sight of the green hills, wishing to sink his hands into the warming earth and plant another year's crops. The fields were a rich springtime green and lay drowsy and peaceful in the late afternoon sun. Except for the dockyards that housed the ships of war and the occasional rows of debris of what had been people's houses before the blitz, it felt like they were leaving home again. Almost all the men had experienced a lavish dose of hospitality in the Scottish city, and it was a homesick crew of boys that lined the decks as they headed away from her.

Perhaps no one on board felt worse about leaving Glasgow than Chester Stanfeld, who had fallen head over heels in love with Margaret Harris. Both he and Jerry had gotten one more pass for shore leave, and Chester had spent every moment of his time with his "bonny lass." Now, watching the green fields slip by, he fell into a miserable silence, obviously pondering how long it would be until he would see his angel's face again and hear her sing another enchanting hymn.

Like Chester, Jerry was miserable, but along with being acutely aware of the seriousness of their mission, he had taken on a heavy dose of melancholy. Maybe it was because three weeks had passed since he'd heard from Marjie. Maybe it was because the Scottish people had been so good to him—he couldn't forget the little old grandmother who had hugged him. Or it might have been because he couldn't come to terms with what had happened in the church meeting. Jerry was certain only that he wanted space and that he didn't want to talk about whatever was bothering him—or about much of anything else.

Jerry had gone off on his own during shore leave, determined to walk the streets of Glasgow and see everything he could see. He had not gotten very far, though. It seemed that every street had a pub that looked too inviting to pass, and their brew was too good not to indulge. In short, Jerry had been lucky to successfully navigate his own course back to the ship. He had been in the bunk a long time before Chester made it back, and he was glad that Chester had not seen him staggering and falling into the sack.

Jerry was getting edgy just being around Chester; in fact, he worried that sooner or later he was going to blow up. All that Chester wanted to talk about was Margaret, her singing, her father's sermon, and the church. He had been annoyed when Jerry wouldn't tell him why he had left the church service that night or why he didn't want to go back again.

Maybe it was the mood of the whole ship that had gotten to Jerry—a contagion of nerves among even the most courageous. Word was out on the flight deck to stay clear of the commander. Captain Jack Reeves, known around the ship as Black Jack, was said to be on a tear, ripping into anyone who crossed his path. Whatever it was, Jerry found himself repeatedly pulling out Marjie's photo and, for the first time, even sneaking a peek into the envelope that contained the locks from her hair. That, he did very discreetly.

Whatever the sailors felt, the *Wasp* had a mission to accomplish. Passing out through the boom from the estuary to the sea, the ship headed down the east coast of Ireland toward St. George's Channel. Night fell on the Irish Sea, and a few hours later Jerry and Chester took to their bunks, hoping to get a decent night's rest. Wherever they were headed, they had a feeling that sleep was going to be scarce.

Chester hung his head over the edge of his bunk and whispered, "What do you hear on the deck? Anybody know where we're taking these planes?"

"I heard some guesses, but it sounds like a goose chase to me," Jerry responded. "Some guys think the Spitfires are going to pull off a special mission on the Germans, but that don't make no sense. If they were going to do any damage, they'd have to send their bombers. And their bombers would fall off the end of this ship if they tried to take off."

"Makes you wonder if the Spitfires can get off the deck, don't it?" Chester asked. "I wonder if they've ever done it?"

"Not that I heard about," Jerry added. "If they're going to take off our flight deck, I'm glad I'm standing at a gun and not sitting in the cockpit."

"You can say that again," Chester said. "Those RAF pilots may be young, but did you see how old they look? Couple more years of this and their hair's gonna turn gray."

"Couple more years and they'll be dead," Jerry countered. "I wonder what their chances are of getting it every time they lift off the ground? Pretty high, I bet."

Chester was silent for a while, and Jerry lay motionless, staring up in the dark. The heavy droning of snores from men in the bunks surrounding them took over for the moment. "The whole thing seems like such a waste," Chester finally said. "Margaret introduced me to family after family who've lost someone close to them. Her brother is somewhere in North Africa, but they're afraid he may be dead. They haven't had any news for months."

The words of the hymn that Margaret had sung came floating back to Jerry. He could see her lovely face and was haunted with the meaning of the phrase, "Did e'er such love and sorrow meet?" It sounded so wonderful, yet it made no sense in a world at war.

"You'd think those people we met would be thinking twice about whether their religion is really working," Jerry stated abruptly.

"What do you mean?" Chester asked. "I've never met people

whose faith was more real than theirs."

"I'm not saying they're not good people, or sincere," Jerry said. "Matter of fact, they're the nicest people I ever met, almost. But nice people can be wrong. Sincere people can be wrong. Maybe they have faith in a religious idea rather than what's true. Obviously, it's not making any difference."

"I think the kindness you felt is an expression of the difference their faith has made," Chester argued. "You realize those people could just as easily be bitter and shut their doors to helping anyone. But explain what you mean."

"Is it so hard to see that I have to explain it?" Jerry questioned. "Where has God been when all these horrible things have been happening to these good people? All the religion in the world hasn't done anything to stop the bombs from falling on their houses. It hasn't stopped their boys from dying. Sounds like it hasn't even saved Margaret's brother. Is that so tough to figure?"

Chester withdrew his head and lay back in his bunk for a moment. Jerry could almost feel him gathering his words, getting ready to try again, and the knowledge both touched and angered him. Leaning over the edge again, Chester whispered, "What if it ain't God's fault? What if it's the result of a terrible evil power in the world that is warring against—"

"Just shut it up, will you!" Jerry broke in. "I'm sick of all this religion talk. It's hocus-pocus, don't you get it? It don't add up, so you twist it around and start blaming something else. If you want to believe it, go ahead. But will you stop trying to shove it down my throat!"

Chester bit back an angry retort. Taking a deep breath, he closed his eyes briefly, then opened them again and continued.

"I'm sorry if you have felt like I was forcing my faith on you," Chester said. "I really didn't mean to, and I'll try to be more careful about it. But you gotta realize—no matter what you think about whether my faith is based on reality or not, it's at the center of my life. And that means that occasionally it's going to spill out of my mouth. If you can tolerate those spills, then I really want to remain your friend, if you'll have me."

Jerry closed his eyes, deeply sorry that his mouth had gotten the best of him. He'd said what he felt, but he wished he could take the words back. If there was one thing that Chester had said that Jerry believed, it was the part about an evil power at work in the world. He felt like some of it resided within him.

He sighed deeply. "Chester, I'm really sorry for what I said. I just don't see it the way you do, and I don't want to talk about it anymore. But I would like to be your friend, if you can stand having me around."

There was only a short silence from the upper bunk. "Friends?" Chester offered.

"Friends," Jerry seconded.

But it would be a long, restless night for Jerry. He and Chester had cleared the air, but he still felt like a jerk. He was afraid their friendship might never be the same again, and he knew that was his doing. Whatever Chester's faults were, Jerry had never gotten along so well with anyone else. And he had to admit that, although he wrestled with the faith he saw in Chester and the Scottish church people, he was attracted to it, too. He wondered what they saw that he did not see. For this night, though, all his wondering did was keep him from sleep.

Meanwhile the convoy of Allied ships was proceeding out toward sea. Once they passed St. George's Channel they would be in the North Atlantic again—and more vulnerable to attack. RAF fighter planes would protect them until they were forty miles out to sea. After that, they were on their own.

To reduce the chances of air attack, the convoy followed a zigzag course. At certain times a signal would be given for all the ships to "zig" a certain number of degrees to port or starboard and at a certain speed. Then, after a set time, they would be ordered to "zag" in another direction, and so on. It was a prescribed routine that demanded immediate recognition and response to the signals, and one misdirection could result in a collision. The fact that American and British ships were zigzagging together made it more complicated because they were used to different signals.

Another concern was that enemy craft had been spotted in the area. A "plot board" had been set up with an ever-increasing number of different-colored pins, indicating the latest sightings of enemy submarines and ships. Should their convoy be spotted, Jerry knew that they would draw a crowd.

As the convoy zigzagged southward, and the sea air grew steadily warmer, details of their mission gradually spread among the crew. Before long everybody on board knew they were on their way to the Mediterranean Sea, to deliver the Spitfires to Malta, and that the fate of the British island stronghold depended on the success of their venture.

Malta, located in the middle of the Mediterranean, was a vital guardian of the sea lanes that were the shortest route to the Suez Canal and the Middle East. Gibraltar, at the Mediterranean's western gateway, was another. British forces stationed on Malta had often blocked German and Italian reinforcements on the way to North Africa. But not surprisingly, Malta was now the target of a concentrated attack by the Axis powers. Malta-based British submarines, in the course of driving most of the Axis shipping from these waters, had suffered fifty-percent losses. Her Majesty's Royal Air Force had also suffered heavily. At one point in the spring of 1942, there had been only five fighter planes left on the island. The Allies also desperately feared that with the German General Rommel pushing the Brits back almost to Alexandria, the whole of North Africa might fall within months or weeks unless their own merchant and naval ships could bluster through more supplies to the Eighth Army in Egypt.

The British, faced with the impending loss of the island, had requested the use of an American carrier to transport planes that could win back air superiority from the Germans and Italians. The Spitfire-loaded *Wasp* was the American response to that request.

It was a rescue mission of grave consequence to the war effort, and the hazards grew as the convoy approached the gateway to the Mediterranean Sea. Twice a day the enemy carried out meteorological surveys from Sardinia and North Africa, and it had been estimated that eight hundred German and Italian aircraft were based on Sicily, incessantly concentrating on the "bombers alley," Malta. Some of that aircraft power could be turned in the convoy's direction at any time. Plus there was the potential for attack by naval raiders and very fast Italian motor torpedo boats that were similar to the American PTs.

Under the cover of another night's darkness, the *Wasp* drew near to the legendary Rock of Gibraltar. Jerry was standing an all-night watch at one of the guns when the first reports came of land sighted off the port side of the ship, and he guessed they must be just off Trafalgar.

Trafalgar. The name had been just a dim memory from his country-school history books until the night before in the mess hall, when two of the RAF pilots had entertained a cluster of crew members with rowdily recounted tales of British sea history. According to the British boys, these very waters had been the site of one of history's greatest sea battles, where the immortal Lord Nelson defeated the Napoleonic and Allied fleets, only to be killed by a French Marines' sniper's bullet.

Jerry laughed to himself when his mental images of Trafalgar merged into memories of "sea battles" he used to enact with his friends in the sinkhole just down the road from the school. At the moment, he would have much preferred a sinkhole engagement to trying to sneak into the Mediterranean Sea on an aircraft carrier without arousing Axis suspicions.

The *Wasp* and her consorts passed through the Straits of Gibraltar in the predawn darkness on April 20. Under orders to maintain absolute radio silence unless there was an emergency, they passed the fabled Pillars of Hercules on the Moroccan coast. Taking their first fix from the navigational lights burning on the Spanish mainland, they soon spotted the lights of Tangier. Once past Europa Point, the ship resumed the normal speed of eighteen knots and returned to its zigzag pattern. As daylight came, the crew spotted the mountainous coast of Spain some twenty miles away.

The tension on the ship mounted with every mile and with the ever-increasing temperature. Jerry stood at battle stations with his old tin helmet on, waiting for the action to begin. There was little wind, and the day was hot and muggy. Below, in the hangar deck the Spitfires were warming up their engines. Then one by one the aircraft were brought up on the after elevator and spotted for launching toward Malta.

Everyone knew the Spitfires would have a harder time taking off than the U.S. naval planes did. The Spitfires had been designed for longer runways, and the RAF pilots, however intrepid, were not trained for carrier techniques, which are at best difficult and hazardous. To improve the headwinds for takeoff, the carrier increased to full speed. Then through the loudspeaker bull horns came the bosun's pipe, followed by "Now hear this! Stand by to launch planes!"

Jerry could hear the many "Good lucks" and "Happy landings" being passed on to the RAF pilots as they mounted into their cockpits. Then the first Spitfire, the acting squadron leader, was flagged the go-ahead to take off. The smooth hum of his Rolls-Royce engine took him down the flight deck and out to sea. The men on the deck held their breath with the launch, and the wobbling of the plane as it left the runway betrayed the pilot's inexperience with carrier takeoffs. Everyone breathed a sigh of relief as the craft steadied and roared off.

One by one the Spitfires sped down the deck, over the forward rounddown and out over the blue Mediterranean. The officers on the bridge and the entire ship's company topside began shouting like football fans, cheering each takeoff.

When the last Spitfire was aloft and winging for Malta, the cheers on deck erupted even louder. The crew was jubilant over the success of the *Wasp*'s "first sting." But there was little time to celebrate. They still needed to navigate their way back through the dangerous Mediterranean. The convoy came about in a wide swing and steamed for safer waters.

Jerry caught a couple hours of sleep that day, but found himself once again standing at his gun that night under a star-speckled sky as the ship passed the Rock of Gibraltar. The African shore was lit up as before, and the "Rock" was silhouetted by the lights of Algeciras and La Linia.

Despite his exhaustion and his homesickness, Jerry was overwhelmed by how good it felt just to be alive.

21

APRIL SHOWERS

"Been over a month since we heard from Jerry, ain't it?" Benjamin asked, seeing Marjie trudge back empty-handed from the mailbox.

"More like six weeks," Marjie said in a worried tone. "It's not like him."

"He ain't much for writing," said Benjamin. "I got one letter from him—total. Maybe one of them letter censors thought he was telling too much and stopped some of his mail?"

"Jerry's too careful for that," Marjie argued. "Even his last letter before leaving Norfolk had nothing in it about the war. And that letter he mailed himself; he could have told whatever he wanted in that one. I'm afraid something's wrong."

"Something's wrong everywhere," Benjamin admitted, "but worrying about it ain't going to change it. And now you got me worrying. Them bags under your eyes got me nervous for you . . . and the baby."

"I can't help it," Marjie said. Whether it was her dreams or her imagination, the past nights had brought back the ghastly image of Jerry sinking to the bottom of the sea. "I'm having trouble sleeping at night," she admitted.

"Maybe the doc can give you something?" Benjamin suggested.

Marjie shook her head no. "Don't want none of that stuff,"

she said. "Once you start it, then you can't stop it. Besides, it can't be good for the baby."

"Then at least take a nap during the day!"

Marjie burst out laughing. "Simmer down!" she said. "Your blood pressure's going up again. If I start sleeping during the day, I'll never sleep another wink at night, and you know it. You want me banging pots all night while you try to sleep? Let me work it out, okay?"

"Fine," grumped Benjamin. "Have it your way. But this can't go on much longer. I'm scared you're going to get sick."

"It'll be all right," Marjie comforted him. "Just look at you. Two weeks ago I thought you looked like a ghost, and today you look as fit as a fiddle."

Benjamin's color had returned, and his eyes had held a mischievous sparkle the past few days. He reminded Marjie of a little boy who's up to something he doesn't want his mother to discover. "Didn't I tell you I was feeling good?" he demanded. "You should trust me more."

"Right!" exclaimed Marjie. "I still think you were lying like a rug. And what's come over you, anyway? You're up to no good; I can tell."

"Me?" asked Benjamin innocently. "What could I be up to? I been too busy to do anything but work."

That was true. Fortunately, the weather had held steady, and Benjamin had managed to get the crops in the field. Lately he had spent a lot of time out in his wood shop—said he was fixing some of the equipment. There was still some catch-up work from winter to get to and some fences that needed mending, but he'd even taken time to help Marjie get her garden in. He hated the crookedness of the raspberry row, but she forbade him to redo it. Her excuse was that the plants wouldn't survive another transplanting, but her real reason was that she enjoyed his fussing about it.

"You have been busy," Marjie said, "but you're up to something. It's written in your eyes, you rascal. And I'm going to find out what it is."

Benjamin clapped his hands and laughed. "Well, that's something you and I do agree on. You *will* find out. But you better hurry up before it gets past you and you miss it completely. How about if I give you one hint?"

"Fire away," demanded Marjie, enjoying the challenge.

"April showers bring May flowers."

"What?" she retorted. "That's no clue. You can do better than that."

Benjamin pushed back his hat, squinted his eyes, and wrinkled his mouth. "Sorry, that's all you get. April showers bring May flowers."

"Don't you have a field to plant or something?" Marjie spat out in mock disgust. "Get moving, buster. You stay out of my house until you can be nice."

Benjamin just laughed again, then turned to head back to his work. "I already told you more than I should have," he called back over his shoulder. "And just in case you've forgotten, this fine old house happens to belong to *me*! You better treat me right, or you may be begging your old buddy Gordy for your job back."

Marjie laughed with him this time. He was right of course. The house was not hers, yet she felt like it was. "Have you checked the title to the property lately?" she called. "I have a friend in the county office who is very good with the records."

Benjamin just kept on walking.

Marjie went back to the house to finish the apple pie she'd been working on before she went out to the mailbox. Her favorite dog was lying at the door, snoozing in the warm sunshine. Benjamin had said he was the smartest cow dog he had ever owned, and he'd owned a lot of them. Marjie thought it was funny that she'd started to think of the dog as her own as well as the old house. She eased herself down to pet him before going in.

"Good old Blue," she said as she ruffled the long hair around his ears. His distinctive blue eyes had given him his name, and he sat up to soak in the attention. "You got it real tough around here, don't you. Lying in the sun, snoring like a bum all day. Eating our food. I should have it so good."

Blue didn't seem to mind her demeaning remarks. He hadn't been scratched so well for a long time and wasn't about to protest.

He stuck out his tongue and gave her a good lick across the cheek.

"Mmmm. Nice kiss!" she said enthusiastically.

Marjie leaned back against the door and sighed deeply. She really didn't have anything to feel sad about. She had a roof over her head, food to eat, a baby on the way, and as far as she knew, a husband who was neither dead nor wounded. She just wished she'd hear from Jerry. Once she knew he was truly all right and happy about the baby, everything would be wonderful.

Later in the afternoon, Marjie got a call from Ruth, asking her to come with her to the church the following night. It was a little unclear, but Ruth had said that she was in charge of some meeting, and she could use Marjie's moral support. Marjie decided it would be fun to see how a church meeting of any kind would go if Ruth was in the front stirring up the soup, so she agreed to go.

Benjamin's chores ran a little late that day, and Marjie had just enough time to clear the dinner dishes before Ruth arrived. She told Benjamin that she'd do the dishes when she got home, but of course he went right to the sink and started soaking the plates.

"Just leave them!" Marjie exclaimed as she put on her light coat. "Why can't you just take it easy once?"

"Go on. Ruthie's waiting!" Benjamin returned. "I know my way around here, if you recall. These plates know me better than they do you."

"Try to get them clean, then," Marjie teased. "If you recall, those plates regained their whiteness only after I put you out to pasture in the living room! Gray is not white!"

She turned and headed out the door. As she headed down the sidewalk, she heard the window open and a voice call out, "Have you figured out the mystery yet? April showers bring May flowers, remember? You're running out of time!"

"Just do the dishes, or I'll take away your allowance," she cried back.

"What's that all about?" Ruth asked as she climbed into the car.

"Who knows?" Marjie answered. "He's up to something and

won't tell me. Who cares, anyway? It's probably nothing. What's up, Ruthie? Tell me what this meeting is about."

Ruth started the car and headed down the driveway. It was only a mile to the church. "It's a meeting some of the ladies at the church asked me to put together. It's about marriage and family, I guess you'd say."

"Sounds good to me," Marjie said. "I'm learning about both the hard way!"

Both women laughed, and Ruth slowed for the sharp corner onto the main road. "That you are," she said. "Incidentally, this meeting is especially geared for you. I've been thinking about you all day."

"You're serious, Ruthie?" Marjie asked, a bit bewildered. "I'm glad I said I'd come, then."

"Me, too!" Ruth exclaimed.

There were a lot of cars in the church parking lot when they pulled up. The lights were on in the basement, but the upper part of the church was dark. A few more cars pulled in as the two trotted up the sidewalk.

"Boy, you know how to draw a crowd!" Marjie said quietly.

Ruth grinned. "You better believe it. I'm very good."

Going down the stairway, Marjie thought the basement sounded like a henhouse. This gathering was far more lively than any of the other church meetings she had attended, but then she had never attended a meeting Ruth was in charge of. Curious, she stepped through the doorway.

The meeting room was packed with people, but it didn't look like a meeting was about to take place. The chairs were spread around the room, rather than in the usual neat rows, and a large table at the front was piled with colorful packages and cards. Then Marjie glanced up and noticed a bright banner that proclaimed: "Marjie and Jerry and little _____!"

Marjie stopped dead in her tracks, and Ruth turned with a huge, beaming smile. "It's that April shower Benjamin told you about!" she screamed. Marjie screamed as well, and the whole place erupted with laughter.

Looking around the room, Marjie decided that every woman

in the church was there; she even saw ladies she had not seen before. She was so overwhelmed that she didn't know what to do or how to respond. She just followed Ruth meekly to a chair near the long table of gifts and sank down gratefully. At the moment, sitting felt safer than standing.

It turned out that Ruth had organized the shower to celebrate Jerry and Marjie's wedding as well as the coming baby. There was a very short program, with Ruth talking mostly about how nice it was to have Marjie as her friend, then the usual coffee and cake was served, with most of the women stopping by to talk with Marjie and welcome her to the community. Then it was time for Marjie to open the gifts.

There were so many presents and cards that it took Marjie a long while to open them all and to thank each one who had given them. With the hard times of war following the Depression, she was amazed at all the beautiful things. Many of the cards contained cash, which would help pay the doctor who delivered the baby. Some of the women gave lovely soft baby blankets, others tiny little jackets they had knitted or crocheted. A few of the boxes held expensive crystal bowls and vases—wedding presents. Marjie wondered what she'd ever use them for, and the thought flashed through her mind that the givers might not have been able to use them either. Then she put that idea out of her mind. They were beautiful, and the party was wonderful, and she was happy.

Ruth was handing her the gifts and seemed to have them in the order that she wanted. The pile finally dwindled down to two boxes. One box was larger than any that had been opened all evening.

Ruth gave her the smaller box and said, "From me."

Marjie smiled and tore the paper free, then carefully opened the flaps of the box. In it were a dozen white, fluffy diapers and attached to the top were two large safety pins. She pulled them out, and the group gave a warm cheer.

Marjie hugged Ruth and kissed her on the cheek. "It's just like you, Ruthie!" Marjie exclaimed. "So practical. Thank you so much."

Then Ruth raised her hand to quiet the crowd. "Now," she called out, "before Marjie opens the last gift, I must first call for the giver to come to the front. Will 'Mr. April Showers Bring May Flowers' stop peeking around the curtain in the back and please come forward."

Every eye turned to the back partition and out stepped a very embarrassed Benjamin. He'd snuck in through the back stairs and had enjoyed watching Marjie open the presents. Ruth had told him it was all right to come, but she hadn't warned him about having to be in the front when Marjie opened his surprise. Now it was too late to retreat.

Another cheer erupted, the loudest of the night, as Benjamin sidled up toward the table. Marjie gazed out at him with tears flowing, and the always practical Ruth handed Marjie one of her handkerchiefs. She had brought two, but she needed one for her own tears.

Benjamin stepped alongside Marjie and gave her a timid hug. Then he pointed to the big box, although he was far too choked up to find any words.

The place went silent as Marjie pulled the wrapping loose and then noticed that the large box was slit down one side. Pulling there, it opened neatly to reveal the most beautiful wooden rocking horse she had ever seen. Fashioned of oak with black-painted features, perfectly shaped leather ears, and a frayed rope tail, it shimmered in the basement lights with its new coat of varnish. It was something from a child's dream.

Whatever escaped Marjie's lips was covered over by the loud gasps and exclamations of the larger group. She reached out to touch the horse, then rocked it gently. It was perfect.

Benjamin now had tears on his own face and begged to leave, but Marjie would not let him escape. They hugged and cried, and Ruth found her way into the warm embrace as well. And the crowd gave one last cheer. They had gotten their money's worth out of this shower.

For an hour or so that night, joy and happiness enveloped a church basement that was usually somber and reserved. The war was forgotten for a night as the majesty of love and family was celebrated. And Marjie's happiness was full to overflowing, with only one little complaint:

"I just wish Jerry were here."

22

THE WASP STINGS TWICE

Unfortunately for the Spitfires that had flown in to replace the dwindling numbers of British fighters on Malta, they were tracked on the way by efficient Axis intelligence and their arrival was pinpointed. The Germans launched heavy air raids that caught many of the new planes on the ground and destroyed them. It seemed that the rescue mission was for naught.

Fearing that Malta would be "pounded to bits," Prime Minister Winston Churchill asked U.S. President Franklin Roosevelt to allow the *Wasp* to have "another good sting." Roosevelt approved the mission, and a second ferry run was scheduled with the code name, "Operation Bowery." The primary difference in this mission was that the British aircraft carrier HMS *Eagle* was scheduled to meet them at Gibraltar for a specially appointed "fly-off" position. She was to launch her nearly twenty RAF aircraft at the same time that the *Wasp* launched hers.

The *Wasp* hugged the west coast of Scotland, then proceeded once again up the estuary of the River Clyde. A day later they were tied up alongside the King George V dock in Glasgow, and another contingent of Spitfires were being loaded, inspected, and lowered by elevators to the hangar deck. It didn't take much for the ship's crew to figure out what their next assignment was, and there was a marked calm on the ship as compared to their last stop.

During the few days they were docked in Glasgow, Jerry and Chester once again got shore passes and made the most of them. Knowing what they would be heading into during the coming days, both men left the ship hoping to find a few hours' escape from the tension. Jerry joined up with a group of his gunnery mates and proceeded to the closest pub, where the stiff Scottish whiskey was flowing. Chester made tracks to spend every second with Margaret Harris.

Next morning, Jerry was in a sorry mood. Drinking way past their limits, he and his friends had made fools of themselves; a couple of the men had even been arrested for disorderly conduct. Jerry had a ringer of a hangover, and he was angry that the mail had not gotten through. The last piece of mail he had touched was in Norfolk. He had been so busy that he hadn't gotten off a letter either, and he felt guilty that he had blown his evening when he could have been writing. He determined that during the hour he had off that day he would write something and get it in the mail.

Nursing his sore head as he crossed the flight deck that morning, Jerry nearly ran into a handsome officer, who stepped neatly aside and cut him an amused, understanding glance. Walking away in embarrassment, Jerry was shocked to realize he had just crossed paths with Douglas Fairbanks, Jr. Jerry had heard that the famous movie actor was now a lieutenant in the navy and had come aboard for this mission, but it still was a surprise to get so close to someone so famous. He remembered going into Preston with Marjie to see *The Corsican Brothers*, back before Pearl Harbor was hit. Marjie had made a big fuss over the swashbuckling Fairbanks. *He doesn't look all that special up close,* Jerry groused to himself.

That night shore leave was forbidden for the men on the ship, so Fairbanks had agreed to arrange some entertainment for the men. He had gone into Glasgow to find the great Scottish music hall entertainer Will Fyffe, who had costarred with him in *Rulers of the Sea*. A crowd of more than two thousand sailors packed the hangar deck as Fairbanks introduced the roly-poly Scot with the red-veined, bulbous nose. Fyffe then stepped up to the microphone and proceeded to steal the show. He told Scottish stories and sang without accompaniment and kept the sailors laughing, singing, and cheering for two or three hours.

Chester and Jerry and their friends enjoyed the night, but Jerry was curious that Chester had not even mentioned what happened on his shore leave. After the entertainment ended, Jerry determined to find out.

"You've been real quiet about your time with Margaret," Jerry said. "How'd it go?"

Chester gave Jerry one of his funny smiles and said, "Pretty good, I guess."

"That's it? Pretty good?"

"Well, I don't know what to say about it," Chester said.

"Anything would be good for starters," Jerry egged him on. "Am I supposed to take it that you'd rather not talk about it? Don't tell me that Margaret met another young preacher and . . ."

"No, no, no," Chester stated. "Nothing like that. It's really the opposite. Okay, I thought about telling you, but I'd like to keep it quiet for a while. Can you promise to keep a secret?"

"Yes. Tell me," Jerry demanded.

Chester pushed his sailor's cap back and looked around for any eavesdroppers. "I went to Margaret's house. I talked. She talked. I told her I loved her. She told me that she loved me. I asked her to marry me. She said she would, but she had to have her parents' approval. I talked to them, and they approved. So now I am engaged to the most gorgeous creature God ever made. What do you think of that?"

Jerry was completely undone by the news and could only stand there staring at Chester, trying to put the pieces together.

"You got engaged to Margaret?" Jerry asked.

"And it's all your fault," Chester said. "You made me do it."

"I didn't make you do anything," Jerry said, still reeling.

"You sure did," Chester countered. "I would have never met her without you."

"You're engaged to Margaret!"

"Absolutely! I'd marry her tomorrow if we weren't pulling out of here," Chester said, finally breaking into a huge grin.

Jerry tossed his cap into the air and shouted, "Congratulations!"

Grabbing Jerry by the mouth, Chester tried to silence him. "You promised to keep it a secret, blabbermouth. Now half the ship's wondering what's going on."

"Sorry. I'm sorry," Jerry apologized. "I won't tell another soul. But really, congratulations, Chester. I'm really happy for you. That girl is worth traveling around the world for. I wish you the best."

"Thanks," Chester said. "You think I'm crazy? I've only been with her three times."

Jerry threw his head back and laughed. "You're asking me if I think you're crazy?" he asked. "Sounds like one mental patient asking another one if he thinks he's sane!"

Jerry slapped Chester on the back, and the two friends laughed as they headed for their bunks. As much as they would have liked to celebrate, they would be underway in the morning and needed all the sleep they could get.

Plans for the *Wasp*'s second sting were much the same as for their first trip. Passing out through the estuary of the River Clyde early on the morning of May 3, they headed down the east coast of Ireland and proceeded out to sea. By May 6 they would be joined by an escort of the *Renown*, the *Charybdis*, four British destroyers, and four U.S. destroyers. Maintaining a careful vigil for submarines, the *Wasp* proceeded unmolested.

On the evening of May 6, the ship received an official communication that the U.S. forces had surrendered to the Japanese at Corregidor in the Philippines. While not unexpected news, it nevertheless had a deeply sobering effect as the sailors considered the fate of thousands of their comrades on the other side of the globe. General MacArthur, it appeared, had been caught unprepared despite repeated warnings after Pearl Harbor, but he, his family, and his staff had escaped in a squadron of PT boats and were heading for Australia.

As the convoy drew near to Gibraltar, they hit heavy seas, and some of the escorts had difficult going. Everything on the *Wasp*—aircraft and anything else movable on or below decks—had to be battened down. Jerry tried to eat his lunch sitting on the floor of the mess hall, but even that proved difficult as the ship rolled and pitched. When he set his plate of beans down on the floor to take a drink, it slid across the room.

The damp, eerie night of May 8 helped them sneak through the narrow straits into the Mediterranean and on past Europa Point. Before dawn on May 9, the convoy was joined by the hardy old HMS *Eagle*, who took her position astern of the *Wasp*. When all was in order, a message was blinkered across: "From HMS Eagle to USS Wasp: The aging lady looks with envious eyes at her smart younger cousin and sends her greetings and best wishes."

A swift reply came from Captain Reeves: "Thank you. There seems to be plenty of life in the old girl yet if I may say so."

Now the entire convoy was sailing single file through the dark waters—first the eight destroyers, then the antiaircraft cruiser *Charybdis*, the flagship *Renown*, then the *Wasp*, and then the *Eagle*.

In the dark predawn Jerry was at his battle station on one of the twenty-millimeter cannons and as nervous as a cat. Men moved about topside in the busy blackness, feeling their way by memory and instinct as final preparations were made for the operation. The air was very still and muggy, and Jerry had already popped four aspirin for a sinus headache.

The plan was for the twelve U.S. fighters to take off first and patrol the skies during the launching of the Spitfires. Then a dozen or more Spits were to take off at intervals of twenty seconds. When the deck was clear, more Spits would be brought up, one at a time. Then the last group would come up and be spotted for takeoff. There would be about fifty in all.

Just after 6:00 that morning, their radar picked up a plane some twenty-two miles away. They were too far from Gibraltar by now for it to be British, and Jerry could hear men praying that in the dark cloudy dawn it would pass by. Fortunately for their mission, it did.

At 6:18, both carriers were ordered to keep heading directly into the wind. Five minutes later the loudspeaker blared out, "Now hear this! Stand by to launch planes!"

Flight deck crews unlashed the wing lines and pulled the wheel chucks from beneath the navy Grumman fighters. At precisely 6:30 the white GO flag was substituted for the red warning flag and the order, "Launch planes" rang out. One at a time, a dozen Grummans roared down the deck and out over the water. A few minutes later the first dozen Spitfires revved their powerful Rolls-Royce engines and made their wobbly launches.

The HMS *Eagle*, running along her prearranged course, three miles off the *Wasp*'s starboard quarter, began launching her aircraft at 6:40. By 6:45 a second group of Spits had begun their shaky ascent from the *Wasp*.

One of this second group started his run but was obviously not getting enough power from his engine to manage a liftoff. Jerry's heart began to race as he watched the RAF pilot appear to change his mind two or three times on the way down the deck. He applied his brakes, then gunned his engine, still did not get full power, then began to weave to port side. Again he gave full throttle, but it was too late. As if in slow motion, he rolled right up to the end of the flight deck and dribbled off the bow and into the sea. As it fell, the plane turned over on its back, breaking off a wing. The *Wasp* rammed it squarely in the middle, driving its two halves and the pilot down beneath the ship.

There was a loud blast on the emergency signal from the bridge, and Jerry hung on as the ship swung first hard right and then hard left, hoping to clear the Spitfire. But as the ship passed over the spot where the plane had fallen, there was no sign of an aircraft—just the dark-blue Mediterranean and the wake of the ship.

Then the command came from the bridge: "Continue to launch planes." Faces were sheet white, but the job continued without respite. Flag hoists and blinker signals passed between ships while they rejockeyed their positions into the wind. Soon the second group of Spitfires—minus one—were off and into flying formation before heading eastward to Malta.

Despite the tragedy, the entire ship topside had once again begun shouting and cheering each plane as it made its way down the flight deck. By 7:30 the last of the Spitfires had left both the carriers. Then they spotted two lone Spitfires still circling the ship. As the last formation group headed off, one of the stragglers fell in with it. He had apparently lost his bearings and waited to rejoin the later group. The second Spitfire had accidentally released his auxiliary fuel tank as he climbed to two thousand feet. Without his auxiliary, there was no way he could reach Malta, and his only alternatives were to try landing on the *Wasp* or to ditch and take his chances in the water.

The bullhorns roared to life: "Clear the flight deck! Fire fighters, get ready! Start pumps on fire hoses! Prepare for a crash landing!"

The RAF pilot turned his plane toward the *Wasp*, knowing that without a tail hook to catch the cables on the flight deck, his chances of landing successfully were slim. The landing signal officer stood at the end of the flight deck with his flags and signaled the Spitfire to land. The pilot came around low and fast and looked like he would crash into the stern. The officer desperately waved his flags in an effort to urge him higher. But the long, high nose of the Spitfire blocked the pilot's view of the deck, and only in the last split second did he catch sight of the flags. Like a sudden roll of thunder, the Spit's engine answered the throttle as he swerved his plane hard to the left. His wing nearly scraped the edge of the flight deck as he zoomed up and off. The landing officer had to jump into his net off the deck's side to avoid being hit.

Jerry and every other sailor topside were riveted by the drama and speechless as the Spitfire circled again and again to get into a position to land. Finally he came in at a perfect height, though at about ninety knots, a bit fast. Finally he set his craft down—a perfect landing, but quite a ways forward of the spot he should have used. His speed, however, was still so great that his brakes could do no more than check him momentarily. He continued to roll on, releasing and reapplying the brakes and slowing himself a little more. Still, inexorably, the plane moved to the end of the deck. About fifteen feet—no more—this side of eternity, the pilot brought the plane to a stop.

There was a second's hush; then a great cheer went up from

all hands. Jerry whistled, applauded, and shouted his delight at such skillful handling of a craft under impossible conditions. The young British pilot was taken up to Captain Reeves immediately and seemed unshaken. He only wanted to have an extra tank put on so he could get off and rejoin his mates. A message from the commander of the *Renown* approved the spirit but disapproved the request. He was "to stay and live to fight another day."

The *Wasp*'s fighters returned a little before 8:00 that morning. One Spitfire radioed back that he was lost and asked for an emergency homing signal, but due to security precautions that signal could not be given. They heard no more from him.

Turning the convoy around, they headed back for Gibraltar at a brisk twenty-two knots. The following morning, the *Renown* passed along all the news from Malta. Almost all the Spitfires had managed to make it to the island to find a fierce air battle in progress. The new arrivals had refueled and returned to battle many times during the day. In the day's battle, thirty enemy planes had been shot down, and only three Spitfires had been lost.

The following day the *Renown* passed along another message, this one from London. It read: "From the Prime Minister to the captain and ship's company of the USS *Wasp*: Many thanks to you all for the timely help. Who said a wasp couldn't sting twice? Winston Churchill."

On the morning of May 15, the *Wasp* was instructed to "drop the hook" at Scapa Flow. Operation Bowery was completed, and the *Wasp* was destined for another war theater.

23

OLD TOM

Warm May showers had greened the farmside landscapes of southeastern Minnesota, and spring was slowly giving way to the first heat waves of summer. As Decoration Day approached, the first crop of alfalfa had grown luscious and heavy, the oats were a brilliant green, and the field corn was well rooted and off to a good start. Mix in the white blossoms on the apple trees and the rich variety of birds returning to nest, and even the most cynical curmudgeon would have difficulty holding a frown.

Benjamin would never admit it, but getting the crops in the ground by himself had been a struggle for him. True to form, he had put his head down and just kept pushing until it was complete. He hoped that he wouldn't have to go through it again the following spring, but with Jerry at war, there was no reason to think it would be any different. Still, watching the crops come up and doing so well delighted him, as it had for fifty years. Nothing pleased him more than walking his fields on a breezy spring day and studying their progress.

Benjamin was more than a little worried about Marjie, though. Physically, she was doing fine; in fact, the country spring had left her healthier than she had been in years. Not a day went by that she was not out working in her garden, soaking in the sun's strength. And despite Benjamin's protests, she was often out in the fields, taking him lunch or helping him with smaller jobs that required extra hands. Her pregnancy was going very well, and though she was more than five months along, she was not as large as he had expected she might be by now.

The clouds of April, however, had never really cleared from over Marjie's head. Although she said she was learning to cope with her worries and fears for Jerry, he knew she still tossed through many long, restless nights, and there were moments when a wall of fear would collapse upon her and leave her near panic. Marjie seemed powerless to fight those moments, and he feared that one day the fear would overwhelm her.

During the second week of May she had finally gotten a letter from Jerry addressed from Scotland. She said it was very brief and didn't really say anything except that he thought the Scottish people were very warm and friendly and that Douglas Fairbanks, Jr., was not as handsome as she claimed. And it said nothing at all about the baby. The letter left Marjie confused and disappointed. Benjamin knew what she was thinking: Was Jerry so unhappy about the baby that he couldn't write about it?

Benjamin suspected that it was only the majesty of the spring sunshine and the activity of helping around the farm that had kept her from tottering over the edge into chronic melancholy. And try as he might, Benjamin simply could not find the words to drive away the darkness. When Ruth managed to find time to visit, Marjie's day would always brighten up, but school kept Ruth so busy that her visits were short and too few.

Benjamin was especially concerned about how Marjie was going to handle Decoration Day. Every day had its difficult moments for her—especially mail time—but a day to honor those who had died in combat was exactly what the doctor had not ordered. Benjamin determined to find a way to transform the holiday into something positive for Marjie, but it wasn't until the last moment that he came up with an idea he thought would work.

The day before Decoration Day, with the help of a couple of neighbor boys, Benjamin had managed to get the last of his first crop of alfalfa into the barn. Now, after supper, he and Marjie sat relaxing in the living room and listening to the radio for any war reports that they might pick up.

"That was the finest first crop I've seen in years," Benjamin was saying. "Those boys were really dragging their tails by dinnertime, weren't they?"

"You worked them like dogs," Marjie said. "I hope you pay them a decent wage. Did it ever cross your mind that you could have saved some of the work for another day? And don't give me your 'make hay while the sun shines' line. The weather report is for another beautiful day tomorrow."

Benjamin laughed and sat forward in the chair. "I couldn't do that," he said. "Tomorrow's Decoration Day."

"Don't remind me," Marjie sighed. "So what does the holiday have to do with it? Last I checked, there's no law that keeps you from haying on Decoration Day."

"That's true," he stated. "But we've got plans for tomorrow," he stated.

Looking away, Marjie said, "I'm not going anywhere—period. If you've got plans, that's fine. But don't include me in them. I'd rather not think of any memorials, if you don't mind."

Benjamin had not anticipated this reaction and thought for a moment that his plans were washing down the tube. But he tried again, this time with a more direct approach. "Didn't you tell me once that you like to go fishing?" he asked.

"I could live on the river," Marjie answered. "Why?"

"Well," he explained, "I was thinking the whole time we was putting the hay up that it would be great to celebrate getting it done by going fishing, and I thought that tomorrow would be a good day for it. What do you think? The hay's in the barn. Let's celebrate."

Marjie stared at Benjamin and tried to read his poker face. "Are you pulling my leg?" she asked. "Since when did you celebrate anything? And since when did you become a fisherman? You don't even have a pole around here, do you?"

"Wait, now!" Benjamin exclaimed. "You've lived here so long that you know everything I like and don't like? Why, there's nothing I like better than sitting on the bank of the river and listening to the water and the birds sing. I don't care much if I catch anything, but I love to go. Trouble is, most summers slip by and I've been too busy to get there. So I thought maybe I'd go early, just this once."

Marjie was still skeptical. "Where're the poles?"

"Turn the yard light on, and look out by the car. They're a bit on the worn side, but I think they'll work."

She went out to the back porch and flipped the light on. Leaning against the car were two cane poles and a disreputable-looking container that could pass for a tackle box.

"So what do you fish for?" Marjie asked.

"Suckers mostly," Benjamin answered. "But there's trout in the Root River. Big ones, too. You ever see a big brown trout, Marjie?"

Benjamin was really starting to talk Marjie's language. "I never have, but I've caught some nice bass down in the Upper Iowa," she said. "I can handle a cane pole, easy enough. Just one problem, though."

"What's that?"

"It may have slipped your attention, but have you forgotten that I'm over five months pregnant?" she asked. "Won't it be a little unsightly to have me rolling around on the bank?"

"Ah, who gives a rip?" Benjamin said with a snort. "And I know a spot where not very many fishermen go, anyway. Nobody's going to bother us, believe me. Now, are you coming, or do I have to go alone?"

Marjie smiled. "You push all the right buttons, don't you," she said. "You're a sly old fox. What time're we going?"

———— ∽ ————

"This is the spot," Benjamin proclaimed as they rounded a big bend in the Root River. "Right out of a magazine, ain't it!"

Marjie, exhausted from the long hike through the woods, stopped at the edge of the clearing and caught her breath at the peace and beauty of the place.

It was one of those rare places a mile or so back in a farmer's cow pasture that very few people ever see and that could capture an artist's imagination for a lifetime. The clear trout stream, sheltered by a thicket of maples and oaks and elms, tumbled musically through white-water rapids, then entered a wide expanse of water that resembled a huge, slow-motion whirlpool, then finally exited through more rapids on the other end. The swirling pool of water looked dark and deep and was surrounded by high, grassy banks except for one side, where the land and water drew nearly level. The slow-moving water and the surrounding trees worked together to create a hush that made normal talking seem almost like a violation of nature.

Benjamin was lugging the old cane poles, a bucket of night crawlers, the tackle box, and their basket of food. He was huffing and puffing from the strain, but he refused to let Marjie help carry anything. Heading for the one patch of bank that was closest to the water, he called back to tell her she could easily fish from the bank without strain.

"If this wasn't the prettiest fishing hole I've ever seen in my entire life, I'd be upset with you for dragging me so far back into the woods," Marjie declared when she finally reached the spot where Benjamin was already resting. "I guess I don't need to worry about anyone fussing about a pregnant woman on the river. Looks like we got the whole place to ourselves."

"That's what I love about it," said Benjamin, wiping the perspiration from his forehead. "It's just too far back for most folks to walk, and I've never been more relaxed than when I'm here. I can't imagine Old Man River ever finding a more perfect spot to quiet the soul than this place."

"We should put a cabin back here," Marjie suggested, pointing up the hill. "We could live here all spring and summer, then at the farm the rest of the year. Live off the land, you know."

Benjamin nodded in agreement. "Thought of that a few times, myself," he said, pausing to study the surroundings. "Many's the time I wished I could lay it all down and just sit by the river the rest of my days. I think that's what this spot's made for, don't you."

"That and fishing!" Marjie exclaimed, grabbing one of the poles. "First one in the water gets the biggest fish!"

She quickly unloosened the line, bobber and hook, then grabbed the bucket and pulled out a big, juicy night crawler. "This one should do it," she called out. "Bet there's a dozen trout out there waiting for a meal." Giving the line a toss, she had her bait in the water before Benjamin had gotten up off the grassy bank.

"You handle that pole pretty good," Benjamin commented, pulling his gear apart. "But I don't think you got that bobber deep enough to get down to the big boys. Watch me now—this is the perfect depth for the trout. Now, hand me that bucket."

Marjie passed him the bucket, and Benjamin was soon in business. Their bobbers floated gently in the light current and then found a spot where they seemed content to not move. He said, "Watch my pole so it don't get pulled in while I get us something to sit on."

Benjamin put his pole down on the bank and rustled around in the fallen trees behind them. It wasn't long before he was dragging pieces of logs that would work for a poor man's chair. With a grunt and a sigh he pushed a log over for her and finally sat down to rest.

"I ain't as young as I used to be," he conceded. "I'm all played out already."

"I thought you did pretty good for an old man," Marjie teased. "When's your birthday coming up. Next month?"

"The thirtieth of June," Benjamin said. "I—"

His words were cut off by a monstrous swoosh just up current from their bobbers.

"Whoa!" Marjie exclaimed. "What was that?"

Benjamin's eyes sparkled in the sunlight, and a delight from some long-gone day danced across his smile. "That is the reason we came here," he said. "Didn't I tell you there are huge trout patroling these waters. That was Old Tom, just letting us know he's still the king of the pool."

"There's no trout in this county that big," Marjie argued. "Must be a carp."

"Last night you told me you hadn't ever fished for trout, and today you tell me I don't know a trout when I see one?" Benjamin countered. "That was a trout, my dear, and his name is Old Tom."

"How do you know?"

"I've come here for years," Benjamin said. "If I was blind, I could still tell you whether that was Tom simply by the swoosh. He does it several times a day. You just watch the surface, and sooner or later you'll see that old monster come up and give you a wave with his tail. He does it to torment you. I'd guess he's around ten pounds of solid brown trout, and there's none finer in these parts. He's like a living legend."

"You ever hook him?" Marjie asked, starting to believe.

"Me? Shoot no," said Benjamin. "All I ever catch are suckers, but they're good eating if you don't mind the bones."

Marjie's bobber started twitching, then it sank under. Giving a sharp tug with her pole, she hooked into a fish that dove straight for the bottom, but to no avail. Marjie just kept the tension on, and up came a foot-long sucker.

"That's a big one!" she exclaimed, jerking the fish up on the bank. "Clean-looking, too. Must be the cold water. The suckers in the Upper Iowa get sort of muddy looking and taste that way, too, but these are nice. Say, what are the long marks on it?"

"Those are Old Tom's tooth marks," Benjamin said. "Every fish you catch here is marked, just like he owns them. Think of that. He can slip a twelve-inch sucker in his mouth without a problem. You'd think you had a northern pike in there."

"Wow!" Marjie said, shaking her head as Benjamin tied the fish to a stringer and tossed it back into the water. "What are we going to do if Old Tom takes one of our night crawlers? These old bamboo poles look pretty shabby, and when's the last time you put some new line on? Suppose I hook the king and then your rotten gear lets him get away."

"Don't you worry about a thing," Benjamin stated. "If you hook a big one, I'll put him in the frying pan."

"Promise?" she asked.

"I promise," he answered. "Now, why don't you get busy and pull me out some food. I'm starving. I'll take a cup of coffee, too."

Marjie gave him a defiant smirk. "You don't seem to understand. Tomorrow I'll bring you a sandwich and coffee. Today, I'm going to show you how to catch fish. If you've got time to worry about your stomach when you could be yanking fish, then you've got time to find your own grub."

"All right, all right," he groused good-naturedly, reaching for the basket while she turned back to the pond. "I know better than argue with a woman."

The two Macmillans had a great time. They caught several more suckers and added them to the stringer, keeping a close count of how many each had caught. Then they sat back and relaxed for a while, soaking up the wonder of the place. It was so peaceful that it was difficult not to fall asleep to the gentle gurgle of the pool.

By midafternoon they were both getting tired, and Benjamin suggested they pack up and head home for evening chores. He picked up his pole and pulled in his gear.

"I believe I caught one more than you did," Benjamin stated, declaring himself the winner for the day.

"I don't believe I'm quite through yet," Marjie retorted, standing up and taking her pole in hand. "You just watch me, and I'll show you a technique we used on the Upper Iowa. I believe it's going to fool one more fish today."

Holding the long cane pole out as far as she could, Benjamin laughed at Marjie as she walked along the bank, dragging the night crawler slightly faster than the current. "Are you watching?" she called to him.

"Draggin' bottom's what it looks like," Benjamin yelled with a laugh. "Hope you catch a big old boot or a tire!"

"You just wait until—"

Suddenly her pole nearly jumped from her hands, and the tip of the pole dipped sharply down in the water. Marjie let out a scream, and Benjamin dashed to her side.

"Hang on!" hollered Benjamin. "You got Old Tom on!"

The fish took off running parallel to the bank, and Marjie had all she could do to follow. Then he made a big circle and headed back the other way.

"Take the pole!" Marjie cried. "I can't keep up to him!"

"Play him yourself! He's your fish, not mine!" Benjamin called back. "Just don't give him slack. He'll snap you in a second."

Old Tom seemed to tire for a moment and slowly rose toward the surface. Even Benjamin was awestruck at the size and the strength and the shimmering beauty of the big brown trout as he flashed in the sunlight. Then the fish shook his head and dove straight down. Marjie's pole nosed toward the water and then bent and bent.

Suddenly there was a sharp crack, and the cane pole snapped in two. But Benjamin had seen it about to break and made a fast stab for it as the broken half went shooting off the low bank. His grab was successful. But his motion propelled him clear over the edge and into the river with a mighty splash!

Benjamin completely disappeared into the water's depths while Marjie stood watching in shock. Before she could think to react, he bobbed back up to the surface, gasping for air, and started yelling for help.

She grabbed a long stick and thrust it out to Benjamin. He caught hold, and Marjie tugged him slowly to shore. In the confusion Marjie did not notice that Benjamin's right arm was firmly locked to the broken piece of cane pole, and somewhere in the depths Old Tom was still hooked on.

"Help me up the bank!" Benjamin sputtered, clinging to the grassy edge with one arm.

"You need two hands!" Marjie cried. "Let go of the stupid pole!"

"Are you crazy?" Benjamin screamed. "There's no way that fish is getting away! Give me a pull, and I can make it."

Marjie got his arm and tugged with what strength she had. Benjamin got up high enough to get a solid toehold and rolled back up on the bank. Surprising even himself, he jumped up and started to bring Old Tom in.

By this time the big brown trout was too weary to fight much and drifted slowly to the surface. Benjamin let out a "gosh!" and reached over the bank, taking the fish by the gills. Iridescent in his multicolors and rich brown spots, Old Tom was clearly the granddaddy of the river, but now he lay as still as a babe, as if acknowledging defeat at the hands of someone more determined.

Dripping with water and still panting for air himself, Benjamin knew he should scoop Old Tom out of the water before he revived, but that seemed too rough a treatment for such an august fish. Benjamin just stood there, content simply to pay Old Tom his utmost admiration.

"Pull him up before he gets away," Marjie suggested, although she could see that Benjamin was in no hurry. "Let's take him to town and weigh him. You'll probably get your picture taken and your name in the paper. That fish has to be over ten pounds."

Benjamin did not answer, but just continued to hold his grand old fish. Then he shook his head, reached in his pocket, and pulled out his jackknife. Handing it to Marjie, he said softly, "Open it, will you?"

"You're not going to—"

"Please, just open it," Benjamin said. Then he took the knife and gently found the spot to release the hook. With care he made a slight cut, and the hook came loose. Then Benjamin released his hold. The mighty fish slowly turned from his conqueror and swooshed his tail goodbye, then descended to the depths where he would reign as king for another day.

Benjamin sat back on his log. Long strands of wet hair dangled down around his eyes, and he was muddy from his waist to his old work shoes, but he had the most contented look on his face that Marjie would ever see.

Then it dawned on them both how hilarious the whole situation was. They broke into a simultaneous laughter that rocked the quiet woodlands and sent squirrels fleeing for their lives.

And before they left that spot on the trout stream, a mighty thunder was heard echoing down through the river valley:

"I CAUGHT HIM! I CAUGHT OLD TOM!"

24

THE PHONE CALL

When the *Wasp* arrived back at Scapa Flow on May 15, she reboarded her torpedo planes and dive bombers and prepared for her long trip back across the Atlantic. Unfortunately for Chester, there was no stop in Glasgow; he would have to depend upon the power of his pen to continue his romance with the lovely Scottish lass. Being so close and yet so far away from her, and knowing that the ship might never return to Scotland again, he found every hour nearly unbearable.

It was a markedly different story for Jerry. Two months' worth of mail had arrived, and the first letter he opened delivered the overwhelming news that in a matter of months he would be a father. It was such a numbing event that he immediately picked up his neat stack of letters and slipped away to a relatively quiet place on the ship's hangar deck where he could be alone. Then he pulled out the tattered envelope a second time and reread it to see if it really said what he'd thought it said.

Jerry wondered for a moment if he should go get Chester and have him read it out loud to make sure his eyes weren't playing tricks on him. The news just didn't seem to want to sink in. Like the light signals from distant ships at sea, somewhere on the outer limits of his mind he was sure it was saying, *You are going to be a father*. Ever so slowly the words kept tumbling through his mind, getting closer and closer to being consciously understood. Then reality finally struck!

"I am going to be a father!" he shouted as he leapt to his feet. "Marjie's going to have a baby!"

"Hey, what's the matter with you?" yelled a mechanic who had jumped down from his work on one of the planes. "You okay?"

"I'm not sure," Jerry said stupidly but truthfully. "But I'm okay. Sorry I scared you. I just found out that I've fathered a child!"

"Oops!" responded the mechanic. "Too bad for you. Which port is she in?"

"No!" Jerry exclaimed. "It's my wife. She's pregnant!"

"Oh" was all the mechanic had to say, and he turned back to his work, obviously uninterested in more of the story.

Jerry was bursting to find someone who cared, so he galloped away from the hangar deck to find Chester. He'd last seen his friend lying in his bunk, mumbling something about Margaret.

Racing into their sleeping quarters, Jerry reached up and grabbed Chester by the shoulders, then pulled him straight down out of the bunk. "What's wrong with you?" Chester yelled as he tumbled down and his own mail spilled to the floor. "You gone crazy or something?"

"It's Marjie!" Jerry cried out, trying to catch his breath.

"She's gone crazy?"

Grabbing Chester by the shoulders again, Jerry hollered, "She's going to have a baby! A baby! Do you know what a baby is, Chester? I am going to be a *father*!"

"Are you kidding?" Chester yelled back. "You and Marjie? Are you sure?"

"Read it for yourself," Jerry said, handing Chester the letter.

Chester sat down on the edge of Jerry's bunk and read it slowly. "Can't you read faster?" Jerry admonished.

"Goodness, me. Wow! You old son of a gun. Congratulations, Jerry!" Chester exclaimed, shaking Jerry's hand and patting him on the back. "I'll bet I can get you a cigar from the canteen. Wow! That's exciting . . . I think."

"Yeah, I can't believe it. Two nights and—what do you mean, 'I think'?" Jerry asked defiantly.

"Nothing, really, you know," Chester said, regretting he'd let the words slip. "It *is* exciting, you being a father and all. It's great! But, well, it just seems like it's not going to be so easy for Marjie with you away."

Somehow the reality of the difficulties that the pregnancy might have created for Marjie had not soaked into Jerry's consciousness yet. His face went pale, and every ounce of enthusiasm drained out his feet. If Chester had shot him with a gun, the response would have been similar. He asked Chester to move off his bunk, and then he crawled in to think it through.

Jerry's eyes focused on a spot under Chester's bunk and they did not even blink. He found himself suspended somewhere between glorious elation and utter despondency. And once again he found himself agonizing over his helplessness to change or affect what already was set in stone.

"I'm sorry I said anything," Chester apologized, standing awkwardly beside the bunk. "I'm sure everything will be okay."

"It's all my fault," mumbled Jerry. "You'd think a grown man would have realized. I never even thought about Marjie getting pregnant . . . not once."

Chester didn't know what to say, so he said nothing.

"She's over halfway along with her pregnancy, and I didn't even know about it until today. What am I going to do?" Jerry wondered out loud. "She's got no money, no home, and a no-good husband who's a zillion miles away. Maybe if I shut my eyes, it won't be happening." He closed his eyes for a while and muttered over and over again, "You stupid fool, you stupid fool . . ."

Chester picked up the letter and finished the last couple of paragraphs. "Did you read all the way to the end, Jerry?" he asked.

"Yeah. Why?"

"Maybe she said something that would help," Chester offered.

Opening his eyes, he gave Chester a blank stare. "Such as?"

"Well, she says not to worry because everything's working out okay," Chester said, looking down at the letter. "Your dad and her are getting along fine. But most important, she calls the child a gift of the love between you. That's a real powerful thought, Jerry."

"A gift, eh?" Jerry sputtered. "A gift for what? Seems to me that it's more like the result of my stupidity."

"Don't you ever say that to Marjie!" Chester warned. "You're going to hurt her bad if you keep talking that way. You need to think about it for a minute. Is the child the result of your love for Marjie?"

"But I didn't think—"

"That's not what I asked about," snapped Chester. "Just answer the question."

Jerry was surprised that Chester was getting so upset. "Okay. Yes, Marjie is pregnant because of my love for her. But—"

"Because of your shared love, a new life is coming into the world," Chester argued. "Something wonderful happened there, Jerry. Something special. There's never been and never will be another person like this baby. That *is* a gift, and I'm going to tell you that it's a gift from *God*, even though you made me promise not to push God at you. You can say you didn't plan it, and you didn't, but I'll venture to say that Someone bigger than you did have a plan. Just because it's not going to be easy doesn't mean it's not a gift. And if Marjie believes it's a gift, well, I just suggest you give it a chance."

With that, Chester spun around and stomped away. Jerry didn't move a muscle from his bunk. At the moment he really didn't care if Chester was mad at him. He knew that Chester was right that he could hurt Marjie if he ever said the baby was anything but a gift, but Jerry wasn't sure he could feel that way himself. He certainly had not planned on or chosen a child to come into the world yet . . . and he felt that the child was the result of his poor decisions. Now he had made a mess for his wife that he could do nothing about.

———— ✐ ————

The end of May brought a long ride across the Atlantic for both Chester and Jerry. Chester missed Margaret so much that he spent most of his spare time writing letter after letter. And Jerry wrestled the whole way with his doubts. When he could muster up the faith to believe what Chester had said, then he caught a sense of the joy of coming fatherhood. But those fleeting moments of happiness were dwarfed by a towering sense of personal failure.

When the proud *Wasp* steamed into the Norfolk Navy Yard for repairs and alterations, many of the men on board—Chester included—were delighted to get their first four-day passes. Because the trains were too slow to get him to Minnesota and back in four days' time, one of the chaplains who had befriended Chester asked him to come home to Pennsylvania with him. It wasn't like going home, Chester explained to Jerry, but anything beat staying on the ship.

Meanwhile, Jerry was only given a two-day pass. And the first two days that Chester was gone, Jerry spent working nearly around the clock reprovisioning the food supplies and ammunition of the ship. The long, hot hours seemed only to intensify the wall of frustration he felt inside.

Although Jerry did not know what he would do during his two days of leave, he determined that the first thing he would do was call Marjie. Just the thought of hearing her voice after six months' silence was so tantalizing that he could hardly wait to get off duty. And no matter what he was feeling, Jerry was going to tell her he was delighted they were going to have a baby.

Finishing his final shift, Jerry grabbed a quick shower and a change of clothes, then dashed away from the ship to an office section of the naval yard that had telephones the sailors could use to call home. He was so excited that he wasn't quite sure that he'd be able to get the right information to the operator. But he managed somehow, and before long the call was being patched through.

Jerry waited anxiously for Marjie to pick up the phone, but he heard nothing—not even a hint that her phone was ringing. Then the line went completely dead. Disgusted, he called the operator again and explained what had happened. She told him she would try again, but that the connections were not good and he would need to be patient.

Muttering under his breath, he held the receiver and waited. And waited. He could hear clicks, and occasionally he thought he could hear voices, but then the line went dead again. "Shoot!" he yelled and slammed down the receiver.

A tall, lanky sailor a couple of phones away looked over and shook his head. "You, too?" he asked. "I been trying to get through for two days. It's like playing roulette. You gotta be real lucky."

"I got no luck," Jerry growled, starting to sweat. "None. Everything goes wrong for me."

Nevertheless he continued to try over and over, getting angrier with the poor operator at each attempt. A few times Jerry thought the phone was ringing, and once he even thought he heard a voice answer, but then the line went dead again. None of his calls would make it through the long distance telephone wires that should have connected him to Marjie.

Finally the operator could take no more of his abuse and hung up on him. Jerry marched out in a rage and headed straight for the bars. He figured he could try again later, and maybe his luck would change. Just a few cool beers, he reckoned, could at least help him feel better.

But the bars were packed with men who were just as frustrated as Jerry. They were homesick to the bone, bored, angry, and desperate to have a good time in their few hours before heading back to war. It was a bad crowd that only seemed to fuel one another's passions. Most of the men were drinking hard, many of them were trying to pick up women, some of them were looking for a reason to fight, and whole groups would leave together for the red-light district.

Jerry made fast work of one beer and then a second before he said a word to anyone else in the bar. But the brew was so smooth and cool that it washed down easily, and he felt himself unwinding. He asked for a third beer and started talking to a sailor named Marvin who was sitting on the stool next to him at the bar. Marvin was also there to drink away his woes, and he was as sad and lonely and frustrated and angry as Jerry. He bought Jerry a fourth beer, and the two men shared the darkness of their melancholy. Before they became intoxicated from the alcohol, they were stone drunk on the wine of self-pity. Combine the two, and the picture gets ugly.

Sometime between the fifth and sixth beers, Jerry and Marvin spotted a booth and claimed it for themselves. Shouting above the loud din of the music, the two slowly lost count of how many brews they had poured down. Marvin talked freely about some of the women he'd been with and the fun he'd had on this leave. He seemed to make sense when he argued that his wife would understand that a man like himself needed to "pay a little visit to those pretty red lights." He said he was heading there one more time if Jerry was interested.

Jerry wasn't interested—at least he didn't think he was interested. He had no idea what he wanted except to feel good. Having been cooped up so long on the carrier, he felt he deserved to have a little fun. Finally drunk, he didn't feel great, but he didn't feel awful anymore, either. Maybe another beer would do it. Maybe something else would.

A couple of women had come into the tavern and were standing at the bar. Marvin waved at them to come join them at their booth. Jerry wasn't sure what they looked like; his eyes refused to focus despite his best efforts. The women brought their drinks and sat down beside the heavily sauced sailors.

"You boys looking for someplace to spend the night?" the dark-haired one asked, putting her arm around Marvin and squeezing him tightly. "We got a cozy place where the prices are right, and you can call it home tonight."

The blonde who was next to Jerry leaned against him, whispered something to him that he could not understand, and then puffed some cigarette smoke into his ear. Although he was barely coherent, Jerry suddenly realized he was trapped on the inside of the booth. He heard Marvin saying, "Sounds good to me. Let's get out of here. You coming, Jerry?"

Jerry felt like he was lost in a fog as he tried to get his mouth to say no. But the blonde had kissed him on the cheek and then had found his mouth. He had all he could do to shove her away, and the delayed reaction of his revulsion and his words came out loud and obscene and nearly violent.

The dark-haired woman got mad and poured her drink on Jerry, and he made the mistake of trying to shove her back as well. Marvin gave a yell for him to stop, the blonde dove out of the booth to escape, and then the mammoth bartender who doubled as a bouncer corralled Jerry by the neck and walked him to the door. A final shove landed him face down on the sidewalk.

Try as he might, Jerry could not get off the concrete for several minutes. The only thing that kept him from passing out was fear that the military police would pick him up and toss him in the brig. Finally another sailor stopped and helped him to his feet.

Jerry somehow made it back to the ship that night. But when he woke up in his bunk the next morning, he could not remember anything about how he managed to get from the bar to the *Wasp*. He was still wearing his clothes from the night before, and there was blood and booze on his shirt. Reaching into his pants, he discovered his last fifteen dollars were gone. Maybe the blonde had taken it. Maybe somebody else had. But he would never see her again, and he would never recall anything of his pathetic journey. He wondered if any of the other men in the large room of bunks had seen him stagger in, but he didn't ask around because he didn't really want to know.

Jerry lay in his bunk for nearly the whole day. He felt sick, but he was mostly sick of his life. He recalled Chester's story about the town drunk who would buy teenagers booze, and Jerry could see himself being sucked down that same drain. But as wrong as it all had been and as bad as he felt, there was still an inner voice telling him it was understandable, that probably a thousand other men of the ship had done the same thing that night, and what else was there to do to find a good time, anyway?

But he knew it was not a good time, and the familiar voice was beginning to sound hollow to him. *I'm gonna find something better*, he told himself. He did not know what it was, but he knew it would not be found in a bar or with other women. No matter how lonely he felt, he decided he'd rather sit on the ship than try to find pleasure that way again.

Then he thought of the Bible Marjie's mother had given him. It had been weeks since he had even looked at it. Idly he sat up and pulled out his footlocker, rummaging for the big, black book. Then he sat back on his bunk, idly turning the pages.

He could not fathom finding something in religion, but he also could not shake the heavy guilt from the previous night's adventure. It was a deep purple guilt. So in the quietness of his bunk, he started once again to read the story of Jesus in John's Gospel. And for the first time he wished he could have been there to see and hear what happened. He was sorry that it had taken place so long ago and that it was just a nice memory for grandparents and a few good people like Chester.

Nevertheless, he resolved for Marjie's sake to reform his soul. He could not allow himself to become less than the man she first agreed to marry.

25

THE LETTER

The sun was just peeking through the morning rain clouds as Marjie made her faithful trip down the farm driveway. The mailman so consistently arrived at 10:10 every morning that she thought she could set her watch by him. She was careful with every step to avoid the small worms and night crawlers that were still working their way across the gravel. Spotting a cardinal in the pines to the south of the driveway, she stopped to admire the bird's brilliant red sheen in the misty sunshine.

In this second week of June, it had been three months since Marjie had written to Jerry about the baby. Over the weeks that she waited for his response, she had experienced every emotion in the book as she made her daily pilgrimage to the mailbox. One day she was full of anticipation, the next of dread fear, the following of relative calm. This particular morning, with every step she took, Marjie replayed the angry lecture she would give Jerry if he just happened to be in the car with the mailman.

Jerry was not in the car, but when she flipped down the metal lid to the mailbox she found a very fat envelope from him. Marjie screamed so loud that the dogs lying by the barn started barking and came racing down the driveway to see what the disturbance might be. Benjamin came hustling out of the machine shed, wiping the grease from his hands, and breathed his relief to see that Marjie was not hurt. She waved the letter high over her head, and he knew the agonizing wait had ended.

The envelope contained an astounding dozen pages written the day before the *Wasp* was to pull out of Norfolk—Jerry did not know to where. Because he had mailed the letter from Norfolk and did not need to go through a censor, he recapped in detail much of what had happened on their trips to Malta and their return to Norfolk. And he shared deeply about his loneliness and frustrations and his love for her.

All that news was very welcome, but it was the final three pages she had been waiting for. In them she was amazed that Jerry could find such perfect words for his true reaction. She cried for joy when he told her that he was thrilled to be a father, and the words were truly from his heart. But Marjie was also glad that he did not gloss over his personal frustration with not being there to help support her or his feelings of failure in not having planned for this possibility. Knowing Jerry so well, she had been sure that he would experience both reactions, but his words gave her confidence his negative feelings had not overwhelmed him.

By the time Marjie had reread the letter to her complete satisfaction, the clouds had been driven back by the sun's powerful rays and a breeze was lightly shaking the raindrops from the dazzling green trees. It was turning into a perfect summer day— not too hot, not too cool, and just enough wind to bring all of nature to life.

Benjamin finished the work he was doing on a hay wagon and left the shed to join Marjie on the front steps of the farmhouse. He figured she had had enough time by herself, and he couldn't wait to find out what Jerry had finally said.

"Must be some good news in that letter, I reckon," Benjamin said with a smile. "You're looking mighty happy at the moment."

"It's a wonderful letter," Marjie said, rearranging the damp handkerchief on her large lap. "Jerry says he's thrilled about the baby, and I believe him because he also says he's real frustrated by the circumstances we're in. That's just like my man."

"Did he say what the dickens kept him from writing you sooner?" asked Benjamin. "He deserves a good tongue-lashing."

Marjie laughed. "Believe me," she said, "I've given him plenty of whippings in my mind. And now I find out that he didn't get his mail for two months! He couldn't get a letter off before they left Scotland and arrived in Norfolk. Then he even tried to call but couldn't get through."

"He's in Norfolk!" Benjamin exclaimed. "And we missed his call! Probably didn't even ring here. I hate that lousy phone."

"Before you go getting upset," Marjie said, "why don't you read the letter? He gives a lot of details you'll like. They were transporting British Spitfires to rescue Malta—can you believe they dared send a carrier into the Mediterranean?"

"No!" Benjamin said, already visualizing it. "I'd love to read it, but it's personal stuff between you two, Marjie. I got no business sticking my nose in there."

"If the mushy stuff bothers you, just jump over it," Marjie instructed. "Were you as romantic as your son?"

Benjamin tried to hold back a smile but couldn't. "Shoot," he said. "Let's just say that I wish I was a young man again. Martha got charmed right off her feet."

"I'll bet she did," Marjie said, trying to imagine what Benjamin was like in his courting days. "Why don't you sit here and read the letter while I go get the washing machine going? This breeze is just too good not to get the clothes out on the line. When you finish the letter, would you have time to pull the sheets from the beds and bring them to the basement? They are due for a wash."

"Be glad to," Benjamin said. "I can't do much in the field yet, anyway. Should be dry after lunchtime, though."

Benjamin did not anticipate that Jerry's letter would move him so deeply. He loved the details of the *Wasp's* travels and missions, but it was the tenderness of Jerry's love that got to Benjamin. For the first time in his life he could see straight into the heart of his son, and what he saw made him proud. There were so many ways in which Benjamin felt he had failed with his son, so much that had been left unsaid. And yet Jerry had still grown up strong and loving and responsible—the best son he could ask for.

Marjie finished a couple of batches of wash and wondered

what was keeping Benjamin. She took the basket of wet clothes out through the cellar door, hung them on the line, and then came around the front to see if he had forgotten her request. There he sat, puffy-eyed and staring off into the valley below.

Marjie did not need to ask. She just sat down beside him, and the two Macmillans hugged each other and cried, whispering of the love they each had for their missing hero.

In the late afternoon, Ruth stopped by and made Marjie take a rest. Although Marjie argued that she could easily bring the wash in herself, Ruth insisted on doing it for her. By the time Marjie woke up from her nap, Ruth had the clothes folded and ready to put away. She'd even gotten Benjamin's sheets back on his bed.

"You're going to spoil me rotten, Ruthie," Marjie said, somewhat embarrassed. "Don't tell Benjamin everything you did. He'll up my rent."

Ruth laughed. "You should be charging him! He's getting a good deal."

"Under the circumstances, I think it's been good for both of us," Marjie agreed. "He's like a dad and a friend wrapped in one."

"He's a changed man, Marjie," Ruth said quietly. "I've known him from a distance since I was little, but the past six months something's different about him. It's written over everything he says and does."

Marjie nodded reflectively. "He's changed since I've known him, that's for sure," she said. "Sort of like a turtle getting rid of his shell. Some of it I can understand, and some of it I can't."

"Say," Ruth said, noticing the time, "when do you usually have dinner ready?"

Marjie looked at the dining room clock and jumped up. "Why didn't you tell me it was after six? Here I've been—"

"Hold on!" Ruth interjected. "I raided your garden and picked some peas and lettuce. You fry the chicken, and I'll get the rest ready. We'll make it in time."

And sure enough, by the time Benjamin made it into the

house, the table was set and the food was steaming in the serving bowls.

"Smells like a feast," Benjamin called out as he finished washing his hands. "You ladies must've been cooking all afternoon. Ruthie, you come on over anytime you like. Marjie never feeds me like this when she's alone."

The two women laughed, and Marjie said, "Look, buster, you get what you pay for. I haven't had a raise since I got here. And you never paid me for those pigs you sold at a pretty penny. You're a rich man today because of me."

The women expected him to fire back a bantering reply, but instead his smile retreated for a moment as he sat down. He nodded and sighed. "I am a rich man," he said. "Richer than I could've ever dreamed. After we finish eating, d'you think I could tell you about it?"

Ruth and Marjie were caught off guard and just looked at each other, but Ruth recovered quickly and answered that they'd love to listen. Marjie had been joking, and now her mind was racing through all the events she could recall from which Benjamin might have come into some money. The pigs had brought a good price, but she knew that money had been used to pay for the seed corn and oats. If he had inherited something, she had not seen or heard a word of it.

Ruth kept the dinner conversation rolling. Benjamin was quiet but polite. And Marjie was stuck on wondering where Benjamin had found the riches.

They finished their meal, and Ruth cleared the plates while Marjie poured them coffee and brought the cream and sugar for Benjamin. The dishes would wait for more important matters.

"Okay," Marjie said as she sat down, leveling her sights on Benjamin. "The suspense is killing me. The only rich man I know around here is the banker. I suppose you're going to tell us that you struck gold in the woods."

Benjamin gave a crooked smile, but he did not laugh. Something had been brewing in him for a long time, and he seemed to have difficulty speaking about it.

Ruth caught his eyes and studied their expression. "It's about your faith, isn't it?" she said understandingly. "About you and God."

"And how'd you know that?" Benjamin asked quietly. "I ain't said nothing to no one. Didn't I tell you to listen to this girl, Marjie?"

"I'm confused," Marjie confessed. "Will you please just say what's on your mind? I don't like this guessing game."

"Okay, but you'll have to be patient," he said. "Do you remember a couple of months ago when you asked me what was different about me, and I couldn't explain it then?"

Marjie nodded.

"Well, I know now, and I want you to know, Marjie," Benjamin said. "Ruthie, I want you to know as well. If you think that I'm crazy, I want you both to tell me. Agreed?"

"Of course," Ruth said solemnly.

"This is gonna sound strange," he began. "It even sounds sorta strange to me. But over the past several months, something's been happening to me—and it's either changed what I believe about God, or it's taken what I did believe and made it come alive. I ain't never heard of something like this happening to anyone, so I didn't dare say nothing before."

He hesitated, then Ruth asked, "What has happened? Your secret is safe with us."

"It's really pretty simple," Benjamin acknowledged. "It's just that every place I go and everything I do, it's like this voice inside is speaking messages to me—and they're all about parts of my faith that've been a problem my whole life. At first I thought it was my mind telling me things. But after nearly sixty years of not being able to understand this stuff—what would make my mind capable of figuring it out now, when I ain't even been thinking about it?"

"You feel that God has been specifically speaking to your heart?" asked Ruth.

Benjamin squirmed a bit in his chair. "That's it. Almost sounds sacrilegious, don't it? But that's what it feels like. And the only reason I even dare hint it might be God talking to me is that I've been reading in the Bible every night before I go to bed, and I keep finding that it says right there in black and white what I've been hearing during the day."

Both women listened intently, but Marjie was worried. She could tell that Benjamin sincerely believed what he was saying, but it sounded crazy to her.

Ruth didn't seem worried at all. She said, "So nothing you feel you are hearing from this inner voice contradicts what you read in Scripture. So why not stick with Scripture?"

"I am," Benjamin stated. "But you know, I've been involved with Scripture ever since I was a little boy, and now it's like I'm hearing it all over again for the first time. And it's like I'm hearing these amazing sermons in my mind while I'm working that help me understand what the verses say."

"I think I understand," Ruth said, "but I've never experienced anything like that. What exactly do these messages sound like? Can you give me an example?"

"Sure," Benjamin said. "This is one of the messages that keeps repeating over and over—it's like I can't hear it enough times. You see, I've always believed that my faith in God is important. But along with it I've also believed there was a pile of things I had to do to keep on God's good side—you know, like believing in God and going to church and reading the Bible . . . praying, giving money, doing good to my neighbor, and all that. There was this long list in my mind that only got longer as I got older. And the more I failed, the more I felt that God was really mad at me. Sometimes I even got to believing that Martha's death was a punishment for all my failures. Anyway, I never could please Him—that's the way I felt."

Benjamin stopped for a moment and closed his eyes. His knuckles were white where he had gripped the table, but the pain on his face was mixed with wonder.

"I can't begin to explain exactly how the message has come to me about this," he went on, opening his eyes, "but the meaning is always the same—and it's just like in the Scripture. You know, 'For by grace are ye saved through faith . . . it is the gift of God: not of works, lest any man should boast.'

"That's the message, Ruthie. God has just taken away that

whole long list of stuff I thought I had to do to get Him to love me. He said that none of the things I've ever done, none of the things I'm doing, none of the things I'll ever do—none of that counts for nothing. It's grace that does it—just God's grace alone. He loves me, and He accepts me just the way I am, and that saves me. Nothing else. Absolutely nothing else."

Benjamin leaned his hands on the table and shook his head. "You know, all that's there in God's Word. But in all my years in the church I never heard or understood it—not once. Whether it's the preachers' fault or mine, I don't know. But I had this legal religion of works that God says He hates. What He says is, I'm supposed to love Him most of all, and when I do that, the works'll come. But I kept hanging on to that list of dos and don'ts.

"It was like I was so blind to the truth of Scripture that God has had to speak directly to my heart to help me understand. Do you think that's possible, Ruthie?"

"Do you believe that God is sovereign?" Ruth countered.

"Absolutely," he answered.

"Doesn't He have the right to speak to someone's heart directly if He wants to?" she went on.

Benjamin nodded.

"And if that someone is you, shouldn't that be okay?"

"I hope so," he said. "All I know is, it's changing my life. The Word of God has become a spring of life in my heart. I have come to understand what it means to say God is my Father, and I'm not afraid of Him anymore."

Once again Benjamin closed his eyes, but this time he cupped his hands around his cheeks and covered his eyes.

Marjie was still shaking her head in confusion, but Ruth was wiping away tears. She knew the same heartbeat of faith, and it was the profoundest joy to see the fullness of the Master's handiwork in this simple man she had known all her life.

"Is there anything else?" she asked, touching his hand.

"Well, yeah, but I gotta show you . . ."

He went to get his Bible, and Marjie excused herself from the table. She told Ruth she'd do the dishes and clean up the kitchen while the two of them talked. Ruth protested, but Marjie said she really didn't understand anyway, and it was more important that Benjamin have someone who could respond to what he was saying.

But while she was doing the work in the kitchen, Marjie could hear most of what was being said, and she would not forget the power of the words. It still all sounded foreign to her, but the simplicity of Benjamin's faith and the genuineness of Ruth's joy were nudging her closer to the loving Father who was at their center.

26

BILLY

"Well, whaddya think?" drawled Jerry's crew mate Roger Ogle. He wiped a gritty forearm across his face and stared out at the wall of concrete that loomed before them. "Y'ever see anything like it?"

"We got locks on the Mississippi back home in Minnesota," answered Jerry. "Used to fish up by them all the time. This one's a lot bigger, though."

"You ain't kiddin'!" Roger exclaimed. "When I first laid eyes on the *Wasp*, it was the biggest manmade thing I ever seen. But this here Panama Canal . . . well, I just ain't never seen nothing like it."

Jerry left his crew mate staring at the massive locks and returned reluctantly to his scraper. He was back to his least favorite duty of scraping and painting on the ship's topside. The tropical heat and humidity made the work nearly unbearable, so whenever he could, Jerry stopped to rest and watch the activity of the intricate Panama Canal lock system. He wasn't quite as awestruck as Roger. But he hadn't seen anything like this, either.

It was June 10, four days after the *Wasp* had departed Norfolk in the company of the new battleship USS *North Carolina* and a gathering of other ships making up Task Force 37. They had a new skipper now, Captain Forrest Sherman. More important, they were headed for a new theater of war, the South Pacific.

Early in May, almost simultaneous with the *Wasp*'s second run to Malta, the Americans had strategically turned back the Japanese thrust at Port Moresby, New Guinea, in the Battle of Coral Sea. One month later, from June 4 to June 6, an extremely undermatched American carrier force had smashed its Japanese counterpart in the pivotal Battle of Midway.

Those two victories severely weakened the Japanese naval strength—two Japanese carriers damaged at Coral Sea, four lost at Midway—and broke Japan's dominant position in the Pacific. But they also cost the United States two of its precious carriers: the *Lexington* at the Coral Sea and the *Yorktown* at Midway, leaving only the *Enterprise* and the *Hornet* operational in the western and central Pacific.

If they could get two more carriers in the Pacific, the American naval strategists felt they could finally take the offensive against the Japanese after having been on the defensive since Pearl Harbor. Four American carriers could be pitted against Japan's two remaining large carriers and a handful of lighter carriers.

The *Saratoga* had just arrived at Pearl Harbor from San Diego on June 6, after having been laid up for five months of repairs. That left a need for one more carrier. Thus the call had gone out for the *Wasp* to be hurried down to the Panama Canal and into the Pacific.

Before the ship left Norfolk, Jerry had finished what he wished he had done the moment his two-day pass started, and that was to sit down and write Marjie a long letter. It had taken him hours to think through every sentence and then to laboriously scrawl it down on the paper. But when he finally closed the missive with words of love and dropped it in the mail, he felt better than he had in weeks.

Chester had come back from Pennsylvania full of talk. For the better part of an hour he had chattered about the rich farm country and the huge dairy herds and the big, roomy barns he had visited. He had said it was worth the train ride just to walk the cornfields and smell the new-mown hay. But most of all Chester had talked about going to college and seminary after the war.

"There's just something inside me, Jerry," he had tried to explain, "telling me I'm supposed to be a pastor, and I talked with Chaplain Thornburg about everything that's involved in the ministry, and now I really do think that's what I'm supposed to do. I haven't written Margaret about it yet, but I just know she'll be pleased . . . I'm not sure how it's gonna work to be married and go to school at the same time . . . but I bet it's gonna work out, and . . ."

Jerry smiled, remembering Chester's excitement, just as he heard a shout from Roger. He wiped the sweat out of his eyes as he went to join his crew mate at the rail. The huge gates were gradually opening, and a smooth lake spread out before them.

"That's Lake Gatun," Roger told him confidently. "Jim Garvey told me all about it. And once we get past it we keep on following the Canal all the way across to the ocean. The other ocean, I mean."

They stood together for a while, gazing out over the warm, quiet waters and thinking of what awaited them at the end of their journey. Finally Jerry sighed. "Well, I guess we'll get there soon enough. Meanwhile, I got work to do."

But Jerry's work came to a standstill several more times as they followed the twenty-two-mile channel along what once had been the Chagress River Valley. Lush greenery loomed on either side of the canal like a green tunnel, and exotic-looking creatures kept poking their heads out to get a view of the huge carrier. Jerry and his crew mates stared back, fascinated, and fell far behind on their painting.

Eventually the ship passed through the Galillard Cut and two more sets of locks that lowered the vessels back down to sea level on the Pacific side. It had taken them more than eight hours to travel a little over fifty miles, but the trip had taken them from the Atlantic to the Pacific.

Once they were in Pacific waters, the convoy became Task Force 18, with the *Wasp* flying the two-starred flag of Rear Admiral Leigh Noyes. By now the ship had received the triumphant news of the Battle of Midway, and word had filtered down that at the moment they were headed for San Diego. But they were acutely aware that whatever their specific assignment was at the moment, their long-term destiny was before them in the warm, salty waters of the Pacific.

That's what I want, mused Jerry. *That's what I've been waiting for—a chance to pay those Japs back for all they've been doing to Americans. To pay 'em back for what they done to Billy.*

His boyhood friend had been increasingly on his mind since they got the word that they were heading for the Pacific. One of Marjie's letters had mentioned that Billy had been sent to the naval hospital at the San Diego Naval Base to recover from the burns he'd suffered when the *Arizona* was sunk. That letter was several months old, but Jerry hoped he might be lucky enough to locate Billy before they left San Diego.

Arriving in San Diego on June 19, the carrier immediately went to work taking on the remainder of her complement of aircraft, ten Grumman fighters and a dozen Douglas Dauntless dive bombers. Over the next few days the aircraft carrier was in and out of the naval base, running tests on the new planes. Once that was accomplished, they would be ready to sail to their next assignment.

All the time they were running the qualification tests, Jerry was nearly dying for the chance to take shore leave and try to find Billy. When he finally managed to get a pass, he came ashore and made a beeline for the naval hospital. He was so excited over the possibility of seeing his friend that he nearly started to hyperventilate along the way. But his excitement was mixed with dread. What would Billy look like? What had his injuries done to him? Jerry had seen a man once who had recovered from severe burns, and he recoiled at the memory of masklike skin and scar tissue. He hoped he could manage to control his horror if Billy looked like that.

"I'm looking for a sailor named Billy Wilson," Jerry said at the main desk of the hospital. "He was burned bad at Pearl Harbor and I heard he was in treatment here. In the burn unit."

"Just one minute," the woman at the desk said, fingering through a notebook of papers. Pushing her glasses back up on her nose, she looked up and said, "I'm sorry. There's no patient named Billy Wilson here."

Jerry shook his head in disgust, then he said, "How about William Wilson? That's his real name."

Looking back down, she said, "No. There's no one by that name. When was he supposedly here?"

"It had to have been in the last two months," Jerry said hopefully.

"We've had a lot of men pass through these doors," the woman said, not unkindly. "If you're willing to wait, though, I'll have one of the girls in the office go back through the records."

"Thanks," Jerry said. "But if she can—"

"—hurry, you'd appreciate it because he's your best friend and you're only here a few hours," she finished for him. "I hear it twenty times a day, sailor. Take a chair over there."

Jerry watched every second that ticked off his watch for the half hour it took the secretary to track down the whereabouts of Billy Wilson. She was still studying the paperwork when she called him to the desk.

"It looks like you're in luck, sailor," she said, looking up. "William Wilson finished treatment here two and a half months ago, but because of his injuries he was not reassigned to ship duty. For the time being, he's volunteered to stay in the burn unit and work as an orderly. My guess is that you'll find him there."

She gave Jerry a set of complicated directions and he ventured out, hoping he could navigate his way through the maze of long hallways. It was a sobering walk. He saw men who were badly maimed, and he heard moans and cries of pain from the rooms that lined the corridors. *Hope I never find myself in one of those beds*, he thought.

Finding the burn unit, he stopped and asked for his friend at the front desk. He was told that Wilson was helping in the whirlpool room and that he'd have to wait until he was available. But when Jerry explained his story, the woman pointed down the hallway to an open door. "Go right in."

Jerry could feel his heart pumping in his neck as he approached the door. He stopped and peeked around the corner into a chamber that held several low tubs with whirlpool jets at the front. At the farthest one, apparently waiting for the patient lying in the bath, stood Billy. He was looking out the window, his back to Jerry, but Jerry knew him immediately.

Jerry froze in position, overwhelmed with emotion at the sight of his best friend. He could see no sign of disfigurement on Billy; he looked just like the same kid he had played catch and gone fishing with a thousand times during their childhood.

The heartbeat in Jerry's throat turned into a huge lump as he stepped through the doorway. Then Billy turned around and spotted Jerry. He reacted as if he had just seen a friendly ghost. Something between a moan and a word escaped from his lips, then he broke into a loud cry that nearly sent the patient in the whirlpool to an early grave.

The two men who had been friends since they could first walk gave each other a mighty hug and could find no words to say. Just tears and groans. Then another hug and more tears and groans.

Finally Jerry was able to sputter out, "You're alive . . . thank God!"

"Just barely . . ." Billy whispered. "Us Greenleafton boys don't die easy! But I can't believe you're here. How'd you ever find me?"

"Marjie wrote and—"

"Excuse me!" a short, bulky nurse snapped as she came pounding through the door. "Is this a naval hospital or old home week?"

Billy jumped to attention. "Sorry, sir, but—"

"No apology required, Seaman Wilson," she broke in again, then smiled. "I've already heard the story about Seaman Macmillan. I'm ordering you to take the rest of the day off, and we'll cover for you. Understand? Get out of here, on the double!"

"Yes, sir . . . ma'am," Billy muttered, still reeling from the joint surprise.

"Gotcha, didn't I!" she said and laughed again. "You owe me, though, and don't you forget it, either. Now, get!"

It was when Billy took his first steps ahead of Jerry that the limp became noticeable. The faster Billy tried to go, the more pronounced it became.

"How long you got?" Billy asked, turning around toward Jerry once they had emerged into the hallway. "I'm telling you, you look great—must've put on twenty pounds. Guess that's what married life does for a guy, eh?"

"I've got till ten o'clock," Jerry answered. "And it's what navy life does, not married life; I was only with Marjie two days before I left for boot camp. You look great yourself. I was afraid you'd . . ."

"Look like the Phantom of the Opera?" Billy said, finishing the sentence. "It got my legs pretty bad, but somehow the top part of me didn't get burned."

"And the limp?" Jerry asked.

"It's paid for," joked Billy, then turned serious. "It's with me to stay, Jerry. No more double-play balls for me, I'm afraid. I'm lucky even to have legs."

Jerry asked, "Where can we go to talk? We've got a lot of ground to cover and not much time."

"There's a restaurant that's close," Billy answered. "There are some bars a bit farther down, but that's beyond my walking distance these days. Don't much care to go in 'em anyway."

"I like the restaurant," Jerry said. "The last couple taverns I've been in, I was lucky to walk out of."

It being the middle of the afternoon, they were able to stake out a corner booth in the restaurant and talk without interruption for long chunks of time. Both friends had a million questions for the other one, and they retraced nearly every step they'd taken since Billy left for the navy.

Billy described for Jerry the details he could recall from that fateful morning of December 7 on the *Arizona*. "I'd just eaten breakfast," he recalled, "and I'd gone topside for a smoke. Then I felt this heavy shock and there was a huge explosion. Found out later that was the *Oklahoma*—Jap torpedo keeled that whole big battleship over—trapped four hundred men down below . . ."

He stared into his coffee cup with unseeing eyes, then shook his head and seemed to remember where he was. "Then they hit us, Jerry. I saw flames spurting out of the number-two gun turret, and then the forward magazine just blew up. I saw the foremast start to topple over, and the whole forward part of the ship was on fire. And then my legs were on fire, too.

"Don't remember too much of what happened after that," Billy continued, "but I must've dove off and swam to the docks. I remember lotsa smoke and bombs going off real loud. Somewhere along the way I passed out, and the next thing I know it's midnight and I'm lying on a cot in the hospital with a thousand other guys and my legs're hurting worse'n I thought it was possible to hurt. Got an infection, too, and that complicated things. For a while, they didn't think I'd make it. But they finally got things under control, and that's when they sent me to San Diego."

Rolling his pants up a ways, he said, "Check these babies out. That old bulldog nurse scrubbed my stick legs until those scars finally gave it up. I owe her a lot more than just a couple hours off work."

Jerry was surprised at how good they looked. The skin was red and looked extremely thin, but there were no large patches of scar tissue.

"So why the limp?" Jerry asked.

"My knee got messed up from the infection," answered Billy. "The doc told me it's as good as it's going to get. At one point he thought he might have to take the leg off at the knee. I got a feeling these legs aren't going to appreciate the Minnesota cold. You wouldn't believe how sensitive they are."

"They're gonna have to take it," Jerry said. "I'd hate to think of farming without you down the hill."

"Don't worry about me," Billy returned confidently. "I'll be there. I could have gone home already, but I thought maybe I'd stay for a while and try to pay back the doctors and nurses that've been so nice to me. I had so much therapy that I'm just about an expert at getting scar tissue off."

"I'm gonna make those Japs pay for what they've done to you, Billy," Jerry said somberly. "I swear it!"

Billy looked down and shook his head slowly. "Is that why you joined?" he asked.

Jerry nodded. "Partly."

"I forgave 'em already," said Billy. "Revenge is a sorry motive, Jerry. Defense and honor are different, but you can't never satisfy revenge. Can't live that way and have any kinda life."

He had been staring out across the empty tables in the room, but now his deep-blue eyes locked on to Jerry's. "You gotta forgive them, too, Jerry. You gotta, or else it'll keep you all torn apart."

A waiter broke the conversation for a minute to fill their cups with coffee. He looked a bit miffed that they had stayed so long without ordering another meal, but he went back to the other customers without complaining.

"You seem a little different," Jerry said, still trying to figure out Billy's last statement. "Is everything okay? Except for your legs, I mean."

"Everything's fine," Billy said, running his fingers through his short brown hair. "Whaddya mean? I have slowed down a step, if you'll pardon the expression."

"No—not physical," answered Jerry. "It's like you seem so— so calm, I guess. And all this stuff about forgiving Japs. That's not like you, buddy!"

Billy laughed and nodded in agreement. "Seeing what I've seen and going through what I've gone through—I guess it's helped me see a little clearer what's worth living for. There was a lot of stuff that I was doing that I've found was a waste of time."

"Like what?" Jerry asked.

"Oh, things like wine, women, and song," Billy said with a smile. "I was running pretty crazy when I first got away from home."

"We sowed a coupla wild oats at home, as I recall," Jerry reminded him.

Once again Billy shook his head back and forth. "Nothing like what I got into when I was on my own," he said. "You would have been disgusted with me."

Jerry did not want to agree with Billy, but he had seen a lot of disgusting things since he left home. "So," he said, "you've stopped running wild. Is it because of the burns—what people will say if they see them?"

"No," Billy said. "That's really got nothing to do with it. Matter of fact, some of the other men I've seen that were burned worse than I was leave the hospital and go do crazier stuff than they did before."

"What's the reason, then?" Jerry asked. "You're not going to become a monk or something, are you?"

"Not on your life," Billy barked out a laugh. "Although I hafta admit I've gotten to know a priest here in the hospital. First priest I ever even talked to, and he sure was nice to me. But as to the reason, well, I'm not sure I can explain it well enough that people could understand, so I don't talk about it much."

"You're my best friend, Billy, and you always will be," Jerry said. "I want to understand—at least, try to. What's changed with you?"

Billy Wilson gazed out over the restaurant and ran his finger around the rim of his coffee cup for a long minute, gathering his thoughts. Then he looked intently into Jerry's eyes. "Ever since we was little," he said, "we done everything together. If you went somewhere, I was there. If I went somewhere, you were there. Wasn't nobody could pull us apart.

"But six months ago I walked all by myself into a country that's stuck somewhere between heaven and hell. I can't explain what it's like to stare death in the face at the same time you catch a glimpse into the face of God. It has to be the most awful, wonderful encounter you could ever imagine. I was so afraid I was going to die . . . and never get a chance to see the glory of God again . . ."

Billy paused and shook his head in frustration. "It's stupid trying to explain it," he said. "But let me tell you, Jerry, I ain't never gonna be the same person I was before it happened. Never."

Jerry couldn't do anything but stare. He'd prepared himself for physical disfigurement, but not for this. Fortunately, Billy saw his discomfort and jumped back in.

"You remember when we used to go hunting squirrels in the backwoods when we were kids? Sometimes when we got tired we'd lie down under the trees and just watch the clouds moving across that deep blue sky?"

Jerry nodded.

"You remember what we'd talk about?" Billy continued to question. "You'd be looking up, and you'd ask me if I thought God could see us."

"That I recall."

"I'd always say I didn't know," said Billy. "But I'm here today, and I really do believe it's because of a miracle. And I'm also here to say that He did see us back on them hills, He's been with us in our travels up to now, and He's gonna be watching all the steps we make in the future. I've really come to believe He sees it all, and He cares, too. That's why I've changed my ways, Jerry. It's a whole lot deeper than just giving up the wild life."

They talked until right up to Jerry's curfew, and then Billy walked Jerry back to the ship so they could squeeze in every minute of the precious leave time. Jerry had a hunch that this would be his only shore leave before the *Wasp* headed for their new assignment.

One last hug, and lifelong friends once again said a sad good-bye. Then Jerry stood watching and thinking as his friend limped away.

Billy hadn't said all that much about what had changed his life. But what he said struck deep in Jerry's mind. Deep as the ocean. Deep as a friendship. Soul deep.

27

OH, HAPPY DAY

It was only a few minutes past eight in the morning on the Fourth of July, but a warm, sultry breeze was already cutting through the Macmillan dining room. The parade that was going to be held in Preston later that morning promised an abundance of hot misery under the scorching sun. Despite Benjamin's most persuasive arguments, Marjie had refused to even consider going along with him to town. She had told him she had no interest in collapsing from heat stroke, but the truth was she hated people staring at her now that she was nearly seven months into her pregnancy.

She sat quietly at the dining room table, rereading for the fortieth time the letter she had received from Jerry the day before, and worrying.

The letter was actually quite cheerful. Jerry had written a very brief description of his trip through the Panama Canal to San Diego, and then he had added a couple of delightful pages about his time with Billy Wilson. Marjie had already called the Wilsons and read them that part of the letter.

But what troubled her about this letter was the fact that the *Wasp* was clearly heading for the South Pacific. As soon as she finished reading it for the first time, a chilling fear had drawn its fingers around her. The radio and newspapers had been full of the perilous naval battles that had already been fought with the

Japanese. The tide seemed to be turning for the Americans, but the danger was far from over.

What worried her most were the Japanese submarines that stalked their prey like pack wolves in the South Pacific. They were extremely efficient in silently locating and bringing down their enemy completely undetected. What if they did that to Jerry's ship?

Sleep had escaped her most of the night. Even with the window wide open, her bedroom had been muggy and breathless, and the vision of death that haunted her from the first had made its return in the silence of the dark. It had been so intense at one point in the night that she'd nearly gone to wake Benjamin, but she hated to disturb his rest.

Now, glancing out toward the barn, Marjie wondered what was delaying Benjamin. By this time, ordinarily, he would already be out of the barn, and his breakfast was already cooked and waiting on the stove. At this speed, he was going to have to settle for reheated eggs and bacon.

Marjie opened the letter one more time and studied the deep indents of the pencil work. She wished intensely that Jerry had never left—but then, she had wished that a thousand times since he'd gone. With each new morning, the challenge of having their baby without him seemed more overwhelming.

Her wandering thoughts were broken suddenly by the sound of barking. Marjie looked back at the barn and saw Blue barking from the doorway that led into the milk room. The other dogs were beginning to join in. She looked around to see what he could be barking at, but she saw no cars, no strange dogs approaching. Then Blue headed up toward the house and started barking at the front door.

Marjie got up from the table and went to the screen door. "What's the matter—" But then, somehow, she knew.

"Oh no!" she gasped, shoving open the door and hurrying toward the barn as fast as her seven-months bulk would allow. Blue ran before her and headed straight through the milk room into the milking parlor. It took a few seconds for her eyes to adjust to the shadows, but Marjie knew that all she had to do was follow the dog. He ducked around the back row of milking cows, and then she heard Benjamin's voice.

Dashing around the large Holstein on the corner, Marjie stopped in her tracks. Benjamin was sitting on a stool and leaning with his back against the wall, his faithful companion at his feet.

"What in the world is going on?" Marjie cried, trying to catch her breath. "Your stupid dog scared me to death! I thought I'd find you—"

"Lying in the gutter dead," Benjamin quietly finished.

"Well, what am I supposed to think?" she snapped. "You're late for breakfast, I hear barking, Blue comes running up to the house and raises a ruckus, then he leads me straight to you. It looked like you were in trouble!"

Benjamin sat motionless with a faint smile. "Well, I did send Blue up to get you, although I'm not sure how he figured it out. I ain't feeling too well, Marjie. I thought you best be here in case it gets worse."

"What gets worse?" Marjie asked, the dread rushing back in on her.

"Oh," Benjamin said with a sigh. "It's my left arm again. I got some pain shooting up—"

"You sit still," Marjie commanded. "I'm going to call the doc."

Benjamin shook his head no. "Wait," he said. "It's not that bad. Just help me up and walk me to the house. It'll pass."

"You're going to the doctor!" Marjie insisted. "And you're going to do what I tell you. Understand? Now, sit tight. I'm calling the doc, then I'll pull the car around by the door and drive you to the hospital."

"But—" His words were wasted. Marjie was already on her way out the barn door. Pumping adrenaline drove her to the house and over to the telephone faster than she thought she could move. But she couldn't get through to the doctor. "We'll find him," said the brisk voice on the end of the line. "You just get that man to the hospital as fast as you can." Grabbing her purse, she ran to the car and pulled up outside the barn door.

Benjamin had not moved. He did not complain when she helped him get up. And that worried her more than ever.

"It's going to be okay," he assured her weakly as she led him out into the bright sunlight, opened the car door for him, and helped him climb onto the high seat. His words did nothing to allay her fears.

She ran around the car and maneuvered her stomach behind the wheel, popped the car into first gear, and tore down the driveway, spraying gravel everywhere. "Don't you die on me, Benjamin!" she pleaded, looking over at him. "We need you too much . . . we love you too much! Don't you dare leave us!"

"Then slow down, for crying out loud!" he pleaded back, clutching the door handle as they flew around a corner. "If you're trying to scare me to death, you're doing a great job!"

Marjie did slow down, and they made it safely to the hospital. Doctor Sterling led Benjamin into an examining room, and Marjie was left in the empty waiting room. Every nerve twanged from their breathless journey, and something about the room—the sterile smell, the lifeless, oversized furniture, the high ceilings—made her feel nauseous. Reeling, she stumbled to the desk.

"You can wait out in the courtyard if you like," said the desk clerk in a professionally soothing voice. "It's much nicer out there, and one of the nurses will come get you as soon as we know something."

The courtyard was a lovely shaded spot furnished with a couple of park benches and secluded from the normal flow of traffic by several large elm trees. A nice breeze had picked up and seemed to be drying out the hot, muggy air, but Marjie hardly noticed. Had it been raining, she might not have noticed.

Marjie sat down on a bench and covered her face with her hands. Ever so slightly, her body gently rocked back and forth as she tried to comprehend what was happening. Tumbling through her mind was an avalanche of thoughts: *He's dying . . . I'll never see him alive again . . . Jerry will never get to know his pa better . . . our baby will never meet his grandpa . . . and he spent all those hours making that beautiful rocking horse when he should have been resting . . .*

"Oh, God, please," she whispered, looking up through the rustling leaves overhead. "Not yet. Not yet."

Then Marjie closed her eyes again. She could remember praying these exact words for her own father four years before, and it had made no difference. Once more she saw him lying there, emaciated by disease, tortured with pain; and an intense wave of anger rolled over her, and once again she felt the old bitterness rising within. "It's all your fault," she blurted aloud. "You're responsible, God. You're going to take Benjamin away from me, and then you'll let Jerry die, too. I hate you!"

Not a tear had been shed before that, but the venting of her rage tore loose the dam that restrained the tears. Marjie wept and wept, with large sobs and gasps for air. Wept with the pain of losing her father, and now with the pain of feeling that Benjamin was slipping from her grasp, that she could do nothing to stop it.

Finally the rage abated, and the buckets went dry. Marjie sat motionless, except for the occasional blinking of her reddened eyes. Silence reached deep into her soul and arrested every faculty. Complete silence reigned within. And somewhere in those moments the words that Ruth had asked her to weigh in the balance of truth pressed back in upon her consciousness.

Until this moment, Marjie had refused to consider Ruthie's question: "If God were cruel, or if He did not care, how can I explain Jesus dying on the cross in agony and pain?" It had been so easy to blame all the painful things on a God who stood away with His arms folded. But suddenly she knew she must face a Jesus with His hands outstretched, nailed to the cross.

"Why did you do it?" Marjie whispered.

"For you" echoed from within. "For you."

Marjie closed her eyes tightly, and for the first time she opened her heart to the possibility that somehow, despite all the things she could not understand, God really was love. Then she recalled something else that Ruth had said: "I wanted my mother alive, but that didn't mean it was the best thing for her, or for my dad, or for me. By drawing the straight line of how it had to be, I had set myself up as God. I had to let that go . . ."

The force of those words was like a warm breeze cutting through a frozen river in the spring. All the pieces of her arguments began to break to pieces and wash away downstream. She was tired of trying to hold on and play God. She had to let her father go, and she had to let Benjamin go, too . . . and Jerry as well. She had to trust them into the bleeding, outstretched arms of Jesus. To let Him be God.

"For you" came again. "I died for you."

She bowed her head and was overcome with wonder. "How can you love somebody who has despised you so?" she cried softly.

And then she had another thought, one that seemed to come from outside herself. "It was me, wasn't it?" she moaned. "It was me that put you there on the cross. It was my sin, my selfishness that brought you down. Oh, I'm so sorry, God. How could I have not seen you? Oh, God, I believe in you. I believe in your Son. Please save me from my own darkness."

Now the words were flowing, almost praying themselves. "I give you my dad. And I give you my dear Benjamin. He belongs to you, right now on the hospital bed, but I ask you to share him with us a little longer because we really need him in our lives, if you can hold off for a while." And then she hesitated. "And I want to give you the love of my life, but I ask you to look into my heart and know what Jerry means to me. He is yours, he is not mine, but please, please protect my love. And, somehow— oh, please show him what you've shown me. Please be his God."

Marjie didn't move for a long time. She just sat there, feeling like the weight of the world had rolled off her shoulders and she could breathe again.

She whispered, "I am not God," and though it seemed like a foolish thing to say, she knew that it held the key to releasing her anger and fears.

"God is God" sounded even better. She stood up and called it out, "God is God." And she felt the profound liberty of being free from hate, free from sin and guilt, free to start life all over again.

When the nurse came out later to get Marjie, she met a new person—composed, at rest, and prepared for the worst.

"How is he, Beth?" Marjie asked as the nurse came into the courtyard.

"He's doing fine," the nurse answered with a smile. "The doctor says that Benjamin's been pushing too hard and needs more help. But it wasn't a heart attack."

Marjie shut her eyes and shot up a brief thanks. "Can he go home, or will he need to stay?"

"Doctor Sterling said he can go home if he promises to behave himself," Beth answered. "But he absolutely must cut back, or he could just as well shoot himself."

"You may not have noticed," Marjie said. "But that man's as stubborn as a mule."

"Aren't we all?" the nurse replied. "But you know, I think this spell got his attention this time. At least, it's the first time I've seen him give the doc a listening ear. If you can give him a little push about getting help around the farm, I think he'll be willing."

They went back inside, and Marjie found Benjamin standing by the door waiting to go. He looked as happy to see her as she was happy to see him, and it was Benjamin who reached out and pulled Marjie as close as her swelling stomach would allow.

"That was too close," he whispered.

"I was so afraid we'd lose you," she returned.

"You know," he said, "a few months ago, I was thinking that the sooner I could die, the better. Today, I told the Lord I was hoping for some more time. I don't think my time's up yet."

Marjie hugged him tighter and nodded her head. "I don't think so, either," she said. "But we've got to find a way to help you slow down—that is, if you want to meet your grandchild in a couple of months."

"Please, don't even talk that way."

"Then let's go home and see what we can do about it," Marjie urged.

"We're going to miss all the Fourth of July celebrations, aren't we?" Benjamin said.

"Not all of them," Marjie answered. "There were some fireworks in the courtyard while you were in with the doc."

"Really?" he said. "I didn't hear a thing, and the windows were open."

"I'm the only one who heard them," Marjie explained. "Get in the car, and I'll tell you all about it."

28

GUADALCANAL

The *Wasp* sailed out of the San Diego harbor on the morning of July 1. Jerry stood on the flight deck looking back toward the naval hospital, glad to have found his friend. For a brief window of time, home almost seemed close again. But thoughts of home turned poignant and painful when the reality of where they were heading began to sink in.

When Jerry told Chester what Billy had said about staring death in the face, Chester just listened silently, saying nothing.

"What's with you?" Jerry finally asked, a little irritated.

Chester looked away and took a deep breath. "Look, where we're going, I've got a feeling we're gonna be staring at the same face. And it's a face I'd prefer not looking at just yet. I was hoping to get married first."

"Did you hear something about where we're going?" asked Jerry.

"No," answered Chester. "But we didn't come all this way just to turn around and go back to bonny Scotland. Can you imagine getting into the kind of fighting that happened at Midway?"

"I think I get your drift," Jerry said. And then it was his turn to be silent.

The *Wasp* began its Pacific tour by sailing for the Tonga Islands, serving as protection for five transports carrying the Second Marine Regiment toward an unknown destination. Day and night they steamed steadily south, ever watchful for the enemy, yet seeing nothing but an occasional glimpse of the transport ships they were escorting.

The Pacific, with its vast sweep of gentle waves, was quite a different experience from the choppy, dark Atlantic. Somehow it seemed both friendlier and more ominous. The rains were warm when they washed the decks, and the stars that crowded the skies when Jerry stood watch were both foreign and lovely. It was hard to believe that enemy subs could be gliding beneath the lively, phosphorescent water, that at any moment a Japanese bomber could roar overhead out of the star-studded skies.

It was on these long Pacific days and nights, with their peaceful surface and their dangerous depths, that Jerry began to pull out the Bible in his footlocker more often. The pages always fell open to the point where Marjie's father's ring had indented it— the same ring that now circled Jerry's finger. So he started reading there, with the passage that Sarah had said was Robert's favorite, the ninety-first psalm. It quickly became his favorite as well.

As he stood his watches, especially the long, nervous night watches, Jerry developed the habit of reciting the words of the psalm over and over. He still did not know what it meant to "say of the Lord, He is my refuge and my fortress," but he loved the sound of the words. He clung to the promise that "there shall no evil befall thee, neither shall any plague come nigh thy dwelling." And he hoped that the *Wasp* qualified as a "dwelling."

En route to Tonga, the carrier developed serious engine problems. Chester, still serving in the machine shop, told Jerry privately that he didn't think they'd be able to continue. Somehow, though, the carrier managed to keep moving, and on July 18 they reached Tongatapu Island, where they replaced the ship's starboard high-pressure turbine. Then they headed off, curving around to the southwest and then north again through the Coral Sea.

By that time it had become clear that something major was in the offing. Every level of combat readiness was being stepped up. The airmen worked intensively, practicing day and night operations to hone their skills. And a vast armada of American ships was gathering—carriers, battleships, troop transports. Jerry overheard one of the pilots who'd just returned from a practice run say, "The whole horizon was littered with ships. They were everywhere, all over the sea, as far out as the eye could reach."

Whatever they were headed into, Jerry knew it was big. And then, with ever-increasing frequency, he began to hear the word *Guadalcanal*.

On July 4, the Japanese had reached out from their major base in Rabaul, on an island in the Bismarck Archipelago, and landed on the largest of the Solomon chain, Guadalcanal. Allied planners had realized that if the enemy was able to operate land-based aircraft from that key island, then Allied control of the New Hebrides and New Caledonia area, to the southeast, would be immediately imperiled. Rather than wait until the Japanese got too firmly entrenched, they had proposed to drive the Japanese out of Guadalcanal before they could complete their airfield.

Preparations for the invasion of Guadalcanal had proceeded with the utmost secrecy and speed. The *Wasp*, together with the carriers *Saratoga* and *Enterprise*, had been assigned to the Support Force under the command of Vice Admiral Frank Jack Fletcher. The carriers were to provide air support for a landing by a division of Marines on Guadalcanal and its neighbor island Tulagi.

Now, six weeks after the Americans had turned the tables on the Japanese at Midway, the three carriers were slicing northward through the Coral Sea in company with most of Admiral Nimitz's Pacific Fleet. "D-day" had been set for August 1, but the late arrival of some of the Marine transports pushed the date to August 7.

Providence seemed to have smiled on the Allies as the bows of the carriers turned for the final run to Guadalcanal on August 5. Heavy clouds and rain blanketed the sea on which the assault convoy and the carrier groups advanced, cloaking their approach. Japanese search planes either did not penetrate the weather front or failed to see the armada as it plowed onward.

It was a miserable day to be standing at battle stations, but Jerry had grown accustomed to the rain and stood ready at his gun. About noon he was looking straight up into the sky when the heavy cloud cover suddenly parted for a brief moment. There in shocking full view above the ship flew a huge Japanese bomber, a four-engined Kawanishi flying boat. But before Jerry could even pull up his twenty-millimeter cannon, the clouds closed back down, and the enemy bomber was gone. Not one gunner on the ship had been able to fire a shot, and somehow, miraculously, the bomber had not spotted the carrier. But the men on the deck looked from one to another with widened eyes, severely jolted by the close call.

All it would take, Jerry realized, would be one bomb or one torpedo. In a matter of seconds, it could be too late, and there would be no time to launch the planes or even shoot back. He shivered in the warm drizzle, feeling more exposed and vulnerable than ever in his life. And suddenly the words of the now-familiar psalm ran through his mind. *He shall cover thee with his feathers, and under his wings shalt thou trust. . . . Thou shalt not be afraid for the terror by night . . . nor for the destruction that wasteth at noonday.*

The rain was coming down harder now, and he hunched his shoulders against the pelting pellets of water.

Don't know about the feathers, he thought, *but I sure could use some cover right about now.*

From the time the ship left the Tonga Islands, Jerry felt like all he had done was stand watch on the guns, eat, and occasionally sleep. But he was as ready and as eager for combat as any of the airmen. And as he went to stand night duty on the evening of August 6, Jerry could sense that something was up. No one was talking yet, but the tension among the airmen was running high.

That evening the *Wasp* steamed westward toward Guadalcanal until midnight, screened by the *San Francisco*, the *Salt Lake City*, and four destroyers. Then they came about, and Jerry noticed a change in course to the east. The order had come to reach a launch position eighty-four miles from the island of Tulagi, one hour before sunlight on the morning of August 7. Jerry felt a fresh breeze whip across the carrier's darkened flight deck as the first planes were brought up to prepare for launch. The night offshore was bright, but clouds hung heavy over the assigned objective. All was going well, and no Japanese patrols had been spotted.

At five-thirty that morning, the first planes from the *Wasp's* air group roared down the deck. Sixteen Grumman Wildcats were soon followed by fifteen Douglas Dauntless dive bombers. The formation of Wildcats quickly split into smaller groups that raced off to their assigned hunting areas.

Eight months to the day had elapsed since Japan struck Pearl Harbor without warning. Now, it was the Allies' turn to achieve complete surprise on every front through a combination of sound planning and good luck. The Japanese were caught flat-footed, and the Wildcats, flying in low over the disembarking Marines, shot up all the patrol planes and fighter-seaplanes that were in the area. Fifteen of the Kawanishi flying boats and eight Naka-jima float Zeros were destroyed. The Dauntless dive bombers had been dispatched to attack the Japanese antiaircraft and shore battery sites that had been pinpointed by intelligence reports. They laid their bombs on the money and wiped out the enemy sites in their first attack.

The raid was so successful that as Jerry counted the returning planes, he realized that only one plane from the sixteen Grum-mans failed to return. Later he discovered that pilot had run low on fuel and had elected to land on board the nearer *Enterprise*.

But that was not all for the day. At a few minutes after seven, twelve Grumman Avengers took off, loaded with bombs for use against ground targets. When the initial landing forces encoun-tered resistance, they had called for help. The dozen Avengers went in and blasted enemy troop concentrations, effectively si-lencing the enemy.

The first day's operations against Guadalcanal had proven a triumph, and the stories from the air crews spread like wildfire among the sailors of the *Wasp*. Some ten thousand Marines had been put ashore on Guadalcanal and met only slight resistance. On the island of Tulagi, however, the Japanese had maintained a stronghold, and by nightfall they still retained about one-fifth of the island. The three carriers and their screens called it a day and retired to the south.

As dawn came on the morning of August 8, Jerry had finally gotten a decent night's sleep and was once again at his battle station. Although the first day had gone well, no one expected the Japanese to let them have their way for a second day's running. The *Wasp* returned to its launching position and settled in to maintain a continuous patrol of Grumman fighters over the marine transport area. Suspecting a counterattack, a scouting flight of twelve Dauntless dive bombers was also launched.

Early in the day, the *Wasp*'s planes met only minor altercations. Later, word came that a large flight of Japanese planes was heading in the direction of the marine transports. The *Wasp* and her sister carriers accordingly cleared the decks for action, and the Wildcats began to roar out over the ocean in close formation. The enemy aircraft were successfully turned back before getting to the American transports. But the price was high. Out of ninety-nine fighter planes originally launched, twenty-one had been lost.

The orders for the carriers to withdraw came shortly after six that evening. Vice Admiral Fletcher had not only become concerned about the large numbers of enemy planes that had been sent out on attack and the loss of his fighter planes; he was also alarmed that the carriers' fuel supplies were running low. By sundown, the *Wasp* was powering south and east along with the *Saratoga* and the *Enterprise*.

"Well, we did it!" Jerry enthused to Chester as they lay on their bunks, trying to calm down enough to sleep. "Got those Marines there, and wiped out our fair share of Japs, too. But I hafta admit I'm glad to be getting out of that area. Had enough danger for one day."

"Yeah," Chester agreed. "But you know, I can't help wondering if we're pulling out too quick. The enemy's not just gonna lay down and let our guys take over the island. Seems like they might still need us."

"I know," Jerry admitted. "I was thinking that, too. Hope they can hang on."

"I imagine they could use some prayer," said Chester from his bunk.

And Jerry didn't argue.

The next day, word came that their suspicions had proved true. Early on the morning of August 9, a Japanese surface force had engaged an American one off Savo Island and retired with minimal damage to themselves. The Allied force had lost four heavy cruisers off Savo Island. These losses, coupled with the carriers' absence, would jeopardize the success of the entire Allied operation in the Solomon Islands. Although the Japanese had reacted sluggishly to the initial push by the Americans at Guadalcanal, they soon began pouring reinforcements down to contest the Allied forces. Only after six long months of heavy fighting would the Japanese finally surrender at Guadalcanal.

Meanwhile the *Wasp* spent most of the next month patrolling and covering operations for convoys and resupply units headed for Guadalcanal. Ordered south by Vice Admiral Fletcher, she did not participate in the Battle of the Eastern Solomons, which cost the Americans the use of the valuable *Enterprise*. The *Saratoga* took a torpedo a week later and was forced to depart the South Pacific war zone for repairs. That left only two carriers in the entire southwest Pacific: the *Hornet* and the *Wasp*. A sailor on either ship did not need to be a military expert to realize that they were now the prime target of the Japanese.

Jerry was surprised by the courage that the words of Psalm 91 seemed to give him during this time. Sarah had said that she thought he would need "a secret place under the Almighty's shadow" someday, and he could feel the dark day approaching like a bad dream.

And Jerry was far from alone in his sudden interest in finding a source of strength for the difficult days ahead. All over the ship, sailors were wiping the dust from Bibles stashed deep in their lockers. Whether they read it openly like Chester or secretively like Jerry, a very quiet revival began to take place on board ship. Many men stopped telling their dirty stories, and the profanity on the ship dropped to an all-time low.

"The destruction that wasteth at noonday" seemed to have cast a long shadow of fear across the ship and had turned hearts heavenward for the first time.

But it would not be the last time.

29

TEDDY

In the humid stillness of the early summer morning, Marjie sat at the dining room table with pen in hand, trying to wrap up the last of her correspondence to the Chief of Naval Personnel at the Naval Operating Base in Norfolk, Virginia. As she sealed the envelope, she hoped this was the last letter that the war department would require.

More than a month had passed since the scare with Benjamin, and the intervening weeks had been both difficult and productive for Marjie. Despite the extreme physical discomfort she had been feeling since the dog days of summer rolled in, Marjie had been far more troubled by the dilemma of what to do about Benjamin and the farm.

They had been able to hire a teenage boy from a neighboring farm to come over twice a day to help with the choring, but that help would only last through August. Fortunately, the field work had been light, and Benjamin was feeling much better. But late in July he had made a decision that promised to drastically change the direction of their future. Unless something changed, he had told Marjie, he just couldn't keep the place going through another winter. Once they got the field corn picked and stored in the crib in the late fall, he was afraid he would have to sell out.

When Marjie first heard Benjamin say it, she had been speechless. She had already been thinking about the same thing herself, but she hadn't known how to say it to Benjamin. To hear the words from his own mouth was nearly unthinkable.

It was Ruth who had come up with a plan of action for saving the farm. She had read of some young men who had returned from the war because of the hardships caused on the farm due to their absence. She had called Marjie and told her to contact the chairman of the county war board and explain the problem. Ruthie thought they might have a chance of getting Jerry home.

Marjie had written to Jerry immediately after the incident, but she had no way of knowing if the mail had gotten through to him. Rather than wait to hear, she had proceeded to contact the chairman of the county's war board. Hearing the details of Benjamin's health, the status of the farm's production, and Marjie's imminent motherhood, the man had agreed it might be possible to bring Jerry home. But it would be a complicated process.

The chairman had explained about the affidavits she would need to type and send to the naval personnel office in Norfolk. He, Marjie, Benjamin, Doctor Sterling, and two neighboring farmers would all need to testify to the situation and sign the papers. Even then, the affidavits would only be seen as supporting documents. Jerry himself would have to file a special-order discharge request.

The affidavits had taken a while to complete, and the wording had to be changed twice. But Marjie was hopeful, as she walked out to the mailbox with the last one, that the war department would look favorably upon their request. She thought they had made a good case that Jerry would be rendering an important service to the nation by keeping the farm in operation. After all, a forced sale of the Macmillan farm would also mean the loss of the farm's war units—the portion of crops and livestock pledged to the war effort.

I just hope Jerry gets my letters and sends that form in, she thought. *Guess I've done all I can do, though.* And she was surprised again by the unfamiliar sense of peace that persisted even behind her worry.

As she walked slowly back down the shady farmhouse driveway, she felt a sturdy punch, and her hand moved involuntarily to her abdomen. Since the heat wave had hit, the baby seemed to be constantly moving, stretching, kicking. The activity would have made sleeping through the night a near impossibility—if the discomfort of her extended stomach were not already keeping her awake. It seemed to Marjie that in the past weeks she had doubled in size. And while she wasn't looking forward to the labor pains, she was in a hurry to stop being pregnant.

Nearing the house, she heard the phone ring and did her best to get inside quickly. Still puffing, Marjie picked up the receiver. "Hello, this is the Macmillans'."

"Marjie," her mother said. "How are you doing? Nice and cool there?"

"Beautiful! Just like an iceberg. It's going to be such a scorcher that I can already hear the field corn snapping and popping," Marjie answered. "I'm doing okay, for someone who feels like a whale. I think I've got twins in here."

"Wouldn't that be jolly?" Sarah said. "Just what you need, another mouth to feed. But that's not why I called. I was wondering if there's any chance you could come over this morning."

"Well, let's see," said Marjie. "I don't think there's any problem. I need to get some food together for Benjamin, but after that I guess I can come. Something wrong?"

"I need to talk," her mother answered quietly.

"Is everything okay, Ma?"

"I can't talk about it on the phone," she said. "Somebody on our party line is probably listening in right now. This is private."

Marjie's mind raced to think of what might be going on. "I'll be over in a little while," she closed.

She had Benjamin and the neighbor boy's breakfast ready by the time they finished the chores, and then she made some sandwiches for Benjamin's lunch. He told her he was going to lie low for the rest of the day; it was just too hot to do anything. Marjie liked the fact that he had voluntarily slowed down. Especially on a cooker like today, she did not want to worry about him being out in the fields.

Pulling the car onto the gravel road, she noticed that the cows were already heading for the shade of the burr-oak trees. With the windows down and the breeze, it wasn't too bad inside the car as long as she kept rolling. But the size of her stomach made driving so uncomfortable that she soon wished she had asked Benjamin to drive her. She could barely reach the pedals, and when she did, she had to press so tight against the steering wheel that the baby kicked in protest.

Twenty-five minutes later Marjie was pulling into the Livingstone farmyard and parking in the shadow of the trees. She had noticed from the road that Teddy was out in the hayfield working on the fence, and she hoped he'd at least taken along some water and salt pills. It was a heatstroke day if there ever was one.

Marjie heard the screen door bang shut and saw her mother standing on the wooden steps. As usual, she was wearing her long gray dress, white apron, and heavy black shoes. "Did you say you had a whale in there, or just that you felt like a whale?" Sarah asked and laughed. "Maybe you do have twins!"

"I think so," Marjie agreed, giving her mother an awkward hug. "You should try driving a car in this condition."

"Not fun," her mother said. "Let's go inside and have some cold pink lemonade. You look a little flushed."

"Oh, I'm okay," Marjie replied. "But the lemonade sounds great."

Going into the dining room and sitting at the table, Marjie took a sip of the cold drink and thought back to their conversation at the table some eight months previous. What a sweet memory it held for her!

"So, you've been working on that special discharge for Jerry," Sarah said, reading Marjie's thoughts. "How's it going?"

"I put the last of the paperwork in the mail right before you called," Marjie answered. "Now it's a matter of either my letters getting to Jerry or else the war department contacting him. His signature on the request is the missing link. But the county chairman thought it would get approved."

"How's Benjamin doing?" Sarah asked.

Marjie smiled. "It's kind of strange," she said. "He made the decision himself, and he's perfectly relaxed about it. You wouldn't believe it, Ma. Benjamin has changed so much; I'm not sure Jerry would even recognize him."

"Sounds like your pa," Sarah whispered, tipping her glass and looking into Marjie's eyes with a significant expression. "People do change—sometimes for the better. You've changed, Marjie. And it's good. I wish you'd tell me more about it."

Marjie had seen Sarah once since the Fourth of July and had already told her what she experienced in the hospital's courtyard. Her mother had simply listened, and Marjie wasn't sure what Sarah thought of it. And she wasn't sure what she could add to what she'd already said.

"Maybe we'll get back to that," Marjie said, "but I came over because you had something you wanted to tell me. I've been going crazy since the phone call trying to figure out what's wrong. Please tell me about that first."

"Would you like some more lemonade?" Sarah asked, rising and heading toward the kitchen. "Tastes good on a day like today, doesn't it."

"What's the problem, Ma?" Marjie asked in mild exasperation, putting her hand on Sarah's deeply tanned arm as she sat back down. "You're worried about Paul in the army, aren't you? Have you heard news?"

Sarah took Marjie's hand and stroked it lightly with her heavily callused fingers. "I'm worried about Paul, yes, and about Jerry as well. I think of them almost every minute of the day. But that's not why I called."

"So what is it?"

"I shouldn't have called you," Sarah said. "It's just that this morning I sorta forgot that you had your own load of problems to carry."

"Ma, the next words you say better be the problem you called about," Marjie warned, "or the child I am carrying may never be driven over here to visit her grandmother."

Sarah gave a weak smile, then a somber stare. "It's about Teddy."

"It's about Teddy what?"

"That Markett girl he was crazy about—the one he's been

talking about proposing to," Sarah said. "She dumped him and ran off with some stranger and got married last week. Teddy's in a bad way."

Marjie didn't know what her mother meant by a "bad way," but she was silently pleased that Linda Markett was out of Ted's life. Marjie had heard that Linda was running around with a lot of guys, but she couldn't talk with Ted because he always got so mad when anyone got involved in his life.

"So Teddy's upset?" Marjie asked, hoping for some details.

"More than mad," her mother said quietly, looking out toward the barn. "He's hitting the bottle—bad. Every night since he found out, he's gotten drunker than the night before. Last night I had to help him get from the car to his room. Then he threw up all over the bedroom floor."

"Whew!" Marjie exclaimed in disbelief. "What have you said to him?"

"He's like a walking bomb, Marjie," her mother said sadly. "I say anything and he blows sky high. He's hurting bad inside, but he's like a wounded animal. I can't get that close."

Marjie shook her head, wrinkled her forehead, and gave a tired sigh, then sat up as the anger rose inside. After all the agony her mother had been through in her life, she shouldn't have to cope with this. "So there's nothing you can do?"

Rubbing her hands together, Sarah suddenly seemed to age in front of Marjie's eyes. "Nothing" was all she said.

"Maybe he'll get tired of it and quit?" Marjie suggested. "Or find another girlfriend."

Sarah nodded her head. "Or maybe he'll drink himself to death or get killed in a drunken car accident. You remember your Uncle Arty, don't you? He drank for forty years and finally rotted his liver.

"I'm too old for this, Marjie," she went on. "And I'm too tired to keep crying about it. But I don't have the power to take it away. I'm even scared that Teddy'll find out that I told you about it. He's doing crazy things."

Marjie had no idea what to say to her mother, but she reached over and hugged her as tightly as she could. Watching her uncle as a child, she knew full well the horrors that followed the path of a drunk. She shuddered to think that Teddy might end up hooked on the bottle.

Sarah whispered to Marjie, "The last time we talked, you told me about how you had to let go of your pa, and Benjamin, and Jerry. I've been doing a lot of thinking about that, and I think I need to try and do the same with Ted. I made peace with God a long time ago about your pa dying, but I was hoping you would help me with Ted."

"How?" Marjie asked. "Should I go out to the field and talk with him?"

"No," her mother answered. She was quiet for a long moment in her daughter's embrace. Then she ventured, "I'm embarrassed to ask, but I was hoping you would pray with me. I've been trying on my own, but I don't seem to be getting anywhere."

"You should have hinted to me on the phone," Marjie whispered. "I would have brought Ruthie along. She's real good at praying. Or Benjamin. He's so—"

"Shhhh," Sarah broke in quietly. "Ruthie's real nice, and Benjamin, too. But I want to pray with you."

"But I don't—"

"You prayed, and God heard you, Marjie," said Sarah. "Didn't you?"

"Yes, but that doesn't mean—"

"No one other than me loves Teddy more than you do, Marjie," her mother continued. "If Ruthie and Benjamin want to pray later, that's good, but today, now, please, let's you and me pray. I need you to help me give Teddy to God."

Marjie finally nodded. She knew her mother was right, that this was a prayer for a mother and a daughter, not for anyone else. They bowed their heads to pray their simple prayers. And the moment they closed their eyes God filled the room with something of His presence and glory. Neither woman could explain it later, but they knew that He was there, reading the deepest cries of their hearts, so that their words were a mere formality, an offering rather than a necessity.

Sarah would describe it later by saying simply that "God

came near." Marjie could not improve on that explanation. The effect it had was to bond them together closer than they had ever been, and it brought a richness of comfort to the depths of Sarah's heart. In a way far beyond her own understanding, she could truly trust that Teddy was in the hands of God, and God was free to be God toward Teddy.

That was the best thing she could have asked for.

30

TORPEDOES

Late in August, Jerry received a cluster of letters from Marjie that brought the distressing news about his father's "spell" as well as the special-order discharge request. Apparently the mail had been piling up until a ship that was heading out their way could bring it. Jerry had worried about his father's health from the day he enlisted, so the news did not come as a shock. But he was still upset to hear it, and deeply disappointed by the prospect of having to go home before his tour of duty was up.

He talked the situation over a couple of times with Chester, but from the moment he read the letters he had known he needed to file the form and request the discharge. His family's welfare and the farm were at stake, and he knew in his heart that by keeping the farm operational he would be serving his country even better than by manning a battle station.

He took the papers in to Captain Sherman, who read through the copies of the affidavits, briefly listened to what Jerry had to say, and nodded. Then he and Jerry signed the papers and sent them to Norfolk. The captain was sure that getting the papers approved was only a matter of formality, but he warned Jerry to be patient. In the navy, he said, nothing that involved paperwork ever went fast—except enlisting, of course.

The *Wasp* had once again drawn the duty of escorting military transports that were carrying reinforcements to Guadalcanal.

She and the aircraft carrier *Hornet*, the battleship *North Carolina*, and ten other warships were the covering forces for the five transport vessels bearing the Seventh Marine Regiment. Late in the second week of September, the convoy was thrust into known submarine waters. Tension on the ship mounted with every move.

During the day of September 14, and into the early afternoon hours of September 15, reports were pouring in of at least one Japanese carrier and two battleships, plus many cruisers and destroyers, prowling in the vicinity of Guadalcanal. It was also reported that a flying boat sporting the red-disk insignia of the Japanese had scrutinized the convoy about 11:00 that morning. Admiral Turner assumed this sighting had blown their cover and jeopardized their mission. Gauging the picture as "not reassuring," he resolved to withdraw temporarily and wait for a better opportunity. But he did not know how bad the situation really was.

Jerry was on watch on the port side aft that afternoon when he heard the frantic call from the lookout: "Three torpedoes—three points forward of the starboard beam!" The *Wasp* put over her rudder hard to starboard, but it was too late. Only moments later, two of the torpedoes rocked the ship on her starboard side forward, with catastrophic effect.

One warhead tore into the gasoline storage tanks, and a second exploded abreast the forward bomb magazine. Both hits unleashed convulsive shock waves. Aircraft on the flight and hangar decks were thrown around like toys and dropped on the deck with such force that their landing gears snapped. Spare aircraft secured to the overhead in the hangar slipped their moorings and collapsed onto the planes below, puncturing fuel tanks and sending rivulets of high-octane peril across the decks to mingle with fuel hemorrhaging from the fractured gasoline pumping system. Flames reared up on the hangar deck and began to play among bombs, depth charges, and ready-use ammunition.

The terrific jolt of the initial explosions threw Jerry to the deck, smacking his head hard against a pipe. As he lay dazed on the cold metal, he could feel a ceaseless series of additional explosions along the deck and inside the forward part of the ship. Intense fires were detonating the air tanks in torpedoes, powder magazines, and ready ammunition all over the ship, and the *Wasp* had taken a ten- or fifteen-degree list.

By the time Jerry was able to get to his feet, the pungent odor of smoke and the sight of flames leaping forward had become full reality. Suddenly furious, he flew to his battle station, but there was nothing in the sky overhead to shoot at.

All around him now was furious activity. Pilots scrambled to their planes, but there was no way to get either aircraft, gasoline, or ammunition off the deck. Some tried pushing their planes over the side to keep their bombs from exploding, but that proved impossible. Fire fighters raced to their hoses, but the water mains in the forward part of the ship had been broken by the force of the explosions. A heavy haze of smoke rolled over the rest of the ship, and an inferno was clearly raging below.

Hot pieces of metal began whizzing by Jerry, and he crouched down as low as he could by his gun. The ready-service ammunition under the flight deck had begun to go off, sending shrapnel skimming parallel with the deck; he felt like he was in the middle of a machine-gun barrage. He saw sailors on the flight deck crumple down, some burned, some with shrapnel wounds. While the fire raged on the deck, the explosion of a pair of two-ton aerial bombs blew the bomb tower high into the sky.

Captain Sherman slowed the *Wasp* to ten knots and had the rudder put to port to try to get the wind on the starboard bow. He then went astern with the right rudder until the wind was on the starboard quarter, attempting to keep the fire forward and to get the ship clear of burning oil on the water. Despite tempests of flame and a lethal rain of exploding ammunition, courageous officers and men continued to grab hoses to fight the fire, but only a trickle of water could be brought against the conflagration. Then all the communication circuits went dead.

Just after three o'clock, a huge gasoline-vapor explosion blew incandescent gases skyward on three sides of the ship's superstructure, burning Admiral Noyes about the hair and eyes. About five minutes later the number-two 1.1-inch gun mount was blown overboard, and the corpse of the gun captain was thrown onto the bridge, landing next to Captain Sherman. Three additional gasoline vapor explosions rocked the ship, and Captain Sherman appraised the situation with his key subordinates.

Although flooding presented no immediate danger, flames had enveloped the entire forward half of the ship, and the sundered gasoline tanks and forward magazines were in volcanic action. With many crewmen already dead or injured, there was no way to fight the fire effectively. And they were a sitting duck for any Japanese sub that might decide to aim another torpedo into their side. Just twenty minutes after the first torpedo hit, Captain Sherman made the painful decision to abandon ship.

Jerry was incredulous when he heard the two words being passed from sailor to sailor. "Abandon ship?" he yelled over at another gunnery seaman. "Is that official?"

"Sure is. Direct from Captain Sherman. Loudspeakers are out—pass the word."

The fires and explosions had played havoc with usual abandon-ship procedures, but a group of seamen were already carrying injured to the port side, and Jerry hurried to help. Running over to a burned pilot who was completely unconscious, Jerry picked him up over his shoulder and headed through the smoke. Sailors were cutting loose the rubber life rafts and letting them drop into the water. By this time splotches of black oil could be seen in the water near the stern; on the starboard side forward, the oil was already burning furiously.

Half a dozen able-bodied seaman went over the side and scurried down the ropes into the life rafts. Jerry and other seamen worked together to gently lift the wounded, place them in a wire stretcher with a rope through its center, and lower them over the side into the waiting hands of the men below. Some of the wounded were so badly burned that Jerry didn't think they were going to make it.

Once the injured men were safely in the rubber rafts, Jerry grabbed a life belt and was about to grab a rope and go over the ship's side with the hundreds of other sailors already sliding down ropes from the deck. Then he thought of Chester. There was no way, in the confusion of smoke and fire, to tell whether his friend had made it out, but Jerry felt he had one shot at finding him. If he had managed to escape the fires below, Chester would have had to come out on a corner of the hangar deck that Jerry thought he could still reach. If Chester was not there, Jerry figured he could go overboard on that deck and have the advantage of being forty feet closer to the water.

Covering himself as best he could with a fire blanket, Jerry descended a pitch-black, smoky stairway to the hangar deck. He had taken these stairs so many times that he knew every step and turn, but the smoke got him coughing so badly that he almost didn't make it. A port of light led him forward, and he rolled through the opening onto the devastated hangar deck, gasping for air.

Only a few men from the hangar deck were still making their way over the side from this deck. Jerry looked around to see the battered remains of dozens of planes, along with the bodies of several sailors who had been blown to bits.

Chester was nowhere in sight, so Jerry headed for the far corner of the deck. He figured he would come down in the rough water at a point that was farthest from the burning oil slick. But as he ran, he thought he spotted a movement by a pile of big tarps that had been thrown around in the explosions. Turning toward the movement, he saw first a boot and then a leg sticking out from under one of the tarps. And the leg moved.

Adrenaline pumping, Jerry tossed the heavy tarp aside and looked into the ashen face of his friend. Chester's hair was singed, and black smoke marks ringed his nostrils and eyes, but he was still breathing—slightly. A deep gash had ripped Chester's leg, and the blood had pooled around it on the deck.

"Chester!" Jerry screamed, dropping alongside his friend and taking his head in his arms. "Chester! It's me, Jerry! Can you hear me? Answer me!"

Chester's eyes fluttered, and for a brief moment he smiled. One eye opened slowly, and Chester coughed and sputtered back to consciousness. Finally he whispered, "I never thought I'd see you again. When that tarp hit me, I thought the grim reaper had me."

"Save your stories for later," Jerry cried. "We gotta get you over the side as fast as we can. The ship could blow at any second."

"I'll never make it, Jerry," Chester said, shutting his eyes again. "You go! You've got Marjie and the baby to think of. I'm not afraid to die."

Jerry shook Chester again and shouted in his face, "If I have to carry you down myself, you're coming with me! You hear! If we die, we die together. Now sit up!"

He pulled Chester up to a sitting position, and Chester shook with a coughing fit. But then he seemed to revive a bit more, and his eyes struggled to focus on Jerry's face. "And you said your dad was a stubborn old cuss," he said. "I can't let you die, Jerry. Go on now, or all the boats will be gone. You can't swim."

"They're probably already gone!" yelled Jerry. "Don't you worry about me swimming; I'll take care of myself." He pulled Chester up and lifted him onto his shoulder. "Now hang on!"

Jerry was so pumped up that Chester felt like a light bale of hay as he carried him to the corner of the hangar deck. There was no one left to help him get Chester down; Jerry knew he was on his own. He propped Chester against the rail and studied the chaos in the water below the ship. He wondered if he could make it down a rope with Chester on his back, but it was obviously too far. Then he got an idea.

Pulling up one of the ropes that was hanging over the side to the water below, Jerry tied it around his friend's waist. Then he helped Chester to stand.

"Can you hold the rope and keep yourself up if I let you down the side of the ship?" Jerry asked.

"I can try," Chester said weakly.

Helping Chester over the rail, Jerry carefully lowered him down along the side of the ship. Chester was able to hang on to the rope and helped with keeping himself vertical. When he touched down into the warm water, Jerry retied the rope onto the rail so his friend wouldn't sink if he passed out again.

Chester waved up to Jerry that he was all right.

Then Jerry took one last look around the mangled inferno, grabbed another rope, and made his descent over the side of the mighty *Wasp*.

31

A Sweet Package

The first labor pain came while Marjie was standing at the kitchen sink in the early evening of September 14. It was a short contraction, but the combination of its intensity and the surprise nearly doubled Marjie over. She gasped and grabbed the countertop, wondering if Benjamin had heard her from the living room. She had planned not to say anything to worry him until she felt it was time to make a move for the hospital.

Marjie had been anticipating this moment for the past weeks and had tried to rehearse several scenarios of what she would do when the first contraction came. But until the pain subsided, she couldn't remember any of them. As the muscles relaxed, she took a deep breath, put the last of the dishes away, and turned to see if she could make her plan work.

Stepping into the living room, Marjie was surprised that Benjamin had already dozed off for a quick cat nap, still holding the local newspaper in his hands. *If he only knew*, she thought. She coughed slightly to see if she could resurrect him.

Benjamin's eyes popped open, and he smiled a bit sheepishly. "Just closed my eyes for a second," he said. "Was I snoring?"

"Like a trooper," Marjie said and laughed. "No. You weren't snoring. But you were drooling."

"Cotton picker," he said, reaching up to touch the corners of his mouth. Then he shook his head and knew he'd been had again. Both he and Marjie laughed this time.

"Listen," Marjie said. "I'm beat. I think I'll head to bed a little early. Big day ahead."

"Sounds like a good idea," Benjamin agreed, as she had hoped he would. "I think I'll head that way, too, soon as I finish this paper."

"At the rate you were going, it's going to be a late night for you," Marjie quipped and started toward her bedroom door.

"Say," Benjamin called out, and Marjie turned. "What's the 'big day' tomorrow? You got something planned?"

Marjie had known the minute she said those words that she might have blown her cover. She had to think fast. "Going to town, aren't we? Didn't you say you had to pick something up at the lumberyard? And I'm low on groceries."

"Oh, that's right," he remembered. "Guess I didn't think of that as too big a day."

"Guess you aren't nine months pregnant, are you," Marjie joked, hoping Benjamin wouldn't keep on talking until a second contraction came.

"Since I started eating your cooking, some folks might think I am," Benjamin commented, patting his stomach. "How you feeling tonight?"

For a moment Marjie thought he must have heard her gasp in the kitchen, but he didn't look too concerned. "So far so good," she said honestly. "Just a little tired. Good-night."

"See you in the morning," Benjamin said. "Should I be pulling the car up by the sidewalk, you think?"

"No," she said reassuringly. "We'll have plenty of time when it happens. Good-night."

"Good-night," he closed.

Marjie ducked through the bedroom door and shut it quickly. Then she lay down on the bed, figuring the next contraction would come in a matter of seconds. But fifteen minutes went by and nothing happened. She wondered for a while if it had simply been a false alarm and she had retired early for nothing. But five minutes later, another pain came on with a short burst of fury. Marjie held her breath and bit her lip to hold back a yell, but then the pain subsided, and she took another deep breath and looked at the clock on her bedside table.

The doctor had told her she needn't bother coming into the hospital until the contractions got regular. But now that she had a taste of what was ahead, Marjie seriously doubted she could keep her secret from Benjamin till then. The house was so quiet you could hear a mouse running across the hardwood floors. And it would take just one moan from Marjie for Benjamin to be revving up the car as well as his blood pressure.

She got up and changed into her housecoat, figuring she might as well get as comfortable as possible and ready to go, if need be. Stepping quickly out of her bedroom and into the bathroom, she brushed her teeth and turned sideways to get a good look at her stomach in the big mirror. "Unbelievable," she whispered. "Time to get you out of there."

As Marjie stepped back into her room, she noticed that Benjamin had drifted off again. She closed her door with a thud, and she could hear the papers rattle as he came back up for air. Pretty soon she heard the light click off and his steps plodding up the stairway to his bed. *So far, so good*, she thought.

Marjie had read everything she could get her hands on about the delivery process. She knew that labor could vary drastically from woman to woman, but she was fairly confident that she understood the basic steps her body was going through. She knew she'd need to be patient until the contractions started coming regular. That, she suspected, was easier said than done.

Grabbing the extra pillows that she had stashed under the old metal-framed bed, Marjie positioned them on the bed in such a way that she could sit up and read and yet recline enough to relax. Getting back into bed, she reached over to the nightstand and picked up the copy of a novel by Grace Livingston Hill that Ruth had given her. Marjie had read a previous book by the same author and liked it, so Ruth had passed along her copy of this newer book.

She turned pages for a while, but she couldn't concentrate on the story; too many thoughts were whirling through her head. Finally she put the book back in its place and got up to shut the light off. Then she stepped over to the window and gazed out.

In the moonlight, her garden was framed by the silhouettes of the tall pines that formed a natural windbreak behind it. The neat rows—except for the raspberry plants—were now withered and spent; all that remained to be brought in were the potatoes, but Marjie hated to add the chore of digging them to Benjamin's list of work. He had taken over choring by himself again, now that the neighbor boy was gone, and there simply weren't any young men in the country to hire for help.

She had heard nothing from the war department since she sent the affidavits, nor from Jerry since he'd left San Diego. Marjie accepted the fact that communicating in war was very difficult. But tonight more than any night, she ached to have Jerry with her. She'd gotten by so far, but this was the moment she needed him by her side.

Where is he tonight? she wondered. *Is he thinking about me, about the baby?* And then the feeling struck her almost as strongly as the labor pain: *Something's wrong. He's in danger!*

And then she thought of all those nights she had lain awake, tormented by visions of the man she loved sinking into the sea.

I gave that up, she reminded herself. *I gave those worries to God. And I've got to keep doing that. I've got to save my strength for the baby.*

Aching with loneliness and fear, Marjie stared out the window, reaching deep inside for the comfort she had only recently begun to know. Standing there in the quietness of the cool fall night, Marjie prayed for Jerry and for Benjamin, then for herself and the baby, that all would go well.

She stood at the window until the third contraction began, and she clutched the window frame to get through this one. As soon as it passed, she climbed back into bed and tried to relax. She figured she had better be lying down next time, or she might fall.

It became an endless night for Marjie, marked off by the bedside clock and the wrenching pain. She would have two contractions that were six minutes apart, then several contractions that were spaced by fifteen minutes. She would doze off to sleep, then suddenly be wakened by the oncoming wave of agony. She got up and walked between some of the pains, but that didn't seem to help much either. A couple of times Marjie gave muffled groans, but her concern about Benjamin's waking was unwarranted. She could hear him snoring away like a hibernating bear in the bedroom above her.

The first hints of daylight on the horizon came as a great relief; somehow, the brightening sky seemed to promise that change was on the way. The contractions, though still very erratic, were getting longer and harder.

About six that morning she heard Benjamin's alarm go off. Then she heard his footsteps as he put on his barn clothes, clomped downstairs, and headed out to do the chores. Once he was out, Marjie rose and went to the bathroom to wash her face and try to gather her hair into some semblance of decency. The water felt refreshing, but when she toweled off and opened her eyes to look in the mirror, she was not impressed with the woman before her. *Maybe this is why Jerry headed for the navy!* she thought. *I'll scare the doc to death when he takes a look at me.*

Marjie wasn't hungry, but she went to the kitchen to fix herself some toast and grab a cup of milk for nourishment. While she was staring out on the dimly lit windows of the barn and eating her toast, a very strong contraction took hold, and Marjie doubled over. Without Benjamin in the house, she let out a yell and held on to a chair. This one felt like it really meant business.

Wishing she hadn't been standing, Marjie headed back for her bed and lay down again. It wasn't long until another contraction hit, followed by another, and then another. Eight minutes apart. Then it jumped back to twelve minutes. Then to eight minutes again. There were no more lulls. If they started coming any faster, she wondered if she could make it out to the barn to get Benjamin, or if she should call Ruth, who would still not have left for teaching school.

By seven-thirty, the labor pains were steadily rolling in at seven-minute intervals. In between the contractions, she got up and called the hospital, telling them she'd try to be there in an hour or so. The nurse reassured her that the doctor would be there and that she was probably still a ways from delivering. Marjie also called her mother, who promised to be there as soon as Ted could drive her.

When the farmhouse door opened at eight o'clock, Benjamin stepped into the entryway and was surprised not to smell the eggs frying and the coffee brewing. He knew instantly what was going on. Rushing to Marjie's bedroom and looking in, he cried, "It's time?"

"It's time," Marjie said as calmly as she could. "My water just broke."

"I'll call the hospital first," Benjamin said in a panic. "What's the number?"

"I've already called."

"What's the number? I don't know the number!" he cried again.

"Benjamin, listen!" Marjie raised her voice. "Now you've got to settle down, or your blood pressure could give you trouble. Listen to me. I have called the hospital."

"Okay! Why didn't you say so?" Benjamin said, trying to settle down. "I'll get the car."

"Wait!" Marjie pleaded. "Take this suitcase out with you. Pull the car up. Then come back in and help me walk out. Got it?"

"Got it!" he said, grabbing her tattered leather suitcase and hustling out the door.

Marjie heard the doors slam, the dogs start barking, the car roar to life and spin gravel as it pulled in front of the sidewalk. Meanwhile she had gotten up and moved into the dining room, sinking into a chair. The front door banged, and Benjamin flew right past her and into her bedroom. "Marjie!" he yelled, then peeked back around the doorway.

It was all just too funny, and Marjie broke into laughter. Benjamin walked back into the dining room slightly dumbfounded, but her laughter seemed to break through his confusion. He flashed her a grin and said, "I'm ready if you are."

Benjamin gently helped Marjie to the car, and fortunately there were no contractions until she got into the seat. Benjamin looked on with concern as she let out a moan and grimaced. He shut her door, ran around to his side and hopped in. Popping the car into gear, he took off down the road.

"Why didn't you tell me when the labor first started?" Benjamin asked as he poured on the gas down a straight section of road.

"I thought one of us had better get a good night's sleep," Marjie said. "You never know if it's false labor, anyway. You could sit all night, and then the labor just stops. Who knows? Maybe they'll tell me to go home."

"Nobody's going to tell you to go home," Benjamin said. "No matter what, you're going to stay there till you have the baby. You should have told me, though. It makes me mad."

Marjie laughed again. "I love you, Benjamin. You're the most wonderful father-in-law I could have hoped for. But be thankful for the night's sleep. Soon as the baby comes home, you can kiss sleeping through the night goodbye."

"That's what you think," he said with a return laugh. "I can sleep through a tornado."

They pulled up in front of the hospital, and one of the nurses was waiting with a wheelchair. With a little tug from Benjamin, Marjie was out of the car and heading for the delivery room. She kissed an anxious-looking Benjamin goodbye at the desk, then waved back at him as she rolled down the hallway. "Go downtown and get yourself some breakfast," she called to him, then gasped as another contraction hit.

Once in the delivery room, everything went much quicker than Marjie had expected. They got her a gown, and the doctor came in and casually chatted with her about her progress. Her contractions were down to three minutes and harder than ever. He told her he'd like to check on her dilation, and when he did his inspection, the relaxed look on his face turned to a serious frown.

"You should have come in sooner," the doctor said to Marjie and looked over at the nurse who was watching. "We're going to have to hustle on this one. Beth, get the gear! This baby's on the way. I'd say within half an hour."

Both the doctor and the nurse moved with lightning speed as

they collected instruments and supplies. Meanwhile the contractions came even closer together, and it seemed like one was coming on top of another; there was nearly no let-up. Then Marjie's back started to hurt, and she found herself gasping for air.

The doctor reached over and said, "Here. This will help you relax. You've got to relax and let the contractions do their work. Take a deep breath."

He put a mask over her face, and she breathed in. The effect from the gas was immediate. "That was wonderful!" Marjie said dreamily. "Do it again."

"Not until you need it," he answered. Then he stepped out of the room, leaving Marjie and the nurse together.

"Do you think the baby's really close?" Marjie asked.

"You better believe it," Beth assured her. "You're fully dilated."

Ten minutes later the doctor reappeared, obviously ready to go to work. A couple more whiffs of laughing gas and Marjie was completely relaxed. "This isn't so bad," she said. "I should have had some of this at home last night."

"We save it for the end," the doctor said, positioning himself for the delivery. "Now, when the next contraction comes, I want you to push. The baby is ready to come."

"I'm not sure I can feel a contraction," Marjie said.

"You'll feel it, believe me! Get ready to push," commanded the doctor. "I can feel the baby's head. Here comes the contraction—push now!"

Marjie was amazed at how good it felt to push. She gave it a mighty surge.

"Now, relax," he said. "Save your strength for the next one."

Marjie shut her eyes and felt her head whirling like a top. She took several deep breaths and then came the command, "Push!" She did, with all her strength.

"Okay, relax!" the doctor called. "It's coming now. One more push and I think we'll have ourselves a baby!"

"You're doing great," Beth whispered in Marjie's ear. "One more push! Give it everything!"

"Ready, Doc?" Marjie called out.

"Not yet," he said. "Wait . . . wait . . . okay, now!"

Marjie pushed with all her might as Beth supported her from behind.

"Almost!" cried the doctor. "A little more!"

Marjie let out a scream, and it was over. In the doctor's hands was a little pink bundle of wiggling arms and legs.

"It's a girl!" he announced. "It's a beautiful girl."

Releasing every muscle in her body, Marjie sank back down on the delivery table and began to cry. The baby let out a cry as well, and the doctor handed the baby to Beth, who went to work cleaning her up. After she had the baby wrapped in a soft, white blanket, she placed her in Marjie's arms.

"She's perfect," Beth assured her.

Marjie looked on with wonder and tears and took the tiny person into her arms. She gazed at the little pink face with its big eyes and wise, old-woman expression. And she stroked the silky dark hair. She could find no words for what she was feeling. She only wished that Jerry could share this moment and the newness of life she cradled against her chest.

"Do you have a name picked?" Beth asked.

Marjie nodded her head yes, then she found her voice again. She said quietly, "Her name is Martha. She's named after a very wonderful woman that I never had the chance to meet. When you go back out and see my father-in-law, would you tell him the name? It's going to be a bit of a surprise for him."

32

TIME STANDS STILL

When Jerry dipped into the salty water, he immediately realized that the coarse rope he'd made his descent on had burned all the skin off his fingers. But the burning and the pain from the bleeding wounds soon went away when he took a look at Chester. His friend was still clinging to the rope, but his face looked pale and bloodless.

"Chester!" Jerry called out, reaching out with one loose hand and pulling Chester close. "You're going to make it, buddy! Hang in there!"

Chester shook his head. "I'm not doing so good, Jerry," he whispered. "Take off while you can. If the ship goes down, she'll suck you down with her if you're too close. Go now. You've done everything you could. I'll just hang here and see what comes by."

All around them the waves were rolling, and the water surface was coated with a film of oil. Though he had his life belt on, Jerry knew he could never get Chester away from the boat and stay afloat long enough to be rescued.

Chester was right. They'd both go down if they tried to go together.

Men were swimming in every direction around the ship, looking for an escape route. Jerry looked down the ship's edge and was surprised to see one last rubber life raft coming by, piled thick with men. Unless he could get Chester on that raft, he knew his friend was a goner.

Jerry called and called, but the seamen in the boat were focused solely on getting away from the ship. His only chance was to intercept the raft somehow.

In a split second Jerry decided he had to risk it. He let go of Chester and then, fighting a suffocating burst of fear, let go of his rope. The life belt did keep him afloat. He made some feeble strokes, then thrashed wildly, and finally made some headway against the waves. He bobbed and paddled and jerked, and finally got close enough. "Help!" he screamed.

"We've already got too many on!" one of the drenched seamen called back.

Jerry pointed to the side of the ship where Chester was now slumped down unconscious. "It's my friend! He's gonna bleed to death."

The sailor yelled to the others, and the lifeboat turned back toward the ship. Two of the men jumped from the raft and swam past Jerry to Chester. By the time the raft pulled alongside, one of the seamen had cut Chester loose, and the others pulled him aboard. The two men in the water waved for the rafters to pull away, and they took their chances clinging to the side of the raft.

In the confusion and rush, Jerry had been forgotten, and now he bobbed in the waves that quickly pushed him back against the side of the *Wasp*. He wished he could have grabbed hold of the raft as well, but it was too late now. Already exhausted from his first attempt at swimming, he grabbed one of the hundreds of ropes that were hanging down from the ship's rails and took a rest.

Jerry knew he couldn't just relax and go with the current of the waves, for they would carry him around to the side of the ship where a burning oil slick was consuming everything on the water's surface. There was also danger from the ship itself. Ammunition was still exploding on board. Now and then a white-hot piece of metal, like a tracer bullet, would come soaring out over Jerry's head and drop into the water with a sharp hiss. He feared that any moment the whole ship would blow and scatter him to the sharks.

But it didn't seem possible to get away from the ship, either.

As he hung there on his rope he watched many of the men trying over and over to swim against the current, only to exhaust themselves. Even the best swimmers could only get so far from the ship before a big wave would roll them back again. One sailor without a life belt managed to get far away from the ship, but it wasn't long before he tired and slipped beneath the waves.

There seemed to be no way out, no way to escape certain death. Helplessly, Jerry bowed his head and hoped that God was looking down as Billy Wilson had said He was. He closed his eyes. And then the nightmare surrounding him was suddenly and completely shut off. Jerry could not tell how long the silence reigned; it was almost as if time stood still. And there, in the silence of his mind, he watched a painful parade of all the worst things he had ever done.

One by one his sins marched past him, filling him with regret and sorrow. There were the unkind words he had said to his mother, the fights he had had with his father, the thoughtless taunts of the fat boy at school, the broken window he had never reported. Even his beloved fantasies of revenge against the Japanese joined the procession, and now they looked tawdry and shameful.

When the vision cleared, Jerry did not open his eyes. Come what may, he was not going to die and take those sins to a deep ocean grave without at least trying to talk to God about them.

But then came the problem of what to pray. He could not think of what might be appropriate to say to God. In fact, he could only think of one prayer, so he thought he'd try it.

There by the burning inferno of the *Wasp* hung a penitent sinner, clinging to his rope and bobbing in the water. Only one ear could hear the words being whispered, but it was the only ear that counted:

Our Father which art in heaven,
Hallowed be thy name.
Thy kingdom come.
Thy will be done
On earth, as it is in heaven.

Give us this day our daily bread.
And forgive us our debts,
As we forgive our debtors . . .

Jerry didn't finish the prayer. When he said the phrase about being forgiven, he knew instantly and beyond any shadow of doubt that his prayer had been answered. It was an explosion in his heart—an explosion of peace with God in his heart. Jerry knew that if he did not survive this day, he was ready to meet his God.

Popping his eyes open, Jerry looked out on the sea with new vision. His soul was calm, and he could think clearly again. But nothing more had changed, except that the men trying to swim away from the ship seemed to be approaching exhaustion.

He thought for a moment about making one big push to escape the ship and perhaps get lucky. If he could make it out to open water, maybe one of the destroyers in the convoy would pick him up. But then his favorite words from Psalm 91 came back into his thoughts: "There shall no evil befall thee, neither shall any plague come nigh thy dwelling."

He wondered what those words might mean, if they meant anything now. They surely hadn't meant, as he had hoped, that the ship was safe from a torpedo. But what if they meant that the safest place was right where he was now? He had seen sharks out in the distant water, their dorsal fins slicing the waves. Besides, he knew he could never paddle strongly enough against the waves. Jerry hoped the verse from the psalm might apply, and so he decided to stay put. Maybe the other ships in the convoy would make a rescue attempt.

Tiring from holding the rope, Jerry tied several of the overhanging ropes together and fashioned a kind of swing to sit in. This way, he figured, he could save his energy. Also, should the ship begin to go down, the position of the knots would tell him of the change, and he'd be able to make one stab at getting far enough from the ship to avoid the sucking vacuum of water it would create as it sank.

An hour passed, and one by one the seamen who had tried

to swim away gave up and drifted back to the ship. Jerry found himself busy tying ropes and knots together for the most exhausted men and pointing others to where they could join hold as well. Quite a gathering of salty dogs—more salty now than ever—were soon hanging off the sides of the crippled carrier.

Finally, after more than two hours in the water, the stranded sailors cheered to see a whaleboat from one of the destroyers make its approach. A seaman on the whaler tied a line about his waist, dove in, and swam toward Jerry.

"You men all right?" he sputtered as he neared the *Wasp*.

"We're here," Jerry answered. "But we'll be happier when we're someplace else."

He grabbed the rope and held it while his drenched crew mates moved toward it. Then the rescued men and their single rescuer clung to the rope and pulled their way to the small craft. Some of the men were too tired to pull, so Jerry and the seaman from the whaler collared two men each and held on for dear life as the men on the whaleboat pulled them in. Once over the side, Jerry collapsed in the bottom of the boat, too exhausted to sit or to stand. But even as he lay there, he reflected on how wonderful it felt to be out of the water.

The whaleboat took them to the destroyer *Salt Lake City*, where the magnificent crew welcomed them warmly. First they had risked great danger by staying in the submarine-infested waters to pick up the survivors; now they offered showers, clothes, and delicious, steaming coffee.

Dusk was coming as Jerry joined many of the men on the main deck. The *Wasp* was still a beacon of fire two miles away. When darkness fell, Jerry could see the flames more clearly as they devoured the ship before his eyes.

The destroyer *Landsdowne* had drawn the grim duty of destruction, and around eight o'clock that night she fired five deadly torpedoes toward the dying ship's fire-gutted hull. Three hit, but the brave old girl still refused to do down. By now, the orange flames had enveloped the stern, and the carrier floated in a burning pool of gasoline and oil. Finally, at nine that night, she rolled over on her side and sank, bow first, to her early grave.

Wherever Jerry looked or went on the destroyer, seamen from the *Wasp* were either talking together in hushed tones or standing by themselves, gazing back to the spot where oil continued to blaze on the water's surface. Many of the men wept openly as the ship had gone down, carrying some of their friends with it. All of them felt a strange mixture of grief for those who had perished and tremendous joy that they were still alive.

Jerry was told that a large storage room in the lower part of the ship had been set up for the rescued sailors to sleep in. But instead of heading for bed, Jerry sought out the sick bay to look for Chester. Jerry did not know which destroyer might have picked up his friend, and he wondered if Chester was even alive, but he could not sleep until he checked.

The sick bay was packed with men who bore varying degrees of injury, from superficial scratches to massive burns. All the medical personnel were too busy tending emergency cases to bother with knowing who had been brought in, so Jerry just walked into the bay to see for himself. He saw many men he either knew or recognized, but no Chester. Then he came around a white screen that housed another gang of the injured.

"Looking for somebody?" a voice called out. There, beaming a smile from ear to ear and propped up a bit on his cot, was Chester.

Jerry rushed to his friend's side and dropped to his knees alongside the cot. "You made it!" Jerry exclaimed, giving Chester the hug of his life. The two just stayed that way for quite some time. It was a typical sight around the sick bay that night.

"You saved my life," Chester said passionately. "I was shark bait hanging there."

Jerry was too overwhelmed to speak. All he could do was hang on to Chester and shake.

"I owe you everything," added Chester.

"Don't you ever say you owe me again!" Jerry finally was able to say. "You'd have done the same thing for me. Besides, you helped me more than you know."

"How's that?" asked Chester.

Jerry pulled back and fixed Jerry with a big grin. "All that fancy preaching of yours finally paid off."

"What?"

"I met God in the water, Chester!" Jerry exclaimed, not knowing what words to hang around what had happened. "Or God met me. Anyway, I was ready to die, just like you said you were."

Chester looked on with wonder. "You're not pulling my leg—"

"Nobody pulls your leg, sailor," broke in a navy doctor who had apparently sewn up Chester's wounds earlier and now had appeared from behind the screen. He was obviously less concerned about happy reunions than about Chester's health. "Now, you've lost a lot of blood, and you've got to rest—friends or no friends. We patched you up without a transfusion because we're out of blood. If you get weak again, we're going to have to get some fast."

"What type do you need?" Jerry asked.

"O positive," said the doctor. "Got a spare pint or two?"

"Coming right up," Jerry said, rolling back the sleeve of his newly donated shirt. "O positive. Take as much as you need for this man. Where's the needle?"

As it turned out, Chester did not require the blood that Jerry gave, but another seaman who was in a lot worse shape would not have lived through the night without it. "Two lives saved in one day," he joked with Chester.

When the exhausted Jerry finally stumbled down to the dark, overcrowded room that was filled with sleeping cots for the men from the *Wasp*, he was not prepared for what he saw and heard. As he lay down to sleep, all around him seamen were on their knees giving thanks to God, and a few men were standing with their hands uplifted. Jerry remembered hearing someone in a tavern in Norfolk say that there were no atheists in a foxhole. Now he knew what they meant.

It only seemed appropriate that he give thanks as well. So in the darkness Jerry Macmillan dropped to his knees and joined the most thrilling prayer meeting he would ever go to for the rest of his life.

33

So Far Away

When Benjamin walked back into the hospital after venturing downtown for breakfast, he couldn't believe that Marjie had already given birth—and that the baby's name was Martha. He was so delighted with the news about his granddaughter, especially that she had been named after his own dear wife, that he nearly caused a scene at the hospital. Even from her room down the hall, Marjie could hear Benjamin whooping and shouting.

He got so excited that he didn't make it home that afternoon much before choring time. First, he kissed and congratulated Marjie. Then the nurse let him sneak in and hold little Martha for a minute. He greeted Sarah and Ted at the desk and proudly escorted them to see the new mother and baby. And then, on the way home, he stopped at the house of just about everyone he knew to tell them the wonderful news.

Soon Ruth and a score of the neighborhood people had stopped by to see Marjie and the baby. Marjie wasn't so sure if they were coming because of her or because Benjamin had acted so giddy. Everyone who dropped in said that Martha was the most beautiful baby girl they'd ever seen, and Marjie found it easy to agree with them. If Martha wasn't the most beautiful, she unquestionably had the sweetest disposition of any baby that had ever been born.

The three days Marjie and the baby spent in the hospital went by far too quickly, but she was still happy to come home to the Macmillan farmhouse. Marjie couldn't imagine a time when the farm wouldn't be home for her, although she knew that, unless something changed, they might be moving. There was still no word from Jerry or the war department. She had called the local war board chairman, but all he could say was that the paperwork was all accounted for and he would check on its progress.

Just as soon as she felt strong enough, Marjie had written Jerry with every detail about little Martha's birth. But she couldn't shake the nagging feeling that had begun the night before the baby came—the feeling that something was wrong. Still, neither the radio nor the papers had reported anything related to the *Wasp*. So although the nagging dread stayed with her, she said nothing to Benjamin.

Except for the lack of news from either source, the month following Marjie and the baby's homecoming was truly a wonderful time. The summer heat had retreated to the deep South, and the Minnesota countryside exploded into a spectacular red and gold autumn. Marjie spent most of her days taking care of Martha and the house, and she loved every minute of it. She had never thought she'd like the solitary life of a housewife on a farm, but now she could not imagine wanting to be anything else.

The biggest surprise of the fall was Grandpa Benjamin. Marjie had all she could do to kick him out of the house once in a while. All he wanted to do when he came in from choring in the morning was hold little Martha. Hour after hour he would sit in his chair and rock the baby to sleep. From the kitchen Marjie could hear him singing and humming and talking to Martha, and occasionally she'd find the two of them fast asleep together. She wished she had a camera, but she was sure they couldn't even have afforded the film. There were days when Marjie had to ask Benjamin for her turn to tend the baby.

Benjamin chalked his doting attention to the fact that he'd never had a little girl before, but Marjie suspected he had simply concluded that other things could wait. That was fine with her. Benjamin had worked like a dog all his life, so why shouldn't he take the time to enjoy his granddaughter. Her theory was verified in late October when he announced to her that he was going to pay a crew to come in and get the corn out of the field for him. He actually admitted that his time with the baby was more important to him than the extra money it would cost to bring in the crop.

The *Salt Lake City* took the rescued seamen of the *Wasp* to the military base in New Caledonia, where they waited for transport back to San Diego. Jerry spent most of his time making sure that Chester was getting the care he required, and he was anxious to find out whether they might get a chance to go home before their next assignment. He was especially concerned to find out whether Marjie had delivered the baby yet; he knew her due date was already past. At the moment, however, there was little he could do but wait for their next ride out.

They had been ordered to maintain complete silence about the sinking of the *Wasp* until the official communique was given by the Department of the Navy. Because there had been no Japanese surface ships or planes in the vicinity of the torpedoing, the navy hoped to keep the news from the Japanese as long as possible. With the loss of the *Wasp*, the United States Navy was left with only the aircraft carrier *Hornet* to face up to six operational Japanese carriers. It was a golden opportunity for the Japanese to exploit.

Finally the transport ships came in, and the rescued seamen began their long and still dangerous journey back to the States. The transports were slow, and there was next to nothing for the extra hands to do. By the time they finally arrived at the San Diego Naval Base on October 19, the men were nearly going crazy.

It was a wild scene as the sailors got off the transports and headed for the command base to get their orders. All the men had lost their belongings with the ship, so they had nothing to slow them down. Jerry stayed behind to help get Chester checked into the naval hospital, thinking it ironic that his good friend Chester might be spending time with his best friend Billy Wilson while he left them both behind.

He got Chester situated in the hospital, and they said at least temporary goodbyes—hoping to see each other on furlough before long. Then Jerry stopped by to see Billy.

He found it awkward to not talk about the *Wasp* when it was obvious that something disastrous had happened. Jerry did take time to tell Billy that he was absolutely right about God watching out for them, and Billy understood perfectly without having to hear any of the details that he knew Jerry could not tell. They promised to talk about it later.

When he finally made it to the front of the line at the command base, Jerry was first given a handful of mail that had been collecting while they were in limbo. Then he was given a new set of clothes as well as a couple months' back pay, which meant he was no longer penniless. Next came the official notification of a thirty-day furlough with a free rail pass. After that he was to report to Norfolk by November 26 to join up with the new aircraft carrier *Essex*, pending a special notification from the Naval Personnel Office.

Jerry asked if the "pending" meant that his special request for discharge was in the works. But no one there had any way of knowing, and with the line so long, no one had any time to check on it. They did tell him to contact his county chairman of the war board as soon as he got home. And he was told again to maintain complete silence about the downing of the *Wasp* until the official story was released.

Jerry hopped the next crowded bus that was shuttling seamen to the railroad station and then found his way to a ticket window as fast as he could. He figured his best bet was to take the train as far as LaCrosse, Wisconsin, and then take a bus on to Preston. Once he got there, he'd call his dad to come take him the last twelve miles.

The train he needed to catch was just loading, belching its black smoke and getting ready to pull out. He ran like a deer to catch it. Because it would take several days to get to LaCrosse, he was especially glad to find that the sleeping compartments were open to the military men.

As the train pulled out, Jerry looked down at the packet of

letters in his hand. He was desperate for rest and something to eat, but most of all he needed to find a place to sit and read his mail, hoping that one of the letters would tell of the baby's arrival. He decided to go to the dining car and get something to eat while he dug into his mail. Sitting down and ordering a hot-beef sandwich, he opened the packet of letters and set aside the ones from Marjie to read first. With a table knife, he slit open the letter postmarked September 17, the thickest letter and the one closest to her due date.

Pulling the letter from the envelope, Jerry could feel his blood pressure rising, and he could hear his heart pumping in his ears. For a second, he wasn't sure that he dared read the news. Gently folding the letter open, he was greeted by the familiar, delicate handwriting and the wondrous words, "Dearest Jerry, Your daughter is waiting to see you!"

He jumped up and opened his mouth to yell, then remembered he was in a public place. Slowly, ever so slowly, he sat down and then read the words like he was eating the finest chocolate, savoring the taste of every syllable. It was too wonderful! And he was only days from being with them!

Despite his desperate efforts, he could not hold back the tears. Down they poured, and Jerry tilted his head and put his hand over his forehead, trying to cover up. Little Martha Macmillan was waiting for him! She was perfect! She was beautiful!

The skinny waitress came back and put his sandwich and coffee down on the table. Jerry tried to give a muffled "thanks," but his soaked napkin gave him away. "Dear John letter, eh?" she said in a hard voice.

"No," Jerry rasped out. "My wife had a baby! I'm a father, and I'm going home!"

"Well, congratulations, sailor!" she said, warming up with a smile. "Hey!" she yelled to the other diners. "One of our fine men in blue just had a baby. Let's give him a big hand!"

The startled diners had looked up when she yelled, and hearing the news, they gave a cheer and a hearty congratulations. Jerry finished wiping the last tear and waved his napkin in thanks. Many of them patted him on the back when they exited the dining car.

It was the most wonderful news Jerry could have possibly been given, but it made the rest of the trip an absolute misery. He could hardly sleep a wink, and the train seemed so pathetically slow that he wanted to get out and push. But at least the unending clickety-clack of the train told him that the distance between him and his family was shortening.

Jerry arrived in LaCrosse midmorning on Monday, October 26, and hopped on the next bus to Preston.

"Got a new baby waiting for me at home," he told the friendly driver. "Little girl. I've been at sea, and I've never seen her."

"Well, then," the driver replied. "I'll have to see what the old engine can do this trip."

"Thanks," Jerry rejoined. "But I'm afraid there's no way we're gonna get there that's fast enough for me."

The crew pulled in to harvest the corn on Friday, October 23. And Marjie knew that however long it took them, it would be a very busy time for her. Benjamin didn't do much of the hard work, but he hauled loads with his tractor and watched to make sure things were done to his liking. That meant that Marjie had to take care of Martha alone as well as cook for the table full of hungry men that formed the crew. Unfortunately for her, they did not finish that day and had to reschedule to come back on Monday, October 26.

Marjie called and asked her mother to come over and help on that Monday. She really didn't want to knock herself out again tending all the help. Plus, Marjie loved to watch Sarah with the baby. It was good to see her so happy after the many years of heartache.

All that morning, Marjie chopped and stirred while Sarah played with her granddaughter. At lunchtime, the hungry crew descended like locusts on her piled-high table, then headed back out while Sarah helped Marjie clean up. Finally, in the early afternoon, the crew of men got the last of the corn in the cribs and headed out. Marjie sighed her relief to see their vehicles pull out of the driveway; she was in a hurry for things to settle down. It took Benjamin a while to finish out in the barn, but by afternoon coffee time, he was seated at the table once more, making faces at his prized granddaughter.

With the radio chattering away in the background, the three talked around the table long after their coffee was finished. Finally Benjamin reluctantly handed the baby back to Sarah and said he needed to get on with the evening chores. She replied conversationally that she figured Teddy would be pulling up at any moment, and they'd be getting back to their chores as well.

As Benjamin went to the door, he stopped to listen to the weather report that was coming through the static-filled radio. Marjie asked him something, but he held up his hand, and silence fell upon them as the always important forecast was read. But before they had a chance to make any more noise, the crackly voice announced that a special communique had come through from the navy department.

As the bus rolled down the long, winding hill into Preston, Jerry was rocking back and forth in his seat, unable to sit still any longer. He grabbed his few belongings, excused himself to the man sitting next to him, and lurched to the front of the bus.

"I'm sorry," Jerry said. "But you gotta let me stand here. I swear I'm going to blow up if I sit down for one more second."

The bus driver just laughed and turned the bus toward the main-street section of town, pulling up to the bus stop and jerking the door open. Jerry was out before the driver could wish him well.

Heading straight for the only pay phone available, Jerry was upset to see someone already on it. "Shoot!" he moaned. Then he heard a voice behind him.

"You need a ride, Jerry!"

He turned to see John Bates, one of their neighbors, who had just picked up his daughter from somewhere.

"Boy, do I!" he yelled back. "How fast does your car go?"

"Hop in, and I'll show you!" John cried. "I take it you're just getting home?" And with that, Jerry was only twenty minutes from his dream of being home.

The Bateses were eager to give him news of home, but he asked them not to. He wanted to wait to get home before he heard any more news about his family. They understood. All they said was that his little girl was a beauty.

When they rolled around the last gravel corner to the Macmillan farm, Jerry asked them to stop and let him out. The house was still about an eighth of a mile away, but he wanted to look the farm over first and take the last steps at his own pace.

The car stopped, and Jerry stepped out. The Bates family waved and pulled away, leaving him alone on the quiet corner overlooking their lower property.

Jerry took in a deep draft of country air and let it fill his lungs. He surveyed the golden valley below and the farmhouse tucked behind the pine trees that lined their driveway. And then he closed his eyes and breathed a quick prayer of thanks.

Seaman First Class and Catwalk Gunner Jerry Macmillan had made it back alive!

Benjamin jumped to the radio and turned up the volume, and the sense of dread that Marjie had carried for more than a month swelled in her throat.

"The United States Navy has officially divulged the loss of the aircraft carrier USS *Wasp* on September 15, in the South Pacific. The carrier was protecting the movement of marine reinforcements to Guadalcanal and was torpedoed and sunk by a Japanese submarine. While no official account has been given, the navy has announced that most of the *Wasp*'s personnel were saved."

The stunning blow rolled through the room and left them in a state of total paralysis. Marjie could not move or breathe; she felt at the total mercy of the phantom voice in the box to tell her that her love was alive.

Sarah Livingstone held little Martha with one arm and put

her other hand on Marjie's trembling arm. "We have to be strong, honey," she whispered.

Kneeling on one knee in front of the large radio, Benjamin was staring into its lighted dial as if he could see the face of the broadcaster by focusing hard.

Marjie was the first to move. She got up, walked to the picture window in the dining room, and stared blankly out on the valley below. Her only thought was that her intuition had been perfectly accurate—to the very day the tragedy had occurred.

She turned to look at her mother and said, "I knew it the night before Martha was born. I knew it."

Marjie numbly looked back out the window. But then she thought she heard a voice calling, "Marjie! Marjie!"

She shook her head, fearing she might be losing her mind. But she heard it again, and then, out of the corner of her eye, she saw Blue come racing out of the barn and head straight down the driveway.

"Dear God!" she cried and rushed to the door.

"What's the—" Benjamin called, but Marjie had already flown through the door and was following the dog across the lawn to the driveway.

34

A Dream to Hold

Marjie was sure she had heard Jerry's voice . . . but she was also sure that it couldn't possibly be.

And then she saw him . . . by the mailbox . . . with an ecstatic Blue jumping up and down at his side.

It couldn't be a ghost. It was him!

Marjie froze in utter disbelief, fearing that if she moved he might disappear. Jerry froze, too, so overwhelmed that his legs refused to move. Then a simultaneous yell broke the silence, and the two lovers raced down the driveway to meet each other.

Jerry scooped Marjie into his arms and twirled her around in a dance of joy. Then he gently set her down and cupped her face with his hands. "I was afraid I'd never—"

Marjie did not let him finish the sentence. Her arms went around his neck, and she kissed her husband like there was no tomorrow.

Down the driveway behind them, Benjamin and Sarah made a very slow approach with little Martha, eager to see Jerry, but unwilling to interrupt what seemed to be a miraculous reunion. But then Benjamin could stand no more. "Son," he bellowed out, and wrapped his arms around the two who refused to let go of each other. "Welcome home, son!" he said again through laughter and tears.

Jerry got an arm around his father and squeezed as hard as

he could. All three were mumbling words, but nothing made any sense. It sounded like Jerry was trying to say, "I love you, Dad!"

Then Sarah's voice cut through the revelry. She said, "Aren't you forgetting someone special?"

Jerry wiped away some tears, looked over at Sarah, and stood transfixed at the sight of his daughter. Sarah had wrapped her in a delicate hand-knit blanket, and Martha was staring out at him with big, dark eyes, her tiny arms jerking as if she wanted to come to him.

"Meet the sweetest baby in the world," Sarah said, handing the baby to Marjie.

This was the moment Jerry had traveled thousands and thousands of miles for, and suddenly he didn't know what to do. "How do I—"

"Here," Marjie said, taking Martha and placing her safely in Jerry's arms. "There, now . . . tuck the blanket around her. See? There's nothing to it. She's been waiting for you, Jerry. She's a beauty—and she's ours!"

A little stiffly, but with infinite tenderness, Jerry cradled the tiny new acquaintance. His face was full of awe and delight, but all that came out his mouth was a muffled, "God . . ." He looked down at Martha, then up at Marjie. Down at Martha, then up at his father. Down at Martha, then up at Sarah.

It was far better than any dream, and yet it was a dream fulfilled.

The sound of a car on the gravel turned the celebrants around as Ted Livingstone pulled into the driveway. He stopped by them and hopped out, then stopped again in disbelief.

"Jerry, is that you?" he asked. "Son of a gun! I just heard the radio saying your ship had been sunk!"

Teddy gave Jerry a big handshake and a welcome home.

"So the official announcement was made?" Jerry asked Teddy.

"Five minutes ago."

"I hope you didn't hear it before I got here," Jerry said, turning to Marjie and his father with a look of dismay.

Marjie nodded her head. "It was horrible," she whispered,

"but then I was sure I heard your voice. At first I thought I was having a nervous breakdown!"

The whole group roared with laughter, and little Martha jumped in Jerry's arms. "Oops!" he said, drawing her up toward him and kissing her cheek. "Forgot about you, didn't we? Well, we won't be forgetting any longer. You're more beautiful than I could have imagined. You look just like your mother!" Then he kissed his little girl again, and kissed her mother as well.

"How long you home for, Jerry?" Teddy asked.

"Got a thirty-day furlough," he answered, "then I'm supposed to be back in Norfolk. That is, unless something happens with the discharge request. You heard anything?"

"Nothing," Marjie answered. "I've talked with the county chairman several times, but he keeps giving me the runaround."

"For tonight," Jerry declared, "I don't want to talk about going back. We've got some time to figure that out. Didn't somebody famous in our family once say that 'it always works out'?"

"I believe she did," Marjie said, smiling at Sarah.

"A wise woman, no doubt," Sarah said and laughed. "Let's get back to the house before that child catches a cold."

The group moved up the path, but Sarah and Teddy said they needed to get home to their chores.

"Come back after dinner," Marjie invited, but Sarah declined.

"We'll try to get back tomorrow sometime," Sarah said, looking at Jerry. "You folks need some time together. But you have to promise to retell your stories for us, all right?"

"Gladly," Jerry answered. "By the way, the Bible you gave me helped save my life. But it went down with the ship. I'm sorry."

Sarah stopped and looked into his eyes. "Don't be sorry. I got a feeling that Robert would like the story behind that. Will you promise to tell it tomorrow?"

"You better come early," he said. "I'm a slow storyteller."

"Real early," Marjie said. "Be here for lunch. I'll put a hen on to bake, and we can celebrate Thanksgiving early!"

"Sounds good to me!" Ted echoed. "We got a few stories, too, Jerry. Wait till you hear how we got your old friend, Gordon Stilwell."

Jerry laughed. "You sure you don't wanna come back tonight?"

"Tomorrow's soon enough," Marjie cut in. "I want you to myself, tonight. Understand, sailor!"

"Yes, sir!" Jerry barked, scaring the baby again.

Sarah and Teddy turned back to the car, then drove away in a cloud of dust. Benjamin walked them to the house, but then remembered that he needed to get to choring, too. The milking cows were bellowing in the barnyard, impatiently waiting for the doors to open so they could get to their feed and water.

Entering the farmhouse alone, the reunited family went into the living room. Marjie took little Martha from Jerry and carefully laid her on a puffy blanket on the floor.

"She'll be fine," she declared. "Now it's my turn!"

She shoved Jerry down onto the couch and jumped into his lap, snuggling in tight. "Do you like her?" Marjie whispered.

"I love her," Jerry whispered back. "I'm sorry I was gone."

"I've missed you every moment you've been gone," she said, stroking his arm. "You should have seen her when she first came out."

Jerry nodded his head. "And I missed you till I nearly went crazy," he said. "Out there in the night . . . in the dark . . . somewhere in the middle of the ocean . . . I must have called your name a million times."

"But now you're home," Marjie said, looking into his face. "And you've got some lost time to make up for. Think you can handle it?"

"No problem," he said, "but I'm a bit rusty."

"You better be real rusty," she teased.

"Totally," he said with a grin. "Now stop talking and kiss me."

Ten months of separation seemed to melt away in a matter of minutes, and after an explosion of kisses and hugs, Jerry and Marjie sat quietly holding each other. There was so much to say, but it was hard to know where to start.

Then little Martha started to fuss a bit, and before long she was crying.

"Feeding time," Marjie said regretfully.

"This is going to be complicated," said Jerry, sliding aside as Marjie stood up to take care of the baby.

"That's right," said Marjie with a twinkle in her eye. "And I need to get supper going as well. Life on the old farm."

"Do you mind if I change clothes quick and help Dad with the chores?" he asked. "He looks a lot older now . . . since I've been gone."

"Go right ahead," Marjie answered. "We need to talk about him. I'm not sure if you're going to know him anymore. But he could use a hand. He's not supposed to be doing the chores by himself, but we can't get anyone in to help."

Jerry kissed Marjie on the forehead, then went upstairs. His old barn clothes were still hanging on their nail in his old bedroom. Tattered but familiar, they felt good to get on again. He was outside in a manner of minutes.

Stepping into the milking parlor, he looked around the two dimly lit rows of cows. Nothing had changed. He could see his father working between two Holsteins on the first row, so without saying a word, he grabbed his gear and set to work on the second row that used to be his anyway. Except for one of the cows who turned and gave him a good looking over, it only took a few moments before the two men were back to their old routine.

Jerry didn't want to talk for a while, so he just kept on moving. When he was nearly finished, he turned with a bucket of milk and idly noticed the half-grown heifer peering at him from the pen behind him. Something looked familiar. Then he recognized a little black spot like an eyebrow, a look of lopsided surprise. It was the same little Holstein who'd been there coughing when he left for the navy.

"So, you survived," he murmured to the young cow. "I wondered if you'd be here when I got back."

"And she wondered if you'd come home," Benjamin said with a smile. "I kept her just special for you, but she's near outgrown that pen!"

And then he sat back on his stool and beamed. "It's good to have you home, son."